THE MONSTERS IN YOUR HEAD

KITTY OLSEN

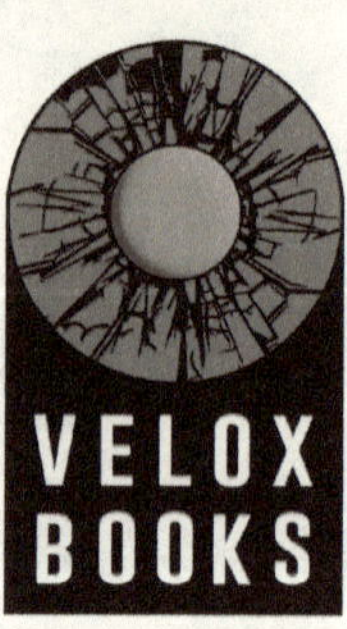

YOU'RE READING ANOTHER TERRIFYING COLLECTION FROM

**FOLLOW VELOX TO KEEP
THE NIGHTMARES COMING:**

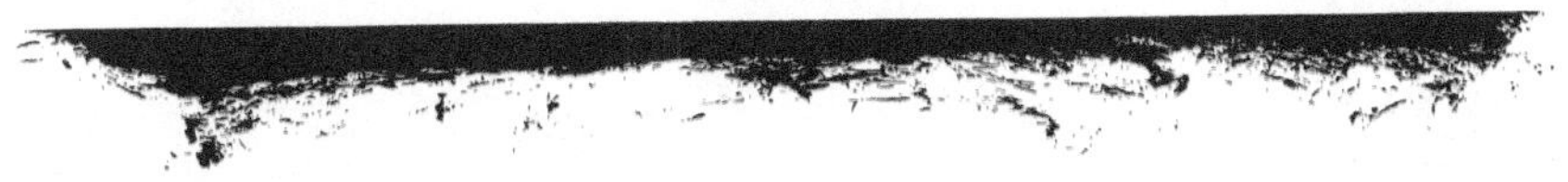

CONTENTS

THE WORST WEDDING I'VE EVER PHOTOGRAPHED

I've been a wedding photographer for nearly ten years, and I thought I'd seen it all. Trashy, beautiful, tragic, hilarious, or just bizarre. I have *stories*. I have the typical groom getting caught getting it on with the maid of honor, family getting into brawls, brides OD-ing in the bathroom, gay couples having no one attend their wedding (or worse, the one uninvited homophobic relative crashing to just be a dick) stories. But we aren't here for typical stories. If we were, we'd be here all day. We're here for the wedding from last October.

Fall weddings are probably my favorite, if I ever get married, I'll probably get hitched in the fall. It was the parents of the bride who came to me, asking for my services for a wedding in two weeks. Their original photographer apparently up and quit on them and they were desperate to have their darling daughter's wedding immortalized in picture format.

Luckily for them, I had a clear schedule. I did charge them quite a bit extra for the suddenness of it all, but judging by the father's Rolex, it wasn't that big a deal. One thing I'm good at guessing is a family's wealth status. And once again I was on point—the Seawrights were *rolling* in dough.

Not that I really liked them, though. I'm not required to like my clients, although it does make things easier. Harold Seawright leered at my chest whenever he thought I wasn't looking, and Carol was the epitome of the trophy wife that was over the hill, looking more like she was made of plastic than flesh. Nothing wrong with plastic surgery or Botox, but there's gotta be a cutoff at some point.

Day came and uh... oh boy, I realized I was getting into something I didn't want to be a part of right away.

First time I saw the bride, Tanya, I immediately thought 'you're too young for this'. She could've been sixteen, she could've been *just* eighteen, but she definitely didn't look over twenty-one. I've seen young marriages when it's a shotgun affair, but then I met the groom, Marcel Wingate. Marcel was not a day younger than forty. And Marcel was just... something felt off. He was a bamboo stalk of a man, thin and towering over me, let alone Tanya. With his long, pale face and sunken eyes, he could've been the perfect casting for Lurch from the Addams family.

When he shook my hand and introduced himself, I barely repressed a shiver. But years of practice helped me to smile and act like there wasn't something slimy about all of this.

Tanya never said a word when she was made over for her big day. Only Carol did, chirping and twittering about 'how about you make her hair a little bigger' or 'make her eyes pop, she has such pretty eyelashes'. Luckily Carol had to go have a smoke every fifteen minutes so the make up and hair people could have a moment to actually work. By the time it was all over, Tanya looked like a princess in her white ballgown styled dress. A tiara was placed in her strawberry blonde hair, cheeks colored a perfect blush pink. But unlike most brides, she still hadn't said a word, and sure as hell those weren't tears of joy she was holding back.

I'm sure you've heard about the 'first look' photo fad. I find it great to get that perfect expression a groom makes when he sees the bride in her dress for the first time. This was the first time I'd shot a first look photo where I believe it was the first time the bride and groom had actually looked at each other.

Marcel did seem to have his breath taken away by his lovely bride, but her expression was less than thrilled as he took her hand and give it a tight squeeze. She flinched as he leaned in to give her a kiss on the cheek and my stomach turned at the sight.

It's time I put a pin in the myth that arranged marriages only happen in foreign countries, and only people from certain cultures take part in it. They happen all the time in the US, and more often than not it's an old man who wants a 'virgin' bride, and by virgin I mean 'still in highschool'... or younger. This wouldn't even be the first one I was hired to photograph, just the first one I'd not been able to back out of in time.

I managed to catch Tanya alone in the room she got ready in, sitting next to the open window and twirling an unlit cigarette between her fingers. "Need a light?" I offered.

"No thanks. I don't smoke, but they say it makes you feel better, right?" She said, looking up at me with her doll like blue eyes.

"It also gives you lung and throat cancer." I took the cigarette from her and lit it up for myself. "But I'm a bad example, so do as I say, not as I do."

Now that got a smile out of her, even if it only lasted a second. "How often do you smoke?" she asked.

"Depends on the day. Usually I have two or three. On bad days I can have a few more." I lowered the cigarette and looked down at her. "How old are you, Tanya?"

"Nineteen. Twenty in a few weeks. I have a baby face." She poked one of her cheeks and I had to bite my tongue to avoid saying she was still a baby. "Why do you care?" I glanced at the door to make sure Carol wasn't going to barge in. "Tanya, are you not okay with this? The wedding?" I asked quietly.

Tanya's eyes widened. "Damn, you're good." She also glanced at the door. "... Harold, my stepdad, arranged all of this back when

I was fifteen. If he had it his way it would've happened then too, but Marcel kept delaying. He tried to delay another year but my dad implied he had other offers." She shivered and wrapped her arms around herself. "If I said no, Harold would kick me out of the house and cut me off. I'd have nothing and no one, and... I don't know what I'd do if that happened." I reached into my purse and pulled out one of my business cards. "Flip the card over, it has a number for a woman's shelter—they specialize in helping women escape from dangerous home situations. Hides them, helps them get started in a new city if need be. If you just need to talk, below that is my personal phone number, okay?"

Tanya took the card and clung onto it tightly before tucking it into her bra. "You might be the nicest person I've ever met," she murmured.

I gave her shoulder a squeeze. "I try," I said before extinguishing the cigarette on the windowsill. "If you need to escape any time tonight, just ask me to help you go to the bathroom. We can pull a whole runaway bride," I joked.

That got another laugh out of her, just in time for her mom to pop into the room. "Well, what's taking so long? Hurry up, the wedding's going to be starting in fifteen minutes, and I don't want you to cry and make your face all blotchy and ugly!" she whined.

Tanya's brief joy faded, and she gave me one more sad look before following her mother out.

The ceremony would've been so much more beautiful if I didn't know the dirty little secret behind it all. Tanya didn't smile once. I don't think any of her bridesmaids was an actual friend of hers, or at least not a sincere one. When the priest said 'you may kiss the bride', Tanya let one tear slip down her cheek when Marcel leaned down to kiss her.

I considered calling the cops, but what could they do? Tanya would be too scared to say that anything was wrong, and since she wasn't a minor they couldn't label Marcel a pedo and her stepfather a child seller. It still didn't make the situation any less shitty. All I could do was snap pictures of the worst day of Tanya's life.

But things changed after the first dance between the bride and groom.

At first, Tanya was stiff as a board, reluctant to even touch Marcel. But he leaned down and whispered something in her ear. Her entire demeanor changed in a blink of an eye to one of surprise and I managed to read her lips- 'really?' Marcel nodded and I managed to catch a picture of the first smile Tanya had since she said 'I do'. By the end of the dance, she was even starting to get into it, resting her head on his chest as they swayed back and forth to 'A Thousand Years'.

It was a complete 180 from earlier. Tanya was now one of the happiest, and dare I say it, flirtiest brides I've ever seen. She even leaned up to kiss him on the cheek as they sat down, something that took Marcel by surprise judging by how his chalk white cheeks went pink.

I started to wonder if Marcel slipped something in her drink when Carol started to nag me about where her husband was. She was the kind of mother who forgot this was her child's wedding instead of her own and she wanted pictures of her and 'Haaarold'. I told her I'd go find him to get her off my fucking back. He'd been hitting the open bar hard that night, I assumed he was in the bathroom either throwing up or cheating on his wife.

When I approached the men's room, I heard something that sounded like gargling or swallowing. Ew, I know, but I kinda hoped to ruin this nasty mother of the bride's day with the news that her garbage husband was cheating on her, so I opened the bathroom door with my camera at the ready.

I made eye contact with Harold.

Or rather, I made eye contact with Harold's *head*.

It was sitting in the sink, expression twisted in abject horror. The room was soaked in blood, body parts strewn around the floor. Meanwhile, Marcel had stripped out of his tuxedo and was currently swallowing Harold's arm. Whole.

Now I was wondering if I'd had something slipped into my champagne. Humans can't just unhinge their jaw like that, each gulp taking Marcel's arm deeper down his throat. I saw the tips of Harold's fingers disappear with a small wave of goodbye... and then I dropped my camera.

Yes, I heard something break. No, I didn't care. I just saw the groom *eat the goddamn father of the bride.* Marcel's head shot up and I was frozen in place by his gaze. Before now his eyes were a dull, watery gray, now they were mottled brown and red with slit thin pupils. Predatory. *Inhuman.* "Oh, I'm terribly sorry, one moment."

Marcel turned to the sink that was free of a man's head and vomited. I heard several things clatter on the porcelain before he fetched them out and washed them off. With an embarrassed clearing of his throat, he walked up to me and pulled me into the bathroom.

I thought I was dead, but instead Marcel placed several small, hard objects in my palm. "For the camera, I didn't mean to startle you," he said. I glanced down and parted my fingers to see he'd given me several diamonds that were still damp from having bile and blood washed off of them.

"Uh huh," I managed to get out as I stared at the literal handful of diamonds. "... Why did you—"

"Devour Harold? Oh, I've wanted to do that for years." Marcel chuckled as he grabbed some paper towels to wipe off his chin, like that would take away from the fact he was still completely naked and soaked in blood in front of me. "Taste is relative to the person. You would taste terrible. It'd be like swallowing nails. Meanwhile, a man who offers his stepdaughter as a sacrificial lamb to something he *knows* eats humans, he tastes like the richest cut of steak, tender enough to be sliced with a butter knife and seasoned to perfection."

Jesus Christ, this twisted situation had taken on a whole new level of fucked up. "Wait, he seriously—"

"Oh, absolutely, and he'd do it again if he had another daughter. All for what happens when my stomach processes human bone."

The diamonds dug into my palm as I clutched them tightly. "... You're not going to hurt Tanya?" I asked.

Marcel shook his head. "God, no. I kept delaying the wedding in hopes that she'd manage to find a way out, but I think Harold was getting bored with my cold feet. There would be plenty of other people willing to pay for her, even if my payment would be easily thrice what others would offer."

I was starting to feel a little dizzy from the stress and the smell of blood. Here I was, talking to a man eating groom. I glanced at the door behind us and a horrible idea entered my brain, one that scared me because I knew I'd suggest it. "So if I told Carol she could find her husband in the men's room...?" I trailed off.

Marcel was puzzled for a second but caught on quickly. He nodded and picked up Howard's head before he tossed it into one of the stalls. I heard it splash in one of the toilets and I almost started giggling, this had to be hysteria kicking in. "Go right ahead. I'll be waiting," he said as he kicked more limbs out of sight.

I left the bathroom and almost immediately bumped into Carol in the hallway. "Well, where is he?" she snapped.

I just pointed a thumb towards the bathroom. "Think he's not feeling so well," was all I could say before I was nearly bowled over by her.

I watched long enough for her to open the door and for a scaled tail to shoot out, wrap around her arm, and drag her into the bathroom before I headed back to the wedding.

The problem was solved after that. Marcel came back after some time, clean but saying someone had made quite a mess out of the men's room, so it was out of order the rest of the night. Tanya no longer had to behave a certain way to please her mom, so she started to actually have a good time. I used my back up camera to make sure to get all the pictures of her smiling. Carol and Harold vanished into thin air, never to be seen or heard from again. And those diamonds paid for quite the nice new camera.

Like I said, it's been a year. I sure as hell haven't forgotten that wedding, but what prompted me to share it was that I got a friend request from Tanya on Facebook. I normally don't accept friend requests from previous clients, but this one time, I chose to make an exception. She does look so much better, she's going to college, she now sculpts and paints, she regularly volunteers at the woman's shelter I directed her to when we first met, and every Friday night is group date night at the local arcade with some of Marcel's friends that now appear to be her friends as well. Apparently, Marcel is quite the Dance Dance Revolution master, but is terrible at shooting games.

Her most recent picture was her and Marcel, smiling. And she was holding up an ultrasound picture.

UNDER THE BACK PORCH

As a kid, I lived with neglectful parents at best. At the worst, dad would turn his screams and fists on me, but I learned quickly how to dodge the worst of it. Mom wasn't much help, she'd just smoke in the kitchen and bitch at him for staying out so late.

At the time, we lived basically in the middle of nowhere. Our nearest neighbors were a long walk away for a six-year-old and we had trees between us. There was no one to run to for help. But I was pretty small for a kid my age. I learned I could fit pretty much anywhere. The closet. Dryer. I think even once I tucked myself under my futon in such a way I could still get some air, but no one could see me.

I was a master at hiding. But it wasn't for a good reason.

One night, though, one night I chose to do something different.

I could hear it in dad's yells, he was pissed and was about to get violent. Mom wasn't helping either, just pouring fuel onto an inferno of a flame. So I knew I had to find a good hiding spot. I'd gotten the idea a few days before, when I realized the lattice covering the bottom half of the back porch had a hole in it. Not big enough to fit a full-grown man, most likely, but it could fit a skinny six-year-old no problem.

So wrapping myself up in my blanket and grabbing my hippo stuffie, I snuck out my window and ran into the backyard. It was the middle of autumn. Meaning it was forty degrees with the temperature steadily dropping.

I crawled under the porch, scraping my elbows and getting splinters in my palms, but I fit inside. It was actually quite spacious compared to most of my hiding spots. I couldn't sit up all the way, but I had plenty of room to spread out my limbs.

Of course, I was also getting covered in dirt. It'd rained a few days ago, so the mud was still a little wet. I wrapped myself in my blankie the best I could and settled in for the night.

But soon, even with my blankie and my hippo, my teeth were chattering so hard I could barely breathe. I didn't want to go back inside, though, knowing if my dad caught me, I'd be in for the whipping of my life. So I had to tough it out.

"Honey, are you cold?"

That voice was not the voice of my mother, scratchy from all the smoking and screeching she did. It was sweet, like honey. I turned over to see the dim outline of a woman lying on her stomach next to me. She had a pretty butterfly necklace and was just as dirty as I was.

I nodded, not wondering how she'd been down there without me noticing.

The woman belly-crawled forward, wrapped her arms around me and suddenly I became warm. It was like I was sitting next to a campfire. I snuggled into her arms, not minding the mud, after all, we were both dirty.

"You've gotten so big," the woman said, examining my face. "How old are you now, Alex?"

"Six."

How did I know this woman again? I didn't think I did.

"Six!" The woman gasped. "You're all grown up then. I'm so happy." She sighed pleasantly and stroked my hair. I'd never felt so cozy in my life.

"What's your name?" I asked.

She smiled, I could hear it in her voice. "I'm Lily. What's your favorite thing to do?"

I had to think for a second. "I like board games. And coloring."

Lily chuckled. "Just like me then. Could never get enough of Scrabble. But I guess you're still too young to play that, huh?"

I nodded. "Lotsa words. I wanna play it though. I like the tiles. Would you play with me?"

I heard Lily sharply inhale. "I... I don't think I can. Your daddy put me under here, and I can't leave... but..." She thought for a second. "Alex, could you do me a favor?"

"Of course!" This lady was oh so nice. Why wouldn't I do her a favor?

"When you wake up in the morning, go to the police station. Ask for an officer by the name of Lowell Joyce. Tell him where to find Lily, okay? Under your back porch. He'll come and he'll get me, okay? And... and then maybe we can play Scrabble."

Yippee! I was too excited about the possibility of playing Scrabble to notice how Lily's voice caught at the end. I nodded vigorously. "I'll do it! We can be on the same team, right?"

Lily softly laughed.

"I'll help you understand the rules. Goodnight, Alex."

When I woke up the next morning, I heard Lily's voice.

"Go now. Your dad's gone to work. I'll tell you how to get to the station."

Rubbing my eyes, I crawled out from under the porch and went into the house to grab my shoes and a coat. I shivered in the frosty cold. But I thought Lily was right behind me.

After my shoes and coat were on, I started walking. It was long enough to get to the neighbor's house. I really can't remember how long it took to get to the police station, although I have no idea why no one pulled over to see what the hell a six-year-old in dirty pajamas was doing walking alongside the road. Lily kept guiding me onward.

"Wait. Okay, cross the street now."

"Turn right here."

"Keep going! You've almost made it!"

I nearly collapsed with exhaustion by the time I walked into the station. The guys out front chatting and having a good time didn't see me until I almost made it to the front desk.

"Whoa! Kid! You okay?" One of the officers knelt down to my level, eyes wide.

I nodded. "I'm okay. Can I speak to Lowell Joyce?" I asked.

One of the other officers picked me up. "Sure kid, sure, let's just get you someplace warm, holy shit, your lips are blue..."

I remembered quietly scolding the man about watching his language. 'Shit' was a bad word.

I was given some warm cocoa and wrapped up in a blanket by the time an old man with a graying mustache sat by me.

"Hey kid. I'm Sheriff Joyce. What's your name?" he asked.

"Alex." I set down my cup and looked him straight in the eye. "I was told to tell you that Lily is under the back porch. You need to go let her out so we can play Scrabble."

I had never seen a grown man turn pale before.

Lots of things blurred together at this point. I remember being taken back to my house and there were a lot of police cars and people around. The back porch was surrounded by yellow tape, and someone was taking a black bag away while my dad was in handcuffs.

After that, I lived with my grandparents. Sheriff Joyce and his wife.

I tried to ask about what happened and who was Lily, but I always got shut down. I was too young to know.

But life got better. A lot better.

Grandpa was the best man I could've hoped for in my life. We went out on weekends to the movies where he let me have the giant soda, even though I'd have to pee in the middle of the movie. When I asked if I could drink when I was thirteen, he let me try a beer. I spat it out and didn't touch it again. He never judged me for my love of art, letting me paint my own bedroom multiple times over the years. I felt safe around him. He never laid a hand on me.

My grandmother was amazing too, over the week she'd homeschool me along with teaching me things that you wouldn't learn in a school, such as how to respect others but not take their crap. And cooking. Lots of cooking. I could make my own birthday cake by the time I was twelve. But I usually just made them for my friends. I got a lot of those, after I was free from my dad.

When I turned sixteen, Grandpa took me back to my dad's house.

The whole thing had been bulldozed over. But I could still see the yellow tape wound around a few trees, faded and torn.

We sat together on the back of his truck. He opened a beer and drank half of it before setting it down and grabbing me an orange soda.

After I'd drank it, he told me.

"Lily was your mother."

Good thing he didn't tell me as I was swallowing, I likely would've had it coming out of my nose. "My mom?" I questioned, confused.

"Your actual mom. The woman who lived with your dad was not your mother." My granddad grabbed another beer. "Lily was my daughter. I loved her so much... but when you were around six months old, she vanished."

My stomach dropped. "My dad just imprisoned her under the porch?" I asked, starting to feel sick.

Grandpa took a deep breath before setting his unopened beer down. "That's... something I've never been able to understand. Lily told you to find me? And that she loved Scrabble?"

"Yeah. She kept me warm that night. I probably would've frozen to death if she hadn't been there." I was a stupid kid, even I knew that.

Grandpa went dead quiet before he opened that beer and slammed the whole thing. "... Alex, Lily had been dead the whole time she was gone. When we dug her up, she was bones. Experts confirmed it, and your dad confessed to what happened. They'd gotten into a fight and he threw her down the stairs. She... broke her neck." He clenched his fists. "I knew he had something to do with her disappearance, but I never had proof until you walked into my station, covered in dirt and telling me she was under the porch."

I was floored. I couldn't breathe. All I could do was shake my head.

"But—I saw her! She was alive! She had this butterfly necklace..." I trailed off when Grandpa pulled an evidence baggie from his pocket.

There was that butterfly necklace, all right. Rusty, and parts of the paint had chipped off, but I remembered it as clearly as I remembered Lily's voice.

Grandpa took a shaky breath as he pressed the bag into my hands. "... Lily loved you so much. 'ts why she stuck around that bastard. You were her whole world. She was constantly taking pictures and sendin' them to us in the mail. Sometimes a mother's love can accomplish things that no human can do."

My eyes overflowed with tears as I clutched the necklace to my chest. Choking on sobs, I leaned against Grandpa. He held me tight, and I swear I felt a few of his tears land on the top of my head.

And for just a brief moment, I swear I felt that warm love I felt that night under the porch.

SHE'S A KEEPER

That's what my dad always used to say, with a chuckle and a pat to my head. 'She's a keeper,' he'd say to a grocer or clerk at a convenience store. People used to fawn over the cute pigtailed gal by her daddy's side, always said her pleases and thank yous, never threw a tantrum, was an absolute angel.

Maybe this is why when I grew up I always needed someone giving me a pat on the back. If I'm not getting compliments about how I look or how well I did at work, I'm gonna assume I did something wrong or I had a piece of lettuce stuck in my teeth all day.

This hasn't always worked out for me. I'm a keeper, but I can also be a sucker. Like what's been happening with my boss.

I love working as a secretary, it's a job that makes me feel really fulfilled. It does make me into a bit of a stereotype with how I melted when Jonathan Price, my boss, complimented my blouse and my work ethic on my first day. I told myself that the silver ring on his left hand and the picture on his desk with his children and wife meant that I shouldn't read too much into it. Jonathan was perfect though, and over time I realized I read him just right.

I never wanted to be the other woman. I just wanted to be loved. And being around Jonathan, working late nights just to have a moment to talk with him, having drinks after work... the inevitable happened. He kissed me after a few too many beers, and we ended up going back to my place. We slept together.

I poured my heart out to him after that, how I'd liked him for so long, and that I really felt a connection with him. He just smiled and brushed the hair from my eyes, telling me that I was the kind of girl you didn't just let get away.

Of course I believed him.

Of course I swallowed the lump in my throat whenever I saw Mariana coming to visit her husband. My lover.

Of course I ignored how I was the chosen topic of office gossip, how the guys smirked and the other women gave me the side eye and cold shoulder.

Of course I listened when Jonathan said he was going to leave her soon. He just needed to make sure he didn't hurt her.

And of course, whenever he called me to meet him at our typical meeting spot, a hotel in downtown, I was there with bells on.

Yeah, I know what you're thinking of me. I think it too. I'm not the brightest bulb in the package. Like I told you, I'm pretty easily manipulated. But I love Jonathan, I love his work ethic, I love how he takes care of his kids, kids that he learned soon enough I couldn't have. I wonder if that was part of my appeal to him. That he couldn't accidentally knock me up.

He doesn't... didn't love me. I was just an easy lay, a stereotype in every sense of the word.

I only started wising up last week, when it occurred to me that Jonathan really wasn't slowing down his relationship with his wife and certainly wasn't preparing for divorce proceedings. She was pregnant with their third child. I saw the pictures he posted on Facebook of their anniversary dinner.

It hit me like a semi-truck when I read his status about enjoying their fifteen years together and couldn't wait to see what the next fifteen will bring.

I cried. I drank a lot of wine. And then I asked him to come to my apartment. That we needed to talk.

Scary words for a guy, right? Took Jonathan a while to drag his ass over, which by then I was even more drunk. I don't drink often, and certainly not in excess, but can you blame me? I'd just had that reality shattering realization I was just his pet to call on whenever he wanted to fuck and spew nonsense words at. Nonsense words I fell for.

Well, I did what I should've done about six months ago—I called him out on his bullshit. Said that he was never going to leave his wife but he wasn't going to stop stringing me along either. He tried, oh he tried to calm me down, but I wasn't going to bow down to his pretty words this time. "Either pick me or stay with your wife. Else I'll call her and let her know the truth."

My ultimatum I'd spent the previous hour preparing. I felt super proud of it when I spat it out, expecting him to pick at least one of the options so this nonsense could end.

Jonathan's face went white, then red, and then... he picked a third option.

He killed me.

Jonathan picked up the empty wine bottle while he muttered something about me being too much trouble, and then brought it down right on the top of my head. It caved my skull in on the first smash, sending shards of glass all over my living room. I dropped like a rock. But I guess Jonathan was just still pissed off, because he used the remains of the bottle in his hand to keep stabbing me, again and again, in the throat and neck. I was almost decapitated by the time he came to his senses.

Of course Jonathan panicked. He just scrubbed the blood off his hands and wiped down the bottle before escaping the apartment. Left me there. All alone. My head nearly taken off my shoulders, my living room a mess of blood, wine, and glass. Man, you should've seen the look on his face when I came into work today. I was at my desk by the time he came in. He looked like hell, understandably, he had just killed a woman two days before. But he froze in his steps when he saw me sitting at my desk, tip tapping away on my keyboard while scheduling another appointment later that week.

I just waved to him real quick before going back to work. Out of the corner of my eye, I saw Jonathan bolt for his office and slam the door.

Oh, that felt so good. Watching him be the one to run in fear. Was he doubting his memory? Was he trying to convince himself that he'd just had a really bad dream?

I clocked out after that, complaining about a cold, it'd been passed all around the office. But I didn't go home.

I went to Jonathan's home. A nice house, in a nice part of town. I saw his wife working in the small garden out front and after adjusting the scarf around my neck, I got out and walked up the drive. She didn't see me until I was right behind her. Marianna was a pretty woman, even now with a smudge of dirt across her face, no make up, and her auburn hair held back with a yellow bandanna.

I cleared my throat, and she nearly dropped the flower bulb she had in her hands. She glanced up, immediately recognizing me. "Oh, hi, Nicole. Is something wrong?" She got up, brushing off her hands and smiling from ear to ear. She was just starting to show, her belly slightly round with the new life that she and her rat bastard of a husband had made. "Can we talk inside?"

"Oh sure, sweetheart. The kids are at school, won't be back for a few more hours. Are you all right? Your voice sounds a bit raspy." "I'll be fine."

I waited until she was sitting down before I began the most difficult conversation of my life. And I got the hardest part out of the way first.

"Your husband and I have been having an affair for almost a year."

It was so sad to see how Marianna just sighed and nodded. I wasn't the only woman that he'd been twisting around and around.

"I figured, with all the late nights at work and business trips that didn't take him out of town. I was about to hire a private investigator to start checking in on him, so you saved me a chunk of change. Are you still sleeping with him?" I shook my head. "No, I figured that ended when he about took my head off with a wine bottle," I said.

Her brow knitted in concern, so I decided to show her. I undid the scarf around my neck and showed her what I'd been hiding all morning at work.

My neck was quite the sight, all purple and black, the decaying flesh all sliced up. I can't even imagine how the smell must be to someone not used to it. The putrefaction had spread down to my chest, which I showed her by unbuttoning my blouse. I'd had to start tearing my skin off to get any sort of relief, you can't imagine how horrid the itching gets when your flesh starts rotting off the bone with your skin struggling holding it all in. I even removed my gloves to show off the pus filled sores and bubbles growing in my wrists and fingers.

Marianna went white as a sheet as she took it all in. It look so wrong, my face perfect as it always has been but from the neck down I resembled roadkill more than a living woman. When the wave of stench rolled over her she bolted for the bathroom. I could hear her violently throwing up from where I continued to sit.

I'd just about buttoned my shirt back up when she came back, teetering a bit and still looking pale but managing to remain steady. "Wait. Show me again."

I shrugged and unbuttoned my shirt again. If she wanted a reason to barf again, she was welcome to it. But she didn't. She sat beside me, her expression of disgust melting away into one of wonder. "... Before Jonathan insisted I take care of the kids full time, I used to be a surgeon. I've never seen this kind of necrosis before, at least, not unless it was on a cadaver. You... you shouldn't be alive. You *can't* be alive. Are you a ghost?"

"No." I shook my head. "This just happens sometimes. I'm surprised it happened after your husband killed me, I thought I was a goner. But then I woke up with my body falling apart, maybe I was due for a shedding, maybe this just happens when I get hurt real bad, I dunno."

"Jonathan..." She shuddered and shook her head, "He's a bastard, but he wouldn't-"

"He beat me with a wine bottle, Marianna." I pulled the bloody shards out of my purse. "And then when it broke, he stabbed me in the neck. All because I told him the affair was over.

Now she was crying. Tears rolled down her cheeks as her bottom lip wobbled with her sobs. "No... no... oh my god, I'm so sorry, sweetheart. I never thought... I never-"

"I need your help."

I rebuttoned up my blouse, but I left the scarf on my lap. "It'll take me a few weeks to really come back together, but my daddy told me of a way to help me heal faster. His sister was like me. Fell apart, rotted like a corpse, and then looked just as pretty as ever in a few days. It took longer, though, much longer... before she started working as a mortician."

It didn't take any effort at all to convince her to help me. The kids are having a sleepover at grandma's tonight, they really are cuties. There's a wine glass laced with sleeping medication ready for Jonathan when he gets home, and I'm waiting in the basement, passing the time by ripping off more rotten skin, wondering what human flesh will taste like. Marianna's already said I can stay here while I recover. She wants to study me. I'm something she's never seen before, and she's fascinated.

She says I'm a real keeper.

LITTLE DEAD NANCY

'Little Dead Nancy,
Sitting on the bench,
One eye long,
and one eye gone,
Little Dead Nancy,
The red swing's open,
come take a seat,
and swing with me!'

I almost completed the summoning of Nancy back when I was a kid. I was somewhere in the second grade, I'd just moved to this new school. Long story short, parents divorced, mom got custody, and now instead of playing with my friends, I was surrounded by strangers.

I'd almost made the mistake of sitting on the red swing during recess when I was tackled into the sand by two other girls. "Don't sit there, that's Nancy's swing!" One of them managed to get out as I squirmed free.

"Who's Nancy?" I glanced around the playground, almost as if I expected to see a kid with a name tag that said 'Hi, I'm Nancy!'

The two girls looked at me like I was an idiot before they looped their arms in with mine and escorted me to the jungle gym.

It was there one of the girls, a gal with red pigtails named Leanne, told me the story of Little Dead Nancy.

The legend went that Nancy was a lonely little girl who had no friends and whose parents hated her, all because she was missing an eye. One day, after being beaten up by the school bully, Nancy went up to the swingset and used the red swing to hang herself. Ever since, that swing belonged to Nancy. If I used the red swing, I was just asking to end up like Little Dead Nancy. If one wanted to speak to Nancy, you had to repeat that little poem while you swung on the green or blue swing. Apparently she'd start swinging next to you once you recited it. It was unknown what she'd do to you, but I think the common conclusion was that she'd murder you.

So my immediate response to this was to go back to the swingset, plop my butt down on the green swing, and start reciting. I attracted quite a crowd with this daring stunt, and I'd gotten to the second 'Little Dead Nancy' when the teacher called us back in.

Quite a bummer to everyone who'd hoped some zombie child would show up and murder me, but I did end up bonding with Leanne about it. By the next day, I'd all but forgotten about the poem and just settled with playing House with Leanne and the other girl, Aileen.

I still kept my distance from that red swing. As I got older, I heard a bunch of stories of what happened to Nancy. Although the most common story was that she hung herself, some people said she was murdered by her parents, who were tired of having an imperfect daughter. Another story said it was just an accident, that Nancy had been trying to do a loop over the top of the swingset and ended up strangling herself that way. You know, good old kid stuff to keep us spooked.

As a sixth grader, I finally went and fact checked Nancy. Much to my surprise, there had been a death on the playground back in the seventies. But it wasn't 'Nancy', it was an eighty something year old teacher named Georgia Smith. She just croaked while pushing one of her students on the swing. I did share my findings with

Leanne, who had almost entirely forgotten about Little Dead Nancy and got a real kick out of my sudden morbid curiosity.

I didn't really have any friends other than Leanne and Aileen, and after Aileen ended up moving to Florida, all I had was Leanne. It was okay, we always just got each other. When my first dog died, she helped orchestrate a funeral. I comforted her after she had her very first break up. I thought we'd end up being friends until we were little old ladies.

Then last week happened. When Leanne was murdered, I almost got killed with her.

She was walking me back to my house after a study date when this gaggle of college aged dudes walked up behind us and started whistling and cat calling us. We're sixteen, so, gross. Leanne just stuck her head up and looped her arm in with mine as we picked up the pace.

This didn't settle with one of the guys, who sped up with us and grabbed Leanne's arm, calling her a bitch and asking what her problem was. I could smell the booze on his breath, and I tried pulling Leanne with me, saying that we have to get home as I had curfew. A lie, as my mom doesn't really care where I am ever, but I hoped this freak would get the hint and just leave us alone. It didn't work. This guy refused to let Leanne go and kept asking her to come with him.

I can't remember what Leanne said that set him off, but the next thing I remember was my head meeting the brick wall and the agonizing punch of pain of being stabbed in the back.

I was lucky. He only stabbed me once. When the cops came to investigate a disturbance, Leanne had been stabbed over twenty-three times. She was already dead. I was getting pretty damn close to it.

But I lived. Fucking hell, I'm alive and my best friend's dead.

The funeral was last Sunday. Our whole school came. People liked Leanne. She was popular. Could've done great things. I, on the other hand, was the social recluse who had no future and no friends. Other than Leanne. Who always made time for me.

No one has the nerve to blame me face to face for her death, but the only reason she was out that night was to walk me home. Note, I say face to face. I think I'm up to twenty-four death threats on Facebook from nine different people. Might be ten, but I think two of the accounts are the same person as they both wrongly spell bleach as 'bleche'. As in, 'drink bleche you fucking wore'. I think they mean 'whore'.

I've spent a lot of time walking around in the dark since the funeral. Maybe I wanted to see that bastard again, the description I gave was shoddy and whoever his shitbird friends are aren't selling him out. Maybe I just wanted to die and was too much of a coward to do it myself, so I wanted to find that bastard to finish the job he started.

But last night, somehow, I wound up on the playground.

Most of the playground equipment had been replaced, the slide, the merry go round, the sandbox... but the swing set was still the same, a rusted testament to the first day I met Leanne.

I brushed my fingers on the chain of the red swing, almost laughing as I remember her tackling me to the ground. That almost laughter turned into sobbing as I sank to my knees. Why couldn't God have taken me too, you know? We were best friends, going to be till the end.

I found myself sitting on the green swing without even re-membering why I did, as I slowly swung back and forth. The playground was unnervingly quiet. I couldn't even hear any birds.

"Little dead Nancy, sitting on the bench..."

I glanced at the bench the poem had to be talking about, it had also been replaced with a much nicer looking one. When I went to this school, I think one of the legs had been replaced by a brick.

"One eye long, and one eye gone..."

What did that poem even mean, one eye long? Kids were fuck-ing stupid.

"Little dead Nancy, the red swing's open..."

I hiccuped, another tear weaving a path down my cheek. That was as far as I'd gotten the time I'd recited. I remembered Leanne's face, eyes wide with anticipation. Anticipation for what, I really don't know, did that little girl really think that a zombie was going to tear me apart in front of her? Again. Kids are dumb. But they don't really mean it.

"C... Come take a seat, and swing with me."

Nothing. Of course. I shook my head and stared up at the sky. "I guess I got the answer for what happens when you ask Nancy to swing with you, Leanne," I murmured.

"Excuse me?"

I nearly froze as I heard the quiet voice behind me. I whipped my head around and nearly fell off the swing as I saw a little girl standing there.

Not a little girl. Nancy. Nancy was standing there.

She was a cute little thing, blonde curls, round face... well, would've been cute, if one of her eyes wouldn't have been just a black hole and the other one dangling from the socket, bobbing up against her bruised neck. She fiddled with her pink skirt before reaching into her pocket and pulling out a tissue. "You look like you need this," she said.

I slowly took it, expecting for her to lunge forward and bite me, but she just smiled as I wiped my face off and blew my nose. "T... thank you... you're Nancy?" I asked, just to be sure there wasn't another little ghost girl with a missing eyeball.

She nodded before taking her seat on the red swing, kicking her little white Mary Jane shoes back and forth. "That's my name, don't wear it out. I remember you," she said. "Can you push me? It's really hard to get going."

I don't know why I stood up and began gently pushing her, but I did. It was like touching an ice cube rather than a little girl. I swear the temperature around her had dropped to thirty degrees and Nancy herself was even colder. "You remember me?"

"Yupyup!" Nancy giggled as she began to swing back and forth. "Push me harder, you won't kill me. I do remember you, you almost completed the poem. Rarely anyone does the full thing, and I can't remember the last time someone did it when they were alone."

"Huh." At this point, I was wondering if I was seeing things and just pushing empty air, but this week had already been fucked enough, so I didn't really care. "Do you remember the little girl with me? Red pigtails?"

Nancy hummed before she bobbed her head up and down. "She seemed nice."

"She got murdered by a creep. That's why I was crying."

"I'm sorry." The apology sounded quite genuine, which made the next thing that came out of her mouth seem even more 'what the fuck'. "Are you going to kill the creep that killed her?"

I laughed. I couldn't help it, I was talking to a goddamn ghost child and now she was recommending homicide to fix my problems. "That would land me in jail probably forever, even if the jury would agree that he would deserve it. Plus, I don't even know his name. Can't kill a guy if I don't know who he is."

"His name is Garth. Garth Strickland. He's twenty-four years old, drives a two-door gray car that's clearly on its last legs. He's currently hiding out at his friend's house in the woods with all the other witnesses. Waiting for this problem to just go away because he's a spineless coward who is trying to reason that it wasn't his fault, he was drunk, she called him names, she was dressing like a slut, so she deserved what she got."

I nearly passed out. I stopped pushing her and slowly walked out to her side. "H... how do you know?"

"I know lots of things!" Nancy chirped, pumping her legs back and forth to keep up the speed. "I know exactly where to find him. I know how to take him and his bitchy friends out too. Eye for an eye," she reached up and flicked her dangling eyeball, "Tooth for tooth. I can help you kill him and gut him so he can't do it again.

You think this is the first girl he hurt? This is just the first one he killed."

"Okay, you're not a little girl, are you?" I crossed my arms. "What will it cost me to get these creeps?"

Nancy laughed and at the peak of her swing jumped off, landing neatly on her feet before turning around. "You're pretty smart. You know there's never been a dead kid on this playground, well, not one within the last few centuries at least. No, I'm not a little girl. I can be helpful, though. All I ask in return is you let me tag along. I've gotten *no* action these past few years, and the old bird that croaked here a forever ago doesn't count—she just happened to accidentally see what I actually look like and her ticker couldn't take it."

I'd like to say I took my time to think about it. This was serious after all, and I sure as hell couldn't trust 'Nancy', whatever the hell she was.

But I knelt down to her height almost immediately, offering my hand to her. "Deal. I'll take you back to the playground when we're done, though."

"Of course. I do like it here after all, there's a reason I'm a legend among the kids."

Nancy took my hand, and she changed. She grew in size, blond curls turned into red hair, the dangling blue eye turned to a shade of hazel.

I nearly started crying again when I saw Leanne kneeling in front of me. She cocked her head to the side before she wrapped her arms around me. The icy temperature gave away that this wasn't my friend, but god, just for a minute I was going to pretend. I threw my arms around her and hugged her tight. "I'm sorry," I said.

"It wasn't your fault. Don't ever think that ever again... Thank you for being my best friend," 'Leanne' whispered in my ear before I felt her chill enter my own skin. I closed my eyes as the cold crawled into my bones, deep in my heart, freezing me to my very core.

When I stood, I was alone. But I could feel the grief inside of me turn to the coldest rage.

Nancy is still inside of me. Every breath I take is borderline painful due to the chill. I imagine touching me would be like putting your bare hand on frozen metal. I had to 'borrow' my mom's car to get here. But I'm in the same town where Garth is, along with all the witnesses that stood by and did nothing while he murdered an innocent girl.

I'll stab each and every one of them twenty-three times. And each one is going to be for her.

———

'Little Dead Nancy,
Sitting on the bench,
One eye long,
and one eye gone,
Little Dead Nancy,
My friend lies dead,
Come along, join me,
let's go see Garth together!'

Doesn't nearly flow off the tongue nearly so well as the first verse, but it gets the point across.

We waited in the woods for a long time, she and I. It was cold out at night, but it wasn't colder than we were. It was strange not seeing my breath on every exhale. But I wasn't bored. We had a lot of time to talk.

The first instinct was to move in the minute we got there, but Nancy made known that we needed to wait. We needed to make sure we could get them all in one fell swoop.

So we waited for three days. Until the storm came.

It was a doozy. The rain came down in sheets, hail smacked against the windows of the cabin where the boys were lying low, and lightning lit up the sky. The roads were certainly going to be washed out. Now was the time.

The first victim was Rick. He went on the back porch to smoke. Nancy told me he was Garth's best friend. His family was the one that owned the cabin. Rick was somewhat nice, but he didn't care that his best friend was a murderer. That's not the sign of a good person.

He was smoking a blunt on the back porch, watching the rain, back turned towards me. He never saw us coming.

Too bad he didn't go for a haircut before this. It probably would've stopped us from grabbing him by the hair and dragging him off the porch. The cabin itself was surrounded by a drop-off into a steep ravine. He took one too many steps back and took a tumble down. When we caught up to him, he was pretty fucked up. A sharp piece of bone was jutting out of his thigh and he kept bitching about how his back hurt.

I flicked the knife around in the air and Rick's eyes went so wide I thought they might pop out. "W-wait! Please, don't do it-"

I didn't give him the chance to beg for his life. We had a lot of time to sharpen the knife. I plunged it into his chest as many times as Garth stabbed Leanne. The rain washed the blood down the hill as we got back up.

Luckily for us, his keys were on his belt. Said keys were now ours.

I hiked back up that hill and got back to the cabin. Luckily no one seemed to be missing Rick—they were partying it up. Guess they figured that the heat was finally dying down. Soon they'd go home.

Only, they wouldn't. They'd never leave this cabin.

Liam was digging through the fridge for more munchies. Liam was the most loyal to Garth. It was his idea to go into hiding while things died down. His sense of humor was rape jokes and those prank videos where you grope or molest innocent women. Thankfully, he also didn't realize the footsteps behind him weren't those of his friends. He asked me when we were going to make another beer run.

It was quick, that deep slash across the throat, but I didn't want him to scream. It wasn't as quiet as I thought it would be, though. Liam thrashed about with a gurgle and his neck sprayed blood everywhere. He fell back with a crash, and I heard someone yell from the living room, asking if Liam was okay.

I hooked my arms under Liam's armpits and dragged him out the backdoor. He was nearly done for by the time I managed to get him partway down the hill. I finished him off the same way I finished off Rick, and then kicked his body the rest of the way down.

I slipped around front, hearing a horrified commotion coming from the kitchen. I imagine seeing a bloody kitchen would make anyone lose their shit. I listened into the conversation from the living room for a while, enjoying their futile attempts to call 911. Their signal was already shit during the clear weather. It was nonexistent during the storm.

One of them, Cody, turned his head to the kitchen entryway and made eye contact with me. His jaw dropped when saw me standing there in bloodstained clothing and holding a knife. I made sure to dive away by the time he got everyone else to look over.

I hid in the bedroom as they split up to find the psycho in their house. I crawled under the bed and waited for my moment. My luck, Cody was the one who made it into the bedroom. Cody once filmed a girl being sexually assaulted at a party when she was passed out drunk. Cody thought he didn't do anything wrong because he never laid a finger on her.

I plunged the knife through his foot as he approached the bed. He screeched as I pulled myself out from underneath, grinning before I stabbed him... well, in the dick. What, I was still kneeling and it was all I could really reach! You can't say he didn't deserve it either.

His screams reached a whole new octave as I pulled the knife back out. I couldn't take the time to savor it, though. I had a job to do and no doubt the final two guys in the house heard that scream. I drove the knife into his chest, pierced his heart, and that was all she wrote.

Garth and his final breathing friend, Xavier, broke into the bedroom just as the knife went in the twenty-third time. Panting, I got to my feet. I could feel my clothes becoming crusty with blood, not to mention my hair.

Neither man looked at me with recognition in his eyes. I cocked my head to the side and smiled. "So, who's next?" I asked.

Garth never stopped being a coward. He shoved Xavier forward and bolted. I heard him run up the stairs and slam the door behind him.

"Garth, you *dick*!" Xavier turned to run after him but stopped when my thrown knife embedded itself in his back.

This was an unfortunate mistake on my part. By throwing the knife, I lost my weapon. And a human filled with adrenaline will do whatever it can to survive.

Xavier pulled the knife out of his back and came at me with it, bellowing like a bull and nearly taking my head off. I ducked and dodged, but got slashed across the chest and the face. It hurt like hell, but what *really* hurt is when he managed to get me in the eye.

I screamed in rage, clutching my bleeding face, Xavier smiling like an idiot as he thought he had the upper hand.

Then I did us both a favor and popped that eye out of my skull. Xavier pissed his pants at the sight, me raising that gore-covered eyeball up to stare at the creep's face.

You remember how Cody filmed a girl being assaulted? Xavier was one of the assaulters. Is it really rape if she's unconscious? Well, obviously, yes, but not in Xavier's mind.

The moment of shock was all I needed to charge and chomp my teeth right into Xavier's throat. Not a graceful kill, but I was out of options. And, hey, it worked. He couldn't even scream.

He dropped the knife. I picked it up, and in just a little while there were twenty-three holes in his chest. Xavier was the tough one, but I still won.

I was on the final stretch. One more and Leanne would be able to rest in peace.

I kicked open the door and found Garth cowering in the corner. He screamed as I walked in, my popped-out eyeball bouncing off my cheek as I crouched in front of him. "What do you want!? Just leave me alone, I didn't do anything wrong!" he shouted at me.

I obviously laughed, because that was far from true. "You don't remember the girl you stabbed in the back?" I asked. "You don't remember the girl you stabbed before you turned on her friend and butchered her?"

Now he remembered. He whimpered as his back pressed against the wall. There was nowhere for him to go. "You? Wh... how did..."

"Well, it's not that girl, either. Well, kind of not." I hummed the tune of an oh-so-familiar schoolyard chant and Garth remembered.

All the kids that went to my school do. My legend dates back to 1973, the same year the school was built. Back then, I was nothing. But the kids named me. The swing set became hallowed ground, or, should I say, desecrated ground. Say my prayer next to the red swing and there I'll appear before you. I'll offer you power, but I always ask for something in return.

Garth never said the chant. He never went near my swing. Swings were for girls, after all. And to be a girl was to be weak in his mind.

It was clear that he was the weak one, begging for his life, offering me anything I wanted if I spared him his life. But I had what I wanted—I had a body, and I had the souls of four sinful bastards.

And now I would have five.

Garth died in the exact same way Leanne did. I made sure each stab would match the marks left on hers perfectly. Then I added one more. One more for the girl whose body I was possessing.

Did you pick up where I stopped referring to myself as 'we' and 'us'? Well, my dear host might have been angry about the death of her best friend, but the moment she raised the knife in the air to stab Rick, she realized she didn't have what it takes. So I decided to take over and handle it from there.

Little Dead Nancy had to tell you this story of glorious and ever-so-satisfying revenge that you all wanted to hear. I've dealt with the bodies, the evidence. They'll never be found. Or maybe they will, years and years and years from now, but they'll be nothing but John Does. Their families will never have peace. They don't deserve it.

My host still sleeps, but I placed her eye back in her head. It'll be blind for the rest of her days, but that's a minor inconvenience considering I could take up permanent residence if I wanted to. And believe me, it was something I considered.

But I'll be back on my bench near the swings by tonight, my host in control of her body once more.

I'd miss the kids too much. My youthful congregation, spreading the legend of Little Dead Nancy, the dead little girl on the swing set.

Just remember, my friends, there's never been a dead little girl on the playground.

MISMATCHED EYES

I have heterochromia.

My mom has it too, only hers is sectoral heterochromia. A part of her left eye is brown, while most of it is blue. Mine's complete. My right eye is brown, the left is blue. As a kid, I'd get the most excited reaction out of the adults—

"His eyes are so beautiful!"

"Wow, they're different colors!"

"How stunning!"

I'd like to say that my eyes are only one part of myself, that it's just a slice of the pie that makes up me. But really, the only fascinating part of myself is the heterochromia. I'm average in grades. Height. Strength. IQ. Not much stunning charisma either—I tend to stick to myself.

But in the end, it's my eyes that saved my life. And maybe the lives of a few others.

The killings started my sophomore year. A young couple going out to smooch in their car was found dead, mangled by some wild beast. Their faces had been eaten off, their tongues ripped out, and their eyes completely gone.

I didn't know them, they went to the private school. All the same, the stories started up about the Gosbecks Knoll Beast.

My mom laughed when I told her about it. Apparently the 'Beast' was around in her highschool days too, two people turned up dead before it stopped. Conveniently, at the same time a bear was brought down in the area. She told me just not to go smooching any girls around there and I'd be fine.

Of course, this is when I corrected her and said 'boys' but this really didn't take her by surprise. Mom's good like that.

However, this time, The Beast wasn't content just to gnaw on the faces of horny teens on our Lover's Lane.

When I'd gotten to school about a week after the first incident, I knew something was wrong. Everyone was quiet, and a lot of people were crying. I found my friend Trent and asked him what was up. He criticized me for not checking my Facebook before he told me.

Douglas Stafford. Better known as Doug. Senior. Everyone loved him. He was a nice guy. Heck, even to lil ole wallflower me. I'd gotten lost on my first day of freshman year and he pointed me in the right direction, even offered to walk me there. I never talked to him again, but damn. I felt like I'd been punched in the gut.

He'd turned up dead in his parents' garage. His face gnawed on, just like the pair from earlier.

The next day there was a school assembly where the principal even teared up a bit and told us that it was okay if we were upset and if necessary, we could take an absence from class to talk to the school counselor. Doug's girlfriend Cathy was in the front row bawling. They'd dated since their freshman year, and it was pretty obvious they would've one day gotten a house with a white picket fence and a dog.

Cathy was the last casualty of the school year, a few months later she was found dead in the forest. The Beast hadn't been the one to kill her though—she'd hung herself and apparently Beastie helped himself, at least according to the rumors.

During the summer, everything went quiet, and soon the talks of dead teens faded into the background. I think Doug's parents started up a fund for depressed youth. I spent ninety percent of the summer in my bedroom playing way too many video games.

I also came out on Facebook. I got a lot of approval. A lot of 'you're perfect the way you are'. And a lot of 'dude it was OBVI-OUS.'

However, Trent didn't see it as most people did. He unfriend-ed me almost immediately and when I got back to school, he'd apparently been badmouthing me to our mutual friends. None of them wanted anything to do with me anymore.

I won't lie, it hurt a lot. But I chose to ignore it for the most part. So I lost all my close friends. Big deal. I could get new ones.

Yeah, no, not happening.

Like I said, my social skills suck. The only reason Trent and I were friends in the first place was because we were assigned to be project partners in the fourth grade. We got a B. And now whenever he talked to me, every other sentence had the word 'fag' or 'queer' thrown in someplace. Shows how little I knew about my best friend, right?

But this is when the murders REALLY picked up the pace.

The first victim of junior year was Camille Dunn. She'd missed her bus home and decided to walk. The next morning a dog walker found her stretched out on the sidewalk, eyes gone and face eaten off. The Beast was back.

Clearly there was some madman or wild animal on the loose and everyone put up their guard. But now I think this is when the Beast got really cocky. He realized he could get away with this shit.

The next victims were in their own damn *house*. An elderly couple, John and Beatrice. They lived across the street from me. When I woke up the next morning to sirens, my heart sank. I thought Beatrice's heart finally gave out on her.

Noooo, the Beast just decided to up his game by ripping out that heart. It was the same thing though- ate their faces and ripped out their eyes. It got into the house through the back window and left the same way, judging by the bloody prints. Kids whispered about how supposedly the prints looked like a human's but with claws at the toes. Sightings of The Beast grew in number, and a description came together of a freak that had fangs and glowing eyes, his only desire being to hunt and kill.

Of course, my mom immediately implemented a curfew and kept the house secure. At night I'd hear her wake up and walk around, as if to make sure we were safe.

I believed in the Beast when she saw it too.

I woke up to hear her scream and I ran to the source. My mom was white as a ghost, her hand on her heart as she stared out the now empty window.

"It... it was there. I don't know what it was, but—fuck, fuck, call the police, call the police right *now!*"

My mom doesn't cuss. She's a classy lady like that. I grabbed the junior baseball bat I used as a kid and called 911. Cops showed up surprisingly fast and mom told them what happened while her eyes still darted to the window on occasion.

She'd gone downstairs because she couldn't sleep, and it was at the window. Its shape was vaguely humanoid, but its eyes did in fact glow. That's when she screamed. It must've not expected her to see it as it took off running. And sure enough, when I went into the backyard the next morning, its feet were indeed clawed. I didn't bother collecting evidence, as I'm sure everyone would've thought I faked it, but I knew the Beast was real.

Two days later I got kidnapped by my so-called 'friend'.

I was walking home from school when Trent ran up behind me, acting all buddy buddy until he got close. Then I felt a switchblade press against my side. Trent was still smiling, but it was cold, dark.

"Start walking, you fucking queer."

The biggest 'well shit' moment of my life.

I didn't try to be the hero and get the knife, Trent was bigger than me and I didn't have a prayer. We walked until we got to his car, where he pushed me into the backseat and he duct-taped my hands and feet together.

He drove us out of town to this abandoned old shed. Two other guys I didn't know were waiting there, and I saw more knives. I was close to pissing myself while still being neck deep in denial. Surely this had to be a joke, though. Just a prank to scare me.

Trent dragged me inside and slammed the door.

It was dark and I couldn't see a thing. I got whacked in the stomach and the air whooshed out of my lungs.

"You fucking fag. How many times did you touch me when I slept over, huh?" I could hear the sneer in Trent's voice.

I groaned as I was shoved to my knees. "Never, Trent. You're not exactly my type," I said as I struggled against the tape.

I got kicked across the face and I hit the floor. I felt one of my teeth come loose and blood start to pool in my gums.

Trent squatted down next to me. I could barely make out his silhouette in the cracks in the shed.

"Fucking liar. You're a freak. And now you're gonna be another victim of the Gosbecks Knoll Beast, old buddy."

I felt the blade press right beneath my blue eye.

"Hope your mommy doesn't miss your creepy ass eyes, faggot!"

I wanted to shut my eyes. Hoped that he'd drive the knife right into my brain so I didn't have to feel it. Instead, my eyes stayed wide open as the blade glinted, and I suddenly made out Trent and his three goonies...

Yeah. *Three* goonies. There were only two outside the shed.

Guess the Beast really doesn't care for copycats.

I heard the scream before the tallest of the figures slammed the other two heads together. When standing straight up he almost reached the ceiling. Trent whipped around and the blade nicked below my eye.

"What the fuck-"

Another whack and Trent was on the ground. I heard him choking and realized I smelled blood.

The figure moved onto me and he hoisted me up to his level. I felt claws tear my shirt. I was certain I'd be dead.

Then I felt the monster pause.

"... Eyes?"

I passed out.

When I came to, it was now dark outside, and we were no longer in the shed. Now we were in a cabin, lit by a lantern.

And I saw the Beast in his entirety.

He looked vaguely human, wearing what looked like a loin-cloth, had pale skin and black stringy hair that hung down his back. His skin was occasionally broken up by patches of scales, and his fingers looked like a tiny blade stuck out of each. His spine was lined with thin bristles that would rise and fall with each breath.

Trent was hung up in the corner by a hook, awake and filled with terror. I could smell more blood. The Beast examined Trent's face thoughtfully before his middle finger carved through his cheek.

I shut my eyes tight when I heard Trent scream.

The Beast made almost no sound at all, other than a soft hum as he worked on carving off Trent's face. When I took a peek, I saw the gleaming white of Trent's cheekbones.

My eyes shut again.

Finally, when the screams went quiet, I heard footsteps approach. Felt his huge presence kneel over me. His hair smelled like pond weeds.

"... Open. Open your eyes."

I did, although I'm not sure why.

His face was kinda human. Had a strong nose and gaunt features. But it was his eyes that caught me.

They glowed all right. But the left one was yellow, and the right eye was violet.

The Beast inhaled sharply before his hand reached up to my face. I flinched and tilted my head away, but he only hushed me as he lightly caressed my cheek. His claws didn't even break skin.

"... Eyes. They don't... match."

I swallowed. "N... neither do yours," I pointed out.

The Beast grinned, his crooked teeth flecked with blood. "No. No they don't," he said, almost if he was trying not to laugh.

I don't know what possessed me to do this, but I reached up to touch his face too. His skin was oily, it almost reminded me of a fish. "They uh, look good though?" I offered. Play nice with the monster, maybe you can go home.

This comment struck him, he looked shocked. Then he pulled me into the most uncomfortable hug of my life.

"... Only one. Thought I was the only one," He sobbed, I felt his greasy tears hit the top of my head.

Really not sure of how to handle this, I patted his back, careful to avoid the spines. God knew they were probably poisonous. Thankfully the Beast seemed to appreciate this.

I'm really not sure *how* I fell asleep with a giant stinky monster practically spooning me, but when I woke up, the police were there. According to them, someone called 911 from my phone and told them where to find me.

Trent's body was found strung up in the other room with the other two guys. They'd been almost entirely butchered. It was a miracle I was alive, according to the police.

I attended Trent's funeral. I don't know why, but I did. His sister apologized for all the bullshit he did to me. I saved her the knowledge of the fact he was going to murder me and make it look like the Beast did it.

When I got home late that night, I found mussel shells on my windowsill. I took them inside and let them rest on my dresser.

Top of my dresser's covered with little 'gifts' now, from snake skins to smooth rocks to glass beads. I haven't seen him since that night but sometimes, I catch a glimpse of those mismatched eyes, glowing from my backyard.

THE DANGERS OF TATTOOS

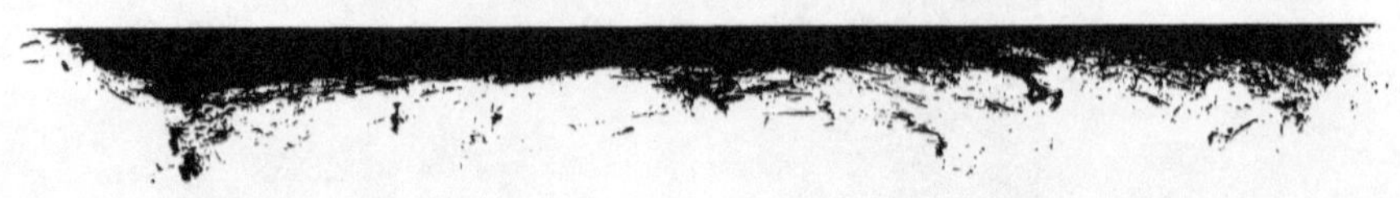

Out of the nine guys at Dillan's bachelor party, I'm the only one who's still alive. And I don't know how much time I have left.

Dillan was a friend from my highschool days. We weren't close, but we hung out when all our other friends were busy. I was happy to hear he was getting hitched to his girl Heather, they were good for each other. When he asked me to join him and a few of the other guys for his bachelor party, I happily accepted. One last crazy night before he said I Do.

We'd all gotten pretty buzzed when Mickey threw out this brilliant idea:

'We should all get tattoos!'

I'd never gotten a tattoo before, but I was probably one of two guys who hadn't been in the group. Mickey in particular was covered in ink, full sleeves on both arms, and he had proudly shown off the progress made on one over his ribs—the inked outline of a Kraken. He and his artist were going to start putting in color in two months.

Like I said, I'd never been inked, but I was in awe. And to my drunk brain, getting a tattoo with the guys sounded fantastic. And whadya know, just down the street there was a parlor.

Unfortunately, they didn't tattoo people who weren't sober. The guy was incredibly patient, just pointing to the sign and saying if we wanted to get a tattoo after our hangovers, he'd happily help us out. The only one to get cranky about this was Derek, Mickey ended up dragging him out by the ear as the idiot cussed out the artist. Yeah, the artist said that all of us would get inked if we wanted, *except* for Derek. Genius move, Derek.

When we were all on the street again, talking about getting more drinks, that's when she just... appeared.

I didn't hear her walk up, although I'm not sure how, she had heels that could put a man's eye out. The only reason we even knew she was there was because she cleared her throat. I whipped around and she was like two inches behind me, way too much in my personal space for me to be comfortable. I yelped and slipped on some slush, landing on my ass. Everyone laughed, but she just sighed and helped me to my feet.

She was wearing a puffy green coat and black skinny jeans, but even with her skin mostly covered, I could see ink on her neck. Half her head was shaved, and I saw three piercings in her exposed ear, not to mention the several on her face—eyebrows, septum, lips, this girl had it all.

"So, Phillips says you're too drunk?" She grinned and chuckled pleasantly. "I'm Lacey. Come on, I'll take you to my shop. I think I can work something out." She turned around and started walking down the street.

Mickey whistled. "She's so fucking *hot*," he murmured.

"You hear her though? Tattoos, man! Plan's back in action!" Derek whooped and took off down the street after her.

Sober, I realized how sketchy this was, but drunk me was just excited to get a tattoo. So I followed the herd. Like a moron.

The girl led us down a few side streets and took so many turns there is no way I could find my way back. But finally, she led us down the side of a building and down a set of stairs to a metal door with one word stamped on it:

'Coven'

"Come on in, boys," she grinned and opened the door.

It actually wasn't nearly as sketchy looking inside. I expected no ceiling, maybe one chair that reeked of mildew, but it was a legit tattoo shop. Pictures were all over the walls of the shop's previous works, and there was another woman with firetruck red hair and huge gauges in her earlobes texting away in one of the leather chairs.

"Hey, Barb, we got customers," The woman shrugged off her coat and threw it on the rack, revealing that she was only wearing a tank top and yeah—she was *covered* in ink. From the chin down it was just a myriad of pictures.

"Kay, Lacey," Barb got up and glanced over. "Sooo, y'all gonna be matching or..."

I glanced over at Dillan, who nodded. "I'm getting married in two days, we're just out partying!" he said, trying to sound bold.

Barb just smirked. "Cute. All right, I'll take the bachelor, Lacey, mind taking the shrimpy guy? I think he's a fainter," she nodded at me, and I was offended but only had a moment for that because Lacey grabbed my hand and yanked me to the chair.

She took a seat next to me and smiled, and I suppose she was quite pretty, although I wasn't sure how old she was. "It's gonna be fine, dude. Your first tattoo?" she asked. I heard Barb talking with Dillan quietly about what he wanted everyone to get.

I nodded. "Yeah. Never been really into them, but why not, right?" If I really regretted it, I'd just get it lasered away, I reasoned.

"Just remember to breathe," she looked up at Barb, "Did he decide?"

Barb nodded and lifted a pic in the air of a symbol that looked like two triangles next to each other, a dot in the middle. Lacey giggled.

"Oh, love that choice! All right, buddy, where do you want it?"

I chose my upper arm. After that, everything kinda blurs together. I don't even remember pain, I just remember stumbling out the door feeling kinda nauseated and trying to get an Uber.

I woke up the next morning, my arm hurt like hell, and I had fifteen missed calls from the guys last night and twenty-one texts in the group text. Although my head was pounding, I managed to make out the point—

'Dude, where tf is Mickey?'

'his girlfriend said mickey didn't make it home last night did any of you see where he went'

'GUYS THERE WAS AN ACCIDENT LIKE TWO BLOCKS FROM COVEN DUDE GOT PANCAKED BY A SEMI TRUCK'

'What the FUCK was it Mickey'

'they literally cannot tell who it was the guy was in pieces'

Jesus Christ. My arm ached, and I didn't even know where to start with these texts. I popped some pain meds and called Dillan. He didn't answer, so I tried Derek. When there was no answer, I had a bad feeling starting to form in my stomach.

After two more calls, I got a response from one of the guys I barely knew, Toby. He was Dillan's cousin and was just in the state for the wedding.

"Hey man, I'm sorry for calling so early-" I was cut off by Toby quite quickly.

"I was starting to think you fucking dropped off the edge of the earth, dude! You okay?"

I groaned. "Maybe? Tattoo hurts, but that's normal I think. Was the guy last night Mickey?"

"I think they managed to ID him from some of the tattoos... I'm sorry man, I know he was a friend, I didn't really know him but... god." I heard Toby quietly gag. "From what I understand, he was just smashed. The driver said it was like an explosion. The guy's gonna need some therapy. Um, wedding's today, are you going to-"

"Hell no." I felt two seconds from hurling. "I don't wanna upchuck on the bride and I didn't really get an official invite. You have a good time."

I hung up and ran to the toilet to puke my guts up. I swore I was never going to get that drunk again as I crawled back into bed with a bottle of water to sip from.

I woke up again about an hour later to my phone going off. I managed to grab it and answer it on the fourth ring.

"Hello-"

"We fucked up! Holy *shit*, I think I'm gonna be sick again, oh my god, oh my god-"

I could barely recognize the voice as Derek, he sounded so hysterical. "Slow down, what the fuck happened?" I said as I sat up.

" Dillan blew up."

My immediate response was to snicker.

"What are you saying? Did he open his mouth to say I do and blew chunks all over Heather's face?"

"No, I'm saying that Dillan opened his mouth to say I do and *literally fucking exploded*."

I laughed again, although it was forced this time. "Really funny dude. What the fuck are you talking about?"

The next thing I heard was Derek start to sob. Like, legitly bawl his eyes out. The bad feeling from earlier returned tenfold.

"He'd... he'd been complaining about his tattoo all morning, it was getting itchy, and Toby just said it was healing, so just don't touch it. Middle of the ceremony, he just opened his mouth before his eyes just bugged out and he grabbed his chest... and that's all she wrote. It was like someone set off a bomb. Blood and guts just. Everywhere. Heather passed out, Toby took off running and when I went to go find him, it was the same thing. Blood everywhere. Oh my god, we're going to fucking die. Those bitches put a curse on us or something, we're all gonna fucking die!"

I looked down at my arm and slowly peeled off the bandage covering my tattoo. It looked innocent enough. Just a few simple black lines.

I heard Derek gasp.

"I... I don't feel so good, it's getting really itchy..."

I heard a gurgle before Derek screamed, only to be cut off by a disturbingly wet splatter and the phone dropping to the ground.

I ran to the bathroom to puke again.

I tried calling all the other guys. Only two picked up, Mark and Reece. Mark had been at the wedding and seen the whole damn thing, Reece had been sick in bed like I was and had slept through all the phone calls and texts. We agreed to meet up at Reece's place.

I sorta knew Mark, we had a single class together when we went to highschool, but I only met Reece last night. I rolled up my sleeve to show off my tattoo, which had yet to itch but every little twitch had me thinking 'this is it, I'm gonna go kaboom'.

We all sat in Reece's kitchen while Reece was messing around with something on the counter. Mark legitimately whimpered as he showed off his tattoo on his chest. My blood ran cold when I realized the ink itself was starting to turn crimson. "I think it's like a timer, the closer to red, the closer to... oh god, we're so fucked," he said, running his hand through his hair.

"You're not going to fucking *die*," Reece said, turning around. I yelped as I saw a knife in his hand.

"Jesus Christ, what are we doing with that?" I asked.

"Not we, you two."

Reece sighed as he pulled down the neck to his turtleneck to show off the damned tattoo. "Listen, if it's the tattoo making us blow up, then just get rid of the tattoo. I don't know if I can skin my neck without actually killing myself, but you two stand a chance." He sat down and continued sharpening the kitchen knife. "I'll help you first, Parker. You'll probably scar, but this means you won't be dead, right?"

I swallowed as I stared at the sharp knife before I shook my head. "Shouldn't you do Mark first?" I asked.

"I think we still have time, and I'll feel better if I fuck up on your arm than I would if I accidentally stabbed Mark in the chest."

He gestured for my arm. "Faster we do this, the faster it's over with. Gimme your arm."

Christ, I felt time stop as I slowly offered my arm to this stone faced guy. Reece positioned the knife just above the tattoo before the knife went down.

The worst pain lit up every nerve on my arm, and I screamed. Mark had to hold me down as Reece to slice off my skin to stop me from accidentally punching Reece. It was like someone was burning me alive.

I passed out sometime during this and when I woke up, I was surrounded by blood.

Not my blood, both Reece's and Mark's. Sometime when I was unconscious, they'd both blown up. It was like someone stuck them in a blender and then splattered them all over the walls. Even their clothes were in tiny little bits.

And to make matters worse, the tattoo isn't *gone*. It penetrated all the way through my skin to my muscle... maybe even my bone.

I can't tell how much longer I have, but I'm not going out without a fight. I'm sharpening more knives, I got some vodka out of Reece's kitchen and I'm preparing myself for what I have to do. I will probably die doing this, but I definitely will if I don't do this.

If the tattoo is on my arm, then I guess my arm will just have to go.

THE CAT LADY

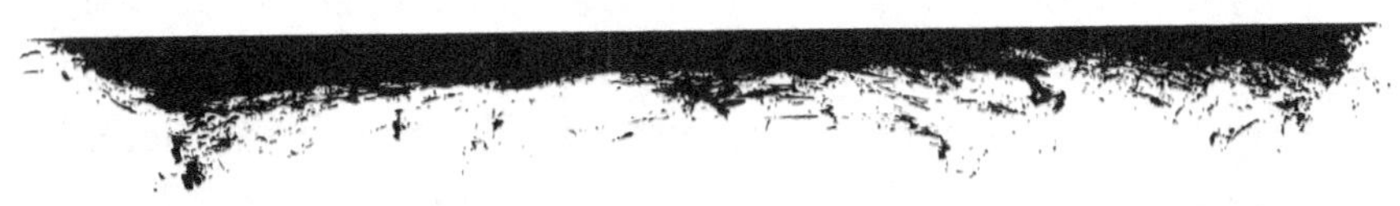

I used to have three beautiful cats. Chloe, Jewel, and Mercy. My sweet girls. I had the perfect family. My husband Greg, son Dylan, and of course the cats. Jewel was the snitch, always pacing around the table, warbling for whatever we had. She had developed a taste for green beans. Mercy was the prim lady. Always cleaning herself. Always sitting on the bookshelves. And always found where I hid the cat treats.

Chloe was my favorite, though. Whenever my lap was available, you'd find her sitting there. At night she'd sleep at the foot of the bed. In the morning, she'd wake me by kneading my chest. Greg would laugh and say she was just making sure my heart hadn't stopped. Her version of kitty CPR.

Greg and I were considering getting just one more when the accident happened. Greg was on the way to the clinic with the cats to update their vaccinations, and... well, I'm almost thankful that my babies didn't suffer.

I lost my cats and my husband all at once. Dylan was already a grown man, and after barely four months after the loss, he took off for college. I was all alone in my house, and my broken heart showed no sign of mending. Dylan barely came to visit, and after the first five years, I was lucky to get a card for Christmas.

I became the 'old crazy witch' on the block with the dead husband. The kids made up their stories, I mostly just sat on my front porch and enjoyed the sun when it came out—the heat made my sore joints feel better.

Then I met Goliath.

My neighborhood is very close to a wooded park. On my days off from work at the grocery store, Greg and I used to walk down those quiet paths. But there was also a feral cat problem there. I'd catch only glimpses of their skinny bodies and wild eyes.

But while I knitted on the front porch one morning, a streak of fur caught my attention, and I saw him. Immediately I dubbed him Goliath.

He was enormous. A tomcat that was bigger than some dogs, he had a mean face, matted long fur, and torn up ears. But he had the same coloring as Chloe, black with mottled orange and brown.

He came to a stop in front of the porch and froze, staring at me. I stared back. His tail twitched. His amber eyes bore right into mine.

" Here, kitty kitty."

Goliath slowly stepped closer to the porch, stopping at the steps. When I got up and tried to get closer, Goliath darted away and ran into the bushes. He didn't trust me.

But I was so lonely. Even a big old mean cat like that could give me some sort of companionship.

I went inside and got some canned tuna, opening it up and setting it at the steps. After I retreated to my chair, Goliath returned. He smelled the tuna. He licked his chops and stared at the can, but was nervous around me. So I went inside. When I came back a few minutes later, Goliath was focused on licking out the can.

I made a friend that day.

Goliath took forever to get used to me, the mistrusting kitty who had never seemed to have felt a human's touch. But he didn't leave, he took to sleeping in the tire swing in the front yard. Greg never got around to taking the damn thing down when Dylan grew too old for it. Goliath showed up for lunch every day, I'd feed him tuna and chatter to him. He'd purr like a semi-truck.

Then one day he brought a date—a gray tabby with a short tail and a missing eye.

I went to the store that night and invested in bulk bags of dry food and the canned stuff.

Duchess, the gray tabby, didn't hesitate to make herself at home in the tree outside. Neither did the others. It was a trickle, and never consistent. One day I'd just have Goliath and Duchess, the next there would be six or seven meowing babies ready for lunch.

For the first time in years, I felt whole. Like I had a purpose again, to take care of these innocent creatures. Most wouldn't come close, but Goliath had become my friend. While I watched the sun set, Goliath would sprawl across my lap and would purr when I scratched his ears.

But of course, the new neighbors didn't take so kindly to my new friends.

It was one family in particular, the Hubbards. The Hubbards had five boys between seven and fourteen. All of them were incredibly ill behaved. This was the same family that tried to claim that the lovely Hakim family was building bombs in their garage (their eldest daughter was actually building an automatic feeder for their dog) and that the reason that one house down the street wasn't selling was because we had Alec and Derek living together 'in sin'. The poor couple actually moved away from how awful the harassment got.

So when the wife Carla saw me with my cats, she threw a fit. She slammed her trash bin shut and marched over to my yard. The shyer cats ran off to the backyard, while Goliath sat content on my lap, unamused by this intruder.

"What is with all these cats?" she snapped.

Goliath just yawned and licked his paw.

I nervously smiled. "Good afternoon, Carla. These are just some strays I like to take care of. They're harmless, maybe a bit flea bitten but they do no harm."

Carla huffed and glared at Goliath. "That one looks like a wildcat, he could hurt my boys! And why are you wasting money feeding these... these strays, when you could have been donating to the church food drive?!"

To calm my nerves, I stroked Goliath's ears. "Goliath won't hurt a soul that won't hurt him. And I did donate."

"Well clearly you had some to spare." Carla flipped her hair over her shoulder, looking down her nose at me. "My son already says the neighborhood calls you a witch. Stop attracting these diseased animals or I'll be forced to call the police!"

Goliath tilted his ears back and hissed. Almost instantaneously, all the other cats turned and started to circle Carla, lurking, hair standing up their backs and growling. The scene was unnerving, to say the least. Carla backed away, growing pale, before she screamed, "Get away from me!" She kicked Kirk across the lawn before she dashed off.

The cats immediately gathered around Kirk, licking his face and purring to soothe him. I got up to check on him. Nothing was hurt except for the neutered tom's pride. I reassured them, the police wouldn't do a thing about my babies, they weren't destroying property or using the other yards as their toilet. They didn't even meow loudly at night.

Well, at first they didn't.

That night became an entire chorus of yowls. I looked out of my bedroom window to see a whole clutter of cats gathered in the Hubbard's front yard. There had to be at least twenty-five to thirty. In front was Goliath, I could make out his quivering hollers out of the rest.

The minute a light would go on inside the house, the cats would scatter, leaving none in sight. I think a few times I saw Carla's husband John pitch something out of the window, probably a bottle considering the crash of glass, but as far as I could tell, none made it close to a feline target.

Even though it was wrong, I giggled like a schoolgirl before shutting off the light and going to bed. I'd had cats in the past. I could sleep through it.

The next morning, Carla was banging on my door, clearly exhausted after a night with no sleep. A paper was shoved in my face, I almost got bopped across the nose.

"Your neighbors aren't happy with you, Doris." Carla had the nerve to look smug. "We petition that you take care of your cat problem, stop feeding them, hire an animal control service, just do it!"

I took the petition and read down the list of names. There wasn't as many as Carla would make me think—and the families that did sign up were her lackeys, the ones who kept their negativity to themselves until someone spoke up about it.

I sighed and lowered the petition. "Carla, it wasn't anything I did that made the cats loud last night. They were in your yard, weren't they?" My turn to look smug.

That knocked the wind out of Carla's sails. She stammered for a second before snatching the petition out of my hands. "This is your last warning. If you don't do something about these cats, I will!" With that, she stormed off, and would've looked awfully haughty... had not Goliath darted from the bushes and tripped her. Carla fell flat on her nose and Goliath ran up to me, rubbing himself against my ankles and purring before entering my house.

That was the first time Goliath entered my house, I'd never tried to take him in. But I was determined to keep him. A trim of his fur to get out the worst of the mats, a bath, and a collar later, Goliath looked like a real prince. A champion of his breed.

He seemed to have a goal in mind, though. That goal was to drive the Hubbards insane. It was war, and Goliath was the general.

The nightly choruses lessened, just enough so that the neighbors couldn't hear so well, but completely obnoxious to the Hubbard household. The grass was dying from cats pissing in the yard, along with piles of dirt from where they handled their business. Dead birds were strewn across their yard, and I heard Carla screaming about the fact a cat had taken an enormous poop right outside her door, ruining her heels.

Goliath got an extra pat on the back for that.

But the Hubbards weren't going to play nice. Every day, their boys would ride past my yard, yelling obscenities and chucking rocks at the cats. The slower ones would get struck and they would mew and cry out in pain. When blood was drawn, Goliath would usher them inside and I'd care for them for the night.

It was a step too far when John put rat poison in his yard.

Duchess, poor Duchess. She'd mistakenly eaten half of the tuna can left in his yard, laced with the deadly ground up pellets. I found her barely alive on my porch.

All I could do was take her inside and make her comfortable.

All the cats came in, through the windows, through the cracked door, I think even some made it up from the basement. There were probably fifty cats, all sitting around me and Duchess as she was curled up on my lap, each breath growing lighter and lighter.

Goliath was the most distressed, pacing around, mewing, licking Duchess' head every few seconds. I never knew a cat could love so much. When Duchess went lax and her breath came no more, he yowled so loudly I'm sure the whole town could hear it. A grieving cat, who lost his friend and love.

It was exhausting to dig the grave, but I had to do it for her. Duchess was nothing but sweet once I'd gotten her to come around. The cats stayed with me, mewing in distress and nudging at the small coffin I'd crafted for Duchess out of a box and some paints. She was a lady, and she was going out in style.

Her body was lowered, the dirt covering the box, and I went to bed. Goliath slept with me that night, and I swore I would occasionally awake to hear him cry.

The next day I could barely get out of bed, but Goliath nudged me awake.

I had to take care of the others still, after all.

Carla was swearing and screaming at her car when I exited the house, and I could barely believe it. A single cat didn't have much strength, but an army? Oh boy. The car was covered in cat pee and feces, the antenna chewed off, one of the windows was somehow broken, and the seats were torn to hell.

She turned and saw me, foaming at the mouth in anger. "You!" She stormed over, her fists clenched. Goliath nudged me back, and I hid behind the door, my throat dry.

"Y... yes?"

I'm sure the woman would have punched me if I hadn't had the door between us. Instead, Carla started screaming. "That was my birthday present! I don't know how you're doing this, but this ends. Now!"

I took a deep breath and stood as tall and brave as a sixty-eight-year-old woman can. "You killed one of them. Rat poison. You asked for it."

"Like you're going to miss that one! What is the matter with you?!"

I heard the chorus of hisses and growls from under my porch, Carla jumped out of her skin and shivered. She took a deep breath and glared.

"I swear, if it's the last thing I do, I'm going to make sure each and every one of these cats ends up in the pound or as roadkill. And I mean it!"

With that awful, awful threat, she stormed off. I stumbled onto the porch and sat on my chair, too nervous to stand. "Oh, Goliath, what am I going to do?" I whispered.

Goliath licked my hand. His way of telling me it would be okay.

That evening I decided to stay out late. Watch the moon and the stars. The cats stayed with me rather than attack the Hubbards' yard. The sun had just gone down when I heard the sound of children's bikes.

It was the Hubbard boys, and they were armed with rocks again, the three youngest aiming at the cats, who darted and dodged under the porch or into my backyard. I'm not sure if the oldest two were aiming for me or it was just an accident, but one rock smacked right next to my head... and the other cut open my forehead.

I cried out as pain exploded across my face and blood started to drip down my face.

Every cat stopped.

Goliath mewed and licked my face before he turned.

The growl he made wasn't a typical cat's sound.

It was like a demon from hell.

Goliath leaped from my lap and trotted closer to the boys, fur puffing out and continuing to growl. The rest of the cats ceased running and grouped up. Some of them I didn't even see leaped down from the tree. I had to have over seventy cats in my yard. I didn't even know so many had ever come to see me.

The eldest boy stopped his bike, the others falling in behind him. He pulled another rock from his bag. "Stupid cat!" He pitched his arm back...

And Goliath went for his throat.

I don't really remember what happened. I think I blacked out. What I can remember is that Goliath grew... big. Even bigger than he already was. Even bigger than a lion. And the rest of the cats swarmed behind him, a hive mind of violence and with only one goal—kill.

When I woke up, it was past midnight.

There was no sign of the bikes. No boys. No army of cats, either. Just a few left, licking at a puddle in the street where the bikes had been abandoned... It was a dry summer. There hadn't been a puddle there earlier.

I stumbled back to my room, the bed cold and empty of my cat. I fell asleep in bed and dreamed of the ripping of wet flesh and the crunching of bones.

The next morning, I woke up and there was Goliath, sleeping across the other pillow. He was fine, he wasn't hurt. I tried to ignore the smell of blood in his breath as he nudged my face to get me up.

There was no sign of any bikes, or puddles. Just a normal plain street like the one I'd gotten used to living on.

There weren't many of the cats today, only four plus Goliath. These ones that weren't present last night, either—Chip, Dill, Biscuit, and Bambi. Bambi had sprawled across my lap and was purring when the police cruiser pulled into my driveway.

Dill hid under the porch while Biscuit and Chip ran up to say hello.

Officer Holly Silva stepped out, with Carla in tow. Carla looked like she'd been crying, but when she saw me, she smirked. I sighed and looked for Goliath, but he was nowhere to be seen.

"Ma'am?" Holly held up her badge, even though she knew I recognized her. "I need to speak with you, please."

Carla's grin grew darker.

I invited Holly inside and we sat at the table together. Carla invited herself in and was standing in the corner, looking around my pristine house. "Thought it'd be more of a mess than this, given the animals you have," she grumbled.

Holly ignored Carla before clearing her throat and looking at me. "Listen, Doris. Last night two of Carla's sons came home shredded up and claiming you sicced your cats on them." Holly took this moment to conspicuously look at Biscuit and Chip played with a ball of yarn, still quite kitten-y. "Her older three never returned home. Have you seen them?"

I reached up and touched my forehead. "I can't really remember, last night I got my head bumped something awful." I looked meaningfully at Carla, who sneered back. "It's not anything serious, but no, I don't remember where the boys went. I think they just rode past the house on their bikes, they were saying some quite nasty things, but that's all I remember."

Holly nodded and wrote that down. "Thank you, ma'am. That's all I needed to know."

"What?!" Carla looked ready to blow her top. "This isn't close to all of the cats she had! My sweet Alexander said there had to be a hundred! Over a hundred!"

Holly snorted and her lips twitched. She somehow managed to remain professional. "Mrs. Hubbard, if Doris really owned over a hundred cats, I don't think she'd be able to hide them this well in this two-bedroom house."

"Well... well..." Carla stammered before she looked around. "Where's that big one? The awful one, the one that attacked my sweet son!"

Goliath. Oh no. Holly looked at me. "Is this all of them? I'm sorry, I have to ask."

I looked around. "Well... Goliath should be here. Goliath? Come here, boy, no one's gonna hurt you."

"The officer is going to put him down the moment she sees that monster, don't you try to pretend otherwise!" Carla's eyes were full of murder, I was nearly about to start crying.

"Mew?"

I looked down.

There was a fluffy kitten, with black and orange fur and bright amber eyes. He jumped into my lap before hopping onto the table and sniffing Holly.

Holly examined his collar. "So, this is Goliath?" She couldn't help it, she immediately started giggling. "The ironic naming style, I dig it. Hey, buddy, do you smell David? He's my German Shepherd, he'd love to take care of a sweet lil thing like you..."

Carla was completely flabbergasted. She opened her mouth and shut it a few times before saying, "No, that... that's not Goliath! Goliath is huge! He's practically a mountain lion!"

"All right, Mrs. Hubbard." Holly stood up and scratched Goliath behind the ears, who purred and teasingly batted at her hand. "That's quite enough, I think your boys probably just are out playing somewhere. Let's go now, you can help coordinate the search."

I saw them out, Carla was fuming and now I was the one grinning. Carla turned to me and hissed, "This isn't over. I will get the gun myself, and when the real Goliath shows up, I'm putting a bullet in his head." With that nasty threat, she stormed back to her house.

I closed the door and turned around.

There was Goliath, sitting so proud, his normal self.

Nervous, I went to my knees. "G... Goliath? How... how did you do that?"

Goliath stepped forward and just batted at my hair. But I swear he smirked.

A few days ago, the bones of a few adolescent boys were found. Picked clean. Carla didn't even try to come over, the marks on the bones were larger than anything a cat could make. The word through the grapevine is that it's probably someone's escaped pet lion. Adopted it as a baby and let it go when it was no longer cute.

But tonight, I'm holding a party. I invited most of my neighbors; I did my hair up all pretty like. I'm no longer going to estrange myself from my neighbors. Holly will be there, with her dog David. So will the Hakim family, the eldest girl is going to bring her boyfriend and his band. I'll have to clear out the dining room to give them enough space, but they're fond of classic rock. Everyone's responded enthusiastically.

Even my son Dylan's going to come home, and bring his wife and twin children.

That should be enough noise to cover up Goliath and his army handling the Hubbards and their goons. In the morning it'll either be interpreted as a mysterious vanishing or written off as another animal attack.

After all... how could a single cat maul a human being?

I MOVED INTO THE CAT LADY'S HOUSE

I bought my very first house last month.

I had to sit in my car for a few minutes, just utterly in awe that this house was really mine. It was one of those things that I wanted since I was kid, as stupid as it is—my very own house. And I got it for a steal, the previous owner had just gone into hospice and her son just needed to get rid of it.

Dylan was waiting for me when I got there, he was a really sweet guy who was just going through one of the roughest times a person can. He welcomed me in, offered to help me sort through the furniture to see what I was going to pitch and which I was going to keep—he wasn't the sentimental type when it came to flower printed couches, apparently.

I had just laughed and was about to tell him yes when something large ran past me and raked its claws down my leg. I screeched, hopping up on a chair and pulling up my pant leg to assess the damage. That was one deep cut, and I looked over at that flower printed couch to see the furry culprit—

A gargantuan calico cat, with the most angry amber eyes and the meanest face I'd ever seen on a cat.

"Goliath! That's where you are!" Dylan attempted to reach for the cat, who just hissed at him and bolted down the hallway and I heard him zip up the stairs.

"Goliath?" I questioned.

Dylan held up a finger before he went to the bathroom and brought me a wet rag to care for my ankle. Then he told me about Goliath.

His mom had apparently always loved cats, but the accident that killed her husband also killed her three cats. Dylan, all sorts of messed up from the grief of losing his father, ended up pulling away from his mom and moved across the country to go to college. By the time he sorted himself and returned home several years down the line, his mother had taken in the feral tom.

"He's always suspicious of strangers, but he'll warm up to you soon enough. When you can get him calmed down, call me, I'll take him to the shelter. I'd rather not have Goliath chew up animal control. Besides, he's a good cat. He saved my mom. I think if he hadn't shown up, she would've died from loneliness."

I don't know how anyone could be friends with that jackass tom. That night when I was about to go to bed, I found him again. Sitting on my bed. Staring at me with a murder glare.

I sat down on the bed, the hair on my neck standing straight up as Goliath growled at me. "Stop that," I shook my finger at the angry cat, "I thought male cats couldn't be calico. Well, they can be, but apparently the few that are are typically infertile or have a bunch of other issues."

Almost as if he understood what I said, the hair on his neck went flat and he stopped growling, like I took the wind out of his sails. That made me snort, but I held firm. "Now, Dylan's going to pick you up the moment he can, whether you like it or not. I don't want a cat. Not now. Capiche?"

Goliath responded by flicking his tail before grooming one of his front paws. I sighed and pulled myself under the covers, feeling a bit silly for talking to a cat. "Goodnight, Goliath," I said.

That first week was a nightmare. Other than that initial conversation before bedtime, Goliath spent all his time hiding under things and waiting for the right moment to come out and bat his paws at me. My ankles and calves were covered in scratches. I complained about his guerrilla warfare to Dylan, but I think he was trying really hard not to laugh even as he offered his sympathies.

It was irritating and I couldn't wait for Goliath to take a damn chill pill so Dylan could send him to the shelter.

It was exactly one week after I moved in that I woke up to hear Goliath yowling.

At first I thought he was just being pissy, and this was his new attack on me. But as it carried on... I felt like he sounded sad. Just really sad. I ended up getting up and checking to see what was wrong. Goliath was sitting on the windowsill in the living room, for a cat of his mass he was surprisingly agile. He continued to cry, and my heart melted. Here I was, being all ticked at this cat, when no doubt he just missed his previous owner.

I don't know what possessed me to pick up Goliath and carry him to the couch for some much needed cuddle time, but he didn't try to hurt me. I stroked his ears and softly told him he was okay, that all was going to be okay. Goliath just repeatedly headbutted me in the chest as his cries quieted, we both ended up falling asleep on the couch. My neck and back were killing me by morning, but Goliath was still asleep as I grabbed my phone off the side table where I'd left it charging the night before and I called Dylan.

"Hey, Goliath's stopped being so angry, I think now would be the time to take care of him," I said, quietly so as not to wake him up.

Dylan was quiet for a few seconds before I heard him take a deep, shuddering breath. "Yeah, um... I can't. Not now... my mom went last night. Just passed away in her sleep. I'm sorry," he said.

I looked down at the sleeping cat in my lap. "Oh, it's fine. He can stay here then for a bit more. I'm so sorry."

He just 'mmhmm'd' before he hung up. I looked down at the slumbering Goliath and decided I was heading to the pet store after I showered. Whether I liked it or not, I now had a damn cat.

I wondered if Goliath knew if he'd lost his owner, that he was mourning her last night.

Now I know he did.

There was another reason I got this house for as cheap as I did—about two years ago, there were a bunch of unsolved disappearances and murders in the area. Heck, the next door neighbors lost their three oldest kids to some sort of wild animal attack before they just vanished themselves. Creepy, but I'm not the kind of person to give a shit about that sort of thing. So someone may have died on this street, big whoop, people die all the time.

But Goliath was different. I think I always knew he was different.

I talked with him all the time and he always seemed to be listening. I usually talked to him about how work was going, or what I was going to make for dinner or what was going on in the book I was reading.

Sometimes we talked about more serious things, about my depression and how hard it made it to get up in the morning sometimes, about how I always wondered if moving out to this small town was really the right choice, how I really wanted to be a writer instead of an accountant but I lived comfortably because of accounting and I wouldn't as a writer. Goliath was a great listener. Never said anything back, but he was a cat after all.

Last Saturday night, though, someone broke into my house. I had fallen asleep on the couch watching Netflix, Goliath had just gone out the back cat door to do his night prowls, I was alone.

I woke up when I heard someone going through something in the kitchen. My half-asleep brain first thought it was Goliath just trying to get into the cat food, so I stumbled my way over there to tell his dumb ass to knock it off. Instead of an oversized house cat, though, I saw a figure with a black ski mask holding one of my kitchen knives.

I tried to bolt back to the living room to get my phone but didn't get too far when I felt something cold slice through my back and impale me through the shoulder. It's not like I had a reference for what being stabbed felt like, I didn't even realize I had been until I fell to my knees, barely able to even breathe, much less scream.

My attacker pulled the knife back out and I looked up, saw the glint of the blood-covered blade preparing to make another strike. I couldn't move. My dumb ass didn't fight or run, I just laid there like a complete waste of space while the knife came down again... or it would've, if Goliath hadn't pounced his arm and sunk his teeth right into his skin.

The guy shouted and shook the infuriated cat off, Goliath smacking into the kitchen cabinet before sinking to the ground. I scrambled as fast as I could to the hallway, blood dripping down my arm as I scrambled to get away.

The sound that came from Goliath as he got back to his feet—house cats don't make that sound. Tigers, maybe.

Goliath growled again, I felt the temperature of the room rise as cats began pouring into my house. Through the open window my attacker had probably come through, through the cat door, hell some even pawed their way up from the basement one way or another. They ignored me as they surrounded Goliath and the intruder.

"What the fuck-"

Goliath roared, his tail whipping back and forth as he paced around his prey. The guy gulped before looking down at me. "Call him off! Call your fucking demon cat off!"

I coughed and shook my head. "He's not mine," I said before I began pulling my body down the hallway. I made it to my bedroom and heard my attacker screech in horror before I lost consciousness. I don't know how long I was out, but I woke up to Goliath licking the wound on my back.

I only saw what Goliath really was for a second. I'd seen tigers at the zoo smaller than he was, his black fur thick as a wolf's and the orange patches now glowing like magma. Those fiery eyes flicked up at mine, I blinked, and he was back to being a normal—if not slightly oversized—house cat.

I don't know what he did to my back, but the stab wound's gone. Just a scar now. I'd want to believe it was a dream, but although my kitchen was mostly clean, there was a few swaths of blood left under the table. And I now have like four other cats living in my house. One of them had the nerve to have its babies under my sink, so I have to find homes for the fuzzy freeloaders.

While I lounged in the living room, I saw one of them hack up what I think was a finger. It scarfed it back up before I got a good look. I turned and looked at Goliath, who was perched on the couch arm. "Just what the hell are you? Did that old lady who lived here before even know?"

Goliath just looked at me, and I swore he winked before yawning and dragging his claws down my couch arm.

At least I don't have a body to clean up. And I'll never need a guard dog with this asshole cat in my home.

I WAS HIRED TO TRANSPORT AN EXOTIC PET TO ITS BUYER

"Come on, man, it's an easy three grand. We just gotta drive through the night."

I stared at Tucker, my best and stupidest friend. "And it's not drugs? We aren't transporting coke or something?" I asked.

"No, dude, it's not illegal," he rolled his eyes, "and it's not drugs or people. I asked."

I chewed on my inner lip as I considered the drawbacks to joining Tucker on another of his poor life decisions. "What is it then?" I asked.

Tucker shrugged. "All the guy said was come by tonight with a friend."

God, this was a mistake. I even knew at the time it was a mistake. But I was out of work, like a lot of other people right now. I just needed a little money to hold me over until I could get another job.

So two weeks ago, I went with Tucker to meet with Mr. Ezra Mack.

Ezra is a portly, short dude with an oversized mustache and droopy eyes. We met with him at a vacant lot just outside of town where the summer fair is usually set up. Of course, that wasn't really a thing this year, so it was just an empty field with a few pieces of garbage fluttering about. After giving me a once over, Ezra just nodded and said, "You'll do. Come on, boys."

We followed Ezra to the other side of the lot, where a U-Haul truck quietly idled away. "Get this to the customer by mornin'. I'll have three thousand for each of you, and probably a few more jobs waiting."

I glanced at Tucker, who was clearly just seeing dollar signs, but I was a little more skeptical. "What's in it?" I asked.

Ezra chuckled before gesturing forward. "Take a peek son, just keep your distance," he said.

Somewhat relieved that he didn't seem all that concerned by me seeing what was inside, I went up to the truck and opened up the back.

All I could make out in the darkness was a cage. Then I saw a pair of eyes looking back, followed by a beastly snarl.

I yelped and fell back on my ass. Ezra laughed it up some more, and he shut the door before I could get a better look. "Exotic pets, people pay an arm and a leg for somethin' that can gobble them and their kids up," he said.

"Is it a tiger?" Now Tucker looked disappointed he didn't get a better look.

"Sure, if that makes you feel better." Ezra helped me back to my feet and patted my shoulder. "Clock's tickin', so get a move on. I suggest you don't think too hard about it and don't take too many stops until you reach the customer. And stay out of the fuckin' back. He's caged for now, but I don't want either of you pissin' him off, I'm not payin' for your hospital bill."

I nodded. I didn't need to be told twice. You know, I was actually relieved it was 'just' a tiger, considering the other less favorable options like drug or human trafficking.

After Tucker and I played a round of rock paper scissors, it turned out I was going to be driving for the first leg. We only stopped for a bit to get a six-pack of Pepsi and a few bags of Lay Chips before we were on the road.

"So how big was it?" Tucker asked after we really got going.

"I couldn't see, probably huge. Hope it's not a man eater," I joked.

Tucker elbowed me before he began tossing potato chips in his mouth. "Tigers were always my favorite as a kid," he said between crunches. "But I don't think they make good pets."

"It's legal in this state... I think. It's like Tiger King."

"Have you even fucking seen that show yet?"

"My ex changed the Netflix pass before I could."

Tucker cackled before an exceptionally loud snarl jerked us both back into reality- even if it was in a cage, there was a very dangerous animal in the back of our truck, only the bars of its cage and the thin siding of the truck keeping it from ripping our heads off if it so pleased. Tucker laughed a bit more nervously before stuffing more chips in his mouth.

I don't really mind driving, not even at night. It's kinda relaxing. Usually the roads are pretty empty and I can just daydream away. Of course, usually I don't have to hear quiet growling coming behind me every few minutes. It wasn't constant, just every now and then. Just as I'd start to relax, I'd hear the growling. Definitely kept me on alert.

Honestly, if we hadn't gotten pulled over, we would've made it to the customer with no problems and I never would've thought twice about it.

But when I saw those red and blue lights in my side-view mirror, my stomach practically dropped into my feet. Tucker had been pretty chipper until that point as well, I swear his dark face went a few shades paler as I pulled over. "What do we do?" he asked.

"Bullshit him until he leaves us the fuck alone," I hissed back.

The cop strode up to the truck a minute or so later, flashing his light in. I could tell right off the bat this was not going to be pleasant. I won't pretend that I know every cop in the world, but every cop I've met has been an insufferable jackass. Especially when they think I'm up to something, which, other than that night, I really haven't ever been.

"License and registration, please," he said.

I just reminded myself he had a gun before I got my license. "Not my truck, officer, I'm doing a favor for a friend," I said.

"What kind of favor?" He eyed the truck.

"Moving things. We've been driving for like five hours already," I said.

The cop 'humphed' before glancing at my license. I prayed for it to be over.

But of course, the tiger chose that moment to start kicking up a ruckus.

I cringed as I heard the growling and snarling kick up full force, and I knew I heard Tucker facepalm.

The cop scowled before handing me back the license. "Stay there," he ordered before he strode to the back of the truck. I didn't bother with the 'But you need a warrant' bit, I knew I was screwed. My lack of knowledge about exotic pets was now coming to bite me in the ass. It probably was illegal to keep tigers in my state and I just didn't know.

Cop threw open the back door. There was a beat of silence. Then a 'What the-'. Then a crash and a scream of terror.

Didn't matter if the guy was a jerk, I immediately leaped out of the truck to go rescue him, Tucker hot on my heels. I skidded to a stop in the back of the truck, flicked on my phone's light, and pointed it into the truck, seeing that the bars had been ripped apart like cardboard before I focused on the 'pet'.

... Yeah, no, that definitely wasn't a tiger.

The humanoid creature back there was nearly big enough to reach the ceiling, his antlers made it the rest of the way. He had the cop crushed between his clawed hands, the man's face white with shock before the creature opened its mouth and smashed down on his skull.

Blood and gore sprayed out from what remained of the cop's head and Tucker did the smart thing by slamming the door shut.

We both bolted for the front of the truck, before I made it I ended up spewing out my stomach contents all over the ground. With trembling legs, I climbed back into the truck, where Tucker was in the middle of a panic attack.

"What... the fuck... was that?" Tucker managed to get out as he hyperventilated.

I shook my head, wiping a bit of puke off my lips. I now missed the growling, it had been replaced by crunching and wet tearing. I glanced at the GPS, we had an hour to go. Just an hour.

I put the truck in gear and drove on, ignoring Tucker asking what the fuck we were doing. In truth, I'm not sure what I was doing. The only thought I could remotely string together was 'get this fucker to his destination and get the hell out of here'.

The chewing became white noise, my focus mostly on the road in front of us. Our destination was thankfully tucked way back in the woods, no more interstate for us, but what was worse was when the horrifying mastication of the body finally drew to a close.

The chewing was replaced by a sound that made the hair on my neck stand on end.

Whispering. From the back of the truck, I swear to god I heard whispering.

I craned my ears in an attempt to make out any distinct words, but it was too muffled for me to make out anything clearly. Tucker began reciting the Lord's Prayer, whimpering in between each breath. I just gripped that steering wheel even tighter and watched the minutes tick down slowly on the GPS.

The house we pulled up to was pretty nice, it wasn't like a woodland mansion or anything, but I certainly couldn't afford it. Tucker bailed from the truck before I even came to a full stop, and I wasn't far behind him.

I speed walked to the front door and didn't even knock before the customer opened up.

He looked so normal, man. Like the average dude you'd pass on the sidewalk and promptly forget in two seconds. Not like a person who was buying monsters. But he glanced back at the truck and his eyes just lit up. "Is he here?" he asked.

"Yeah," I wiped the sweat off my forehead, "The cage is broken though. And it ate someone."

The man sighed and somehow had the nerve to look relieved. "Well, if he's just fed, that'll make things easier. Come on in, put your feet up for a bit. We can handle it from here," he said.

Tucker and I waited in the man's kitchen, sipping flat Pepsi and doing our best not to look out the window where the man and a few other people were getting that thing out of the back of the truck. The man came in about half an hour later, told us they sprayed out the inside of the truck, handed us a few wadded up hundred-dollar bills for a tip ("since you arrived almost an hour before the estimated time", he said), and we went home.

It was quiet in the cab on the way back. Unnervingly quiet. Tucker wasn't cracking jokes, we kept the radio off, and did our best not to stare at the abandoned cop car by the side of the road as we passed by.

No one's ever questioned us about the missing cop, even when we told Ezra what happened, he seemed unbothered. He was more pissed about the cage being broken, saying his boss was going to be ticked to learn that this new cage didn't hold up to snuff. We got paid; I went home, and I did my best to wipe the night's events from my mind.

I hoped it would never come back to bite me either. But of course, I was wrong.

Yesterday I went grocery shopping and came home to Tucker twiddling his thumbs and a woman wearing a flannel shirt with the sleeves pushed up, revealing a nasty scar on her forearm that looked like a bite mark.

"You're Killion?" she asked. Still too flabbergasted about there being a stranger in my living room, I just nodded. "Good. Tucker here told me how well you handled yourself with the last delivery."

She placed a check on my coffee table.

"I'm Beth, Ezra's boss. I'm here offering you full-time work. I promise, they won't all be nearly as rough as that first one."

... Like I said, I *was* out of a job.

MY DAUGHTER'S COMING HOME

When I first saw I was getting a call from an unknown number, I thought it was another sales call. I only answered it on the off chance it was from my friend Irma, I knew she'd gotten a new phone number.

"Hello?"

It was quiet except for someone breathing on the other end. I frowned, but tried again. "Hello, is someone there? Or is this another robot telling me I've won a cruise?"

I heard a quiet laugh, followed by a sob.

"Hi mom."

I nearly fainted. I did actually drop to the floor, phone nearly slipping from my fingers as an almost familiar voice echoed in my ears. My chest tightened as I looked up at the mantle, where all Kendra's photos were lined up. A happier twelve-year-old you couldn't have found, minus those last few months before her disappearance.

I swallowed before lifting back up my phone. "Is... is this a joke?" I asked.

The girl on the other end cleared her throat. "It's uh, not. It's not a joke. I'm Kendra. If you need proof, ummmm... remember when we went to go see that magician, and he called me up on stage? I was like six at the time. He pulled streamers from my pockets, and all I wanted to do was pet the bunny. When he made it disappear in the pile of streamers, I started bawling my eyes out. You had to drag me off stage and console me with ice cream afterwards. I had strawberry, you had cookies and cream. I love that day."

I was shaking. I couldn't believe it. "Kendra... you're okay? You're... where have you been?! It's been eight *years*, I thought... I thought you were-"

"I'm okay. Mostly." Kendra sighed, and I could hear her fiddle with her phone. "I think I can send a picture, did you get it? I took it last night."

My phone vibrated, and I looked at the picture I received.

A good half of her face was hidden by her hoodie, but I could tell it was Kendra. She was holding up a peace sign with her free hand and I could see a smile.

I couldn't believe it. It was Kendra.

I managed to get off the ground and have a seat in my living chair. "How... what have you even been doing? Did you run away or were you taken?" Waking up that morning to see my daughter was gone was the worst morning of my entire life.

"I ran away. Ended up in *California*, somehow." Kendra laughed again. "You wouldn't believe what kind of shit I've been up to. Pardon my language. But my god, I've wanted to come back for so long. I just didn't know how, you know?"

"You're always welcome home," I said. "Are... are you coming home now?"

"Just waiting for the bus to take me on that last leg. I actually should be back tonight. You haven't moved, have you?"

I couldn't stop myself from sobbing. I was still trying to absorb that my daughter was alive. "No. Your dad wanted to, but I couldn't. Just in case you ever came back... what have you been even doing?"

"Oh, that's a story." I heard Kendra shuffle on the other end. "I'll give you the full story when I'm back, but I can give you some of the highlights now? I still got like, an *hour* until my bus gets here.

I hate waiting, but I figured talking with you might help. Lucky I still remember your phone number."

"I made you memorize it for a reason, baby girl." I wiped away the tears and suddenly my soul felt lighter than it had in years. "Tell me everything. I want to hear it all."

And she did. She talked about how she managed to get settled in with a nice couple in California who let her stay as long as she did chores and looked after their kid. When she turned fifteen, she got her GED and began traveling. She'd been all over the states. She'd fallen in love, had her heart broken, she'd slept everywhere from street corners to five-star hotel rooms—apparently it was a gift from 'a really hot old guy with really weird kinks'—she'd waited tables, she'd picked pockets, she'd find temp work when she chose to settle down, but she hadn't really settled. Not ever.

She was halfway through a story about the time she'd shared a hotel room with two prostitutes and their guard dog when she cut off. "Shit! Bus is here, I gotta get going. I'll be home around six."

"Should I have dinner ready? I think I still have the ingredients for your favorite." Honey garlic chicken and rice. She could've eaten that for breakfast, lunch, and dinner.

"Nah, I think I'll eat on the way. See you soon! I love you, mom!"

She hung up and for several minutes, I sat alone in silence.

Then I got up and began cleaning the house. I turned on the Beach Boys as I dusted off all the surfaces, did all the dishes. I hadn't felt this free in so long. I only paused for a moment before I headed into Kendra's bedroom.

I hadn't gone in there since the day she ran away. Nothing had changed—bed was still unmade, an empty fish tank sat on her desk collecting dust. I pushed up my sleeves and got to work. Sheets were thrown into the wash, the fish tank was cleaned out. I was planning on remaking the bed when I heard the door open behind me.

"Dear? What are you doing in Kendra's room?"

I'd completely forgotten to call Greg. I spun around to see my husband, one of his eyebrows raised as he looked around the room. I laughed and wiped away another tear. "I got a call today. From Kendra," I said.

Greg's face went white. "What are you talking about?" he said.

"She's alive, Greg!" I laughed and shook her head. "I just wanted to get the house ready, I'll get dinner started in an hour-"

"Kendra's not coming home, Lauren. She's gone, you know that."

I forced a smile. "Listen, I know it was Kendra. We were on the phone for an hour, she even sent me a selfie, see?" I pulled my phone from my pocket and offered it to Greg.

He took it and I saw his eyes widen before he sneered. "This is a joke. A sick joke. Someone's making fun of you," he lifted back up the phone, "This could be *anyone*. It's been eight years! What took her so long to call? I can tell you why—because it's not Kendra."

My high from earlier crashed. "I was on the phone with her. I'm not an idiot, it was her-"

"I'll show you." Greg hit the call button and turned the phone on speaker. "Whoever this is, I'm going to fucking *kill* them."

"Greg!" I tried taking my phone back, but he waved me off.

The phone rang twice before Kendra answered. "Yeah, mom? Something come up?" she asked. I could hear the sounds of the bus in the background.

Greg's face had gone from white to a startling shade of red. "Whoever you are, you're going to stop, right now. Or we're going to go to the police and-"

Kendra's laughter cut him off, this time they came out harsh and cutting. "Oh, hi, *daddy*. Damn, I hoped I would beat you home. Make it a big ole surprise. Tell me, daddy dearest, why were you so eager to move? Why you're so certain I'm dead? Oh wait... is it because you fucking *murdered me*, daddy?"

Greg went dead silent. I stared at my husband. "What is she talking about?" I asked.

"I wanted to wait until I was home, but I guess this story can't wait." She sighed. "You know, when most people have kids who are depressed, they support them. Ask what's wrong. I mean, mom tried, but you never did. You got pissed when I stopped turning in work. You called me lazy, you said I was embarrassing you. You told me I was going to be *worthless*."

I shook my head. "Is this the truth? Greg! Please, say something."

He shook his head. "She's lying, she's just trying to-"

"Remember the time I was found crying in the library? You were called to school, and you threatened me that if I interrupted your work day again with this 'bullshit' you were going to beat me black and blue. I was so scared, I couldn't tell mom. That's why I tried to run away. But you tried to stop me..." Kendra sighed. "I'm sending you another picture. Take a good long look at me now."

I shook, but I waited for that picture to pop up.

Now Kendra's face was entirely revealed, and I wanted to vomit. No doubt it was Kendra now, but everything looked so wrong. Her skin was almost a pale green, one eye that soft brown of long ago, but the other was like a bright red marble. But the worst part was her left cheek—it looked like it rotted clean off, revealing discolored bone and tooth. I could see her molars all the way to the back.

"You beat me to death, daddy. You finally lost it and you beat me to death, right in the backyard. You panicked. You called a truck driving friend of yours, and he agreed to throw me in the back and take my body all the way to Cali. He threw me in a ditch and considered the job done. A little girl's body, across the country. All alone. But I was found, daddy. Your friend didn't hide me well enough."

Kendra paused to catch her breath. "Their names were Sabrina and Eleanor. They found my body, and they brought me back. I was so scared, so confused, but they were kind to me. They helped me remember my life before, helped me function like a normal person... mostly. There's still some kinks in the system, but that's what happens when you're rotting in the back of a semi-truck for a few days before being resurrected."

"This can't be real," Greg finally managed to stutter out. "This can't be real."

"Oh, but it is. You wanna know why it took me so long to come back?" Kendra giggled again, the sound making my skin crawl. "It's because I was still scared of *you*. Yup. I was scared to face you. Maybe I blamed myself a bit for what happened. Maybe if I tried harder? But no. I've finally accepted it wasn't my fault. It was all you. You killed me. I needed help, and you *fucking killed me*."

"It... it was an accident..."

That's all Greg got out before all I saw was red. I grabbed the lamp off of Kendra's desk. Greg spun around just in time to have it collide with his head. The lamp shattered and Greg dropped to the ground, the phone landing among the glass fragments.

"Mom!? Mom, are you okay?!"

I picked up the phone. "... I broke a lamp over your father's head," I said.

"Jesus Christ, mom, did you kill him!?"

I knelt down next to my husband's limp body. "He's still breathing, so no."

Kendra whistled. "Good, because I call dibs. Just throw him in the basement till I get there, bus is pulling into town now. I'll be home in about half an hour. I love you!" She hung up, and I was alone with my unconscious husband.

All these years, I thought I'd been the only one he took out his temper on. He'd never used his fists. Just his words. But those words were fantastic at making me feel like a monster. Like it'd been my fault our daughter was gone.

Kendra's going to be here any minute now. Greg is locked in the basement. I've heard him beg to be let out.

But he's staying there, so he doesn't miss our daughter coming home.

THERE'S A SEAM IN EVERYTHING

Seven years ago, I met the girl who could find the seams.

"You've *got* to see what Dani can do."

I let myself be dragged across the park, passed the swings and to the big oak tree, where a girl with long black hair sat with a pile of books beside her. She looked up at the small crowd of fellow children surrounding her, sighed, and set down her book.

"Can I help you?"

My best friend at the time, Jacob, beamed and plopped a stuffed bear on her lap. "Do the thing! Luca hasn't seen you do it yet!" he said.

Dani looked at me and my gaze immediately went to my shoes. "You don't have to if you don't want to," I murmured, feeling embarrassed about all the fuss my friend was causing.

Jacob scoffed and crossed his arms. "You don't even know what she does yet! Come on Dani, show him!"

"I don't mind showing you," she said before picking up the bear. She brushed her fingers against its face, and she smiled before she took her middle finger and ran it from the top of its head to its tummy. Like she'd taken a sharp knife to it, the bear split open, revealing white stuffing and the red heart that had been stuffed in there when Jacob got it. She lifted it up to show it to all of us, before plopping it back on her lap and running her finger along the tear. When she pulled her hand away, the bear was whole again, like she'd never ripped it open.

Jacob scooped the bear back up and turned to me. "Cool, right?" he asked.

I shrugged. "I dunno. I guess?" I said, knowing I probably looked less than convinced.

Dani smiled then and got to her feet. "Okay. What do you want to see the inside of?" she asked.

I glanced around the playground before pointing to the swing set. "That. Can you cut that with your finger?" I asked. I might've only been a kid, but I was definitely not convinced by just cloth and fluff.

Dani nodded and walked over, the crowd of kids following her in awe. She patted the chain of the pink swing before her finger sliced right through one of the links. The chain came free and then she proceeded to slice open the plastic of the seat. She picked up the mangled swing, spinning around to show how it really wasn't attached at all, before she reattached it. All with the touch of her finger.

Now *that* convinced me. I probably looked like an idiot, just standing there with my jaw dropped while everyone else just clapped. "How do you do that?" I asked in wonder.

Dani shuffled her feet, a small smile on her lips. "Everything has a seam I can pop open. I can do it to anything," she admitted.

I dug through my pockets and managed to pull out my 3DS. "Can you open this up?" I asked.

For the rest of the afternoon, Dani demonstrated her unique and bizarre powers to us. She opened up my 3DS, showing off all the electronics inside, and once she fixed it back up, it booted up just like nothing had happened. She opened up a Rubix Cube, part of a branch, the monkey bars, whatever we asked she would demonstrate. Only if no adults were close though, one of the other kids suggested she open up one of the cars in the parking lot and she refused.

One by one we all went home for dinner until it was just me and Dani. I was pretty awkward at that age, so we just stood in silence for an uncomfortably long time before I finally piped up with the question on my mind:

"What do you want to open up?"

She stared at me in surprise for a bit before she shrugged. "I... I don't know. I don't really do it for myself anymore. I just do it so everyone else likes me," she said.

I plopped down on the ground and pulled out my 3DS. "I don't have to be home for a while longer, my parents are working late. Want to play some games with me?" I asked.

I don't think anyone really asked Dani to do something with them before that didn't involve her cutting some random object open. But she slowly nodded and sat beside me, and until it got dark we played games. I probably would've stayed out longer if the red light signifying red battery didn't start glaring at us.

"I'll come back and play with you tomorrow, okay?" I said, sticking it in my pocket.

Dani was grinning from ear to ear, her smile filled with joy. "I'd really like that, Luca," she said.

That summer, I spent a lot of time in the park. Of course it was fun watching Dani cut open whatever object we brought her, but it was more fun just.... talking with her. She was a really nice girl, after all, just quiet. There were several times I'd be playing my 3DS while she'd watch and she'd end up falling asleep on my shoulder. She told me most nights she spent wandering around her home rather than sleeping. She never slept well.

Then one day I came to the park while it was raining. I had the stomach ache of a lifetime, but I wanted to see Dani. And she was there, as always. The rain was more of a mist in the air rather than a downpour, but I was more than glad to take a seat under the tree.

Dani, of course, immediately picked up that something was off. "What's wrong? You don't look so good," she asked, pulling her knees up to her chest.

"Stomach ache. Mom said there's a flu going around, so don't get too close," I said.

"What, or you'll barf all over me?" Dani giggled before something clicked in that head of hers. "Luca, you know when you asked me earlier this summer what I'd really want to open the seam of?"

I nodded.

"I lied... I... Kinda want..." She blushed a little and murmured the next sentence so quietly I could barely make it out.

"I kinda wanna see if a person has a seam."

I responded by wiggling out of my t-shirt. "Sure! Maybe you can see what's wrong with my stomach!" I said. I know, what kind of dumb ass move is that, but I was a kid and what kid isn't a little curious about what goes on inside them?

Dani clearly didn't expect my enthusiastic consent, but she did a little dance in place before glancing around. "No one else is out here, but let's go behind the bushes. Just in case," she said.

Excitement brimming between the two of us, we hid behind the bushes as I laid down on the ground, staring up at the gray sky. It was peaceful back here. "Okay, just start checking," I said.

Dani knelt above me, and her cold fingers ran over my chest. I tried not to squirm since I was so ticklish. For several quiet seconds I just laid there, wondering when she'd start. "You can start whenever," I said, thinking she was losing courage.

"I've already started..."

I glanced down and sure enough, she had. I hadn't felt a thing, but my skin over my torso had been opened right up, cut down from the top of my sternum to below my belly button. Skin, muscle and ribs were just pulled open and to the sides so Dani could dig around in my guts. She slit open my stomach, and I saw remnants of digested food, the pancakes I'd had for breakfast. She sealed that back up quickly, so nothing was disturbed as she proceeded to run her fingers through my intestines.

"That's so cool," I whispered, afraid if someone caught us now the little spell she had over me would be broken. "I'm not even bleeding."

It was true, there was not a single blood drop lost. Nothing seemed desperate to pop out of me either. It was just... there. I could see my heart beating, my lungs inflating and deflating with each level breath. I should've been afraid, but I wasn't. I was just fascinated to see what was going on inside of my body.

"There's something wrong."

Dani scowled as she continued to prod, and then I felt a bit of hot pain. "Careful!" I hissed.

"Sorry! I don't really know how, but I think something's really wrong in here. Hold still, I'm putting you back together."

I stayed still as she finished zipping up my chest. I sat up and poked at my chest as if I expected my seam to burst open and everything to come spilling out all at once. "What do you mean, something's wrong?"

Dani shrugged. "I don't know. I really don't. I just looked around in there and something doesn't feel right to me. Go talk to your mom, I think she needs to take you to the doctor. Did you really not feel anything? When I cut your seam?"

I shook my head and got to my feet, grimacing as that pain from my gut flared up. "Not a thing. You're awesome, Dani. I'm gonna go home now though," I said.

"Please hurry."

I went home and somehow managed to nag my mom long enough into taking me to the doctor's office about my stomach ache. Course, I'm sure you guessed by now it wasn't just a stomach ache. Appendicitis. Luckily it was all taken out before anything bad happened, but I was bedridden for two weeks.

When I was finally well enough to play, I couldn't find Dani at the park. Asking around revealed she hadn't been back since that rainy day.

She was gone. And she didn't come back into my life until the beginning of this school year.

I barely recognized her at first. I'm not really a tall guy, but even compared to your average guy, Dani was practically a tree. She cut her hair short, and she'd grown up, but I saw her face and I knew.

"Dani!"

I ran up to her and nearly plowed her over in my eagerness to get to her. Dani nearly jumped out of her skin as she looked down at me, then she realized who I was. "Luca? Is that you?" she asked.

I nodded eagerly, probably looking like an idiot. "Yes! Oh my god, Dani, you're tall!" I said.

When she smiled, I felt like I was a kid in the park, all over again. "... And you're still Luca. I'm so glad... I'm so glad to see you," she said before giving me a quick hug. "Do you have lunch next period? We can talk then, catch up?"

I barely touched my food because I was just too excited to talk to Dani. She was on the girl's basketball team, and was already saving up money for college in a few years. She wanted to be a vet. Meanwhile, all I did was join the school's anime club and still have no idea what I want to do for a living, but she still listened.

We didn't talk about seams. It was a silent agreement between us not to. I knew it happened, it wasn't something I made up. But the seams were something from childhood. We didn't need to open them up again... well, we didn't. Until Dani was hit by a car and left to die by the side of the road.

I only heard about it the following morning, one of her team members actually tracked me down to tell me. Apparently I was the only person outside of the team that was really friends with her. Dani always worked late, and while she was walking home, some drunk joyriders plowed her over. She was found hours later, somehow still alive, and taken to the hospital.

Several bones, including both legs and one arm were broken. Ribs cracked. She was concussed, and she lost a lot of blood. She'd be okay in the end, but there was a lot of recovery ahead of her.

I nearly cried the first time I visited her in the hospital. Gratefully she was sleeping at the time so she didn't hear me sniffling, but I left her a card. It was sitting in her lap when I visited her the next day, and she was awake. But along with her body, her heart had been broken too.

"... I'm never going to play basketball again."

"Don't say that," I tried to soothe her.

Dani snorted. "Even if I can walk again, I'll never walk without a limp. And running will be flat out. It's not a big deal." The way she shuddered when she said 'not a big deal' gave away quickly that it was, in fact, a big deal.

I held her hand, and she squeezed her eyes tight as she struggled not to cry. "I don't know... what to do. They have no fucking idea who hit me, I just know it was a black truck. That's all. They ruined my life, and they're not even going to pay for it," she said.

"Dani, do you remember the seams?"

Dani jolted like I'd hit her with a bolt of electricity. "What about them?" she asked cautiously.

I pulled up my shirt to show off my appendectomy scar. "You were right that day. About what was wrong. I might be dead by now if you didn't find my seam and look inside. I remember them, but do you?"

"I've never forgotten." Her good hand stroked mine, and I watched as the skin split over the back of my hand. Another touch and it sealed right back up, good as new. "It's... it's why I want to be a vet. You know how animals I could save with my gift?

"That's amazing," I said, flexing my hand. "That day in the park. You didn't come back after that."

Dani nodded. "I... I scared myself a bit, after I cut you open. And when you didn't come back the next day, I started having nightmares that your chest exploded and all your organs slid out of you. I wouldn't want to go to the park if you weren't there, anyway." Her brow furrowed. "Why are you bringing this up now? I can't heal myself, I can only close a seam I opened."

I swallowed before leaning in close and lowering my voice. "Does opening a seam have to be painless?" I asked.

It took a second for Dani to get it, but she shook her head. "It can hurt as much as I want it to," she said, her gaze turning cold.

"Then leave the rest to me. You work on getting better, and I promise I'm going to find out who did this to you."

It did take months to track them down. But I got help—the girl's basketball team. They want to help Dani, and all I said was I was going to get her justice. They put their feelers out, and we got something.

Cory. I never really knew Cory, he ran in a different crowd. But he had a black truck, drunk like a fiend, and rumor had it he bragged to a few close friends that he 'ran over that goth bitch'. AKA my friend, Dani.

My first initial instinct was to just go up and punch him in the face, but I knew that wouldn't work. I'd just get expelled. So I did the next best thing. I knew Cory was a shitty student, and we took the same bus to school. I waited until I heard him bitching about struggling with last night's math homework, and then I turned around.

"Hey man, if you need a bit of help, I can double check your work. Fill in all the right answers if you missed any."

He looked baffled, but handed me the paper. I did my best not to cringe at how god awful his handwriting was, but I corrected his work and handed it back just as we got to school.

The next day, Cory slung his arm around my shoulders and said, "Pal, buddy, I got a hundred percent on that last assignment. I think this is the start of something beautiful."

I smiled back at him. "I think it is," I replied.

So yes, for the last month, I became Cory's personal slave. I finished his homework and in return he was somewhat nice to me.

He also blabbed a lot, and it was so hard not to just wreck his face when he told me about the night he ran over 'the goth'.

But I just thought of Dani in physical therapy, doing her damn best to walk again, and I just smiled and laughed.

I got the names of the two other guys in his car, his closest friends Jay and Thomas. I waited. The waiting was the hardest part, and I'm pretty sure my own grades slid a bit while I was doing both Cory's homework and my own. But it was all worth it for tonight.

Because tonight Cory and his friends were at a party, and I swung by at around midnight to see them stumbling out of the house, laughing their drunk asses off. I rolled down my window and called out their names, offering them a ride. They'd no doubt get pulled over in their condition, and hey, I had some more booze in my car. They could keep the party going in the back seat.

Me, I was just the ass kissing nerd that had been doing Cory's homework for the past month. They never even considered that I drugged the beers I so happily handed to them in the backseat. One by one they passed out, and I went on to phase three of my plan.

I'd planned ahead. I'd let three members of the basketball team know that the kind of justice I was looking for wasn't by getting them arrested and serving a nothing sentence while Dani was going to struggle for so much longer with the injuries they gave her. I knew these three would go with it.

They'd set up the perfect place. A basement in an abandoned building. I was impressed by how much effort they put into it, plastic was rolled over the floor and part of the walls, there was a pile of zip ties and three chairs set up in the center of the room. The hard part was dragging their unconscious asses down there, by the time I got the last one down there I was sweating like a pig.

But oh, it was all worth it when I brought Dani there and she saw all three of them, tied up and just starting to stir.

She softly gasped as she looked between them. "And you're sure these are the guys?" she asked quietly.

I nodded and gestured to them. "Do whatever you want," I said.

Dani grinned ear to ear before she walked up to them. Cory was the first to really come to, his eyes fluttering and he groaned before saying, "How much did I drink last night?"

"Too much," Dani chirped, pacing back and forth in front of her prey.

That woke him right up. Cory's head shot up and all the blood rushed out of his face as he recognized the girl in front of him, still walking with a crutch to support herself. He, of course, immediately tried to play dumb. "Do I know you? Cuz I've dated a lot of girls so I can't really keep track of them-"

Dani slugged him across the face. "I'm the girl you *ran over with your truck*," she said, still smiling.

Jay and Thomas had woken up from their beauty sleep by this time, Cory spat out a mouthful of blood before looking up and smirking at Dani. "Sorry, don't remember you," he said, smugness oozing out of the creep.

Dani circled around the trio of hungover morons, watching how Jay flinched every time he heard the sound of her crutch hitting the ground. "I think he remembers," she hummed before she paused in front of Jay.

Jay swallowed before glancing over at the others. "No. I don't," he mumbled.

Dani cocked her head to the side before she lifted up her hand. She wiggled her fingers and then caressed the middle one right up his jawline and over his cheekbone.

Jay barely realized that his cheek was hanging from a last inch of connecting flesh before Dani just grabbed it and ripped it right off. Jay screamed at the top of his lungs, blood pouring down his mangled face and down his neck. I could see his teeth and gums.

The others looked on in horrified silence as Dani dropped the piece of flesh onto the plastic. "Let's fucking try again! Do you remember now?"

"Yes!" Jay wailed, tears sprouting at the corners of his eyes. "Shit! It wasn't me dr-driving, it was Cory! I thought we'd just hit a deer or something, but in the morning we heard about you! I wanted to tell someone, I swear, but they wouldn't let me! I'm so sorry! I'm so fucking sorry!"

Dani hummed and nodded as Jay continued to babble his desperate apologies. "I believe you. So you won't suffer any longer," she said right before she drew her finger right across Jay's neck.

So much blood poured down the front of his shirt, a waterfall of blood splattering against the plastic as Jay's head lolled down. He certainly didn't suffer, he was dead in minutes. And all during those minutes, Thomas and Cory were screaming in terror, any of Cory's smugness had vanished when Dani ripped open his friend's face and cut his throat.

Dani turned her murderous stare onto the other two, still smiling from ear to ear. Thomas glanced down at her hand and realized it first. "Where's... where's your knife?" He stammered.

All she did was raise her hand into the air and wriggle her fingers. "These are my knives. I've always been a bit special," she carefully avoided the blood puddle as she limped over to Thomas, "And even though I'll probably never play basketball or have my full mobility again... you can't take away my gift to find the seam in everything."

With just a brush of her fingers, she sliced through Thomas' jersey, and although he begged for his life, she just slowly dragged her hand from his stomach up to his collarbone while he howled in agony. Watching his skin just split by her touch was mesmerizing, the cut so precise it was like a surgeon's scalpel. Another slice over the gut and everything just... spilled out. This was nothing like letting her find my seam in childhood, where everything just stayed perfectly still. I never knew how really long the intestines were until I watched them plop on the floor, still twitching and alive.

Thomas stared in horror at his disemboweled guts until Dani dove her hand into his chest and I heard the loudest squish.

Thomas' eyes rolled back and he almost immediately expired. Dani pulled out the remnants of his heart before throwing it on the ground.

Cory was crying now, snot dribbling down his lips as he pulled frantically at his zip ties. "Please... it was an accident... It was just an accident, you crazy bitch!" He yelped as she trotted in front of him.

Dani had been smiling until Cory called her a crazy bitch. The smile dropped, and she sighed, crossing her reddened arms across her chest. "Was it an accident that you drove drunk? Was it an accident that you just drove away, didn't even attempt to call 911? Was it an accident you've spent all your time up until now *laughing* about running me over? Maybe I am a crazy bitch. Maybe I am. But if I'm crazy, then you're a downright sociopath. And odds are you'll kill someone else the next time an 'accident' happens."

She knelt down to his level and flicked his nose, watching the tip go flying off and sticking to the wall. Cory crossed his eyes to see the damage and promptly pissed himself, I could see the stain in his jeans.

"Hey Coryyyy," Dani giggled, her smile returning and bordering on maniacal, "You ever hear of a torture called death by a thousand cuts?"

I'm just taking a break, Cory and Dani are still in the basement. Last I saw him, though, he barely even looked like a person anymore—she'd removed his nose, lips, ears, and eyelids. He's bald, cuts covering his entire scalp. Dozens of surgical cuts are decorating his arms, legs, torso... and he's still alive, staring unblinkingly, someplace past begging and tears.

But she's not going to let him die just yet. After all, she's been suffering for months because of that accident.

He can take a few days before she finally lets him go.

FAIRYTALE WEDDING

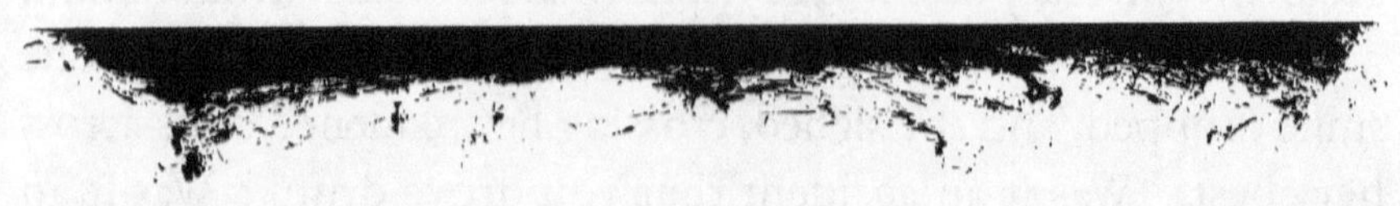

My sister and I... were very different people.

I had what I call 'giraffe proportions', gangly, tall. Amy was average height with the whole hourglass figure. I was a social recluse, she was a social butterfly. I came out as asexual at age fifteen and she told me quite often during our teen years that I was a freak and could never be loved.

Then three years ago she called me out of the blue to invite me to her wedding.

I'd moved across the country, had a decent living working as a freelance photographer, and had just begun to shake off my insecurities when I got the phone call. She'd been dating her highschool sweetheart on and off again since graduation and he finally got the balls to pop the question. After apologizing for our relationship going dead since I went to California, she offered to fly me back home and even to cover the cost of the hotel room.

I chose to bury the hatchet and asked for the dates.

Of course I wasn't surprised when her ulterior motives presented themselves. She knew I was a photographer, and she knew that I wouldn't say no to her asking for wedding photos. She batted her eyes and reminded me that she paid for me to be here. So I said yes. I'd get my money's worth back when I put the pictures on my website, I hoped.

Amy was going to have a fairytale themed wedding. She'd managed to find this meadow in the forest near our childhood home that was absolutely breathtaking. Even I had to admit—if the skies remained clear and the weather was warm, this was perfect for her dream wedding.

I think this is where it started. Amy had been going on and on about how green the grass was when she stepped on a mushroom.

She squealed about how gross it was, and I moved in for pictures. The mushroom was a part of a circle, a phenomena of nature I'd never seen in person.

"What are you doing?" she asked, looking at me like I'd grown an extra head.

I shrugged. "Fairy Ring. That's what they're called. Perfect for a fairytale wedding, eh?" My smirk about her disgust was probably a little too evident.

"Well, we're gonna have to pull them out!" Amy pulled out her cellphone and stepped away from the circle. "I am not going to have mushrooms all over, it'll kill the grass and make it all brown! I'm calling Dane, will you stay to help pull them out?"

Immediately a chill ran down my spine. I shook my head and raised my hands. "No way. Just leave them there, Amy. They'll add to the whole magic theme, I promise."

"No way! They're disgusting!" Amy pulled a face. "You can just go! It's not like I paid for you to get here or anything!"

I pocketed my camera and rolled out. I wasn't going to deal with another of Amy's bitch fits. Besides, I rather liked the fairy circle. It was a shame that my sister was going to tear it up just because it was going to ruin her idea of beautiful.

The next day Amy 'invited' me to take pictures of her in her wedding dress, a small photoshoot before the wedding. Naturally I obliged, to avoid the fuss if I turned her down.

Amy hammed it up for the camera. Puckered her lips, twirled her bangs, she was honestly one of the better models I worked with. She knew how to look good for the camera.

Then she yelped as one of her bridesmaids, I think it was Julie, stood by her. "Julie, what the hell!? Why did you pinch me?" she snapped.

Julie held up both hands. "I didn't pinch you!"

"Then what—ow! Ow!"

I lowered my camera as my sister started swatting at her thighs and arms, no longer the blissful bride. The tie on her hair loosened and came down all over her face, which only succeeded in infuriating her more. Before long the other bridesmaids were dancing around and screaming too, swatting at invisible bugs.

We retreated back to the car while my sister pouted at me. "It's not fair, you won't be in front of the camera, why weren't you hurt?" she said.

I shrunk in my seat. "I don't know? I put on bug spray today."

Julie examined her bare arms, frowning. "It doesn't look like bug bites. Look." She stretched out her arm so I could get a better look.

Her poor arms were covered in nasty welts, already developing into dark bruises. I grimaced. "I hope these heal by the wedding."

"They better or you're not allowed to stand up with me," Amy threatened.

Poor Julie's eyes welled up with tears and she buried her face in her hands as she began to sob. I quickly put the car in gear to get the ladies out of there. I took Julie for a few drinks that night after she got out of her bridesmaid gown and iced her arms. The next morning her welts had turned into mottled purple bruises, but I reassured her that they'd be mostly faded by the wedding.

I went to Amy's house to try to convince her to change the location of the wedding given there seemed to be some sort of insect infestation, but she was furious about something else.

"I just bought it! It's a whole gallon of milk and it's ruined!" She pitched the gallon of milk into the sink, and the container exploded. Chunky milk poured down the drain and the most awful smell filled the room. I visibly gagged and covered my nose as I hurried to open a window.

"It happens, Amy. Listen, let's just have some breakfast, okay? You still take your eggs over easy?"

Amy sighed and leaned against the counter, but gave a short nod. She'd been bitten the worst. Even her face was bruised. "I couldn't sleep last night, I'm sorry I'm being a bitch. I just couldn't get comfortable! My body feels like a giant bruise."

I nodded as I got the eggs out of the fridge and heated up the pan. "It's probably wedding nerves too. Just a few more days and it'll be over."

I cracked the egg and dropped it into the pan.

What's worse than spoiled milk? Rotten eggs.

Amy screamed before she started to gag and threw up in the sink. The egg was horrifying, mottled brown and green and smelled like death. It popped and hissed in the pan before the yolk broke and thick red liquid oozed out. The smell of frying blood was what made me join Amy at the sink, hurling.

"Bad eggs, bad milk, what's next?!" Amy burst into tears and fell to the floor, her shaking legs unable to support her any more.

I scraped the eggs into the trash and as a second thought threw the pan out too—the rotten smell would never come out. After it was all taken care of and the windows were all open, I sat with my sister on the couch, rubbing her back to soothe her and telling her that her fridge was likely the culprit. It wasn't keeping the food cold.

The bruises on the bridesmaids faded in another day, but if anything, Amy's got worse. Awful welts that would swell up and bruise. I swore she got new ones even though Amy claimed she hadn't returned to the meadow.

Amy grew more scatterbrained as the wedding grew closer. She lost her phone, her keys, her wallet, she even lost the necklace she'd borrowed for the wedding. It was a gorgeous silver and sapphire piece that would have complimented the pink parts of her gown perfectly. She couldn't stop sobbing, insisting that she had kept it on her dresser. But it was nowhere to be found. In the end, I had her borrow a simple pearl necklace from me. Something borrowed. But nothing blue.

The day of the wedding arrived, and I got a text from Julie.

'Don't go to the wedding.'

I immediately called her, and it went straight to voicemail. I must've called her ten times before the maid of honor poked her head in and told me to hurry up and get ready.

I didn't wear anything flashy, just a pink skirt and green/white blouse. I looked like a spring princess, Amy was the queen. But god, you could feel how exhausted she was. Make up hid some of the bruising but I felt pained when I saw her back, rows and rows of black and blue marks. I couldn't imagine how much her body ached.

But she was determined. The sooner she got that damn wedding over with, the sooner this would all come to an end.

The ceremony was beautiful, despite Amy's pained expressions between her beautiful bride smiles. She was getting bitten again, I could tell as a new stripe blossomed above her breast. I took pictures of the moments she smiled through it. The good parts of the most special day of her life.

When they kissed, I was grabbed by the back of my shirt and dragged back.

I nearly screamed, but a hand was clamped over my mouth as I was pulled back into the forest and into a car.

When the doors locked, I turned to see my captor.

"Julie?"

Julie looked like hell. The welts on her arms had come back with a vengeance, actually breaking skin and creating horrendous scabbed wounds. In her hands was clutched a pair of scissors and her eyes were filled with madness.

I went pale. "Julie? What's wrong?"

"They're coming. They came for me when I figured it out. I... I don't think they can get in the car but please, please, please Alana, hold onto these with me!" She pushed the scissors into my hands, an old pair of shears that had rust speckled like blood flecks over the blades.

When I attempted to pull back, she grasped my hands and shook her head. I glanced out the window, I couldn't see much anymore given as to where we were parked in the forest, but I could see that the women were prepping for the bouquet toss. "Julie, have you lost your mind?" It was harsh, but she looked insane.

Julie shook her head again, her eyes growing wet. "My family emigrated from Ireland when I was a little girl. I thought something was familiar about the marks, but I didn't put it together until I took a sip of some of the milk from my fridge and it was bad. I'm so sorry, Alana, I'm so sorry..."

I heard a scream, and my head jerked back to meadow. There was a light. A golden light, shining in a circle from where... where the mushrooms once were.

"... Your sister told me about what she did to the fairy circle. There's no hope for her now."

The single scream turned into a chorus of screaming. I saw wedding guests run from the meadow as the light grew blinding. Their clothes were singed, their faces burned red.

I yanked the scissors away from Julie and bolted from the car, ignoring her pleas for my return.

The light was now the same intensity of staring into the sun. I saw members of the wedding party passed out on the ground, their skin the same color of a freshly cooked lobster. Dane was sprawled on the ground, the eyes burned from his head and a silver dagger protruding from his chest. I ran on, to the source of the light.

My sister was being escorted to the light, her white gown whipping about like there was a windstorm. Her bloodless face seemed mesmerized by what it contained.

All I could make out was the torso and the arm extended to her, and I screamed too.

Around the wrist of the arm was the sapphire necklace that she had lost.

Amy slowly took the hand... and was yanked into the light.

I blacked out after that. When I woke up I was in the hospital, Julie was sleeping in the chair next to my bed.

I'd gotten first and second-degree burns on all my exposed flesh, but I was lucky. Everyone else on the ground was dead. No one bothered to try to bullshit what I'd seen, that it was a chemical weapon or some gas leak.

Someone caused what happened to my sister. Her body was never recovered. I lost her.

But why am I bringing this up now?

Well, Julie and I are getting married.

And this morning when I went into our front yard, there was a fairy circle.

In the middle of the circle was the pearl necklace I loaned my sister, with the addition of a blue sapphire at the throat.

Something borrowed, something blue.

THE MAN CALLED DAFFODIL

I thought I grew up in a good neighborhood, surrounded by good people. Everyone said good morning to each other in the morning, my mom was friends with our neighbors, and we all went to church together. In my young mind, that made us very good people.

Then Daffodil came to town and turned my world upside down.

I first met Daffodil when he knocked on our door. Mom was absorbed in a book she was reading so I went to go answer the door. I thought I was mature enough to do so at six years old, and plus, I had Bear—a dog mixed with a million different breeds but was big and looked pretty intimidating. Dad got him for us before he shipped out overseas, for his own peace of mind. Someone to keep us safe while he was off keeping the country safe.

I didn't expect to see a skinny rail of a guy standing on the porch, bouncing on his heels as he waited for someone to answer the door. His cheeks were bright red, he had a short beard and curly blond hair, a guitar that had seen better days was slung over his back, but what really got my attention was that he wasn't wearing any shoes.

"Hello!" He knelt down to my level, grinning broadly. "Is there any chores or work I could do for your family to earn my bread?"

I glanced at Bear to see his reaction to this bizarre fellow. Normally my dog would at least be a little apprehensive around a stranger, but much to my surprise Bear was happily panting away. The man looked at Bear and actually *squealed*. "Oh, a good boy!" He gave Bear's ears a scratch and Bear licked his hand.

I craned my neck in and yelled for my mom, "Mom, there's a man here who wants to do work for bread. Can I have him help clean my room?"

"Sure, sweetie!"

Of course, my mom was distracted. She loved her books. But since she said it was okay, I let the man in. He bowed his head politely. "Thank you, thank you so much. Sun was about to burn me alive. My friends call me Daffodil, what do they call you?"

"I'm Will. Come on, let's go clean my room." Mom said I had to, after all, before I went to go play, and if all Daffodil wanted was bread then what was the harm?

Daffodil was a very efficient cleaner, and I learned quickly he was a complete weirdo, but he was nice. He asked the names of all my stuffed animals, asked about my favorite games to play, my favorite color. When he wasn't asking about me, he was humming tunes to songs I didn't know.

We just got done when Mom popped in to ask who I was talking to and screamed when she saw a strange man in her son's bedroom. "Who—Will, who is that?!" She grabbed me by the back of the shirt and yanked me away.

"Mom, it's the man I told you wants to work for bread! You said it was okay!" I complained.

Daffodil politely bowed his head. "Not to be argumentative, ma'am, but he's right," he said.

My mom was pretty embarrassed, but in the end Daffodil did end up staying for dinner. She came to the same conclusions I did—weird, but absolutely harmless. He was a traveler, just planning on cooling his heels in town for a while.

How long was a while?

"Maybe a week, maybe a century. I'll make up my mind later."

As he left, he gave me a dried-out flower. "Thank you for dinner," he said, before tipping his head once more and skipping down the street.

I still have that flower on my desk.

Daffodil did end up staying a while, several years in fact. He'd typically go door to door, asking for work in exchange for something to eat or a place to sleep. If he wasn't doing that, you'd find him in the park playing guitar for tips or selling pressed wildflowers. His songs told stories of home, of gardens that went for miles and a wife named Rose and another named Dahlia and their dozen children in between them. I rather liked his songs, even though apparently he had some raunchier ones that my mom told me about when I was older. He never sang them around the kids, though.

My mom gave him a pair of my dad's old boots during winter, and I swear he did a little dance and promised to dedicate a song to her. When my dad got home, he was also a little hesitant about Daffodil (I'm pretty sure I heard him ask mom if Daffodil was a queer), but I thought it was impossible not to warm up to such a charming fellow.

I learned better when I got older.

See, Daffodil never minced words. Never pulled any punches. He got into several heated arguments with one of the neighbors, Mr. Robert Miller, about why he wouldn't go to church. Miller was a quite devout Christian, always trying to convince the 'lost sheep' of God to join the flock. Most people knew better than to try to argue with him about it.

Daffodil was not most people.

I was about nine when I overheard one argument between the two.

"Mr. Miller, I am well aware you'll put a roof over my head and food in my mouth if I go to church, but again, I don't think it's very Christ-like to blackmail me like that."

"It's not blackmail. I'm just trying to help you-"

"No, no, you're helping yourself feel good."

"How dare you!"

I enjoyed a good amount of eavesdropping as a kid, so I kept myself hidden behind the fence dividing our two yards as I continued to listen in on this bickering.

"I've been around the block a few times, Mr. Miller, I know how it works. The moment we're done here, you're going to run to all your other little church friends and talk about the heathen that won't hear God, you will pray together and pat yourselves on the back for doing a job well done."

"What is wrong with you?!"

"Nothing. Or a lot of things, depends who you ask. I found my version of god in song and in nature. I'm at peace with that."

"You're one of *those*, aren't you? Is that why you won't go to church?"

There was a pause before I heard Daffodil sigh.

"I am not inclined to share my sexual past with anyone, Mr. Miller. Good day."

"You *are* then! You'll burn in hell, faggot!"

I'd never heard that word before. But the way he spat it out so venomously almost frightened me. I almost asked my mom what it meant, but I lost my nerve, given it sounded like a bad word and I didn't want to get in trouble.

Didn't lose my nerve to ask Daffodil though, the next day while he raked leaves for old Ms. Reed.

"What's a faggot, Daffodil?"

He didn't even miss a beat as he twirled the rake in the air. "A bundle of sticks," he responded.

"That's all? Like a bitch is a female dog?" I couldn't say these words around my mom. But I could ask Daffodil anything and he'd tell me the truth.

"Sorta."

I remember him laughing and performing another twirl of the rake. "Will boy, just know that Mr. Miller meant it in a way to cut me down. It's a nasty word, so don't use it. You can use some of the other bad words when you get old enough, but that's just one of the words you can't."

"Why?" I asked.

Daffodil never got mad when I asked why, but this time he looked a little sad as he reached over and ruffled my hair.

"You'll understand one day."

And I did understand one day. I suppose Daffodil wasn't exactly hyper-masculine, he put flowers in his hair, danced down the street to no music, cried when he was emotional and was not afraid to get excited over things like baby bunnies or dogs. To be totally transparent, though, I don't think Daffodil was gay. He was too much of a flirt with any women close to his age.

Didn't matter though. He was a piece of pyrite surrounded by the asphalt on the cul-de-sac and people didn't like that too much.

It really came to a head when I was twelve. Daffodil was one of my friends, my parents loved having him for dinner and it wasn't often that he wasn't crashing on our couch, snoring like a freight train and his oversized legs hanging over the couch arm. I felt like he was a cool uncle, the guy I could turn to whenever I had a problem or question.

I was doing dishes while my mom was enjoying a glass of wine with Mrs. Miller in the living room. I still hadn't learned not to eavesdrop, so I took a break from the suds to listen in.

"-And I just don't know if it's a good idea to have him hanging around Will all the time."

I heard my mom laugh. "Anna, Daffodil's harmless. Weird, definitely, but harmless."

"Well, you know he's... you know... like *that*. What if Will turns out like that too?"

"Anna, you can't seriously believe Daffodil is homosexual. Really, I think you're making a mountain out of a molehill."

"I just care about you and your son! And god knows what he might have if he is a homo, what if he gives Will AIDS?"

"Anna!" My mom sounded horrified, and I felt the same. I did not like the implication that Mrs. Miller was throwing out there.

"I'm being serious!"

"And I'm being serious when I say, again, Daffodil isn't gay, and he doesn't have AIDS. Besides, I think the neighborhood's done well with him around. You know we haven't had anything really bad happen since he started staying around here? No one's lost their job, everyone has a good looking yard, no one's gotten badly sick or died…"

"What, are you saying he's had something to do with that?"

"Well, maybe he's a good luck charm. Let's change the subject. How's Levi, has his grades improved?"

I went back to the kitchen after the subject changed. I genuinely hoped it was just the Millers with such nasty thoughts, that their venom was contained in the family.

I was wrong. Mr. Miller was a deacon at the church at this time and had the respect of a lot of parishioners. His nasty thoughts had taken root in many people's minds.

I don't know why I was out late that night. It was hot, maybe I couldn't sleep, but I wasn't really the kind of kid to wander the streets after dark. This is the only night I remember doing it. I heard a commotion and followed the sound, curiosity killed the cat, but satisfaction brought it back, Daffodil taught me.

I found a mob of twelve men and all of them had surrounded Daffodil. For the first time in my life, I saw Daffodil look afraid.

"You don't have to do this," he said, hands raised in the air. He wasn't armed. He was defenseless.

I saw Mr. Miller lift up a baseball bat. "We told you to leave, Daffodil. You wouldn't listen. You *forced* us to do this," I swear I heard pure evil in his voice that night.

Daffodil looked down, and then he looked straight at me. I heard him mutter 'stay put' before he looked back at Mr. Miller. "Then I suppose I'll cease to speak. My words have fallen on deaf ears for long enough. Do what you came to do."

They descended on him like a pack of wild dogs, and he never fought back, not once.

I watched them beat him into the ground with bats or golf clubs or whatever the hell they brought. They beat him while he howled in pain, they beat him until he only whimpered, and they beat him until he was still and quiet. When they left, all clearly proud of what they'd done, that's when I crawled out of my hiding spot and hurried to Daffodil's side.

He didn't even look like a human anymore, he looked like fresh roadkill. That friendly face that I never saw without a smile before tonight was swollen and broken, the flowers in his hair were squashed on the ground...

"Daffodil?"

Somehow, Daffodil turned his head towards the sound of my voice. "... Will. Good... good boy, for not leaving your hiding spot..."

"Why wouldn't you let me help you?" My eyes overflowed with tears, they landed on my friend's face.

"Because... I couldn't stand the thought of you getting hurt for me, my little friend."

A shaky hand, one with fingers bent in horrifying angles, reached up and touched my face, smearing blood across my cheek.

"Thank you for listening to me. Thank you... for being my friend."

I waited until he seemed to stop breathing before I dragged him off the road and into the nearby woods. He was far too heavy for me to consider doing this in a sane state of mind, but I was on autopilot at this point. All I could think of was how they might further desecrate Daffodil's body in the morning. How they'll say he deserved it, and then put him in a grave that didn't have a proper headstone and not even a name.

I folded his arms over his chest, like he was just sleeping. I covered him in leaves and flowers. I took one and put it in his hair, tucked behind his ear.

This was the grave he deserved. The best a twelve-year-old boy could do.

I didn't eat for two days after Daffodil's death. I didn't leave my room. My mom was confused as to what was wrong until she realized Daffodil hadn't shown up. Miller claimed he just left town but mom knew he wouldn't have left without saying goodbye.

She managed to pry the real story from me and then she called the police.

Here's the kicker though—the body was gone. They found the grave I made for him, the piles of leaves and flowers, but there was no Daffodil. My mom told me that maybe Daffodil was okay, that he got up and just chose to quietly leave, but I knew I saw him stop breathing.

You know how my mom said Daffodil was a good luck charm, right? I think she was right. Well, half right. Daffodil was good luck to the people that did him good, and their neighbors prospered because of that. But Daffodil wasn't going to give that kindness any longer to the people that beat him and left him for dead.

The week after Daffodil's death, I saw him.

I couldn't sleep. I hadn't been able to sleep well since the incident. I was staring out the window when I saw a familiar head of golden hair walk into the space between ours and the Millers. I couldn't believe it. I rubbed my eyes a dozen times before I got up and pulled the window up, ready to call out to my friend to see if it was really him or if it was just a dream.

The word froze in my mouth when I realized I wasn't sure if this was really Daffodil. Sure, he had his golden hair and beard, but he was... different. Taller, which was quite a feat given he was already a giant. There was this unnatural glow about him, and he wore strange clothes. If this had been a few years later, I'd say he looked dressed to be in a ren faire.

One look confirmed, though, that he wasn't wearing shoes. It was still Daffodil.

He turned to look at me and now he smiled, but there was an unfamiliar mischievousness to it. He put a finger to his lips to shush me before he opened the window and reached inside. Out he pulled the Miller's infant daughter, Rebecca. He cradled her for a brief moment before he turned his head behind him and whistled.

Two women walked out from the bushes. I didn't recognize them. Both were also quite tall, one with hair almost silver in the moonlight wearing a white gown and the other with midnight black hair cut short to her jaw and a sword hanging from her waist. Daffodil handed Rebecca to the swordswoman who bounced her up and down a few times before walking away. I saw the silver-haired woman slip in through the window and a few minutes later left the front door with the Miller's two sons, four-year-old Micah and seven-year-old Asher. Both were still in their pajamas but clung to the woman's hands and looked at peace with her. She walked down the street and vanished in the dark.

Now it was just Daffodil again. He looked at me, still smirking, before he rubbed his hands together before lifting them up to his mouth and blowing on them. I saw sparks fly out from his palms and dance in the air before going black.

The next thing I remember is waking up the next morning to police all over the street. The three youngest Miller children were gone. And the eldest, seventeen-year-old Levi, was dead. Autopsy would later reveal he had gone undiagnosed with brain cancer, even though he'd just had a physical a few months prior and he was healthy as a horse.

Sure, I was asked if I'd seen anything, since my window was closest to the Miller's, but I just remembered Daffodil putting his finger to his lips and told them nothing.

Only one child of the Millers would be found, baby Rebecca, returned to her crib. But a week in and Mrs. Miller looked ready to have a meltdown. A teatime with mom and she confided all about how Rebecca never slept, only cried, and how she swore she heard her daughter giggling whenever she wasn't in the room.

That child was certainly not Rebecca, but once again I kept my mouth shut.

Things went downhill for the Millers the fastest, but they weren't alone. Several other households faced their own bizarre and sudden catastrophes. The Petersons were in a terrible car accident that cost Mr. Peterson his legs and Mrs. Peterson her memory. To her death, she believed every morning was July 21, strangely not the day of the accident but the day of Daffodil's disappearance. The Caldwells had a nasty divorce after Mrs. Caldwell got mysteriously pregnant, even though Mr. Caldwell had a vasectomy. It'd later come out she was approached by a young, handsome man and they had a moment of passion in the backseat of Mr. Caldwell's car.

The Anderson's house burned down. The Rivers were infertile. The Ward's prize garden wilted and died while Mr. Ward wasted away with an illness no doctor could diagnose. The Reeves lost their jobs. I could go on. But I'm sure you guessed by now what each of the families had in common.

Each of those families had someone directly involved with Daffodil's beating.

While everyone else's family was suffering disaster after disaster, ours only prospered. Bear's health held strong until he was nearly sixteen, a long time for a big dog. My parents thought they were out of luck when it came to having another kid, but mom became pregnant with twins. I insisted one be named Daffodil. They compromised and Marie's middle name is Daffodil. They were also approved to adopt, and that's when I got a brother just a few months younger than me, Brian. We became thick as thieves the day he came into our lives and we're still quite close. My dad got an amazing job when he was discharged from the army, mom got some serious promotions, so we got to go on amazing vacations and make amazing memories.

I was eighteen when Mr. Miller finally cracked and hung himself. He'd lost everything—his job after he failed a drug test that he should've passed with flying colors, his position as a deacon after said failed drug test made common knowledge, his wife after she was just done with his bullshit. He just had to give up the car because of the debt he was in and was about to lose the house. In his suicide note, he did confess to Daffodil's murder and named the other conspirators as well. A few of them were already dead from various means, but the others got in pretty deep shit, even though they couldn't be officially charged without a body, apparently.

Sometimes I wondered if I dreamed that night I saw Daffodil outside. Sometimes I even believed it.

But it's been a long time since then. I have a family of my own now, married the love of my life and we have a six-year-old daughter, Iris. I actually own the Miller's house, I got it for a steal because of the suicide. My wife thinks it serves for great inspiration, she's a horror novelist, so that works out.

Maybe I would've forgotten Daffodil one day if my daughter hadn't run to get the door before I could stop her. Girl has no fear, probably like I did when I was her size.

I almost reached the living room when I heard her yell back, "Daaaaaddddyyyy, there's a man asking if we have bread!"

"Erm, not quite, if you have work so I can *have* bread. Close enough though."

I never forgot that voice. I ran for the door, nearly tripping over the dog in the process. I whipped open the door the rest of the way, nearly bowling over Iris in the process.

He looks exactly the same as he did back then. Same beard, same guitar slung over his back, same lack of shoes. He stared at me for a few moments before his eyes widened and he grinned.

"Hello, Will! It's so good to see you again. Mind if I help around the house? I like to work for my bread."

I TOOK A WALK FOR SEVEN YEARS

It was August 9, 2010. I was thirty-eight years old. My oldest daughter Avis was twelve, and the younger pair, Joanne and John, were nine-year-old twins. I'd been married for fifteen years. I worked at an insurance firm. And every Sunday, while my wife and Avis went to church and the twins went to my mother's house, I took a walk.

It was a clockwork sort of arrangement. My wife knew never to push me into going with her, I was an atheist and set on staying that way.

Of course, given what's happened, my views have changed.

It was just a normal day. Avis gave me a kiss on the cheek and told me to not forget my coat, even though it was an abnormally warm day. I'd say it was maybe sixty-five, maybe sixty-eight degrees Fahrenheit. My mom picked up the twins, and I started on my walk.

We lived off the beaten path, so to speak. Our road was never busy and most of the area was taken up by farmland. A truck passed me on the road and I waved. I was pretty sure it was Art, although it could've been one of his sons on his way to church. Either way, he waved back.

I took a turn to the right onto Hensel. Hensel was a dirt road but it was never travelled except by farmers, and today it was quiet. Good time to collect my thoughts.

Every other time before this, I'd turn back around once I reached Art's farmhouse, although occasionally his wife would pull me in for lemonade and gossip.

But August 9 would be the day I took the longest walk of my life.

I was passing by the cornfield when I heard laughter. To be more specific, it was a child's laughter. I paused and looked into the cornfield.

A pair of forest green eyes looked back at me.

The girl looked to be no older than seven, had red hair tied into twin braids, and I assumed she was one of Art's grandchildren. She smiled broadly.

"Catch me!"

She darted back into the corn and I could hear her giggles slowly fade away.

Normally I would've scoffed at going into the field, as I'd have to cross the ditch and I didn't want to get dirt on my pants. But I felt a little bit of concern, a small child running around the field by herself. So with a jump that I knew my knees would feel in the morning, I hopped into the cornfield.

Using the sound of her laughter as a guide, I started pushing through the corn. The dry leaves scratched at my face and hands, and dust kicked up into my face.

I knew she couldn't outrun me for long, even if she was a child with boundless energy, I had longer legs.

However, I exited the cornfield in a place I didn't know.

My house was nowhere to be seen. And there was a light layer of snow covering the ground.

I spun around, but the corn was gone, replaced by frosted evergreen trees. The temperature had significantly dropped, and I was now thankful that my daughter insisted I bring a coat. I shivered and spun around a few more times, trying to make sense of this dream I'd apparently fallen into and where was that little girl?

"Hey! Mister!"

I finally spun around enough to see her, peering past a branch. She grinned.

"You catch me, I'll show you the way out!"

That began the chase.

Getting smacked with tree branches was far worse than the corn, the needles tearing at my skin like knives as I pushed past them to find that little girl. Whenever I got lost, I'd hear her laugh. She was having fun. I was not.

The wet snow beneath my feet made it impossible to gain traction, and forget running—I'd slip if I so much as stepped wrong. With every minute I got colder and colder. My teeth chattered so hard my jaw ached.

Then I broke from the treeline into a grassy meadow.

I didn't expect the change, so I ended up toppling over. The grass smelled sweet as honey. A fat bumblebee trundled past my head and landed on a Black Eyed Susan. It was heaven.

But the peace of the meadow was broken by that girl laughing again.

"Awwww, are you already giving up?"

The warm sunlight made her glow, like a tiny angel, but as I stumbled to my feet, I caught something behind those big eyes I hadn't before.

Malevolence.

She was toying with me and she knew it.

I can't tell you how many times the environment changed. One minute it'd be across a meadow, then a desert during a sandstorm. I'd have to rely solely on hearing her in places like that. Sometimes we'd be back in the cornfield, and I'd shout for Art to get me out of here, but no help ever came. Sometimes we'd be running across barren tundra, where she'd be just out of my grasp.

She wasn't always a little girl either. Sometimes she was a young teen, with a gap between her teeth and who'd hum sweet tunes. Sometimes she was a ravishing model of her early twenties, with fiery hair and a flirtatious grin. And the times she wasn't any of those, she was an ancient crone, with a bent back and arthritic hands that clutched to her cane but still managed to hobble away from me.

She called herself Clarice occasionally. Other times it was Lolita, Dixie, Isabella, Hope... I lost count of her names too. A straight answer was impossible. She'd never lie to me, though, just avoid answering any of the questions I'd ask her.

So I knew she was my key out of there.

It was in the meadow where I finally got her.

She was a little girl again, and her taunting was beyond cruel this time. She'd stop, pick flowers, and run on before I could grab her. She'd throw the flowers about and sing ridiculous nonsense songs and I knew I couldn't ever win like this.

So I dropped to the ground.

The little girl stopped.

"Oh, are you really giving up now? You're sooooo close!"

Nothing. I remained still as I gasped for breath.

I heard her get closer and closer.

"Mister? Are you okay? Do you need a break? You've been going on for a really loooong time..."

Once I saw her shadow, I lunged.

She almost got away but my hand wrapped around her braid and I pulled her back so hard I could've snapped her neck. I embraced her in my arms and breathed out, "I got you."

I'd never felt so successful in my entire life. I'd finally gotten her.

She turned around and smiled sadly.

"Can we play again? We were having fun. You don't have to go back, we can stay here."

No way. I was done with this. "Nope. You let me out of here right now or I'm strangling you with your own braids." A little dramatic, perhaps, but I gripped tighter onto her hair to make my point clear.

She sighed before she kissed my cheek. The same place Avis did before church.

"Okay."

When I woke up, I was in the middle of the plowed cornfield.

It was springtime, the ground was churned to mud and the water freezing cold. I peeled myself off the ground and began stumbling home.

It was then I noticed how tired I truly was. My mouth was as parched as the deserts I ran through. My body was stiff and ached like I'd run a thousand miles, and there was a chance I had. I had one goal in mind, though, and that was home. I could finally go home.

Despite tripping through the mud a dozen times, I caught sight of my house and immediately began to cry. Barely able to move, I just pointed myself to the backyard. My wife should be home by now. She'd see me and come to my aid.

Two teenage boys were on the back porch, one was smoking while the other was playing on his phone. I couldn't recognize either of them. Had my family moved? I raised my hand and attempted to speak, but it came out as a raspy moan.

Both boys jumped out of their skin, the one smoking dropping his cigarette and they backed off. The shorter one raised a hand. "Sir, you're gonna have to..." He trailed off and his eyes widened.

The eyes looked exactly like my wife's.

"... Dad?!"

I passed out on the ground, just a few steps from the back door.

I woke up in the hospital. I'd been cleaned up, had an IV running into my arm, and a woman was sitting next to my bed. Fast asleep. With a tattoo of a bird on her neck. A sparrow, to be exact.

Avis always loved her sparrows.

I'd been gone for a little over seven years. When I didn't return from my walk, my wife reported me missing. At first, law enforcement assumed I'd just ran off with another woman, but when that line of investigation went dry, they realized I'd been the victim of foul play.

Search parties were made. People were questioned. No one was imprisoned. They never found me. And life marched on.

Art apparently died about a year after I went missing. Stroke. The farm went to his sons, who ended up selling the whole property to another family. A family who stayed oblivious to the fact that was the place I was last spotted.

The boys on the back porch were in fact my boys. I just hadn't been around when Joanne announced he was now James, at the age of thirteen. I wish I could've been there to help him become a man.

I apparently had a good replacement, though.

After four years and it looked like I was gone for good, my wife met someone new. His name's Clark. They'd gotten married six months after they met. Clark was a real outdoorsman, hunter, fisherman, and loved to go camping. As I chased a fairy child through her playground, he was taking James and John out on trips every weekend and putting away money to help James afford his surgeries and the like. Clark had two kids of his own, and I was soon a memory in this house. They could survive without me.

Avis was the only one who hadn't given up on me. She pursued every lead. Every dead end. Every chance that I could be there, she was chasing it. Stubborn girl. My girl. But she'd grown from a girl to a woman since I'd been gone, and it was like talking to a stranger. A stranger who had my chin and nose, but a stranger nonetheless.

My wife did want to help me adjust, though, and kindly offered the guest bedroom for me while I recovered. I'd apparently been through hell, bones were broken and healed, muscles torn and strained beyond their limits. I was malnourished and could barely stand without my walker, and I just had nowhere to go.

It was not a place I could stay, though.

Clark's kids looked at me like I was some bogeyman that lived down the hall. Clark and I tried to be polite to each other but things became tense as my now ex-wife was struggling on which name she should officially put down on paper that she would divorce.

I was just in the way.

But the little girl wasn't gone.

Nightly I'd see her outside my window. She'd peer in, with those big eyes, and mouth the words,

"Come with me."

I've told my wife I'm just going out for a walk.

PEEPING TOM

When I was twelve years old, I peeped into a girl's window for the first and last time.

I lived in a pretty boisterous area of town, not too far away from the nearby college. Right down the street was a house leased to a group of maybe five to six girls. The neighborhood didn't mind them, they didn't have crazy parties or trash the place. In fact, one of them had a habit of bringing my mom cookies as a thank you for being so welcoming to the area.

It's how my brother Elliot got the idea in the first place.

Carla was honestly really nice. Had a great smile, always had a joke to crack, and was even nice to me. However, Elliot had a different thought process, having two years of age on me and a little less respect.

"Carla has rainbow polka dot panties, you know."

I nearly rolled off the top bunk of our shared bed. I poked my head down, eyes wide. "How do you know that?" I asked, baffled. Had her jeans slipped down a bit and he just took a peek?

Elliot shook his head no, his smile like the Cheshire Cat.

"I looked through her window last night. She's a babe. I only got to see her back, but... wow." He breathed out, and if there hadn't been a blanket in the way, I'm pretty sure I would've been able to tell how excited he was. "You've never thought about doing that, Archie?"

I shook my head no. Granted, I was more my mother's child. I never really went over to dad's, he just drank beer and looked through magazines that had scantily dressed women on the front. Not my style.

"What, you gay or something?"

"No!" That, however, was not something that could pass.

Elliot made a sound of disgust. "Ugh. Keep your gay shit away from me bro. Night." He rolled over in bed.

The seed had been planted in my mind. I determined myself that tomorrow afternoon, I'd go look through Carla's window.

So I did. I didn't tell Elliot where I was going, I'd just tell him what color underwear Carla was wearing when I got back. He didn't ask where I was going, he was too distracted with working on his newest model plane.

My heart pounding in my ears and my palms starting to sweat, I crossed the four backyards I needed to in order to get to Carla's house.

Thankfully the neighborhood was pretty much dead, and I got there without being spotted. Bent over, I started walking behind the house for the right window. I had no idea which was Carla's bedroom, so I had to keep popping up real quick to see if anyone was inside.

The first window was a bust. No one was in there. Second window had another girl in there, I think her name was Beatrice, and she was napping. Fully dressed.

However, lucky number three, the third window I checked had Carla.

She was in an oversized sweater and jeans, writing at her desk. Her auburn curls hung past her shoulders, and she tapped her pencil against her pink glossed lips, deep in thought. She had no idea I was out there.

I had to admit, I was feeling a thrill. Crouched behind the windowsill, knowing at any moment, I could get caught. Quite an exhilarating feeling.

But soon I started to get bored. Carla was only working on homework, only pausing on occasion to scratch at her chest or back. Nothing like what Elliot saw. I was about to get up and go when Carla threw her arms up in the air and exclaimed, "That's it!"

She stood up in a huff and practically ripped the sweater off.

First thing my preteen self-noticed—she wasn't wearing a bra. I forgot how to breathe. I'd never seen a pair of breasts before. And Carla's set my standards high. Perky, symmetrical, and perfectly round. I'd gotten a step farther than my brother, and I couldn't wait to shove that in his face.

Then I noticed the sore.

It was right in the center of her chest, right below the collarbone. The flesh around it was discolored, pale and almost green. The sore was a dip in otherwise smooth skin, and it looked terribly swollen. How the hell she managed to keep that terribly itchy looking sweater on for so long, I have no idea.

Carla dug her fingers into the sore, and with a shout, ripped it open.

Her skin from the sore to her shoulder came clean off like the breaded skin on a chicken wing.

I still don't know how I didn't scream or run away at that moment. I was frozen. Carla sighed, tipping her head back in relief. The torn flesh oozed yellow pus, and suddenly I was hit with the smell of rot. It was an overwhelming wave that made acid burn my throat and my eyes water.

With a deep breath, Carla set her hand on the wound and tore again. Her right breast fell to the ground with a wet slap. She'd only just begun. Using only her hands and fingernails, Carla clawed off skin and flesh all over her torso. She even ripped out her hair, dropping the ragged locks on the ground.

When she was finally done, she collapsed on her bed, gasping for breath. She'd peeled most of the skin off her top half, and her hair was only a few sparse patches left. She didn't seem to be in pain at all. She seemed relieved. Like she'd finally scratched the itch.

Then she took off her pants.

I remember her panties. Lime green with tiny little frogs on them.

But the crotch was stained with blood. Diseased, brown blood.

I finally remembered I could run away. And I absolutely did. I took off down the street and once I was far enough down the street, I screamed at the top of my lungs. The acid burning my throat finally spilled from my lips as I gagged and hurled the contents of my stomach on the ground. Yellow bile splattered against the ground, and I was reminded of the pus. I threw up again.

That night I had nightmares of the skinless Carla crawling on top of me, wagging her remaining breast in my face and giggling like a hyena. Her pus dripped onto my lips and I was forced to swallow it. When I finally woke up, I'd found out I pissed the bed. I knew my brother could smell it from where he slept, so I hurried to clean it up along with my pajamas so he wouldn't have much to tease me with.

I thought I lucked out when I realized Elliot wasn't in bed. That he'd gotten up to get breakfast or something.

I remember my mom walking in the room to ask why the washer was running, and then her eyes landed on the bottom bunk.

"... Archie? Where's your brother?"

Four words that ended the life I knew.

It was all over the news—boy stolen from his own bed, remaining son left behind. My mother was on the news, sobbing and asking for the return of Elliot. She just wanted her baby boy back.

Search parties were held. Just in case he ran away from home. And I nearly shit myself when I saw Carla again among them.

It was like the whole skin ripping thing never happened. Even her hair was back to its normal thickness. She wrapped me in a hug, and she smelled like coconut shampoo. Not even the slightest whiff of that awful rot remained.

We didn't find Elliot for three months. When he turned up, it was in the creek.

My mother passed out when she identified what remained of Elliot's blood-stained pajamas.

Elliot had been gruesomely done in. His skull had been smashed open and the contents of his brain drained out. There was evidence of cannibalism on his thighs and stomach. I only found these things out because someone leaked it to the news.

I remember spending the night in Carla's room while my mother was handling funeral arrangements.

I laid on a cot next to her, staring at the ceiling. I was still numb. What had happened to my brother? Why had someone hurt him?

"Ya know, Archie. I think someone wanted your brother to be found."

I turned over in my cot, still dry eyed. Carla was sitting up in bed, wearing her adorable hello kitty pajamas. I shrugged.

"Does it matter?"

I remember Carla looking right at me, in the eyes.

" Closure's important. And... and if that person knew how much he hurt you, I bet he'd be super sorry. You're a good kid."

My stomach crawled as my mind played over and over again the smack of Carla's breast on the floor.

I felt my eyes finally fill with tears.

"A... are you really sure they're sorry?"

"Oh, Archie." Carla swept in and wrapped her arms around me. This time, when she hugged me, I smelled it. I smelled the slightest scent of bittersweet rot.

"I'm sure they are the most sorry person in the world."

MY PARENTS DIDN'T BELIEVE MY SISTER WAS PREGNANT

To be fair, I didn't know what to think either. Ellen was a quiet girl, senior in highschool, straight B's, didn't really go on dates, didn't even really talk to boys. She has friends, sure, but not many of the male variety.

She told me while I was reading in my room, clutched in her hands was the positive pregnancy test. She was crying. I felt stunned. I didn't ask about the father, it didn't really cross my mind at the time. I just hugged her after the stun faded and told her we'd be okay. I went with her to tell our parents.

Mom immediately burst into tears, sobbing and shaking her head. My father went quiet, face going a few shades paler. Then he spoke up.

"Why are you lying to us like this?"

Ellen started to cry again as she shook her head. "I'm not... I'm not lying! I'm-"

"Shut up!" My dad slapped the pregnancy test from her hand and stuck his finger in her face, his voice raising to a shout. "I taught you better to lie to us! What is this, you trying to hide your grades from us?"

I didn't know how to react to that. Ellen just sobbed and ran back to her bedroom, slamming the door shut. My dad turned his rage on me next. "Did you put her up to this? Do you think this is funny!?"

I bolted next, I'd never seen my dad this angry, and I didn't want to bear the brunt of his anger. I figured, when they'd calmed down, they'd see reason and help Ellen cope with what was happening.

They didn't.

Ellen tried to bring it up the next morning with just mom around, but her lips pressed together firmly and she refused to answer. Ellen pleaded with her to see reason, but she just told us to pick up some things from the store on the way home from school and left the table. Ellen buried her face in her hands, shed tears and was just confused.

I patted her on the back and told her I'd come up with a way out of this.

That afternoon I googled abortion clinics near us. Made a plan. I technically only had my driver's permit, but Ellen couldn't drive herself back after the procedure so I figured what the heck, might as well try to get away with it. I shared my plan with Ellen and although she was hesitant, I convinced her this was the only way she could get out of this.

When we attempted to go out for 'ice cream' the next afternoon, Dad stopped us.

I forgot to erase the browser history.

He screamed at us, telling us we were both going too far with our little joke and that we were grounded until Ellen confessed to lying. His face was bright red, a vein was popping out so far in his forehead I thought it was going to pop. Dad was always hot tempered, but I'd never seen him like this.

The moment Ellen opened her mouth to say something, Dad punched her in the jaw. Actually punched her. And he's no small guy, so he hits hard. Ellen hit the floor, I saw her spit a bloody tooth on the ground before she started sobbing. I dragged her by the arm as dad screamed after us how we weren't leaving this house for anything but school until we came clean.

I helped clean up Ellen's mouth, wiping away the blood and managing to sneak down for some frozen peas to press against her jaw. She shook her head and looked at me.

"I... I am pregnant. You believe me, right?"

It didn't really matter if I believed her or not, because she was.

Over the next few weeks, Ellen would be nearly knocked over with morning sickness. 'Morning' sickness is giving it too much credit, she had days where she was slumped over the toilet, unable to keep much of anything down. If mom caught her, she'd just say Ellen had the flu, if dad caught her, he'd call out her 'prank' and make her get dressed for school.

It was hell. Actual hell. And I could only stand by and watch.

Ellen wasn't sent to the doctor for prenatal care. I did my best with school computers to research how to help, but the help of a fifteen-year-old isn't exactly much help. I wasn't a medical professional, after all, and that's what she needed.

As her belly swelled, Ellen became a joke of the school. Rumors spread about how she slept with one of the teachers to pass her class, or that she had no idea who the father was because she'd been fucked by anyone who would take her. To her credit, Ellen didn't ever respond to these rumors. She'd just simply carry on with how she had.

I think sometimes even Ellen would doubt her own pregnancy. I'd catch her staring at the mirror, running her hands over the bump with the most quizzical expression, like she had no idea what was really in there.

And no, the baby bump didn't convince my parents either. My mother began to restrict Ellen's food intake, saying that she really needed to 'watch her weight' even though Ellen had probably never been above a hundred pounds her entire life. It was incredibly fucked up to have to sneak her food every night, so she wouldn't be starving. Sometimes it'd be leftover lasagna from dinner, a lot of the time it was only like a pack of raisins or a snack bag of chips. It didn't matter. Ellen was always thankful.

Despite our screwed up situation, it did help me and my sister grow closer. We were just that different in age that it wasn't easy for us to really bond, but I was the only one that really stuck with her. As she became more and more obviously pregnant, her few friends 'drifted away' or simply stopped talking to her.

Months passed. Ellen graduated with passing grades and looked positively enormous, even with the graduation gown. She smiled during pictures, and I think that's one of the last times she sincerely smiled.

Now that school was out, though, there was no leaving the house. We were prisoners in our own home. I could only get on the computer with mom or dad lurking nearby, so no more pregnancy research. I had to rely off the notes I'd managed to take during the school year. I'd keep moving them around my room so that my parents couldn't find them.

When Ellen went into labor, I thought my dad might kill her.

Ellen was on the couch moaning in pain, begging dad to call 911, she needed to go to the hospital. He just stood there, his arms crossed, and he glared down at her. "Enough's enough! You! Are! Not! Pregnant!" he snapped. He wasn't going to get help. He wasn't going to let anyone get help.

What happened next is something I should've done a long time ago.

I attacked my dad. Seeing my sister in pain while my dad did nothing was what sent me over the edge. I grabbed a pair of scissors off the computer desk and charged with a banshee yell. I didn't kill him; I was tempted, but I didn't kill him. I stabbed him in the arm and as he toppled back; I helped Ellen off the couch and got her into her room.

We didn't have locks on our door, but I blocked it off with a chair and prayed that would be enough. Ellen laid on her bed, clenching her sheets and screaming as another contraction shook her tiny frame.

The whole thing was a blur, really. I held my sister's hand until she nearly crushed it, I got her old baby blanket out of the closet, and I told her that she could do this. Her screams shook the windows, at least I thought it was her screams shaking the windows... but I realized that the house was shaking.

I remember thinking that this would be the time for an earthquake when I realized it was time to catch the baby.

My niece was so tiny, so still, her skin was tinted blue and I thought she was dead... until she opened her mouth and cried.

My sister looked up at me, her face white as a sheet and covered in sweat. I did my best to clean off the baby and wrapped her in the blanket, handing her to my sister and smiled.

I heard footsteps behind me and I felt the hair on the back of my neck stand up. Had my dad gotten in during the insanity? I turned around.

I can't quite describe what was behind me, only that it was tall, its head brushed the ceiling. The room seemed to grow dark with its presence, its features hidden by a black cloak that brushed the floor.

I nearly jumped out of my skin when it spoke, its voice low and ominous. "Is the child healthy?" It asked.

I gulped. "I... I think so."

My sister looked up and relief poured over her face. "You're here... I thought you wouldn't make it..." she said, a true smile crossing her face.

"I wouldn't forget you." The creature crossed to the bed and gingerly picked up my sister. I caught a glimpse of what was under the cloak's hood.

Strangely, I think he was rather beautiful, with dusky blue features and eyes pure black. He nodded at me.

"She'll carry a form of your name, child. And for your kindness."

He pulled a small pouch from his pocket, setting it in my hand. I undid the string and sparkling gold pieces poured into my hand.

The strange man walked to the closet, opening it up, I could hear my niece squall and my sister excitedly tell the stranger how happy she was to see him.

The door closed behind him. I got to my feet and opened it up.

There was nothing there, except for a few of my sister's dresses and some mismatched shoes. I sank to the floor, wrapping my arms around myself and allowing myself to cry as my dad finally broke in.

I've never seen my sister again, although sometimes late at night, I can see a small child peering in from my closet... she has my sister's eyes.

MY OLDER BROTHER PAUL

I didn't even know I had an older brother until he showed up outside my school that afternoon.

It was two years ago. I was a sophomore, my little sister Paige was a freshman. The original plan that day was to hitch a ride to a friend's house, where we'd probably team up and knock out our homework as quickly as possible.

That plan changed when we exited the building and someone called my name.

"Parker! Hey, Parker!"

My attention was immediately grabbed, and I glanced around for anyone familiar. All I saw was a guy in his late twenties, leaning against a fancy car parked on the street. He smiled and waved me over.

"Parker, over here!"

Double checking to make sure there were no other Parkers in immediate range, I decided to at least meander over. Paige was practically clinging to my backpack as we walked, she was a little shy and I was expecting any second for this stranger to look away and find that other mystery Parker.

But he didn't. He lit up and looked right into my eyes as we walked up to him.

"Wow. Parker. You're gonna get taller than me, aren't you?"

I frowned and made sure to take a sidestep in front of Paige, just to put myself between this stranger and my sister. "Can I help you?" I asked.

He looked a bit sad for a moment, before he sighed and nodded. "Yeah, I guess you wouldn't remember me. You were only two and Paige here," he stood on tiptoe to look at Paige, "She was just a lil baby."

I must've looked super confused, because Paul reached for his wallet and pulled out a photograph. "I'm Paul. I'm your brother," he said, handing me the photo.

It was so jarring. There was my mom and dad, I was standing in front of Dad with a big old smile on my little toddler face, Mom was holding Paige, and there was a boy standing between my parents, about thirteen or fourteen years old, with the same blond hair that both me and Paige had and a grin on his freckled face.

I'd never seen this photo before. But it was real and in my face and impossible to deny. I looked back up at Paul, who was back to smiling. His freckles had faded away with age, his teeth were straighter and whiter, but he still had the same goofy smile. And I could just about tell we had the same shape of our eyes, the same ears that stick out just a bit... the resemblance was uncanny.

Paul reached out and clapped his hand on my shoulder. "We have a lot to talk about. Come on, you like McDonald's?"

Paige cleared her throat. "We should—we should probably just go home, mom and dad-"

"They're gonna be at work until what, five? Six?" Paul glanced over my shoulder to look at my, well, *our* apprehensive little sister. "If they're still the workaholics I remember, they'll not be home for hours. We'll only be a bit. I just wanna catch up. I'll buy?"

I should've known better. So should've Paige. But even if we did, we still got into the backseat of Paul's car, and he drove us to the McDonald's a few blocks away.

Lunch that day had been pretty garbage, so getting a McDonald's treat was more than welcome. Paige tried to decline, saying she wasn't that hungry, but he ordered her an Oreo flurry and like magic her appetite came back.

As we sat in a booth, I stopped inhaling my burger for a moment to confront that elephant in the room.

"Why didn't mom and dad ever tell us about you?"

Paul was not at all surprised by the question, but he answered with one of his own. "You're a good kid, aren't you? Always home on time, straight A's, chores done without a single complaint?"

"I mean, I have a B in algebra-" I stopped myself before I nodded. "I guess so."

Paul glanced over at Paige. "You too?" he said. Paige also nodded and Paul sighed, nodding with understanding. "Yeah, that's about right. Nothing wrong with that, but I was a bit more... high maintenance."

I pushed my fries away and leaned forward to listen. Paige, despite her apprehension, was looking with just as much interest as I was.

"I guess you can say I had issues? I mean, I was fourteen, but I was already getting myself into heaps of trouble." Paul drummed his fingers on the table. "My grades were awful, got into fights at school, I'd sneak out at night... I mean, once I got out of there, I figured out I wasn't like most kids. I couldn't be parented like most kids. But one day Mom and Dad just... sent me away."

Paige gasped quietly, her eyes going wide. "They sent you away? Where?" she asked.

"Tennessee, to a friend of dad's that lived down there. They took a weekend trip and dropped me off at the door with a suitcase and a note." Paul shrugged. "I don't blame them, I mean, I was a holy terror. But man, it does sting a bit that they never even mentioned me to you guys. I'm still family... or at least, I thought I was."

A wave of sadness and disgust washed over me. Sad that I'd never gotten to know about Paul, disgust that our parents just gave up on him like that. Most fourteen-year-olds go through phases of being difficult, right? It sounded like he just needed some therapy, some freakin' support, and our parents just made him someone else's problem and erased him from our lives.

Paige finally lowered her defenses, reaching across the table and resting her hand on his. "I'm sorry, Paul," she said.

Paul smiled, reaching across the table to ruffle her hair. "Not your fault. Not yours either, Parker. You were just babies, after all. But hey, I'm here now. Let's make up for lost time. Don't waste food, but if you want anything else, let me know. And feel free to ask me literally anything you want. I got nothing to hide."

I didn't want anything else, but Paige did get an order of chicken nuggets. We munched and got to know our older brother.

After Paul left the house he was dumped at, he had traveled all over the states. He 'didn't want to go home without showing he was worth something', he said. He's worked all sorts of jobs, waiter, mechanic, janitor, but it was his most recent job as a manager at a small store that he ran into his girlfriend... well, 'girl friend'.

"Do you guys know what a sugar mama is?"

Paige nearly choked as Paul handed us his phone, a picture of himself and a woman that was probably in her early sixties. Sure, she was pretty okay looking for her age, but damn, she was without a doubt older than our mother. "That's Elaine," he said, pointing at the woman. "Elaine lost her husband a few years before we met, lung cancer. She just wants some company, specifically, she wants cute company." He poked himself on the cheek. "And I happen to be *adorable*."

I couldn't stop from laughing as I picked up the phone to get a better look. "Dude, our parents would *kill* you," I said.

"Listen, in life, you're up to your ears in debt until you die, you start off rich, or you marry into the good life. I mean, Elaine and I aren't married," he laughed at the thought of that, "But I can do whatever I want and she won't care, long as I'm home every now and then and ready for some... snuggles," he gave a pointed look at Paige, who scowled at the innuendo, but I just cracked up.

True to his word, Paul did get us home before our parents, but once we all got out of the car he tossed the keys to me.

"Registration's in the glove box, she's paid off and only got a few hundred miles on her. You have your driver's license, right?"

I was too stunned to do anything but nod.

"Then you're set. Think of it as the present for all the birthdays I missed. See you soon, guys." With that, Paul just walked off in the direction of the nearest bus stop.

Course, our parents had quite a few questions when they came home and all of them revolved around the car in our driveway that was easily worth over fifty grand.

I just waited for them to get out all their questions at once before I looked at Paige, who crossed her arms and said what they needed to hear.

"Paul came to visit."

Their faces were enough to confirm once and for all that Paul was our brother. Mom's face went white and Dad staggered back, falling into his chair to probably avoid fainting.

Mom took a seat on the couch, taking several deep breaths. "He found us?" she asked.

"Found us?" I repeated, that earlier disgust starting to boil up into rage.

"We moved after..." My mom swallowed, "You're all right? He didn't hurt you?"

"Hurt us?!" I snapped. "Are you kidding me? Why—why did you never tell us about him!? He's our brother!"

My dad cleared his throat. "Half brother, actually," he stared at our mother, who just looked at her hands, "And you need to tell him to take the car back. When he comes back, give him back the damn car."

I scoffed. "No way. You can't afford to get me a car, if you want it gone I'll just sell it and save the money for college," I said. "Why didn't you ever mention Paul?"

Mom's head was bowed in shame. "Paige, Parker, Paul isn't—Paul's not *right*-"

I didn't want to hear it. I just stormed out of the room, Paige right behind me. We'd heard all we needed to. Our parents abandoned a kid just because he 'wasn't good enough'. And Paul was actually not so bad now... least, we thought so, anyway.

Paul showed up again the next day, at school, not at home. This time he took us to his condo, which was just as nice as you'd expect from a man just giving away luxury cars. We had a Skype call with his 'girlfriend', and Elaine really was nice, if not a little eccentric.

"If you're Paul's family, you're mine," she laughed quietly, "So if you need anything, and I mean anything, just call me. I'll help you however I can."

After the call, we ordered pizza and just spent the whole afternoon chilling out, playing video games and just getting to know Paul. He was competitive but never a bad winner, just giving tips about how we could improve. He gifted Paige a brand new laptop, perfect for homework and for playing video games. 'I'll get you your own car when you get your license,' He promised, ruffling her hair and then asking what movie we wanted to watch.

When Paul dropped us off late that night, he didn't come into the house, but he did wave at our parents waiting at our front porch. My mom just looked ready to die of embarrassment while my dad... I guess he looked so stern to hide any fear he had. We didn't talk to them, we just went inside to do our homework.

It went like that for a few weeks. Mom and dad would tell us to stop hanging out with Paul, but since he was always outside school at the end of the day, we just hopped in his car and took off for another fun afternoon. Mini golf, arcades, wherever we wanted to go he'd just plug it into his GPS and we'd spend an afternoon having fun. We even spent a whole Saturday at Six Flags. Paul had us take an overpriced picture and put it in an even more overpriced frame as his souvenir. I got a t-shirt, Paige got a stuffed animal that was almost as big as she was.

Meanwhile, our parents were clearly upset, but we barely talked with them. I had resolved that I hated them both for cutting Paul out of our lives and I was going to do the same to them when I turned eighteen. God, the fact they moved after they left him to be someone else's problem so he couldn't find them? It pissed me off. Paige too, her theory was that Dad gave up on him so quickly because 'Paul's not his kid'. It was so tense at home I wanted to spend even more time with Paul, just to escape all that.

One of the final things we did was go out to a movie. By then we were all best friends, Paul, Paige, and I. We had so many expensive gifts, so many fun memories, we weren't even a little bit afraid of him. We'd gotten all the snacks we could carry from the concession stand and settled into our seats when a handful of popcorn smacked into the back of my head.

I turned around and internally groaned to see some unfortunately familiar faces. Paul glanced over to see the popcorn sticking out of my hair. "What the-" More popcorn flew through the air, followed by some pointed snickering and loud whispering.

"Ignore them," I said, pinching the bridge of my nose, "They're just some jerks from school."

Paul's eyes widened. "You're getting bullied?" he asked quietly.

"I wouldn't call it that, especially since Evan is the principal's son," I glanced back at the group and glared at the middle one, who only proceeded to laugh and throw more popcorn, "But they mess with me sometimes. It's fine, they'll get bored sooner or later." I'd gotten thicker skin from this sort of thing. I was already one of the tallest of my class, but I was also the quiet guy who didn't stick up for himself, so I was an easy target.

Paul turned around and I swear it was the first time I saw that carefully placed mask on his face slip. The look in his eyes screamed murder. "Fuck off," he growled at the group behind us.

Evan mockingly 'ooh'd'. "Whatcha gonna do about it?" he asked, smirking like he knew he was untouchable.

Paul responded by getting up and starting to walk back the few rows where Evan and his goon squad were sitting. I don't know what they saw, but I think Evan realized that Paul wasn't just going to sit and take it like I was. He threw up his hands and repeatedly whispered apologies. Paul stopped at their row and leaned in close to the boys that looked ready to shit themselves.

He whispered something I didn't hear, and I think Evan did actually piss his pants a little. Paul straightened up, I heard him mutter 'enjoy the movie', and then he returned to his seat. Back to being fun, big brother Paul, just like that.

At least I wasn't getting popcorn thrown at my head anymore, so I brushed aside any concerns I had.

That night when Paul dropped us off, he didn't stick around long. He said he needed to call Elaine, she had left him a voicemail earlier about how much she 'missed him', and frankly that's all I wanted to hear. Ew.

This time, my parents were waiting in the living room, together. They'd been going at it like cats and dogs for a week now, constantly having whispered arguments, and I think my mom was sleeping on the couch.

"Your mother has something she wants to say," Dad said. Mom just stared at her shoes for several painfully long moments before Dad added, "Or I'll say it, and I won't be as nice."

Paige scowled. "What?"

"You need to know the truth about Paul... so please, sit down," Mom said, her voice barely above a mutter.

I did take a seat across from them, but I probably looked as interested as I did during Algebra. "What?"

Mom looked like a woman defeated. "Like... like your father said, Paul is your half-brother, but that's not the whole story." She swallowed before she sat up straight and finally told us that whole story.

"I met him at camp. I was a counselor. Your father and I were on a break," she glared at him, while he just quietly scoffed, "After he'd cheated on me with his tutor at college. So I was bitter. I was alone. I was... empty. But Paul's father, he was charming? Different, but charming. After camp that year, I realized I was pregnant. Paul's father, we—we couldn't be together, so I went back to your father, and let him think that Paul was his... until Paul was born, anyway. It was impossible to hide that."

Dad shuddered. "You gave birth to a *monster*, Andrea."

"What the hell is wrong with you!?" Paige blurted out. "Just because he's not yours-"

"I wasn't. Being. Metaphorical." Dad glowered at Mom, who seemed incredibly focused on the wall rather than any of us. "Tell them, Andrea."

Mom's eyes welled up. " Paul... Paul was born a few weeks early, and he came so fast we didn't even have time to pack up for the hospital. And when he did, he... he wasn't right. I can't even describe—it's something you'd have to see to understand."

"Paul looks fine to me," I said.

"Because he wants you to see him like that," Mom rubbed the back of her neck, "He can do that. Within minutes he looked like every newborn baby boy. I would've blamed it all on the pain and hysteria if your dad didn't see it too. And sometimes, he'd look like... that, again, if it was only me in the room."

Paige and I probably looked equally confused. "Mom, you're not making any sense," she said.

"I know," Mom nodded before she looked at me. "The scar on your stomach, Parker. Shaped like a triangle. Is it still there?"

I hauled my shirt up to show it off. It had faded over the years, but it was still visible. "From the time I fell?" I said.

"That's not how you got it."

Mom shook. For the first time in weeks, I stopped being angry at her and was now genuinely worried. "Paul was—he was mostly like any other child until you two came along. He was a good boy. But he changed. He changed, and I was afraid, *terrified*, to leave him alone with you. The one time I did... oh my god... I can't, I can't..." Mom broke down in tears, burying her face in her hands.

Dad finally interjected. "He was acting up beforehand, but your mom was taking a nap in the next room over. I came home from work early and found Paul in your room. You were just laying there, eyes glazed over, and he had his mouth on you."

I nearly threw up. "What?" I had to have him repeat it.

"I thought he was just being a sicko and ripped him off, but it—Parker, you were bleeding real bad," Dad shook his head, "You only started crying when his teeth were out of you.

I looked at the scar again. My head was swimming, I couldn't breathe. "He bit me?" I asked.

"He was trying to *eat* you."

When my dad started to shake, it was with pure rage.

"I nearly lost it. He wasn't even *sorry*, Parker. He was just mad that I interrupted his snack."

Paige looked so white she looked ready to faint. "That doesn't look like a bite mark," she managed to get out.

"He bit him with his real mouth." My dad managed to get himself back under control after a deep breath. "What you've all been seeing, it's not really Paul. He's not human, because his father wasn't. I couldn't let him be in the house anymore. I began doing research, and I found someone-"

"I thought you shipped him off to a friend," I interrupted.

"Not exactly." Dad finally looked a little ashamed. "I found out more about Paul, and what he could be. And I found someone who could handle him, teach him to get his hunger under control. But Paul ran away from there after a few months. We'd already moved, but I didn't sleep through the night for years because I was afraid he'd be back to finish what he'd started."

I leaned forward, trying to wrap my head around this. "How is he not human?" I shook my head. "This can't be real."

"It is real," My mom sat back up, wiping away some of her tears, "I never wanted to give Paul up, but—he would have killed one or both of you. We didn't have a choice."

After the room stopped swimming, I got up.

"I need to be alone."

I went into my room and laid in bed for hours, just staring at the ceiling. I knew what I had to do, but I had to wait for everyone in the house to be fast asleep. Even Paige. Even if she was a part of this, I had to do this on my own.

My alarm clock read 12:13 when I finally got up. If my parents heard me start the car, they wouldn't have been out of bed before I was zipping down the road towards Paul's apartment. I probably broke the speed limit, but I didn't want to wait. If my parents were telling a lie that was that out there, I needed to let Paul know they'd freaking lost their minds.

Paul's apartment lights were on, and by then I knew where he kept the spare key, so I let myself inside. It was quiet, but I figured he'd just drifted off to sleep on the couch while binging Netflix.

He wasn't on the couch, though. I walked through the apartment, trying to hear him snoring or something.

As I pressed further into the apartment, I didn't hear snoring.

I heard this wet, squishy sound like someone was wading through knee deep molasses, and it only got louder as I headed for the spare bedroom. He'd used it for storage, he told us, so I never bothered to check it out. The door was cracked just an inch, and despite my better instincts, I pushed it open.

What I saw... god. What I saw. I still can't believe it, even though it's been years, I can't believe it.

I barely recognized the two corpses hanging by their ankles from the ceiling. Both were stripped of their clothes, completely drained of blood and their torsos ripped open, their bodies empty except for some bits of flesh and bones. The third body was still twitching a bit, and still had some color in the face, but it still took a second for me to place him as Evan. I'd never seen Evan so... blank. There was nothing going on behind those empty eyes.

And the thing next to him... I don't even want to describe it. It was humanoid, but barely so. It had two legs but only one arm, its gut stretched out so far it looked ready to topple over. Its skin was baggy and all mottled blue and green, and its arm was shrunken, curled in towards its body like a claw.

Its head was pressed up against Evan's gut, teeth set into his skin as it continued to suck blood and whatever else fluids it could get. I saw its sharp tongue stab into his gut and Evan gasped before his eyes rolled back and shut. His body caved in like the monster was draining a capri sun, liquefied guts spilled into the creature's mouth and some dripping down its chin. It finally pulled off when Evan was hollowed out.

It turned in my direction, his triangular mouth filled with rows and rows of spines that never seemed to end. Its tiny eyes blinked, and so did I... and then there was Paul, standing in front of me, looking entirely normal except for being soaked head to toe in blood.

"Parker?" he said, so softly, sounding so surprised. It jerked me out of my shock.

I slammed the door and ran for it. I barely got to the living room before the back of my shirt was grabbed, sending me flying onto my ass.

"Parker, dammit, wait a second!"

I looked up, expecting to see that *thing* instead of my brother. But it was Paul, out of breath and looking like a genuine serial killer.

"Christ, you know how hard it is to run just after you've had a big meal?"

I thought I was going to die. I wanted to beg for my life, remind him he was my brother, that he didn't have to hurt me. But I didn't have to say any of these things.

Paul crouched down next to me, brushing his red stained hand against my cheek. I flinched, something he didn't miss judging by the hurt in his eyes.

"I wanted to tell you. But then there's just so much more to explain, and I just… I just didn't know where to start. I just wanted to say sorry for what I almost did to you as a kid, so I figured, why not give you something? Something to show I didn't want to hurt you?"

I swallowed, telling my legs to crawl backwards and away from this blood-soaked maniac, but I couldn't move. I was frozen. "What are you?" I asked.

"My father's child. A son of Beleven." Paul shook his head, tears welling up in the eyes that looked just like mine. "I'm so sorry, Parker. Back then I was so, so hungry, all of the time. And I just couldn't stop myself, I couldn't. And those dickwads in there? The world's better with a few bullies gone from it, and this way, I won't lash out at someone else. Someone like you and Paige."

I shook my head. "You killed them…" I glanced into that room, where three classmates were still hanging like meat in a freezer, "You just killed them."

"I did," Paul nodded, and I think I saw what my father saw so many years ago, that apathy for human life. "I did, and I did it for you."

I finally ran. I finally got my stupid legs moving, and I fled that apartment, and Paul didn't try to stop me.

When I got home, my parents were waiting for me on the front porch. I hadn't brought my cell phone, stupid, I know. They thought I'd gotten myself killed.

I just hid in my room. I didn't tell them that I was sorry. That they were right all along. I didn't think I needed to.

Since then, my parents have divorced. I stay with Mom most of the time, Paige stays with dad. We don't see each other except at school or during holidays when we sneak away from our respective guardians. It's rough, but we get by. I've never told her entirely what I saw that night, only that our parents were right all along and that we needed to stay the hell away from Paul. I sold the car, Paige gave away the laptop. One by one, we got rid of his gifts.

Paul's just... gone. After Evan and two of his friends were reported missing, his apartment was vacated, he left without a word or a goodbye. The bodies were never found. I don't know if Paul just ate the rest or dumped them somewhere where they can't be found. I don't know. The nightmares from that night are never ending, the images of Evan just hanging there, letting Paul drain the life out of him without a fight flash before my eyes. Needless to say, I'm a bit of an insomniac.

Why has this all come up now?

Well... because I got a welcome letter for a job I never applied for. Alongside the letter is that picture we took at Six Flags, with the words *'I'm waiting for you'* written on the back. It wasn't signed, but I have a feeling who applied for me and who's the one waiting there. So I'll be accepting the position.

Next summer, it looks like I'm going to be a counselor at Camp Golden Oak.

MY BROTHERS AND SISTERS LIVED IN A SECRET ROOM

Growing up, I knew that my family's arrangement wasn't normal. As I got older, I even had an inkling that it might be wrong. But it was all I knew, and I won't let myself feel guilty for not doing anything about it for as long as I did.

I was the only biological child of my mom and dad. I found albums stacked away in a corner of the attic. The beginnings of baby books. A picture of an ultrasound, sometimes even a happy card announcing, 'It's a boy!' or 'It's a girl!' in blue and pink lettering. Mine was the only one who had pictures of a squishy faced infant with tangled red hair and fat lil cheeks.

My first sibling arrived when I was about four. I'd made the horrible mistake of asking Santa for a baby brother when I sat on his lap. My mother burst into tears when she heard me, and I knew I'd done something horrible. When we got home, mom told daddy about it and he told me to go play in my room while they talked about it. I knew that it wouldn't be right to ask Santa for that again.

Next week on Christmas Day, though, I woke up to hear a baby cry.

I ran downstairs to the Christmas tree only to find nothing there. I was confused until I heard a cry again. I followed the sound to the basement, where the most beautiful sight met my eyes.

My daddy had built a secret room behind the bookcase. My old toys I'd grown out of were scattered on the floor, the crib repainted to look brand new. My mom sat in the rocking chair, smiling so brightly as she cuddled a baby wrapped in blue blankets.

I couldn't breathe. It felt like a dream as I walked up to them, peering to look at his face. His face was all red from crying, and a fat tear rolled down his cheek as bleary blue eyes looked back at me.

I probably almost cried. My dad came up behind me and planted a kiss on the top of my head.

"Merry Christmas, Ella."

They let me name him Robin. I can't tell you why I picked that name, maybe watching Batman cartoons with my dad every Saturday morning had an effect on me. But Robin was the biggest secret I had to keep. I couldn't tell all my friends at school I had a brother. If I told anyone, my dad told me that Robin would have to go away, and I didn't want Robin to go away.

Every day after kindergarten, I'd sneak downstairs and just talk with him. Once he stopped crying all the time he was a real sweetie. I'd cradle him so carefully and talk to him about my day. I was so, so happy. I didn't think I could be any more happy.

Until I got a baby sister. My mom named her Caroline, I just called her Carol. Carol had thick dark curls and the softest skin. I loved her just as much as I loved Robin.

I got five more siblings over the years. Robin, Carol, Andrew, Andrea, Ivy, Ronnie, and Isaac. So many cute little babies. Ivy had a bit of a colic and Ronnie constantly had ear infections, but they were all little dears... well, except Isaac.

Isaac was the oddball out of the kids. He was the only little sibling that wasn't a baby when he arrived. I was about eight when we got him. I remember my dad coming back super late and hearing him walking into the basement. His shadow looked like he was carrying something, and I felt a spark of joy in my chest. I knew this meant I'd have a new brother or sister come morning.

I went into the basement the moment I woke up, expecting to see my mom feeding my new sibling a bottle or for him to be kicking his little feet while relaxing in his crib. I was shocked when I walked into the nursery and found a little boy my age, with a gag in his mouth and handcuffed to his bed.

Confused, I walked over and peeled off the gag. "Are you okay?" I asked.

The boy immediately screamed, straining against his handcuffs as he attempted to struggle free. Judging by the bruises and bleeding around his wrist, he'd already tried this. Instead of trying to help him up, I tackled him, slapping my hand over his mouth. "Shut up! You're gonna wake up our brothers and sisters!" I hissed.

My new brother responded by biting my hand. Hard.

I wailed as I ran back upstairs to my parents. My dad went downstairs to deal with my brother while my mom took extra good care to wash, clean my hand and bandage it up. She explained that Isaac was troubled. It would take him time to adjust to his new home, I just had to work really hard to be a good sister.

But I was never to undo his handcuff, and I was never, ever to let myself get too close. He was dangerous.

I did my best to stay out of arm's length of Isaac. My dad had to build another room to put him in, one that was below the staircase. He wasn't safe to keep around the babies.

I did try to befriend Isaac. For that first month or two, all he'd do is lunge at me and spit or just scream in my face.

When he did start talking, it was the things I didn't want to hear.

"My name isn't Isaac, you know."

I nearly jumped out of my skin when I heard him speak that first time. He was quiet that day, only giving me a sullen glare. I'd decided to leave when he finally spoke up, his voice raspy from all the screaming he did.

"It's Kevin." He turned around to face me. "I want my real mom and dad."

I shook my head. "But my mom and dad are now yours too," I said. I was such a selfless child, I figured, being so willing to share my parents.

Isaac just shook his head. "No. I don't want them. I want mine. Your dad came into my bedroom and stole me."

"You're a liar." I stuck my tongue out at him. "I hate you."

Isaac shrugged. "Just ask him. I bet he killed my mommy and daddy so they wouldn't look for me, either," he said.

I stormed out, slamming his door a bit hard. But what Isaac said got to me. I couldn't stop thinking about it, even when my dad came to tuck me in and kiss me goodnight. I even almost asked him. But I couldn't make myself face the truth.

I barely got any sleep for a week. Every time I closed my eyes, all I saw was Isaac, all alone under the stairs. Thinking about his real mom and dad.

I still didn't do anything until I overheard my mom and dad talking about getting rid of Isaac.

It was late, probably close to midnight. I still couldn't sleep so I was going to my parents' room to ask for something to drink when I heard them talking.

"I told you, Isaac is too old. He's too far gone. We can't help him," I heard my mom.

"Give it some more time, we can still help him!" My dad sounded so desperate, so... so sad.

"I'm sorry. But this was your rule, and breaking it was never going to end well. I'll... I'll take care of it myself tomorrow. Take Ella out while I handle Isaac. We'll just tell her he ran away."

Even at my young age, I knew something really bad was going to happen to Isaac. And even if I hated him, I couldn't let that happen.

I found the key to the handcuffs, ran into the basement, and ripped open the door. Isaac, no, Kevin jolted up in bed. "What's wrong?" he asked.

I didn't say anything, I just slid the key into the lock and freed him. Kevin gaped as he pulled his hand free. " But why?" he asked.

"We need to go to the cops. Come on, hurry!"

I took Kevin's hand, and we snuck out the back. I held onto his hand when we ran down the street, and I kept holding on when we finally came across a cop car. Of course, seeing these tiny tykes at that time of night got his attention.

I told him everything. About the children behind the bookcase, what I heard my mother plotting. All of it.

My life was turned upside down after that. All these children my parents had taken. Just little babies that were taken from their cribs in the middle of the night, the parents awaking to find their child was gone.

Kevin was right, he was the only one whose parents had been killed. Their throats had been cut open. My dad claimed that by the time he'd gotten there, Kevin's parents were already dead, but that really didn't hold up in court. My mom swallowed a bottle of pills before she could be tried, and my dad was sentenced to life in prison.

The last time I saw him, he just patted my shoulder and told me it wasn't my fault how this all turned out.

He hung himself that night in his jail cell.

Now I was an orphan, just like Kevin.

I went into the system, which was just as shitty as it sounds. I've literally done everything from sleeping on the floor to showering with my clothes on because I didn't feel safe. I bounced from house to house until a great aunt crawled out of the woodwork to save me. She really didn't do much other than clothe and feed me, but that's all I needed. By then I was fourteen, I could basically take care of myself.

The last thing she did for me was make sure I got my childhood home back. I know it's fucked up, considering what went down there, but my heart ached whenever I passed it. No one ever bought it. The yard was unkempt, windows gathered dust and paint began to peel. But my aunt, penny pincher that she was her whole life, had saved enough to give me all I needed to scoop it off the market.

I've spent the last month cleaning up the place. It's actually starting to look like a home, and it was only two nights ago that I stumbled across those old albums I told you about.

There was another one, though, for all the kids my parents abducted. It was hidden behind a fake panel in the wall, I only found it because I accidentally kicked the damn thing. I contemplated just leaving it there. A part of my past I didn't need to dig up.

But I went through it anyway... and there was so much I actually didn't remember.

I didn't remember that Robin's eyes glowed ultraviolet in the dark. I didn't remember that Andrew and Andrea never slept. I didn't remember how Carol sprouted a mouth full of needle-like teeth and had leathery wings jutting from her back. I didn't remember that Ivy had patches of pale blue scales breaking up her otherwise dark skin. I didn't remember that Ronnie's ears came to a slender point and that he had a second set of near transparent eyelids. Kevin seemed normal, maybe, but now I'm not so sure. When I think of his hands, I remember how each fingertip ended in a sharp, bone claw.

I've not slept since then. I've stayed up to research those kids, my little brothers and sisters. In the news footage they looked normal enough... almost. If you squint, you could almost see Ivy's scales or Ronnie's ears not looking right. But then you blink, and they just look like normal little kids.

I've dug up their fates. They all went back to their families. However, all their families are now all dead and have been for a while. Ivy's family drowned. That much I confirmed. I think Ronnie's dad just never woke up. The others I'm still researching.

And Kevin? His foster parents had their throats cut out one night. He's never been seen since.

THE STRANGEST ROOMMATE I'VE EVER HAD

This took place all about three years ago. I was going to college at the time and was living with two of my friends, Phoebe and Macie, along with Macie's boyfriend Joe. I'd been friends with Phoebe since we were kids, but only recently befriended Macie within like a year of agreeing to move in together, and Joe was sort of a last-minute addition.

Well, to sum it all up so we're not here all day, Joe was a jackass. He was a lousy roommate, but he was even worse to Macie, who's a pretty meek person and a doormat for Jackass Joe. It was the third time Joe was caught sleeping around that Macie finally snapped and broke up with Joe. He responded by taking off and leaving us scrambling for a new roommate, so we didn't end up losing our place. I think it was Macie who posted the ad on our school's Facebook page as a last-ditch resort. It didn't matter if they smelled like ham or were up all night blasting Marilyn Manson, we just needed someone to pitch in with the bills.

The next day, I answered the door to Miss Dorothy Ball.

I could already tell she was a weirdo off the bat—she was wearing a floor length navy colored dress with long sleeves and a high neck and didn't seem bothered at all by it considering it was almost ninety freaking degrees out. Not a blonde curl was out of place, not a drop of sweat on her paper white skin or rosy cheeks.

Her large blue-green eyes stared at me as I stared at the trunk and suitcase she had behind her.

Her head bowed down, speaking so quietly her lips barely moved.

"I'm Dorothy. I'm here about the roommate ad?"

I only let her in because I felt bad about how hot she had to be in that get up. When she sat across from me, I noticed she even had white gloves on; she seemed to be doing all she could to hide every inch of skin she could.

"I have the money here." Dorothy sat down an envelope on the table. "I intend on staying a full year, minus any unpredictable happenings. I would like to stay in a room by myself. I promise that I will be silent as a church mouse and that the rent will always be on time. Will that be alright?"

I cleared my throat. "I'll have to talk to everyone else." I opened up the envelope and nearly choked on my spit as the crisp one hundred-dollar bills fell into my hand. "Is this for half the year?!"

"Just the first month." Dorothy cocked her head to the side. "I found out the cost of rent, is this too little?"

"You're only supposed to pitch in a quarter-" I cut myself off as I realized Dorothy knew exactly what she was offering. "You're paying for all of it?"

"The first month at least." Dorothy laughed quietly, her lips not even twitching. "My family is quite wealthy. I would just like to live close to the campus and this is such a nice area. I want to show my appreciation for letting me board here."

I had a meeting with the other roommates after introducing them to Dorothy. I showed them the cash. Phoebe's eyes filled with dollar signs as she was clearly imagining what she'd do with all the spare cash she had while Macie seemed a bit more hesitant, but we'd not had any other offers. Most people by now had a place to call home while they went to college, and someone offering to pay all of this month's rent? You'd be an idiot to say no to that.

Dorothy was pleased as punch to be allowed to stay here, even giving us all a hug as she thanked us repeatedly. Phoebe tried to bolt from the hug, but Dorothy insisted on it. We did have to move things around a bit, Macie moved into my room while Dorothy took her old one, but I didn't mind since Macie and I basically had the same sleeping schedules, anyway.

You know how I said I wouldn't have minded if we got a roommate from hell as long as they paid the bills? Well, Dorothy was basically the roommate from heaven. She kept to her promise, she was so quiet she'd sometimes scare me because I didn't even realize she was there. Not to mention she was a neat freak—there was never a dish in the sink or a speck of dust on the shelves. I swear it was how she had fun, well, that and shopping.

There wasn't a week that went by that we didn't have a bunch of packages on the front porch. All cloth or dresses, Dorothy was quite the seamstress. Her closet quite literally overflowed with dresses, all long sleeved with floor length hems. The few that didn't have high necks she'd pair with chokers or scarves, again, she didn't want to show any skin. Not like she minded us dressing how we did, I think Phoebe nearly cried when Dorothy presented her with a crop top she made that was hot pink and had her name on the front. She made me something too, this summer themed dress printed with lemon and lime slices. I still wear it whenever I can, and it fits perfectly. She could guess a person's measurements just by looking at them.

Not to say I wasn't still a bit put off by her. Something was just not right about this perfect roommate. Any time we'd ask a question about her family or her past, she'd give a half-answer and change the subject, usually by offering to buy us dinner. Even though she did that, I never saw her eat, although she enjoyed tea twice a day, once at ten and once at three, like clockwork. I never caught her in the bathroom, although I did hear the shower run late at night when we'd all gone to bed, even Phoebe, who's a night owl and potential insomniac. Whenever she talked she'd bow her head down so I couldn't see her mouth clearly. She'd never complain about being hot or cold, hell, she never complained at all. And her face was practically frozen. She'd blink, but she had no real expressions from what I could tell—again, she'd always bow her head down so I couldn't get a clear view of her face past the curly hair.

Again, all of this is weird, but harmless. I chalked up my willies to just Dorothy's weirdness and did all I could to be friendly to her. I never wanted to be an asshat.

Dorothy was closest with Macie. After Joe left her Macie was pretty messed up, she cried nearly every day, and Phoebe said she was afraid Macie was going to drop out and leave us too.

That changed after Dorothy moved in. I think Dorothy sensed how sensitive Macie was and focused a lot of her energy on becoming her friend. Macie never told me what they'd do when they hung out, but Dorothy made it a habit to enter our room and just... talk with her for hours. I'd usually just excuse myself to the living room to binge Netflix and, well, whatever Dorothy did worked. Macie got out of her funk, her self-esteem shot way up, and she even began going on dates. All the while Dorothy was just basking in her glow, just happy that Macie was happy.

Of course, something did happen. I'm sure you haven't forgotten Jackass Joe from the beginning of this story. For a little more context, Macie's old room was on the ground floor, while my room that I now shared with Macie was on the second floor.

Waking up to hearing Dorothy scream bloody murder at around three AM was not a welcomed sound.

I jumped the stairs three at a time to rush down there, and when we threw open the door, Dorothy was hiding under her quilts while Joe was sitting in the center of the room completely flummoxed.

"I thought it was Macie!" He tried to explain as Phoebe dragged his ass out of there. Naturally, no one was interested, even if it was Macie, it's gross as hell to just crawl into bed with your ex-girlfriend who wants nothing to do with your ass anymore.

I approached the bed, Dorothy still shaking and crying. I tried to draw the blankets back, but the blanket bulge flinched back. "No! Don't take away the blankets!" She screamed.

So I just sat by the bed and waited for her to calm down. Her crying did slow, but she refused to come out.

"Are you okay?" I finally asked.

" He almost saw me."

The very top of Dorothy's head peeked out from under the blankets, I did absentmindedly note how her eyes weren't blood-shot, and her face wasn't red and blotchy, but she was still shaking. "I know... I know if anyone sees what I hide, they will never want to come near me again. And to suddenly have a man in my bed, I... I was frightened. I am so sorry for screaming."

"Don't be, I think most girls would freak out with a stranger suddenly climbing into their bed," I rested my hand on the side of the bed. "It's okay. You're my friend, no matter what you're hiding." I meant it too. Sure, she was strange, but nice. And I prioritize nice.

Dorothy slipped back under her blankets, but I heard a muffled 'thank you' as I exited the room.

Of course, Joe wasn't going to stop being the worst because he accidentally got in bed with the wrong girl. He began harassing Macie, saying he was 'sorry that she felt hurt' and he'd 'never do it again'. A quick Facebook check revealed that he was about to get kicked out of his dad's place for being a shithead, so it made sense he'd try to go back to his doormat ex to get a new place.

Of course, in the few months Joe was gone, Macie had grown a backbone, and she was just not interested. Neither were the rest of us, Dorothy especially. The first time I heard our strange roommate swear was when I heard her call Joe a bastard over breakfast, which nearly made Phoebe choke on her Cheerios. Joe could rot in hell. Joe probably sent over one hundred texts asking Macie to kick out 'the weird chick in your room' so he could move back in. Macie just ignored him, blocked his number and then every social media profile he tried to reach out to her on. She kept blowing him off, and we all figured sooner or later Joe would get bored and leave us alone.

Oh boy. Not even close.

Phoebe was out that night. I just went out to go pick up some frozen pizzas at the corner store, I was probably gone for like ten minutes. When I got back my heart sunk in my chest when I recognized Joe's truck out front. I didn't even enter the house to hear them arguing.

I bolted up the stairs to see Macie and Joe screaming at each other. One of Joe's friends was there too, a guy named Derek. From what I could make out, apparently Joe did find another place, but they needed one more roommate to make it work, and apparently Joe was back to harassing Macie about it. Macie's face was bright red as she yelled at them both to get the hell out of her house. She wasn't interested in ever being near Joe again, and if he didn't leave she'd call the police.

That police threat seemed to really rub Joe the wrong way as he grabbed her arm and squeezed it so tight I thought he was going to break it. I tried to step in, but Derek actually pushed me away, stepping between us so I couldn't get to my friend to help her out. My cellphone was in my pocket and I was considering just running for it to call 911 when I heard someone walking up the stairs.

I turned to see Dorothy, her head bowed so I couldn't see her face. She was dressed in a white nightgown that reached just past her calves. I could make out what I thought was scarring on her ankles and toes as she paused at the top of the stairs for only a moment. The next moment she stormed up to Joe and grabbed him by the arm, dragging him towards the stairs, clearly intent on throwing him out herself.

"Get out of this house. Right now. And never step near Macie again."

Her voice was cold and grating, far from the typically soft mumbles. Joe was probably frozen in shock at first, but he reacted with violence. He shoved Dorothy with all his might, Dorothy stumbling for a moment at the top of the steps before losing her balance and falling down the stairs.

When her body collided with the steps, it sounded like someone had taken a stack of china and thrown them down to the ground.

Dorothy rolled down the rest of the steps, the discordant sound of smashing glass causing all of us to freeze in our tracks. Dorothy finally hit the bottom step with her head and stayed all too still at the foot of the stairs.

Joe shot us all a 'what the fuck' look before Dorothy stirred. With the rattle of broken glass, Dorothy got up on all fours. For a nauseating moment I thought the side of her nightgown had been pierced with a piece of bone, but with a sickening grinding sound, Dorothy grabbed onto her gown and ripped it down the side, grabbed the loose shard of white porcelain in her hand, and began the painful-looking process of crawling up the steps.

Now I could see what Dorothy had been insistent on hiding, now that her gown had been ripped to ribbons thanks to her shattering. Each of her joints was like the ball joint on a doll, a dip in the skin that now made more disturbing grinding sounds as she hauled herself up the steps. Slivers and pieces of porcelain continued to fall from her body, the biggest missing part nearly taking up her entire right side. Inside of her, I could make out incredibly lifelike imitations of ribs, lungs, all cracked and breaking apart. Her right cheek was horrifically cracked, her eyelid hanging half down, unable to fully shut or open. Her chin hung loosely open, her mouth a black, gaping hole. But that still open eye was focused right on Joe, and it was full of loathing.

Macie acted first, bolting into her room and turning the lock. Derek screamed in horror and shoved me forward to act as a shield. Dorothy hauled herself up that last step and I nearly fell on top of her, barely managing to catch myself as I stepped on another piece of porcelain and sliced my foot open like butter.

Dorothy paid me no mind as she managed to push herself to her feet, swaying as she tried to regain her balance before she began to limp over to the terrified men. Joe looked at me and I think I remember him saying 'help me'.

I responded by crawling into Phoebe's room and locking the door behind me.

They weren't screaming for much longer.

I hid in there for hours, clamping my hands over my ears to block out the worst of the wet ripping and tearing. I didn't leave until I heard Phoebe enter the house, call for us, and then shriek when she saw all the blood.

And there was a lot of blood. It soaked the carpet on the second floor, with bits of flesh and muscle embedded in the fibers. But other than that, and the shards of porcelain scattered about the stairs, there was no sign of Joe, Derek, or Dorothy.

We never heard from Dorothy again. An envelope containing enough money to cover a few more months of rent did appear in our mailbox, but the police couldn't even confirm Dorothy Ball was a real person outside of her school registry. I never even told Phoebe the entirety of the story, only that Dorothy had attacked both Joe and Derek.

I still don't know what I saw, not really. The image of her shattered body crawling up those stairs, the hate in her still working eye as she stared at Joe will never leave even as I try to rationalize how on earth that could happen. People don't shatter like... like that.

But I do know Dorothy was real. I know she was.

And I'm thankful for her. She's still my friend, wherever she is.

MY FATHER SURVIVED THE CHAIR OF TRUTH

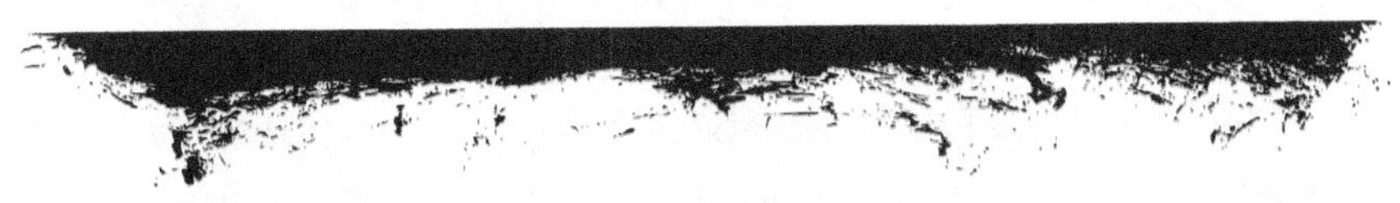

I was the only one home when my father called me in for his deathbed confession.

He wasn't very old in the grand scheme of things, only fifty-eight, but after a violent mugging that took place about twenty years ago, his physical health hadn't always been great. It really took a downhill turn last year. Heart failure. And it just wasn't getting better.

My sister Amber and I were taking care of him as his health deteriorated. Last week though, Amber was running errands for our grandmother, so yeah. I was alone. When dad called for me, I thought he might need a drink or help getting to the bathroom.

Instead, he told me to sit down. He told me I needed to know the truth, the truth about the mugging and about what really happened that night.

After all of this, he'd pass in his sleep a few hours later. I can't ask for any more details. All I can do is relay this story to you... and find out how much truth there really is to it. Below is the confession, word for word.

"You know, if your mother and I weren't in the middle of our first separation, it may have never happened. I wouldn't have been alone in bed that night. Alone in the house, since she took your older sister with her and you were still two months out from

"

being born. That following morning, I was found on the streets, all bloodied up, pockets turned out and missing my shoes. They concluded I had been mugged. I let them maintain that conclusion.

I hadn't even left my house the night before. It was an early night, I was tired from work. I basically passed out on the couch while the TV was on. I don't remember if anyone broke in, if I woke up before they abducted me.

The next thing I do remember? Waking up strapped to a chair, dressed in white scrubs with electrodes plastered on my now shaved head and sitting with a circle of people in the exact same condition.

I only recognized three of the other people there, and I only knew two of their names. One of my classmates from back when I was in high school was to my right, I barely recognized Magnolia since most of the blonde hair had been shaved right off. A few patches were still plastered to her scalp, whoever had taken the razor to our heads hadn't been the most meticulous about it. Perhaps because they had a lot to get done before we woke up.

The other two I recognized were Augusta, an older woman who lived down the street from where I grew up, and the homeless man that I usually saw begging for cash downtown was to my left. I didn't know his name, I only recognized him because he'd been there every day.

There were eight of us in total. The woman right across from me had smeared lipstick and a cut on her forehead, maybe the razor had slipped during her head shave. Next to her was another woman with long, fake fingernails and a natural scowl that was even there when she was unconscious, like she sucked on lemons in her spare time. The most conscious of us was a middle-aged guy with a few more bruises than the rest of us. I imagine he put up a fight, he was a big dude. Finally, there was this portly, smaller man who didn't need his head shaved, since he was already bald as an egg.

Magnolia began breathing faster when she came to full consciousness, glancing around wildly and in full panic. "What the fu—where am I!? What's going on!?" She yanked at the straps, which didn't so much as budge. "Get these things off me?! Help! Someone help!"

The burly bruised guy shushed her loudly. "Quiet down. Don't want to alert the wrong people we're up," he craned his neck around to look at the room around us, it was quite bare other than the circle of people strapped to heavy duty chairs—dark brick walls, a cement floor with a drain in the center. The only light was in the center of the ceiling, and that thing was set on as bright as it could go. Everyone looked a little washed out, pale, sickly.

The one thing I had missed was the speaker, attached to the wall right behind my head. It crackled to life before shrieking with feedback. This definitely got everyone awake, the portly fellow moaning and bitching the loudest while the woman with smeared lipstick being the only one perfectly quiet. Her eyes I remember the most, dark and careful. She was watching everyone in the room.

"Welcome, everyone."

Once the feedback died down, the male voice coming from it was perfectly calm, smooth. It would've almost been soothing if the situation surrounding it wasn't so bizarre.

"I am the Judge."

I flexed against the bindings experimentally. There was no coming loose from them. I was stuck there, here for whatever this 'Judge' had planned.

"You sit here now because you have all committed crimes. Crimes ranging from white lies to ones that may result in... capital punishment."

The scowling woman's jaw dropped. "What do you mean, capital punishment?"

"This is my court room. Where we are, no one will hear you scream. I advise you don't cry out unless you can't avoid it." The Judge didn't even take note of the interruption. "These are my Chairs of Truth. When we are finished, you will pay for what you've done. If you lie or talk your way around the truth, you will be punished. We will start with you, Connie."

The scowling woman sputtered. "How dare you! I'm not a criminal! Do you know who I am?"

"Yes. Of course I do, Connie Andrews." The Judge sounded almost... amused. "I know everything about you. Your first question is this: where do you go every Wednesday afternoon?"

"Are you for real?" Connie looked genuinely baffled.

"We are starting with an easy question. One that has a minor effect on your life, legally or illegally. Where do you go every Wednesday afternoon?"

Connie looked relieved. "Um... I get my nails done," Her fingers tapped on the arm of her chair. "What, is that a crime?"

"We'll come back to that. Frankie? Can I call you Frankie, Frank Smith?"

The burly guy shifted in his chair. "You can," he decided.

"Frank, during highschool, what was the extracurricular you and your wife participated in?"

"I was a football player, she was a cheerleader." Frank cleared his throat. "And who are you?"

The Judge quietly chuckled. "I am not important. I am here only to fulfill judgment, officer," he cleared his throat, "Onto the next. Augusta Armstrong? How many children do you have?"

My neighbor looked terrified, shaking in her chair like a scared Chihuahua. "I have five, they're the light of my life. Please, please, let me go," she whimpered.

"If you answer these questions, we can see about that. Charles Nolan?"

"When I get out of here, I'm going to *sue* you!" The man snapped, lurching in his chair. It didn't so much as budge, it had been bolted to the floor.

"Charles, what is your occupation? No need for specifics, you like those, I'm aware."

"Businessman, I work for-"

Charles suddenly breathed in sharply. I had to crane my neck around the homeless guy to see what had happened. I only caught the glimpse of what looked like a sewing needle exiting Charles' arm and going back into the chair, a pinpoint of blood beading from his skin.

Fuck. I took a better look at the chair, which I'd only assumed was a heavy-duty wooden chair. Now I saw there were holes all in it, some small enough for needles to come out and jab, others thin slats that looked large enough for daggers to come out and slice through us.

"When I say something, I advise that you listen," The judge explained patiently. "Harley Scott?"

The homeless man lifted his head up. I'd never heard his name before then. It was strange, finally putting a name to the face I'd seen so often. "Yes?" he said, barely louder than a whisper.

"Harley, what branch of the military were you in, and what was your rank?"

"A-army," Harley swallowed, "Private."

"Edward Adkins."

I flinched when I heard my name.

"What is the date of your wedding anniversary?"

I actually had to think for a second. My mind was running blank.

"What is the date of your wedding anniversary? Don't make me ask a third time."

I swallowed the lump in my throat. "I—it's June 6," I managed to get out.

I felt genuine relief when he moved on to Magnolia, asking what she did for some extra spending cash, and she responded that she was a babysitter. The final question was asked to the woman with smeared lipstick and careful eyes, her name was Delilah, and it asked where she lived. I don't remember the exact address, but I know it was in a rough part of town. A part of town I'd never go, anyway.

The Judge sighed, sounding pleased with our cooperation. "Very good, so far, only one punishment had to be doled out," he said.

"Oh go *fuck* yourself!" Charles snapped. This got the needle jabbing back into his arm, right where the wound had just begun to scab over.

"These questions are not going to get any easier. In fact, they will be harder. So learn to cooperate and answer truthfully now. It will save you later."

I expected him to start going around the circle again. Instead, the voice surprised me.

"What is your occupation, Delilah?"

"Unem-" Delilah cut herself off, sighing. "I bet that's not what you mean. Fine. Sex worker. Prostitute. Hooker. Whatever you want to call it. That what you wanted to hear?"

"Very well. Charles, how did your friend Rosemary Marshall make so much money from your company's stock?"

Charles shifted. "Good luck?" He tried to lie, so poorly though that no one was convinced.

I didn't expect to hear the crackle of electricity and Charles' eyes to bug out of his sockets, his teeth clamping so tight as his body jolted with electric current running through his veins. When he finally did manage to scream, he flopped back against his chair, screeching and howling at the top of his lungs. The room beforehand reeked of antiseptic, now I could detect a faint hint of urine. The rest of us sat in mostly dumb silence, the only sounds being Charles gasping for breath and Augusta crying. I certainly didn't know how to react.

"Charles? Answer the question correctly."

"I..." Charles swallowed. "I gave her some information... that helped her out. She's a single mom, she needed the money!"

"Which you took a cut from. About ten thousand dollars, a high price from the single mom you claim you sympathize with. Edward?"

Fuck.

"How did you pass your final exam in algebra, senior year?"

I actually sighed with relief. That wasn't nearly so bad as I expected, since I was following up on Charles' question. "My friend helped me cheat."

"Your friend's name?"

"Jordan. Jordan Mills. He was a genius, he knew I needed his help. He gave me the answers."

The Judge paused for a moment before turning on Magnolia. "And you, Magnolia? How did you pass your SATs with such high scores? Remember, I can see the rest of your grades. They're... barely mediocre."

"What!? They're-" Magnolia glanced over at Charles, who still looked like a mess. "... I cheated too," she grumbled.

"Both of you, such poor students, in the same graduating year," The Judge tutted his tongue, "Our future generation is looking so promising already. Frankie, what happened to the cocaine from the raid on the Wolfe home?"

"It's in evidence," the answer came out so fast I think 'Frankie' didn't even consider it a lie, and for a second I thought it wasn't a lie either.

Then the knife came out and sliced clean through the meat of his shoulder. To his credit, Frankie just breathed in sharply, gritted his teeth and took it.

"I presume you want to change your answer?" The judge asked as the knife slid back out, blood now staining Frankie's white scrubs.

"Mm... mmhmm," Frankie exhaled slowly, his body shaking as his face went white. "M-me and another officer took some. S-sold it to someone we knew was a dealer."

"Therefore putting it back on the streets that you swore to take it off of?"

"It's different!" Frankie swallowed, his eyes fluttering shut as his shoulder continued to bleed. "The original punks were dealing with highschoolers, kids! The dealer we sold it to, he only sold it to thugs who have already ruined their lives."

"An interesting point of view, for sure," The Judge said. "Now, Augusta? How did you get your eldest to sleep sometimes?"

"Oh, I'd rock him to sleep," Augusta bobbed her head up and down, "He was always so fussy, and-"

She didn't even get a chance to finish her lie. Her whole body seized up, and she *screeched* as the electric crackle filled the room. It wasn't as long a shock as it was for Charles, but Augusta looked far worse for wear, gasping and coughing as she tried to calm down.

"Augusta. Stop lying."

Augusta wailed before her head flopped forward. "A... little whiskey in his bottle... never really hurt anyone, honest, how could I ever hurt my own children?" she said.

I was blown away. Magnolia cheated on SATs, a police officer dealing drugs, and now one of the nicest neighbors on my block gave her kids alcohol so they'd sleep. Christ.

It didn't get better. That first round wasn't always fair, after all, all I had to answer for was a false grade, and Harley admitted he took part in a military hazing in which the poor victim had to streak across the base naked. Meanwhile, Connie confessed to cheating with a married man and convincing him to leave his wife for her, only to completely blow him off once the wife took the sap for all he was worth. He couldn't spoil her if he was broke, after all.

I only lied once, I learned quickly enough after that. It was over something stupid, about driving drunk and getting into an accident, slamming into a tree. Jordan covered for me that time too, said he was the one driving since I was tanked. I'd never been electrocuted before that day and I never wanted to again. I didn't judge Charles for wetting his pants after that, you lose all control when you get shocked like that and that's all I'll say about it.

It's amazing how often some of them chose to lie, and which ones chose not to. Delilah never once lied, completely blank faced as she told us how she robbed one of her johns of everything in his wallet because he passed out drunk or how she didn't tell her boyfriend that she tested positive for gonorrhea, although the Judge was kind enough to inform her that it was likely him that infected her and not vice versa. Harley only lied twice, once about that hazing and another time about how he abandoned his pregnant girlfriend without even a note.

Meanwhile, Charles had to be shocked and stabbed nearly every other question, and Augusta lied literally every time. The elderly woman I'd thought was the kindest soul admitted to so many shitty things, some I can't even say. All I can say is I pity those poor children of hers, with such a nightmare mom that would beat them for shattering a glass or literally calling the police on her second youngest when he brought his black girlfriend home. She had claimed the girl was trying to rob them. Actual sociopath.

We're all devils, you know. Devils with different sins blackening our hands, tearing up our souls. No one is innocent. And the Judge knew every one of those sins, no matter how some of us tried to hide them. I wish I knew how he knew that Frankie beat a suspect to get a confession, only for it to be revealed that the suspect was innocent all along. I can't even imagine how he found out that Magnolia slashed her ex boyfriend's tires because she was mad at him for dumping her, especially since he dumped her since she was so goddamn controlling he couldn't even see his friends.

For that final round, we all looked fucked up. Shocked, stabbed with everything from knitting needles to steak knives, being forced to reveal our darkest secrets around people that were acquaintances at best, and at most were just strangers.

"It's time for your final question. You will only have one chance to answer this properly. We will start with Augusta."

Augusta definitely looked the worst off. Like I said, she lied every question, sometimes even more than once. I was surprised she was still alive.

"Augusta, how did your eldest two children die?"

Augusta shakily inhaled and my heart sunk to the bottom of my stomach.

"Doctors... don't know... I don't either... mystery illness took my babies from me when they were just six and four years old... let me go home," Augusta whined.

The Judge sighed.

"Augusta, that's not the truth. And I told you, this time you would only get one chance to answer correctly."

The door on the far end of the room and the Judge finally walked out. We finally saw his face. He was tall, well built, probably at least a little handsome, but by that time my brain felt like watery pudding, so all I could do was blankly stare at him. He pushed in front of him a television connected to a VHS player, tapes stacked on top of the screen.

The Judge plucked the first tape up, showing us all the name 'AUGUSTA' written in black sharpie on the front. He placed the tape in the VHS player and stepped back.

It was a recording of medical documents, a lot of them. The camera panned over several paragraphs nice and slow so we could get the general gist. And that general gist? Augusta's children would get sick for no discernible reason, but would recover at the hospital. Once they got sent back home, they'd just get sick again. And one day, they both got just too sick and passed away.

"Munchhausen's by proxy," The Judge said, and I saw true pain in his eyes as he stood by the wall, where eight switches were neatly lined up. Each of them had a name beneath them, our names. "What are your final words, Augusta?"

"I..." Augusta shook her head. "No, I loved my children, I really did..."

She paused to take a breath and that's when the Judge flipped the switch.

Augusta writhed and her eyes went so wide they looked like they were going to fall out of her head. She wailed one last time before her eyes rolled back and then the only movement from her came from the electric current.

The switch was turned off and the Judge looked back at us. Then he raised his hand and had his fingers ready at Delilah's switch.

"Delilah?"

The woman, the truthful one, finally looked up. "Yes?" she asked.

The Judge stared at her. "Your boyfriend. Calvin McLaughlin. Was his murder premeditated?"

"... Yes." Delilah bowed her head. "He had friends in the force. He was getting out of jail for nearly killing me, because none of them believed me. So I just waited for him to get home. I waited for him to get drunk. And I wasn't going to wait for that first punch, so I took a baseball bat and I smashed his head in."

There was a deathly quiet pause before the judge lowered his hand from Delilah's switch. The Judge turned his gaze on Frankie, who went pale.

"How did your wife die, Frankie?" he asked.

Frankie, to his credit, did come off as convincing. "Car accident. She went off the road, killed her instantly," he said.

The Judge did his best to hide any emotion to us, but I did see that look of murderous intent as he grabbed another VHS that had Frankie's name written on it. He put it in.

Another recording of another document. An autopsy report, about how Mrs. Nancy Smith had many injuries that were in different phases of healing. How her ribs had been broken multiple times in the past, and this time one of those rib fragments broke free and punctured her heart. Followed by that were doctor's reports about Nancy's many visits to the hospital, all for 'accidents'.

"Was Nancy that clumsy, Frankie?" The Judge asked quietly. "I highly doubt it. Your last words?"

"You don't understand!" Frankie blurted out. "No one seems to understand how hard our job is, what we see! It takes a toll! It's not my fault that Nancy didn't get it-"

I turned away from this electrical death, and when I heard the electrical chair powered down I looked up to see a froth bubbling from the dead cop's lips, his dead eyes staring at the now flickering light on the ceiling.

"Connie Andrews?"

Connie slowly looked up at the Judge, her face twisted in rage.

"Where did you get the poison for all of the husbands you killed?"

"Fuck you," she spat at him, saliva landing on his clean white shirt. The Judge simply wiped it off, picked up another tape that no doubt had her name on it, and put in the VHS player.

This time it wasn't a document, it was a woman exiting a nail salon and heading into a small drug store that happened to be right next door. It was clear the video was taken from someone's car. Connie exited the store about ten minutes later with a small bag. A newspaper was raised in front of the camera, revealing the date.

"This was two days before your third husband mysteriously passed in his sleep. Your last words?"

Connie went white as The Judge raised his hand for her switch. "No, wait! Don't do it! I'll give you whatever you want! I'll confess! I'll tell the truth!" She yelped.

Click. The acrid smell of Connie's fake fingernails melting was so bad it made my head spin.

Magnolia shook her head wildly as The Judge went to her switch next. "I never hurt *anyone*! What the hell are you doing?!" She screamed, thrashing about so wildly I thought she might actually tear an arm free.

"What did you tell your boyfriend, Zachary Cullen, to do before he shot and killed himself?" The Judge's stare.

"That... that wasn't my fault!" Magnolia shook her head again and again, the strap holding her head in place actually coming loose. "How was that my fault?!"

The Judge held up a finger before pulling a voice recorder from his pocket. "This doesn't need video," he said simply before he hit play.

The conversation I heard... I can't repeat it. It was too terrible. Magnolia telling her boyfriend again and again how worthless he was, how he was such a pathetic waste of space, and how she couldn't wait for him to kill himself because that was the only good thing he'd ever do for himself.

The recording ended with a gunshot. The Judge cocked his head to the side.

"Your last words?"

"How was that *my* fault!?" Was all she wrote. Being right next to the person being shocked, it's... it's so disgusting. I could smell the burning hair and skin, hear every garbled sound that ripped its way out of her throat as she jolted and contorted in horrifying ways.

Charles moaned loudly as The Judge approached the switch. "Don't. Don't ask," he said, even though he knew what would happen.

"Charles? Last month, early morning. Rushing to work because you were late. Did anything happen on that drive?"

Charles didn't even speak, he just shook his head.

Another tape was taken off the VHS player, the Judge flashing the front to show off Charles' name.

This was from a traffic cam. A couple was walking across the street, probably the same age your mother and I were at the time. The collision happened so fast, the car slammed into them and sent the man flying over the hood while the woman was crushed under the car. The car stopped for a moment, just a moment, and I recognized the bald head that poked its way out of the window. Just for a second.

And then he zoomed off, leaving the bodies broken and bleeding in the street.

"Mr. Oscar Long was dead on arrival, but Miss Hannah Garcia? She took longer to die, and she suffered for every minute of it. Do I even need to ask for your last words?"

"It was just an *accident*!" Charles wailed.

I don't need to describe what happened next. I'm sure you know by now. Another human being electrocuted to death, executed by the expressionless Judge.

Harley sighed shakily as The Judge looked at him. "And?" was all the Judge said.

"... I know what I did was wrong." Harley admitted, his head bowed before he raised it and looked at The Judge. "So I will not be confessing today, Judge. I know what I deserve."

The Judge paused, and I caught a glimpse of something. Sympathy. "Being a part of the massacre of a village of innocent people and then covering it up. The act of a cowardly soldier. So, I believe this is the bravest thing you've ever done."

"Just end it already," Harley said, his eyes closing as he prepared for the shock.

"I won't make you suffer."

For a moment, I thought the Judge might have an inkling of mercy in him. Instead, he crossed the room of corpses and grabbed Harley's head. It was so efficient, the twist of his head, the snap of his neck. Harley was dead in less time than it takes to finish a sentence. Perhaps it was mercy in the Judge's mind. It was certainly quicker than what the others went through, that was for sure.

The only people left that were still alive in that room were me, Delilah, and The Judge. I was the only one left who had a final question. He went to his switches. I knew what he was going to ask.

"Why did you kill Jordan Mills, Edward?"

I took a deep breath.

"Because I was in love with his girlfriend. And she wouldn't give me a second look as long as Jordan was alive."

"And the girlfriend?"

"We're now married. Have a daughter. We have another kid on the way."

Delilah stared at me, probably shook that someone else confessed their most dirty secret, their most wicked of sins. The Judge nodded.

"And with that, court is adjourned." The Judge left the room, coming back a moment later with two needles. He jabbed one into Delilah's neck, the woman's eyes flickering as she fell unconscious.

"Why did you do this?" I asked as the Judge walked up to me, tilting my head to the side with the hands he'd just used to murder six people.

"So you never do it again," The Judge hissed before the needle entered my neck.

The next thing I know I'm lying on the street, cops are all around me, asking if I was okay and what happened. I was back in the clothes I'd fallen asleep with, the only sign that anything that had happened was the bruises on my wrists and the memories.

Oh, I know, you never expected me to have taken a life too. I regret it. Jordan was... kind to me. It was a moment of rage, something not at all planned out. I was just lucky no one ever found the body until it was too decomposed to really tell anything. Everyone assumed he fell off the hiking trail and hit his head on the way down, causing his death.

I paid for it my own way, of course. Ever since that night in the Chair of Truth, I've practically been a saint. Paid my taxes, watched my words, donated time and money to help others, and even when your mother finally left me for good, I never held it against her.

Why? Well, it's hard to do anything wrong when you know someone's gone through your life with a fine-tooth comb. The fact that someone is still watching me, no matter what I do, and I feel if

I ever slipped up again, I'd wake up in the Chair. Next time I'd not get away so easily.

And I hope, my son, that you learn from my mistakes... that no matter how well you hide your sins, you will be found out, whether in the afterlife or this one."

VICKY

It happened ten years ago. I was only eight years old. I woke up that morning to the smell of frying eggs and bacon.

Stumbling down the hallway, I was greeted by the sight of a dark-haired woman at the stove, humming some friendly tune as she filled a cup to the near brim with orange juice. She turned to me and I nearly jumped out of my skin. In a sense, she was pretty, but she had a vicious scar running down the left side of her face.

"Andy! You're up!" She beamed as she picked up the plate stacked with a delicious smelling breakfast. "I had to run to the store, but I hope you like breakfast!"

Too shocked to say anything else, I replied, "I don't have breakfast. Where's my mom?"

The woman laughed and set the plate on the table, now cleared off of shredded bill envelopes and clutter. "She's gone, so I'm here to make sure you're alright. You can call me Aunt Victoria, or Vicky, whatever you prefer, I don't mind! And while I'm here, you have breakfast!" she said in a chipper tone.

Feeling like this all might be a dream, I sat down at the table and took a bite of bacon. It was perfectly crisp, not burnt as it would've been if my mom had cooked it. She was always so tired, I normally had to fetch my dinner off the stove myself.

"Is she going to be back soon? My mom?" I asked after I swallowed, it was impolite to talk with your mouth full.

Vicky shrugged. "She didn't say. Clean your plate, then you can show me your favorite cartoons, okay? Only until ten though—that's when we're going to the zoo!" She laughed and tucked a lock of hair behind her ear.

The zoo? I remembered my mom telling me that our zoo trip wouldn't happen this year, she was just too busy with work, but if Vicky was going to take me... I suppose it wouldn't be too bad to let her stay, I figured, as I chowed down on breakfast.

Maybe you think I was a dumb kid, and I'll understand that. Maybe I was. But you have to understand, my mom was a single parent working as many shifts as she could pick up. It wasn't uncommon for her to send a babysitter my way when she couldn't get home in time, although typically they were younger teens that spent all their time on the phone and maybe threw a frozen pizza in the oven for dinner.

Vicky was different in every way for the week she took care of me.

The house was cleaned top to bottom; I helped in the bathroom while Vicky handled mom's bedroom. Every night, meals were freshly cooked and done to perfection. I remember on Tuesday we had a pizza that she made from scratch. I watched her toss the dough in the air like a real chef and asked how she did that.

"I learned from a real chef," Vicky winked and tossed the dough again, "in Italy."

"Have you traveled a lot?" Vicky did have a slight accent, I believe it was British.

She nodded as she set the dough down onto the pan and started adding the toppings. "All over the world. Would you believe that I've met the queen?" She winked, and I realized she was joking.

"No."

"Good. You're a smart kid, Andy. Don't just believe things people tell you." Vicky bit her bottom lip as she cracked open the oven to test the heat. "I never believe what the oven tells me. But this time it's about right for the perfect pizza."

It was the perfect pizza too.

Vicky was almost too good of a babysitter. It was like she wanted to be my mom. To be honest, I think she did want to be. She was... bizarre, in small ways. Ways I didn't think about until much later. She was never home at night, and she always did her laundry in the morning. I could hear the machine banging around when I woke up. Whenever we went out, she slathered her arms and face in sunscreen, almost a ridiculous amount. I asked her about it once.

"I just have delicate skin."

That was all she'd say about it before she'd change the subject. It was late summer, so I accepted the excuse. She made sure I had sunscreen on at all times as well, but even if she was popping out to check the mailbox, she'd grab the tube and start slathering it on. I found over a dozen bottles in the towel cabinet, stashed with the ibuprofen and cough medicine.

Vicky loved to read, we went to the library twice when she was there and would stock up on all sorts of books. Typically horror, but she made sure I picked out at least two books for myself the second time we went. I chose two books from the Boxcar Kids series. My mom had given me a few of her old ones and I couldn't put them down. I still have those books. After everything went down I just never returned them.

It was one of the best weeks of my life, but every night I asked the same thing when Vicky tucked me into bed.

"Did you hear from mom yet?"

Every night, she'd just kiss my forehead and tell me to chase the dream butterflies. I never knew what she meant by that, but I always slept soundly.

The last night I woke up to quiet sobbing. I glanced at my alarm clock, the numbers 1:32 blared back in bright red. I slipped out of bed and into the hall, following the sound to my mother's bedroom.

Vicky was curled up on my mother's perfectly made bed, a photo album open next to her. I slowly walked up to Vicky and set a hand on her shoulder. "You should chase the dream butterflies too, Vicky," I said. Vicky flinched and sat up. The room was dark, but I could tell her mouth was covered in... something. I turned on the lamp.

Her mouth was soaked in bright red, along with her hands and shirt. Blood.

"Oh... Andy." Her voice cracked as she picked me up and set me on the bed next to her, wrapping her arms around me. "I'm something horrible. I've done horrible things."

I remained still in her arms, my eyes flicking open to the page in the album. It was a picture of the day I was born and my birth certificate. My mother proudly showed it to me every birthday and told me how she went through twelve hours of labor before I came into the world. And she'd go through those twelve hours again if she had to, she loved me so much. I might've not quite understood what 'labor' was about, but I knew she loved me very much.

"Are you hurt?" I asked, reaching up to brush some of the blood off her mouth.

Vicky shook her head. "No, sweetheart. This isn't my..." She trailed off and shook, shaking her head. "I thought... maybe, just maybe, I could make things better by taking care of you. I think I'm just making them worse. So much worse. Andy, I'm sorry. Do you forgive me?"

"Forgive you for what?" I asked.

" Do you forgive me for the horrible things I've done to you?"

I frowned. "What horrible things?" I asked.

"The worst thing possible.... No, it's not fair," Vicky sighed and released me from her hold, "It's not fair to ask you to forgive me." She got up. "I have to leave, Andy... can I do anything else for you?"

I had one more question.

"Why do you have a scar, Vicky?"

Vicky reached up and brushed the side of her face. " Horrible things happened to me too, Andy. The worst things. I suppose that's why I can only do horrible things too." She took the quilt and tucked it over me, smiling softly. "Go to sleep now, Andy, and chase those butterflies to the end of the world and back."

I woke up the next morning to a police officer shaking my shoulder.

"Hey... Holy shit—guys, the kid's here!"

Wiping the sleep from my eyes, I sat up and slipped out of bed. The police officer stumbled for words for a moment, whatever he'd been expecting, it certainly wasn't this. "Andy? Are you okay?" he asked.

I looked around. "Where's Vicky?" I asked.

"We'll find Vicky. We need to get you to the hospital."

I think I baffled all the doctors and police with my case. When they broke into the apartment to find me, they expected to find this half-starved kid, scared out of his wits and desperate to find his mother. But instead, they found me dressed and clean, with the house taken care of and with a full stomach.

I think you can guess by now that my mother was dead. I was taken in by my dad, who had no idea I even existed, but he did okay with that. He'd remarried after he and my mom split, and I had three half-siblings that I didn't know existed. It was fun being the big brother and my stepmom Mika was super sweet.

She wasn't my mom, though. And she wasn't Vicky.

I had to pry the rest of the story out of my dad when I was older. The reason police weren't hammering down my door sooner was that my mom was a Jane Doe in the morgue. She'd been found practically shredded to pieces. The cause of death was bleeding out from an artery in her neck. Her body had been discovered a few blocks from her work, all forms of ID were missing, including her wallet.

My mom always had a picture of me and her in there. And they found that wallet, with bloody fingerprints, in my mom's nightstand. Right next to where I was sleeping.

My dad still wonders why my mother's murderer returned to her house only to care for her son, but I don't need to wonder. I know.

I know this is a long shot, Vicky, but I remember you liked horror, so maybe you'll find this story. I know you killed my mom.

But I forgive you.

THE GIRL NAMED BEA

I met her while I was weeding the flower garden.

I had just about finished up when I heard someone clear their throat behind me. They may have been trying to get my attention for a while, I had my headphones in and the only reason I heard anything was because I was in between songs.

"Sorry, sorry," I pulled out an earbud and scrambled to my feet, "I didn't hear you back... there..."

My voice got choked up in my throat as I stared into the soft dark eyes of the most beautiful girl I'd ever seen. Her golden hair came down in waves past her shoulders and she had a smile like sunshine. She quietly laughed. "I wasn't waiting long. You seemed to be enjoying your music, anyway." She offered me her hand. "My name is Bea."

Her name could've been Mud and I would've thought it was the prettiest name in the world. "Um, I'm Cassie, but everyone just calls me Cass," I shook her hand, inwardly kicking myself as I saw I got dirt all over her hand. "Shit, I'm sorry-"

Bea laughed again, just brushing her hand off on her skirt. "A little dirt won't kill me. Sorry, I'm just trying to find the Lakeview Cemetery?"

"Oh, you're not far," I pointed down the street. "Just down the ways, take a right at Petunia Road, it'll be on the left. If you hit Black Street, you've gone too far, and you'll need to turn around."

Bea turned to look, tucking a lock of hair behind her ear. "I see. You visit often?" she asked.

I nodded. "It's where my parents are buried. I try to go every other week. If you need to pick up flowers, Mary's Garden is right nearby. Tell her you're there to pick something up for a deceased relative or friend and she'll give you a good deal-"

"It's you!"

I nearly tripped over my feet to look up at the door. My grandfather was leaning against the door frame, with an expression like he had seen a ghost. "Grandpa, what are you doing out of bed!?" I rushed to his side, all thoughts about the pretty girl in my front yard gone. "You need to be resting." Resting wouldn't change his rapidly approaching fate, but it would make him more comfortable when the time came.

He pointed a shaky finger at Bea. "It's you. I know it's you. How... where's Francis? Is he still with you?" he asked.

The woman blinked owlishly before her eyes widened in recognition. "Robert! The years have changed you, I am terribly sorry for not realizing you were still living here." She looked at me before curtsying. "I'll come talk to you again, I have to be going."

"Bye," I said, waving as I watched Bea return to her car. She opened the door and held it open just for a second to let a young man poke his head out. He wasn't nearly as graceful as Bea when he seemingly recognized my grandfather, his jaw dropping and eyes nearly popping out of his head.

He dived back into the car before Bea slipped in and it drove off. I looked at my grandfather, who looked like he'd experienced a shock. "Do I need to call Dr. Samuel-"

"I just need to be alone for a bit." My grandfather shuffled back to his bedroom, leaving me alone.

It wasn't until the sun was going down that he called me into his bedroom.

My grandfather was a quiet man, I'd never known him to make the outburst like the one earlier that day. Even when I entered the room, he just pointed to his closet. "Check behind the coats, there's a photo frame," he said.

I moved aside old coats and a far outdated tuxedo to find the photo frame. I brought it out and sat beside my grandfather's bed to get a better look.

The picture inside was faded and black and white, but I could recognize a much younger version of my grandfather sitting out on the front porch, his arm wrapped around a black teenager about his age. "I've never seen this picture before," I said, tilting it side to side. When Grandma had been alive, she'd shown me her albums again and again, even as the cancer wasted her away.

"I keep it just for myself. His name is Francis."

I nodded while reaching for my cell phone. "Listen, grandpa, you're a little tired, how about I call-"

"Listen to me, Cassandra!" My grandfather snapped, causing me to nearly jump out of my skin. "You bring up calling the damn doctor again and I'm sending you to your room!"

Even with me being twenty-one, that was a very real threat. I sunk down in my chair, deciding not to question him any more. "Who is Francis, Grandpa?" I asked.

He calmed down and looked back at the photo. I saw a touch of a smile on his lips. " Francis was my best friend. See, his father saved mine. After that, my father referred to him as a brother—white and colored was never an issue. Our families were close, I was just a few days younger than Francis. We never could attend the same schools or play together in the park, but if I wasn't at his home he was at mine. If he couldn't sleep, he would sneak in through my bedroom window and we'd stay up just talking about anything and everything under the sun. I had his back, he had mine. We were just as close as our fathers."

The story was heartwarming, but there was certainly a part nagging at me. "Why have you never talked about Francis before then?" I asked.

That smile on my grandfather's face vanished.

"Because I never wanted to think of him again."

He handed me the frame to hold as he told me the story.

"It was probably a week after this photo was taken that we met her. We were on a walk through the woods, we took a lot of those. Just so we couldn't be bothered by people who thought a black man and a white man couldn't be friends. We were on the way back when we heard a car refusing to turn over. Francis insisted we take the right path to see if someone needed help. I followed, he was always the leader out of the two of us. We didn't expect to see such a nice car way back where we were, but what we didn't really expect to see was the behemoth of a man poking away at the engine... or the girl standing beside the car, her dress spattered in mud as she shivered in the cold. She looked up at us and her eyes met Francis'... and I knew it was all over then. Because he looked at her and he fell in love."

"Was she also black?" I asked.

"She was Bea."

"You mean she looked like Bea?" I asked.

He shook his head. "No, I mean that the Bea you talked to today was the same Bea standing on the road next to the car that wouldn't start." He scowled as he saw me open my mouth. "I'm not crazy, you know I still have all my marbles. You shut it and listen."

I closed my mouth.

"Good girl... now where was I... "My grandfather's eyes went glassy as he was transported to a much different time. "Right. Francis was just about frozen in place, so I had to shout out and ask if they were all right. Turns out they'd stopped for a picnic and when they got back, the damn thing wouldn't start. That's when Francis' brain started working again and he offered his help, he was pretty handy with cars. I just sat with the giant as Francis got to work and started chatting with Bea. I found out his name was Sten, but we didn't really talk, we just watched Bea and Francis interact, and let me tell you—you could tell the attraction was mutual by the way she laughed and how she'd brush her fingers against his arm. I think Francis was disappointed when the car finally got running, but I'll admit I was relieved. I didn't know what was going through her head, flirting with Francis like that."

"I thought the color of Francis' skin didn't matter," I said.

My grandfather shook his head. "Cass, you have to remember where we live. About three years before, a black man was accused of groping a white woman. No evidence, it was just what her brother said happened. What happened to that poor bastard..." My grandfather shuddered. "It wasn't human. Humans don't do that to other humans. I was worried about Francis' safety. I gave him an earful on the way home about it. He was a bit embarrassed, but he realized where I was coming from. I was worried for him. He promised me he'd be more careful, and that was that... or so I thought."

My grandfather took back the picture frame and removed the back. He took out a photo hidden behind the other one and placed it on his lap.

This one was slightly better quality. I now knew what my grandfather meant by behemoth, the one man standing next to Francis was an absolute giant. Next to them stood two women, one crossing her arms and trying to look serious while a woman of Asian descent was practically leaning all of her weight on the serious woman, clearly laughing and having a good time.

"Sten, Francis, Alana, and Lihua."

My grandfather pointed at each of them when he said their name. "So many things you can't see in this picture... Alana's hair was so red you'd think it'd somehow find a way of bleeding into these old pictures. Lihua had the most joyful laugh, when she got going the whole town could hear it. I never saw her without a smile. Sten's arms were covered in these old scars, I never got the story for all of them but he was a warrior, a soldier in another life, he told me."

I leaned in close to the picture. "Who are these people?" I asked.

"They were Bea's."

Leaning back in the bed, my grandfather sighed. "Almost two weeks after we found her stranded on the side of the road, I would've forgotten all about it. But when we were heading home after work, we were suddenly surrounded by Bea's two girlfriends. Lihua looped her arm in with Francis', Alana put hers with mine, and they pulled us down the street towards a car as they chatted us up like we were old friends. I'd thought I was about to get robbed when I recognized who was driving that car—it was Sten. Alana and Lihua drew straws to see who would be walking, there weren't enough spots for us all to sit, Lihua lost and proceeded to call Alana a bitch before laughing and starting to walk. Sten drove us to probably one of the nicest houses in town, and that's when we had tea with Bea."

My grandfather rolled his eyes. "She said she always had a taste for the dramatic. Any advice I gave Francis, he promptly forgot, and the two flirted the whole. Damn. Time. I mean, by then I realized she wasn't just trying to get Francis in trouble, she'd had him brought to her just so they could be on a date. But I still didn't trust her. She was strange. Something about her just didn't sit right with me."

He paused for a while. "But when she came to me, asking for my help to find ways to keep seeing Francis, I couldn't say no. She said she found him... handsome. Charming. Genuine. She called the time we lived in full of sociopaths that would stone Francis if they had any idea they were interested in each other romantically. She promised me she wouldn't hurt him. Promised me that if anyone tried to hurt him, they'd have to go through her first. I told her to get in line, cuz they'd be going through me first. That smile on her face almost seemed a little condescending, but she said that Francis couldn't ask for a better friend.

"They started seeing each other weekly. I was their go between. I'd pass letters in between the two of them, tell them when the other had time to meet. I took that picture right there," he pointed to the one with Bea's friends, "And I watched their romance blossom. I learned more about the world from Bea and the others than I ever learned from school. I considered them friends... but the perfect little secret that Francis and Bea had couldn't stay secret forever."

My grandfather's shoulders sagged as he placed the photograph on his bedside table. "It was just a whisper. I think someone noticed the look in Francis' eyes whenever Bea passed by, or maybe they weren't nearly as discreet as they thought. But when the whispers started, I knew my friend was in danger. People had killed for less than whispers. We made a plan. Dead of night, they'd pack up, head north. I'd accompany them to New York and see them off to France. Hell, I even considered going with them, go see the world... We never got a chance."

I shook my head. "I'm not going to like this story's end, am I?" I asked.

My grandfather didn't answer, instead he continued with his stories.

"Francis and I were heading to Bea's house, our suitcases were packed. Francis was humming love songs under his breath when I heard the gunshot." Grandfather's fists balled up, knuckles turning white. "I saw blood shoot out from Francis' side and he fell to the ground. I turned and saw the sheriff leading a mob of angry men. I could've left Francis then, saved myself from the heap of trouble I was going to be in. But I didn't. I picked Francis up and carried him the rest of the way."

My grandfather reached up and pulled down his shirt sleeve, revealing an old, puckered scar. "They got me once in the shoulder, twice in the leg. I remember you being a little girl and asking why I walked the way I do. I did say I'd tell you when you were older, well, now you know. I don't know how I made it to Bea's house, but I collapsed at the front door. Francis was cussing, I was too. The door opened and out walked Bea. When she saw how bloodied up we both were and how Francis was hurt bad, I saw a tear sneak down her face before she just went dead calm and wiped it away."

For a few moments he was quiet. "Cass, you know I've not lost my mind. I'm sharp as I was back then, maybe even more so. But what I saw... I just wanted to forget all these years, and I never can.

"Bea walked out in front of the mob, followed by the others. She looked at the mob and quietly asked who shot Francis. One of the stupid bastards near the front raised his hand... and then she snapped it off with the same amount of effort it would take to break a twig. He howled before she went for his throat, her canines became sharp as knives, and she'd grown claws an inch long. The others followed suit. Alana ripped open the sheriff's ribcage and stomped on his heart. Sten took a man's head and crushed it between his hands. The man's brains splattered over his face before he roared like a lion and charged into the fray. Lihua caught a coward trying to run away before dragging him into the dark. I heard him scream once for his mother before I heard a crack and nothing else."

Grandfather shook his head. "It was over quicker than you'd think. That mob was about twenty men in their prime, and in about five minutes, each one was dead. Sten licked off each of his fingers before coming to me, picking me up and carrying me indoors while Bea cradled Francis in her arms. I wasn't sure if he was breathing anymore... and that was the last time I saw him."

"What happened after that?" I asked, shocked I could find my voice.

"They disappeared." My grandfather shrugged. "When I woke up the next morning, I was in my own bed, all bandaged up. The whole town was in an uproar. The sheriff and his sons, all dead, along with several other 'upstanding' men of the town. Bea was gone, along with the others. No sign of where they'd gone.

Francis... Francis was also gone. They never found his body, but they went and said he was dead anyhow. Probably for the best, I can't imagine how they'd blame the slaughter on a single man but I'm surprised they didn't try. We all just pretended nothing ever happened. I took care of Francis' little siblings like they were my own brothers and sisters. I never told anyone before tonight about my best friend."

I couldn't believe it. Most of me wanted to reason out how that couldn't have happened. Stuff like that didn't happen.

Instead, when I opened my mouth I asked, "Was the man in the car today, was it really Francis?"

"Looking just like the last day I saw him." My grandfather sunk into the pillow, I could see how tiring this whole experience was for him. "Whatever Bea was must've crawled right up out of hell. You need to know that before you go with her."

"What do you mean?" I asked.

My grandfather smiled sadly.

"Because the way your eyes lit up while looking at her, it was the same way Francis' did when he first saw her... I think I'm going to shut my eyes for now, I'm feeling tired. Go to bed, Cassandra... I love you."

I swallowed the hard lump in my throat before getting up. "I love you too, Grandpa," I said before fleeing the room.

Just before I closed the door, I think I heard the sound of his window being pushed up. But I wasn't sure until I came in the next morning, and it had been left open. My grandfather had passed away with the most content look on his face. He was at peace, finally having revealed his darkest secret.

The funeral had long been planned, nearly everyone in town attended. People came up to me and told me how my grandfather was the most open-minded and kindest of people. I got told stories of his generosity, his good sense of humor.

Hours passed until I was finally sitting alone between his grave and the ones of my parents. My tears had dried up, leaving an empty hole inside me. For the first time in my life, I could truly say I was alone.

I heard quiet footsteps approaching, and I looked up to see her.

Bea was wearing a dark coat and black stockings. Her hair had been carefully pinned back, her eyes reddened with tears. "Can I sit with you?" she asked.

I nodded and patted the ground next to me, the side closer to my grandfather's grave. She nodded before taking her seat, folding her legs under herself. " Your grandfather was my friend. I owe him a great deal. Did he tell you about me?" she said.

I nodded.

"Shot three times, carrying the bleeding body of my dearest love and his dearest friend," Bea's breath shuddered, and she wiped her eyes, "I could never repay that. I offered, but I knew he wouldn't accept the only thing I had to give before he even responded. I'm not sure if he even remembered the talk we had before I took him home that night." Her fingers combed through the freshly turned earth.

"What did you offer?" I asked quietly.

"... Eternity."

She got up and glanced at the other pair of graves next to me. "He's with his wife, his daughter, and his son in law. I think he couldn't live in a world that made it impossible to to see them again, so I am glad he didn't take my gift when I offered it again last night." She looked down at me and smiled, extending her hand. "Would you like to go on a trip? A change of pace might help you."

I knew what offer was hidden behind those words. I glanced at my parents' graves, dead when I was just a little girl. I looked at my grandparents' graves, much newer than theirs.

I took Bea's hands, and she pulled me to my feet. "I think I wouldn't mind visiting Paris. I've always wanted to see the Eiffel tower. Is it more beautiful in person?" I asked.

Bea smiled widely.

"It will take your breath away."

Together we walked to the car, this one was probably a lot bigger than the one my grandfather talked about. Sten was even bigger than the picture suggested, he was sitting in the driver's seat while Lihua took selfies of them both. I think I caught a glimpse of some sort of Instagram filter on the screen before Lihua dropped the phone, she was laughing too hard to hold it. In the back seat, Alana was reading something on a Kindle, absorbed entirely in the digital pages.

The car door opened and there sat Francis. His eyes were also tinged red from tears, but he smiled as he looked at me.

"You look a lot like your grandfather. Come on in, we got space to squeeze in one more."

I'M NEVER SHOOTING ANOTHER SNUFF FILM

You don't start out shooting snuff. You build up to it. To be honest, I never thought I'd let it get that far. And I wish I never did.

I started out wanting to be a legit filmmaker. But that's a hard business to break into when you don't know the right people. Living on your own is expensive, and it gets humiliating to ask your parents for help covering your rent after the second time. My mom was always more than happy to help, but it wasn't like my parents were loaded, and I hated being a leech.

Eating nothing but ramen noodles and cheap mac n cheese is its own kind of misery. Not to mention being unable to go out and do anything with friends. I mean, I survived, but I was miserable. So when the chance to film a porno came up, I jumped at it. I told myself it would be just this once.

Just this once turned into just one more time, then this would be the last time, and before I knew it I started getting deeper and deeper into the taboo. Like Fifty Shades of Grey looked vanilla compared to some of the BDSM I was behind the camera for.

I knew I was getting out of the realm of legality when I filmed a girl cutting open her arms and licking up the blood. I don't know what she was on, but she had to be on something to do this all while smiling and giggling. But that check felt so damn good, so I kept my mouth shut. I was finally in the black. I told myself no one made her do those things, so what was the harm in it?

Then one day I was approached with a once in a lifetime deal. I normally worked with my guy Charlie, he got all the hookups for the weird stuff. One day Charlie came over with this other guy I'd never met before who introduced himself as Noel.

Noel doesn't look like you're probably picturing someone in this scene, he was about five foot six and balding on top. He wore these round wire-framed glasses and made me think of a schoolteacher. The kind of teacher that everyone loved, the one that you couldn't wait for his class every day because he never assigned homework and let you listen to music while you worked.

"I'm a fan of your work, Frank—can I call you Frank?" Noel took out his wallet and counted out a few hundred-dollar bills. "This is your signing bonus. Once the film is complete, I'll give you double that."

My eyes nearly popped out of my head. "How long's the filming going on for?" I asked, already snatching up the money.

"Oh, just a day. Maybe two, if we need to do reshoots. Don't worry, you'll be compensated if it takes any longer than it should." Noel extended his hand. "What do you say? No hard feelings if you feel you're not up for the task."

I shook Noel's hand and asked when I started.

I figured it would just be over the top BDSM when I saw the set, all chains and brick. I had a few drinks with the two male actors while we waited for the actress to make her appearance. Not gonna lie, I got Ted Bundy vibes from the guy calling himself Tommy, but Gabe seemed like another average, fun guy.

When I saw the actress get dragged in, I realized how very deep I was in over my head.

Her mouth had been duct taped shut, she'd clearly been crying and looked pretty banged up. Noel followed the men dragging her and clapped his hands together. "Let's get to work then! Frank, I'd like for you to focus a lot on her limbs. The commissioner is very into legs and arms. You'll only get one chance, but since this is your first time filming this sort of kink, I won't be too upset if it's not perfect."

I should've just bolted then. Gave Noel back his goddamn money and left. Gone to the cops, gone to *someone*.

Instead, I quietly sat behind the camera and treated it like any other porn film.

Lights, camera, action.

I never knew the girl's name. Both Tommy and Gabe wore full leather masks and were armed with hand saws. I zoomed in as they started sawing through her shoulder. Drops of blood landed on the camera and I brushed them off without even thinking. I saw Noel nod approvingly at that natural motion. The arm fell to the ground, and I panned over it nice and slow as it rested on the floor.

They took off her other arm and both legs, her struggles slowly fading and her eyes fluttering shut by the time they got through the final femur. Tommy and Gabe stood, bowed to the camera like they were on stage for a play.

And cut.

I had to run to the bathroom after that. I vomited for what felt like an hour. When I finally stumbled out, Noel handed me the rest of my payment. He patted my shoulder and helped escort me to my car. "It's always the hardest the first time. I bet you had dreams of filming the next summer blockbuster someday?" he said.

I didn't say anything, but I didn't need to. Noel just nodded. "We all had dreams like that. Maybe if things turned out differently, we would've been working on one of those blockbusters together. I'll call you when I need your services again."

I told myself that I wouldn't pick up the phone again when Noel called.

But I did.

I did twenty-five snuff films in total. The money felt so, so damn good. And after a while, you really do become desensitized to it all. For me, it just felt like I was in a dream. A dream with gore and guts and horrible, horrible things happening to people, but it wasn't happening to me. I just saw it through a lens.

The twenty-fifth film was the one that finally made me quit.

I was out drinking with my fellow crew members when Noel came up with this darling blonde on his shoulder. I don't know how he did it as he was pretty average in appearance, but Noel could get the hottest women.

"Gentlemen, this is Rada. Rada, this is Tommy, Gabe, and Frank," he said, gesturing to them all.

Rada giggled and clapped. "Noel tells me you are... actors?" she said, her Russian accent thick on her words.

Gabe puffed up. "Tommy and I are the actors. Frank's the camera man," he said.

"Camera man?" She cocked her head to the side. "Is it fun?" she asked.

I shrugged. "Well, I like it. It pays the bills," I said.

"Very good, very good!" Rada clapped before looking up at Noel. "Could I be in a film? I've always wanted to be an actress."

I nearly dropped my glass. I had to excuse myself from the table, unable to ignore that glint of darkness in Noel's smile.

I got a text about twenty minutes later saying to head to the 'studio'. I stopped by at home to change into clothes that I didn't mind getting bloody before I walked over.

Rada was clearly drunk as she teetered around the set. She poked at the chains on the wall and smiled. "Am I a captive in your scene, Noel?" she asked.

"That sounds about right." Noel helped her into the chains, Rada's innocent doe brown eyes looking excitedly around. This whole thing made me genuinely sick. It was one thing when they were terrified, begging for mercy and sobbing as they realized they were doomed. But the innocent expression on Rada's face, how clear it was she had no idea what was going to happen... I almost walked out then.

But then Noel slipped a few hundreds in my hand, and I just got the camera ready.

"Now remember, Rada, you are terrified. You are in true fear of your life as this man is about to gut you. Don't be afraid to scream," Noel said.

Rada nodded. "I can do that! I'm very good at being scared," she said.

Tommy snickered before he pulled on his leather mask. "This is just too easy sometimes," he murmured to me. I just rolled my eyes.

Lights. Camera. Action.

Rada's bubbly expression changed to one of true terror as Tommy walked into the camera. "Please, why am I here? I want to go home, please," she said as a tear rolled down her cheek.

Tommy twirled around the knife before sliding it down her front, slicing through the front of her dress. Rada whimpered and turned her face away. "I'll do whatever you want! Please, take my money, use my body!" She begged.

The knife nicked her skin, and I saw this brief moment of confusion before she began to struggle in earnest, realizing this wasn't just a movie anymore. "*Nyet*! Unchain me! I don't like this game! Director! I don't want to play anymore!" She shouted.

The knife went into her stomach and her breath caught before she screamed so loudly I felt my ears pop.

Tommy sliced down her stomach, thrusting his hand inside to pull out her intestines. He held them in front of her eyes as she continued to scream actual bloody murder. Even Noel, who was typically quite passive during these scenes, winced and rubbed one of his ears.

Rada's dying breaths came as all her organs were spilled out in front of her. Tommy bowed for the camera.

And cut.

"Incredible," Noel shook his head before he got up and threw Tommy a towel, "You've outdone yourself."

Tommy nodded before I heard a groan.

"Noel, can I go again? I can do better."

I am not lying when I say I literally pissed my pants when I saw Rada's head roll back up, blinking a few times before her eyes focused on Noel.

Tommy screamed like a schoolgirl as he scrambled away, ripping off his mask. "How the *fuck*!?!" He yelped as Rada began to tug at her chains.

The girl groaned before rolling her eyes and smashing her right hand against the wall, I heard bones crack before she pulled it free. She did the same to the left before beginning the impossible task of shoving her organs inside her mangled torso. "Scene... sorry... your language is hard... when I hurt..." She grunted as she popped her large intestine back inside. "Scene would look better, covered in my blood? I can be cleaned," she looked up with a smile as she attempted to pull her skin together.

Noel got up from his chair, I saw him shake as he slowly approached this woman that should absolutely be dead. "What are you?" he said softly.

Rada giggled.

"An actress, Noel. I want to be a very good actress."

We filmed that scene three more times. Rada had to film the rest of the shots naked, but she didn't mind. Only thing that bothered her was how cold the stone under her ass was. After each time she'd get up, put herself back together, and we'd go again. I'd never filmed for so long before, not for one of Noel's films. The sun was coming up when Noel finally said we were done.

I was about to leave when Rada stopped me. "Can I see?" she asked, snuggling into the shirt she'd stolen from Tommy.

Swallowing, I let her have the camera and rewound to the final time we filmed, which Noel had said was going to be his best work yet. She watched silently, nodding approvingly as Tommy tore out her heart and squeezed the beating organ in his hand. "My expressions are believable?" she asked.

"Does it really hurt you?" I asked.

Rada nodded. "It hurts like it would if it would kill me. But like I said, I want to be an actress. Will I be famous in these films? I can change if the director needs me to be a different girl." She looked so eager for my response.

"... In certain circles, you'll be a star."

I left that day and never went back. I never picked up Noel's phone calls. Charlie was as good as dead to me. I cut my lease early and am now living back with my parents in Ohio. I think I'll be going back to school, into something less bloody like accounting. My mom always wanted me to be an accountant.

I never want to film anything again. Especially one of Noel's films.

I wonder if Rada's starring in all his movies now.

MY SISTER DROPPED OFF MY NIECE LAST NIGHT. I DON'T THINK SHE'S COMING BACK.

To clarify, I haven't seen my younger sister Mara in a little over five years. She was a little over eighteen years old, a few months pregnant, and was determined to keep her baby. I told her exactly what I thought—that she was a goddamned idiot and that she either needed to give it up for adoption or I'd drive her to the abortion clinic myself.

We had a screaming fight before she stormed out, saying she was going to stay with her baby's daddy and that they'd be a happy family together.

Like I said, it's been five years. Five years and a lot changed. I tried contacting her probably a dozen times, but when she sent me a picture flipping up her middle finger, I got the message and gave up. If she wanted to live like that, fine by me. She ended up blocking me on Facebook before cutting off both our parents, and I figured I'd never see her again.

When I heard the doorbell, I thought that one of my friends had stopped by to return a book they'd borrowed a few weeks back. They'd told me they were almost done and that they couldn't put it down, so I expected them to give it back any day now.

I opened the door and there she was. I didn't even recognize her at first. She'd gotten a lot thinner and had dyed her hair black, but I recognized that cheap tattoo on her hand and the dimple in her right cheek. It was my baby sister.

And clutching her hand was a little girl with rosy cheeks, blonde curls, and my sister's green eyes.

"Thomas," Her face broke into a tired smile, and she pulled me into a hug. I couldn't respond. I just froze. She stepped back and smiled even brighter. "Ariel, this is your Uncle Thomas."

The little girl waved and smiled. "It's a pleasure to meet you, Uncle Thomas," she said in a chipper tone.

Ariel. Mara's favorite Disney Princess.

I cleared my throat. "H... hi, Ariel." I looked up at Mara. "Do... do you want to come inside?"

"I'd really love that, actually." Mara walked inside. "I can't stay long, but... oh man, when did you get ripped?" Even her laughter sounded tired.

"Uh, three years ago, I wanted to get in shape, do you want something?" I didn't even know what to say at this point, in the light it was clear she'd been through some serious shit.

Saying she'd gotten a 'lot thinner' is understating it. She looked skeletal, her once vivid eyes were now dull and too large, like they were ready to roll out of her skull. Her fists were all bruised up, and she had a black eye that wasn't quite hidden under thickly applied foundation.

"I'm fine. Really. It's just been a bad week." Mara gently pushed Ariel to the couch. "Sit right there, honey, okay?"

I'd never seen such a well-behaved five-year-old in my life. Like a prim little angel, Ariel walked over to the couch and sat, her bare feet dangling a few inches above the floor. I turned back to Mara. "What happened? Where's Bradley?" Just saying the scumbag's name made me feel nauseated.

Mara's gaze dropped to the floor. "He didn't even see Ariel get born," she grumbled.

"Oh shit, I'm so sorry," I rested a hand on her shoulder.

Mara jerked away. "It's fine!" She yelped before coughing a few times. She wrapped her bony arms around herself. " It's fine. I... found someone else to stay with... but I can't... I can't stay there... now. Not right now."

Oh god, what have you gotten yourself into, sis? "Well, you're welcome here. Mom and Dad really miss you," I said.

"Um... "Mara chewed her bottom lip. "Can you do me a solid? Don't tell Mom and Dad I was here. Really, it'd be great if you didn't tell anyone. You work from home, right?"

"Most of the time," I frowned, "Why?"

" Can you please watch Ariel for a day?"

I looked at the tiny girl on my couch. My niece. "What will you be doing?"

"Don't ask me that." Mara shook her head. "Just... don't leave the house. Don't let Ariel near the windows."

"Are you in danger?"

"Just—promise me. Please."

At this point, I had two theories about why my sister was wigging out—either she had gotten in an abusive relationship and was on the run... or she had completely lost her mind on drugs and was a nutcase.

Either way, I knew I had to help.

"Sure. She can sleep on the couch, right?" I don't have kids, I know literally nothing about caring for a kid.

Mara wrapped me in another tight bear hug. "Thank you so much," she sobbed, nearly crushing my ribs before stepping back. "I'll be back tomorrow night, I hope. I love you, Thomas... and I'm sorry. You were right."

With that, Mara slunk out the door and into the night, like she'd never been there.

This whole time, Ariel sat on the couch, her hands neatly folded on her lap as she kicked her feet back and forth. I coughed a few times before sitting next to her. "Sooo... when's bed time?" I asked.

Again—I don't know how to deal with kids.

Ariel giggled, and I saw more bits of my sister in her—the smile, the way her nose wrinkled when she was amused. "You're funny, Uncle Thomas. Can I color?" she asked.

"I might have some colored pencils and paper somewhere..." Listen, I love that they make coloring books for adults nowadays, and I am completely in on the fad. So in about ten minutes, I had Ariel sitting at my dining room table with some paper and watched as her tiny fist clutched onto a bright pink pencil as she drew a shape that could've been a horse or an airplane.

I tried to fill the silence with conversation. That went as well as you'd expect.

"So, what's your favorite color?"

"Pink."

"Do you go to kindergarten yet?"

"I stay with Mommy. She's taught me my ABC's."

"Do you have a pet?"

"We're not allowed to."

"Um, do you like snakes? I have a snake."

That had her pause. She stopped her scribbles and looked up, her eyes wide. "Wow! You have a pet snake?!" she said with a gasp, her face lit up with delight.

"Yeah, his name's Popcorn," Finally, something I could distract her with, "Come on, let's go see him. He's in my room."

Popcorn is a Corn Snake I adopted about a year back, a friend had to move and couldn't take him with. Since then, he's been my little buddy. Ariel squealed as I flicked on the light and ran to the other cage in my room. "Mice!" She pointed at the cage of small white mice wriggling around.

"Yeah, those are my other buddies," I laughed as I walked up to the cage. "Come here, Popcorn... "I carefully lifted him out.

"Are we gonna feed him?"

I turned around to see that Ariel had one of my mice curled up in her hands. "Oh, honey, no," I laughed, the mouse in question seemed content and it wasn't like she was dangling it by its tail, "Popcorn already ate recently and uh, those aren't the mice he eats. Can you put him back in his cage now?"

Ariel shrugged and gently placed the mouse back inside the cage. "Can I see Popcorn now?" She extended her arm expectantly.

"He probably won't want to crawl on your arm, sweetie." I knelt down and carefully lifted Popcorn forward. "He's a bit shy, and-"

Popcorn naturally slid from my hand onto Ariel, twisting around her arm, and I swear he never looked more content. My jaw dropped. "Are you a freaking Parseltongue or something?" I said.

"I don't know what that means. But snakes like me." Ariel leaned her face forward, slitting her eyes and staring at Popcorn, who flicked his tongue out a few times before slithering forward, crawling around her neck and hanging loosely there. "Father says it's because they know I'm their friend."

"Father? I thought your mom said your dad... wasn't around."

Ariel looked puzzled before she burst out laughing. "Oh, no no no! Father isn't my daddy, I don't have a daddy. Father is all of our father."

I felt an unpleasant chill go down my spine. "... What... is this Father like?" I asked carefully.

"He's very kind!" Ariel grinned and nodded her head. "He reads from the Book every morning and makes sure that we all know right from wrong. One of my friends, her daddy is the Father, but he's not my daddy. He wants us all to stick together. Last week, he chose me for something really important!"

"What was that?" I had to know. What the hell had Mara gotten into?

Ariel glanced out the window. "Well, I'm not supposed to say, but..." Ariel giggled and clapped her hands. "I'm going to be the Daughter!"

What. I had no idea what to say to that. "Really," I found myself looking out the window as well, almost expecting someone to be there, "And what does that mean?"

"I have no idea!" Ariel removed Popcorn from her neck and handed him back to me. "I'm hungry, I'm gonna get something to eat," she said before running out of the room.

I settled Popcorn back into his cage and gently ran my finger down his back. "I'm gonna kick Mara's ass when she gets back," I grumbled before heading back into the kitchen.

I saw Ariel peering into the freezer. "Do you want pizza rolls, Ariel?" It might've been close to midnight, but I had no idea when she'd eaten last. "Or chicken strips?"

I heard a crunch and the sound of chewing. "No thank you!" Swallow. "I found something yummy!" Another crunch.

Frowning, I walked up to Ariel. "Honey, you can't just eat something frozen... "I turned her around, and the words died in my mouth.

Ariel was clutching my bag of frozen feeder mice in her hands, her mouth smeared with blood. A small frozen tail was sticking out between her lips. She swallowed, and it vanished. "They're a little cold, could you warm them up?" She handed the bag to me.

What the fuck? "Ariel!" I grabbed a paper towel and wiped off her face. "Jesus Christ, kid, you don't eat mice!"

"Why not?" Ariel cocked her head to the side. "Popcorn eats mice."

"Well, you're not Popcorn, oh fuck, Mara's gonna kill me..." I groaned and put the feeder mice back on the top shelf, she'd have to dig past the frozen bread to get it. "How about we have some pizza rolls instead?"

Ariel pouted and crossed her arms. "I don't want pizza rolls," she grumbled. "Can I go to bed now?"

I ended up just putting Ariel to sleep on the couch. I was done. That was my limit. Children eating fucking frozen mice.

I woke up about midnight to see her standing over the mouse cage. The lid had been taken off and her head was cocked to the side. I almost sat up and asked what the hell was she doing when she opened her mouth and something long and thin fell out of her mouth, plopping into the floor of the cage. For a second, I thought she somehow had Popcorn in her mouth, but a glance confirmed that Popcorn was chilling in his cage under his lamp.

Ariel's tongue slowly felt its way around the cage, slithering about until it touched one of the sleeping mice. I don't know why they were asleep, they were usually jumping around this time of night. Her tongue slowly wrapped around the mouse and lifted it to her mouth. It hung limply in its grasp until she brought it into her mouth. Then it jerked about, and I heard it squeal before she brought her jaws down on it.

That crunch was one of the most horrifying things I'd ever heard.

Humming pleasantly, Ariel skipped out of the room and back to the couch. In just a few minutes, I heard her softly snoring.

I didn't get a wink of sleep the rest of the night.

Ariel's been a normal kid all day, but I can't shake that image out of my head of her tongue just dragging that mouse to its doom. I counted them to make sure and one was absolutely gone.

But what's worse is that Mara's not come back. I've tried texting her, but apparently her phone number belongs to someone else now. And I swear I've seen the same car drive past my house five times today.

I don't know what to do.

And I'm scared of what I'll see if I wake up tonight and see Ariel again.

MR. FERGUSON

I think the whole street breathed a sigh of relief when we saw the EMTs take a body bag out of the Ferguson house. I was only about ten or eleven at the time and it's been a while, so some details of my childhood are lost to time, but I could never forget Mr. Ferguson.

There was never a Mrs. Ferguson in the picture, as far as I know. He lived in the house on the corner, the one with the bright yellow shutters and the gorgeous garden out back. The garden didn't make up for the rotten old bastard he was. I wondered once if he was nicer when he was younger, when he didn't have to walk with a cane and could actually get around without help, but my dad set me straight on that one. Mr. Ferguson had always been a terrible person and the neighbor from hell.

All day long, Mr. Ferguson would sit on his front porch in his rocking hair, grasping onto his black cane as he stared out on the street. If someone walking their dog got close to his yard, he'd start spewing threats about what he'd do if the dog took a shit on his lawn. If a kid put even a toe on his property, he'd get up from that chair and start shouting more terrible things. I learned my first cuss words from Mr. Ferguson, he didn't censor his language even among the smallest of ears. And he wasn't all talk. One of my friend's dogs wandered into the Ferguson yard, just sniffing around as beagles do, and Mr. Ferguson beat that dog bloody. The poor thing had anxiety for the rest of its life and if you so much as passed the Ferguson house with it the dog would lose its mind.

Other than him, our neighborhood was a friendly place. Summers were full of cookouts and pool parties, winters had Secret Santa gift exchanges, and someone was always willing to help shovel out your driveway. You'd never be hard pressed to find a babysitter on short notice, odds are your friend had a teenage daughter willing to make a few bucks to make sure the kids were on bed in time.

But not Mr. Ferguson. People did try to bring him in on the fun sometimes. He'd scoff and tell them to leave him alone in no uncertain terms. Mom said he just wanted to be miserable. I didn't understand how someone could want that and, well, I still don't.

One hot summer morning, though, his caretaker came in to do a check and found him in his garden, dead as a doornail. Probably a stroke or a heart attack.

My mom made us go to the funeral. I don't know why, she probably hated Mr. Ferguson the most, and we were like one of five people that went. One of them being the priest. At least it was short, the priest just said a few words about how we should treasure our lives and be good to others and then Mr. Ferguson was chucked into the ground.

That was that... or so I thought.

The accidents started happening just a week later.

I was at my friend Michael's house, we were playing board games when we heard the crash. It was so loud it shook the house and Michael dropped his soda. Root beer spilled onto the carpet as we tried to figure out what that sound was for a second.

Then we heard his dad screaming bloody murder.

Forgetting completely about the spilled soda, we ran out to the garage where he'd been working on changing the oil in the car.

Michael's dad was pinned by the car against the garage door, face white as a sheet as his head lolled to the side. I saw blood splattered against the off gray color of the metal and I puked while Michael ran inside to call 911.

It was lucky that he survived. He never walked again, and health issues plagued him for the rest of his life, but for a guy crushed by a car that's probably the best-case scenario.

It was an accident, sure, but a weird one. The car just suddenly launched forward as Michael's dad stood in front of it. There was no one else in the garage with him. So yeah. It was just an accident.

But accidents started happening more and more often.

The next one was at the final pool party of the season. We were all at the Benson house to celebrate their brand new hot tub. There were probably like twelve kids running around, the sun was shining, the barbecue was sizzling. I had just gotten out of the pool to grab a lemonade and was chatting with Annie when I heard the pop.

Mrs. Benson and her friends had been relaxing in the hot tub, making jokes and laughing until the pop. Their bodies suddenly went rigid before they began rapidly jerking about and twitching. Mr. Benson shouted if she was all right and I heard this gurgled yell before Mrs. Benson went under.

The kids stampeded out of the pool and I smelled something burning before I realized that the hot tub was on fire.

Mrs. Benson and her sister ended up dying on the way to the hospital. The other woman ended up surviving, but not without some serious electrical burns. Electrocution via hot tub. Just an accident. But there was one more accident we all missed until we returned to the pool to see a little body floating at the top. Three-year-old Maggie had fallen in during the chaos and drowned.

Mr. Benson moved away after that. Losing both his wife and youngest child in that house just killed something inside of him. But after he moved away, we all saw it happen.

His backyard became overgrown by plants. Not over a few weeks, like what happens when a house is uninhabited and there's no one to mow the lawn. The very day after they'd left that house, the backyard was now filled with dandelions, daffodils, lilies. and all sorts of flowers that shouldn't naturally appear in the late summer.

It was like a garden.

Accidents happen, sure. But not like this. Not when a guy who's been working home improvement his entire life ends up toppling from a ladder and breaking his spine. Not when a mom trips and falls face first into the open dishwasher and ends up getting impaled on a knife. Not when a toddler was left alone for just a few seconds and ended up nearly drowning in the bathtub.

Dogs ran into the road and ended up getting hit by cars. Kids fell from their bunk beds and cracked their heads like eggshells on their dressers. Teenagers got into fatal car wrecks. It was a mess.

Two other families ended up leaving our neighborhood and their yards had the same fate as the Benson's—completely grown over. A morbid beauty.

Fall came and the yards grew brown, but the gardens seemed to be even greener. The whispers started about a ghost. A ghost that was such a miserable old bastard in life and was now a nasty poltergeist in death.

Mr. Ferguson had never left our neighborhood.

It all came to a head when a tree was struck by lightning and a large tree limb crashed into our living room. I'd just tripped while picking up my things and suddenly the roof caved in above me. I was lucky I was on the ground. If I'd been standing, well, I'd probably not be telling you this story.

Two nights later, my mom woke me up. She looked grim.

"Come on. We're going to see Mr. Ferguson."

When we walked out of the house, I saw everyone on our street was out, all with the same grim looks on their faces. The deaths, the mutilation, it'd forever tarnished our street and we'd all had enough. We walked down the street, I saw several guys walk into Mr. Ferguson's house with mallets and chainsaws, but we kept going with a few of the others. I saw that several of the adults were carrying shovels and containers of lighter fluid.

We walked into the graveyard, and my mom led them right to Mr. Ferguson's grave. She took a deep breath.

"... Start digging."

It was the frantic endeavors of people who believed they were cursed. Dirt flew in the air and nearly pelted me in the head a few times. I hid behind my mom, who just stood there stone faced.

Even then the accidents weren't over. A man tripped in the hole and his leg snapped like a twig. He wailed as he was dragged away by a few others before they got right back to digging. Someone else got smacked in the face with a shovel and blood poured from his nose as he just kept on digging.

Finally the coffin was reached, the lid cracked open. Mr. Ferguson's body lay inside. He didn't even look dead, it was like he was just taking a nap.

Then they started pouring the lighter fluid in. It covered the corpse's skin, his clothes. They probably added more than necessary. My mom struck the match and threw it in, shielding me from the sudden burst of flames.

I didn't get to see the body, but I swore I heard the old man yelling as his body burned.

It was over after all that. The gardens were all dead by morning. The accidents stopped. And although we'd lost so many of our friends over the past year, we recovered.

New neighbors moved in. We welcomed them into our fold. One or two asked about the property on the corner, the one that looked like a tornado hit it, and we'd just say it was vandals. They stopped asking. We never talked about what we did to Mr. Ferguson's body. And soon we just stopped thinking about it.

I grew up on that street. Even now I only live a few blocks away. And for so long, I wondered why our family was practically the only one untouched by the tragedy. We never got hurt, even when the tree branch came crashing into our living room.

I think I found out the answer. See, my mom passed away a few months ago from breast cancer and I've been going through her things. She's always been such a good, kind woman and it was great seeing pictures of her helping plant the garden behind the church and teaching at the local school.

But in the bottom of the box, hidden under dozens of other albums, was a picture from when she married my dad. Unlike the family picture with the groom, all it was was my mom and an older man. I didn't recognize him until I flipped the picture over.

On the back was written 'Pauline Walters (P. Ferguson) and The Father of the Bride.'

BECOMING A MAN

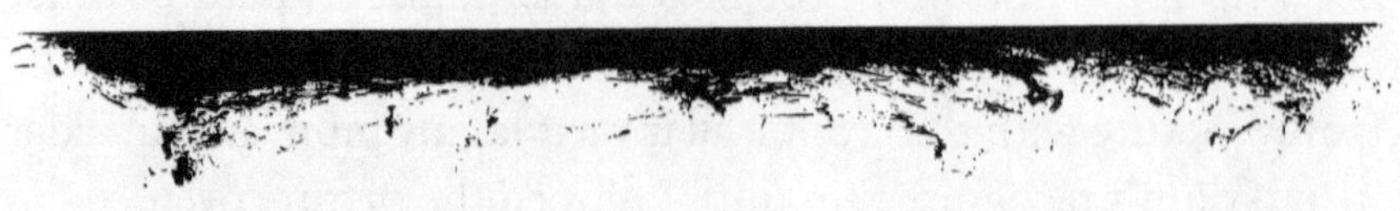

"This is what you have to to become a man, Christian." My dad shoved me out of his truck. I turned back to see him light up a cigarette for my cousin Dave in the backseat.

Dave looked at me and grinned crookedly. "Make sure to wrap your tool!" He teased before reaching forward and pulling the door shut, having to slam it twice to make sure it actually stayed closed.

Well, this was actually happening. I swallowed before I walked down the street, hearing my dad's truck backfire twice before it drove off. I was now alone out here. Granted, I could use my phone and call an Uber, maybe even beat my dad home, but I had to do this. I was eighteen. I had to prove to the rest of my family that I was a real man.

My eyes went from woman to woman, all different flavors of beauty and desperation. One curvy woman with pale skin and crooked teeth whistled and called out, "Sweetie, you look scared, want someone to keep you company?"

I just smiled and kept on walking, looking for that perfect girl.

And there she was, looking like a piece of the night sky had come down and became a woman. Skin darker than midnight, dark curls bouncing behind her shoulders, and hands staying by her sides, neatly manicured nails lightly brushing against her ripped stockings and short skirt.

I felt my hands tremble as I walked up to her. "Hey, um, how much?"

Smooth.

The girl looked over, she was probably only a year or so older than I was. Or maybe she was younger, I couldn't tell. She grinned, quietly laughing. "Oh Christ, you're not used to coming around here, are you?" She leaned closer, grasping my jacket collar to pull me down to her level. Even with those four-inch heels, she was still so much shorter than I was. "You look like a guppy among all these bloodthirsty sharks," she whispered.

I gulped before straightening myself back up. "Yeah, I just... look, do you want my money or not?" I didn't mean to snap, but I just didn't want to lose my nerve.

The girl snorted. "Not with that attitude. Drop the tough guy act, will you? You have nothing to prove to me," she said.

Damn it. I quelled the anger burning in my chest before dropping my gaze. "S... sorry. I'm just a little embarrassed. Um, I'm Christian," I mumbled.

"I'm Diane. Do you have a car or enough extra cash to buy an hour at the joint down the street?" She shot a thumb down that direction.

"I have enough." I fumbled for my wallet and pulled out three crisp fifty-dollar bills. "I want all you can give me."

Diane's eyes widened, and she sputtered for a moment before snatching all three and stuffing them in her bra, clearly visible underneath her sheer pink shirt. "Done deal. Come on, it's cold as tits out here and you look like you need to warm up," she said, looping her arm in with mine before taking me down the street.

I expected her to smell like nicotine smoke or acrid perfume, but as I leaned in I could smell her hair. Green apples. I felt the butterflies in my chest flutter wildly about, beating against my rib cage. She was so gorgeous, I could barely catch my breath. Her chilled fingers interlaced with mine and I gripped on tightly. "I'm not the only one who needs to warm up," I said.

Diane tossed her head back and laughed. "I'm used to it. Come on, we're here. Make it quick, I want to get inside," she said before leaning up to kiss my cheek. I could smell the barest hint of whiskey on her breath, followed by a metallic scent I just couldn't place.

The guy managing the front desk only cared for the money I threw in there, tossing me the keys to room 104 before telling me to be out in an hour and not to make a mess.

Once in the privacy of the room, Diane slipped out of that skin tight shirt and smirked, tilting her hips to the side before sauntering over to the bed. "Come here, Christian. Let's have some fun," she purred.

My first time was just as one would expect. Sloppy, clumsy, and I finished way too fast. But Diane was as beautiful out of her clothes as I expected. There was a scar in between her right ribs, I traced my fingers along it for a moment too long judging by her flinch. But it was beautiful, just like the rest of her.

After we were done, she rolled over to her side to catch her breath, have a few more minutes in the muggy room before braving the cold again. Now came the actual hard part. I pretended to act like I was getting dressed, pulling on my jeans while slipping my hand into my pocket. I gripped the handle of my knife, taking a deep breath before pulling it from the sheath.

This is what it means to be a man. Kill the dirty bitches.

I sat back on the bed and turned to her. She had somehow managed to fall asleep, or at least she looked it.

She looked so peaceful. Like an angel.

She's a dirty whore.

She's so young. So pretty.

She belongs with the rest of them. Cut up and fed to the pigs.

But maybe she didn't.

My hands were shaking so badly that the knife tumbled from my fingers, falling to the floor. Diane startled, eyes shooting open as she sat up. "What's going on, Chris..." she trailed off as she looked down at the floor, the shine of the blade likely drawing her attention. Her eyes widened before she looked up at me, I saw fear.

"... If y... you want your money back, just take it! I, oh fucking christ, why do I always get the-"

"I'm so sorry!"

I sobbed like a bitch as I fell to my knees. Tears and snot dripped down my face as I broke down, shaking as I bawled out my apologies. I was so weak. I couldn't be a man. Not how my dad wanted me to be.

I felt those slim hands rest on my shoulders. I looked up at her, looking probably quite the sight. This scrawny, pimpled boy who had come into this room with the intent of cutting this bitch open and taking her heart to my family.

Diane was smiling.

"Hey... hey, it's okay. You didn't do it. You might've wanted to, but you didn't. You don't want to hurt me anymore, right?"

I shook my head.

"Did someone try to talk you into doing it?"

I nodded.

"Who?"

I sniffled and wiped my nose off on my arm. "My... my dad. My uncle. My cousin. They've all done it before. It's how you prove you're a man."

Diane made a disgusted sound before grabbing a tissue off the nightstand and wiping off my arm before cleaning off my face. "That's bullshit. Complete bullshit. Murdering a helpless girl just because you can doesn't make you a man. Making up your own mind not to though, just cuz they told you to? That's manly as balls."

"They're not gonna accept me back home if I do though." I shook my head. "If I don't come back with a heart-"

Diane shushed me, pressing a finger to my lips.

"Let me get dressed and make a call to my girls. If they've made a habit of killing us, then we're going to return the fucking favor.

Call your dad, tell him something went wrong and that you need all the other family. Trust me, and I'll make it worth your while."

I nodded before I scrambled to finish getting dressed.

I stayed hidden in a nearby alleyway when I saw the old truck pull up. It rattled as it came to a stop and my dad jumped out. "All right, how'd you fuck it up this time, Christian?!" he snapped, looking around for me as my uncle and cousin exited the truck, looking just as pissed.

I blinked and my family was surrounded by several different women. Diane was standing in front of my father. She grinned, and I saw her canines nearly grow an inch in length before she launched herself at my dad's throat. I covered my eyes to avoid seeing the bloodbath, but I could hear their screams.

I waited until it all became quiet to peer out.

There was nothing left of my family except for piles of bones and gore. Diane looked up at me, her beautiful smile soaked in blood, before she gestured me forward. Unafraid, I approached, the other woman parting to let me close to her.

Diane pulled me down to her level to press a kiss to my lips. I now knew what that smell on her breath was from before.

"You're going to make a great guard dog, Christian. Be a real man. Help clean up the mess and we'll take good care of you."

GROWTH

Did you know that one in five pregnancies end in miscarriage?

Some women are lucky. When they conceive, their child is born safe and sound. They grow up healthy and happy, they become doctors, lawyers, maybe even the president someday. Some women are not nearly as lucky, they lose a child the first or possibly even the second time, but then they have their lucky day and they're blessed with an addition to their family.

I'm neither of these women.

I'd never been able to carry a pregnancy to term. Four times I've conceived. Four times I've miscarried.

It's never easy. I get my hopes up every time. I run to Mitchell with the pregnancy test, grinning and telling him that this is the time, this is the time our family will grow from two to three. The first time, my husband spun me around and kissed me several times on the cheek. He did that the second time too.

The third time, he only smiled. The fourth time, the smile didn't reach his eyes. I didn't blame him. I couldn't smile either. Even though hope was attempting to blossom in my heart, I knew I'd never get to hold the life growing in my womb.

I threw myself into my garden to distract myself from my pain. Because of this, I have quite a beautiful garden. I grow vegetables of all sorts, carrots, potatoes, a few stalks of corn, I even grew pumpkins last year. When the harvest comes around, I store what I can and what I can't I end up giving to my neighbors. The little kid next door took the pumpkin I gave them and carved it into the perfect Jack o' Lantern. Well, mostly perfect, its smile was lopsided.

A few months ago, I was in one of my gardening chat rooms when the subject of children came up. My heart ached as I brought up what me and my husband had gone through, and everyone was so comforting. One of the other women, her screen name was AbbyLovesApples, opened up about how she'd also had several miscarriages before she'd had her twins six years back. Twin girls, identical in every way. They were so cute I nearly cried. If only I'd had the desire to keep trying like Abby had.

I nearly signed off when I got a private message from AbbyLovesApples.

'I can help you have a child. Let's exchange email addresses, I can't bear seeing you suffer any longer than you have to.'

Of course, I assumed that she would bring up some sort of expensive medical treatment. Something that my husband and I couldn't even dream of affording, not like he'd even want to try. He was already bringing up getting my tubes tied when our tax return came in.

It wasn't that at all.

Abby sent me a long message about how she'd also given up hope about having children. How her husband had actually left her for another woman because she couldn't give him children. She'd lost all hope and was two days away from jumping off a nearby bridge. She'd made plans, wrote out her will and was finishing up her suicide note when her elderly neighbor came to visit.

That woman saved her life.

The woman had brought her something to help her womb become as friendly as her garden. She'd given very specific instructions and Abby followed them to the letter. With luck and a random man she'd picked up off a dating website, Abby became pregnant and gave birth to Ivy and Iris.

And Abby was willing to guide me through this process, with no payment necessary.

I needed this. I knew Mitchell would never leave me, at least, I hoped he wouldn't. But I had no other option if I wanted to give birth to my children.

In a week I got a box in the mail. Abby's instructions were abundant, but she insisted I had to follow them to the letter. If I didn't, not only would I lose the baby, but I would risk my life as well. Thankfully, the instructions were simple. In the box was a bag of what I can describe as something like white sand. It was ultra fine but had a bizarre smell, almost like copper.

I was to measure out a teaspoon of this stuff, mix it with a cup of water once a day, preferably around the same time, and drink it down. I know, it was stupid to drink something I got from a stranger on the internet, I was desperate. And Abby didn't come off as a nutcase.

It didn't taste bad at least. It didn't have much of a taste at all, just left my throat feeling rather grainy and uncomfortable.

I was to do this until I became pregnant.

It wasn't hard to drag my husband into bed, I didn't tell him what I was doing, but it wasn't much of his business anyway.

When I skipped a period, I knew I was pregnant. I'd stocked up on pregnancy tests beforehand and I took two to confirm. When my husband got home from work, I showed him the test with a hopeful smile.

"Maybe this time, babe?"

His smile didn't have much hope, but he kissed my forehead. He knew I was happy. He didn't know that this time I had a secret weapon.

Now that I was confirmed to be pregnant, I had to up my dosage of the 'sand'. Two teaspoons, one in the morning, one at night, taken with water. My husband caught me taking it at night once and asked what it was, I told him it was some prenatal vitamins that would help the baby. He didn't say anything after that, just turned over in bed and turned out the light.

His lack of excitement was a thorn in my side, but as weeks went by, I realized there truly was a spark of hope.

Now, I had to be careful. Abby specified that I could not, under any circumstance, go to the doctor. Any ultrasounds might interfere with the powder's effects and I'd have gone through all of this for nothing. I couldn't take any other medication that helped with prenatal care. And it was recommended I didn't tell anyone outside of my husband I was pregnant. Hide it for as long as I could.

That last part made the most sense, if I ended up losing the child again I would've gotten up everyone's hopes for nothing. I'd made that mistake twice before, I didn't want to do it again.

The pregnancy went smoothly at first, much to my surprise. I felt my stomach begin to swell, I started wearing baggy shirts just to be sure no one asked too many questions. My husband would carefully phrase questions about how my pregnancy was going, to see if I'd lost the baby yet and just hadn't told him.

I didn't expect anything was wrong until I woke up in the worst pain of my life.

My tired brain initially thought I was on my period until I remembered I was pregnant.

Then I realized I was losing the baby.

I stumbled into the bathroom, shutting the door behind me and twisting the lock. My heart sank. I was losing the baby again. I went over and over in my mind what'd I'd done wrong. Had I missed a dose? Had I accidentally taken too much or too little?

I stumbled into the bathtub and laid down, digging my fingers into the sides and doing my best not to cry out as spasms of pain ripped through my body. I didn't want to wake up my husband for some reason.

I lost consciousness as I felt my child leave my body and when I came to again, blood and fluids were circling down the drain and there was my child.

It was about the size of a potato, a lump of oval flesh that twitched and squirmed. Not comprehending what I was seeing, I picked it up, only to see that there was an eye staring back at me. An eye the color of mine.

I dropped it back and bit the back of my hand to stop from screaming. It continued to squirm.

It was alive. It was fucking alive.

I stumbled out of the bathtub, wondering what the hell had happened to me, when I heard my cell phone start to buzz in the next room.

Terrified my husband would wake up and see the... thing in the bathtub, I hurried out and grabbed it before retreating to the bathroom. Thank god he slept through that.

I answered it with a quiet hello.

"Did you have your baby?"

I didn't recognize the voice, a calm, feminine voice with a southern drawl. But other than my husband, only one person knew I was pregnant.

"Abby?" I asked.

"Yeah, it's me. Listen to me, did you have the baby?"

I looked in the tub at the squirming lump of flesh. "... Yes. What... what is it, Abby? It doesn't look like a-"

"Listen to me, very carefully. This is the part where you have to be more careful than ever, but you also have to be quick. Pick up your baby. How many eyes are there?"

Repulsion wracked my frame as I picked up my 'baby'. I carefully turned it over in my hand a few times, shivering as I'd come across another eye. "... Three. Three eyes."

I heard Abby whistle. "Damn, that's lucky. Congrats, you're having triplets. Go to the kitchen, and find a sharp knife. Have you ever cut the eyes out of a potato before?"

"... Yes."

"Same concept. Flesh is a little different to cut, but it's doable with a sharp enough knife. After you're done cutting out the eyes, plant them in a part of your garden that gives them plenty of space to grow. Keep the eyes close to each other though, they'd not like to be alone. The earth is the womb of the world, but it's still lonely in the dirt. Hurry, you wait too long and the eyes will start to dry."

I nearly puked twice as I slowly cut apart the lump of flesh. It twitched, and I swore I heard it make a sound like a cry, but Abby reassured me that it was just me. I wouldn't have made it through this without her.

I planted my babies in the garden, in a plot I just hadn't had time to plant anything in. I collapsed next to the dirt, the blood between my thighs starting to dry. "It's... it's all done, Abby. I did it," I said, starting to feel tired.

"Good. Get some good fertilizer, water them everyday. Talk to them too. Your baby can hear your voice even when they're like that... I'll talk to you after you get some rest. Goodnight."

I was shaken awake the next morning by my husband, who woke up to find blood all over the bathroom and the kitchen and nearly lost his shit. Not to mention the leftover flesh from the babies. I really hadn't thought of taking care of it.

He thought I'd finally lost it once I'd told him what happened. He threatened to dig up our babies to prove they were just figments of my imagination. That would have killed them. I couldn't let him do that.

I didn't mean to hit him that hard with the frying pan, but perhaps it worked out for the best. I needed good fertilizer, after all.

Abby moved in with me last week. She's about ten years older than me, but we understand each other more than anyone else in the world. The twins are adorable, and very helpful. They love to sing to my garden, teaching their future sisters their favorite songs. Last night, we just finished painting the nursery. It was so much fun, Abby got paint on her nose and after I laughed, she retaliated by dragging her paint covered hand over my cheek.

We've finished right on time too. I can hear my babies start to cry at night, the earth around the place they were planted stirring and squirming. Any day now, they will be ready to be born.

I can't wait to be a mother.

AUTOPSY REPORT

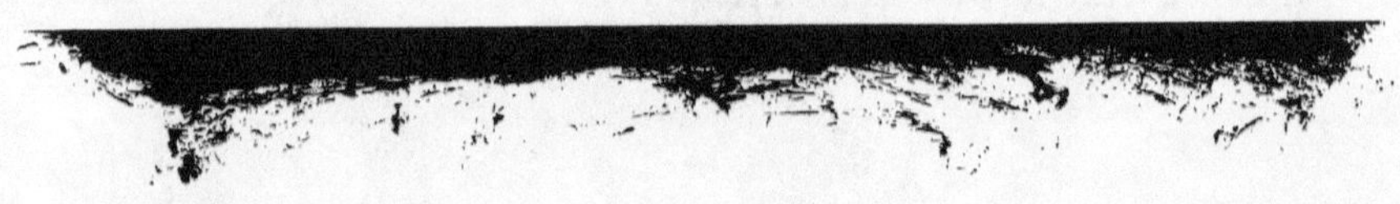

Y ou would not believe what kind of shit I've pulled out of
people.

Hi, I'm Mike. I cut into dead bodies for a living. It's not
exactly the kind of job that gets you laid, but it pays the bills.
Anyway, back to what I was saying. Fucked up shit in dead bodies. The weirdest 'normal' thing I've pulled out of a person was
a hairball out of someone's stomach. And when I say hairball,
I mean it looked like the woman had swallowed a cat. She was
a suicide victim. Probably bit into her hair because of anxiety. I
get it. My little sister has issues with that sort of thing.

Wow. Off topic again. Clearly I've pounded those beers a
little faster than I thought. I'm not here to talk about hairballs.
No. I'm here to talk about something really weird.

Over the course of three weeks, I got three cadavers that
have topped the weirdness scale. I swear, everything I'm saying
is true, and I got no explanation as to how the things got into
their bodies... or why they were in there in the first place.

Forks up a vagina. Yup. Forks. Up. A vagina. Yowza.

When I uncovered the body, I made a few notes. One was in
her late teens, probably a senior in highschool and not much more.
She was probably pretty, when she was alive. I'm not a freak, I think

dead bodies are hideous. You really see all the flaws when someone's dead before they're made to look pretty for the funeral.

Apparently she'd just dropped during algebra with massive bleeding out of her crotch. She didn't even make it to the ambulance before they called it. They sent her down to me, in my cold, dark basement morgue, and I let my sister know I wouldn't be home until late and she could stay at Annie's house tonight.

When I saw the silvery prong starting to edge its way out of her 'lady spot' I wondered if she'd been stabbed and just hadn't gone for help. I've seen things along that line before. I got a hold of it and eased what appeared to be a bloodied, metal dessert fork outta there. I dropped it into the tray and felt nothing but confusion. How the hell had a dessert fork gotten up there?

When I opened her up, I found nine more, all the way up to her cervix. One had even gotten trapped in her uterus. I'm thinking she might've confused it for the worst motherfucking cramps of her short life—she was on her period.

When I told the investigator that the cause of death was massive bleeding caused by a fork up her vag, he laughed in my face. When I showed him the evidence though, he changed his mind.

In the end we had to put the cause of death as something self-inflicted as there wasn't any evidence of someone forcing them up there. Honestly though. Forks. Like the ones my mom used to eat her little cheesecakes and tarts with while laughing with her friends.

The second one was just as weird. Another teenage girl, around the same age. She had a more athletic build, though, probably was in the gymnastics or swim team. She'd started vomiting blood in the parking lot after school. And a little something extra.

Pins.

When I cut open her stomach, it was jam packed with sewing pins. I swear it was bulging with them. I'd never seen so many in my life, cept when I snuck into my gran's sewing room. Old women have a million pins, I swear.

I can't even tell you the final count up. Far too damn many. But again, there was no evidence she'd had them forced down her throat... although this is where it takes a step farther.

There was no evidence she'd swallowed them at all.

I had no answers. Somehow this girl had a porcupine of pins in her stomach, and I had no idea how they got in there. The hospital literally brought in three other dudes, some who have been doing this for a decade longer than I have.

We all turned up squat. I think one of the guys went straight from the morgue to a bar. It was pretty heavy shit.

But the last one is the one that's going to give me nightmares.

By the time another teenage girl's body turned up, I wouldn't have batted an eyelash if I had cut her open and fucking Jennifer Lawrence turned up in there. I was done.

This girl's death wasn't so bloody. She'd just asphyxiated in class. Some students claim they saw something sticking out of her mouth, but at the moment she was on the slab, there wasn't.

Not until I cut open her throat anyway.

The slit I'd made split wide open, and the brown patterned head of a ball python poked out. Like it was breaking free from the egg.

I might've screamed like a little girl and fell back on my ass so hard I bruised my tailbone.

By the time I got back up, the python had mostly squirmed free. The sucker had to be about five feet long, and it was now curled up across the girl's chest, looking entirely unbothered about where it just crawled free from.

Nervously, I extended my arm to the scaly creature. He slithered up and made himself comfortable.

I clocked out early and told the nurse I'd caught the stomach flu. I snuck out the snake in my lunchbox. Lil guy was always good at not making a fuss.

When I got home, my sister had cleaned up her little 'ritual' site, but the dribbles of wax on the ground and the smell of burnt blood still lingering in the air gave away what she'd been up to. I put the python back in her tank and pulled out a few beers from the fridge.

When I get back to work, I'll have to play dumb again. Not like there'd be much to prove there was a snake in the girl's throat in the first place.

RULES OF CAMP GOLDEN OAK

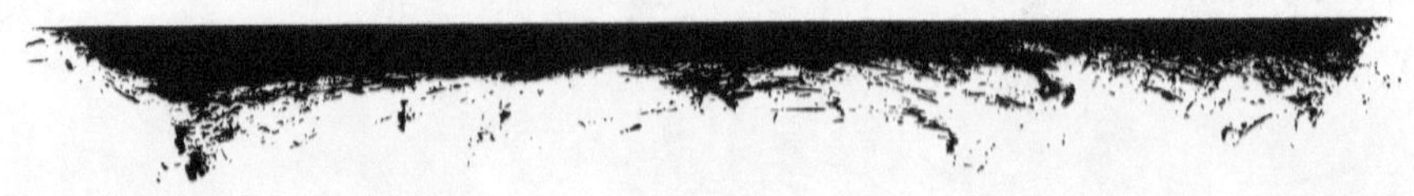

Hey guys, did anyone here go to Camp Golden Oak? It's a long shot to reach out here, but I'm pretty sure my mind's playing some sort of trick on me and I'd like to know I'm not suddenly losing it after years of that place not even crossing my mind.

Let me back up, Camp Golden Oak was a summer camp in Michigan that took place from June to August for kids ten to thirteen. I went there all three years I could, and up until a few days ago I only remembered a few bits, making friends, playing in the crafts room, having the counselor tell spooky stories at night... you know, the fun parts.

I was doing some spring cleaning when I found a box of things from when I was a kid, tucked away behind the skis I said I'd throw out three years ago. It was full of participation medals, report cards, school pictures, that sort of thing, and I also found an old school folder labeled 'CAMP GOLDEN OAK'.

I expected it to be full of pictures and not much else, but I found a lot of things. Pamphlets, notices for counselors, and on a piece of folded up paper signed by the owners of Golden Oak, I found the camp rules. I think the paper was given out during the first week, but... I don't remember these at all. There's some water stains on it but it's still readable. I've written what it says below and yeah, it's fucking weird. If anyone has any input on this, feel free to offer it, I'm just really confused right now. And a little creeped out

.

———

At Camp Golden Oak, we want you all to have the best experience you can. Just follow the few rules below to help keep everyone safe and having fun!

1—Always listen to your counselor. For this week, they're your teacher, your leader, and most importantly, your friend. Don't be afraid to come to them for help. They are there to listen.

2—Be kind to your fellow campers and never be afraid to make new friends. But be respectful, remember the Golden rule!

3—When on a nature hike, don't wander off the trail, even if you see something that catches your eye. No one wants to be a Lost Camper!

4—Never waste food, clean your plate! If you have special food requirements due to religion or allergies, don't be afraid to tell Chef! He'll make a special plate just for you.

5—Please don't start food fights. Sometimes things can get confusing and exciting, and sometimes someone can get hurt.

6—Please don't start paint fights in the art center. Again, people can get hurt.

7—No going out after dark. There are bathrooms in your cabins if you have an emergency. Do not leave the cabin under any circumstance, even if you hear someone calling your name outside. Even if it sounds like a friend.

8—If you get locked out after light's out, immediately head to the cafeteria. Chef will put you up for the night, no questions asked. Don't be afraid to come clean. If you hear someone call your name while you're out, again, keep walking, don't turn around.

9—We at Camp Golden Oak are open-minded and happy to accommodate any camper from any background. However, we do not allow religious jewelry (crosses, Stars of David, pentacles, etc.) to be worn on the grounds. Any form of religious writing must be examined during check-in. If we deem it necessary, it'll be held in Mr. Bram's office for the week(s) you stay at Camp Golden Oak. Don't worry, it won't be stolen, it'll be locked in an airtight safe.

10—If you have any belongings you're afraid of being stolen, you can turn them in during check in and they'll go in the same safe mentioned above.

11—Please do not pray out in the woods. We understand it feels like a reverent place, but it just isn't safe. Pray in your cabins, in the cafeteria, and anywhere indoors, but do not pray to any form of deity outdoors where anyone (or anything) can hear you.

12—The horse corral is a fun place, but only if you follow the rules! Be quiet, be courteous, and mind the horses—they are beautiful and wonderful creatures, but they must be respected.

13—If for some reason you find yourself outdoors and unable to find the cafeteria, under no circumstances are you to go to the horse corrals. The horses may sound like they're frightened or that something's wrong, but they're in no danger.

14—Do not go into the marsh.

15—If during an activity a camper you don't recognize joins in, ask their name and what cabin they stay in. If they

- Are unusually pale with blue lips

- Are unable to look you in the eyes

- Do not give their name

- Change the subject and ask for your name

- Tell you they stay in Cabin 16, 19, or 21

Immediately end the conversation and tell your counselor that there is a Lost Camper in your group. They will end the activity and likely take you to the cafeteria. The Chef will keep you safe until the situation is handled.

16—Under no circumstances do you tell a Lost Camper your name. Under no circumstances do you follow them to any of the following locations:

- Any of the mentioned cabins above, they are unused and unsafe

- The Horse Corral

- The marsh

- The Arts and Crafts Room

17—If one of your cabin mates goes missing, tell your counselor immediately. We may be able to save them from becoming a Lost Camper.

18—If you feel anything is not right, anything at all, tell your counselor.

19—If you feel your counselor can no longer be trusted, talk to the Chef.

20—And remember to have fun!

Mr. and Mrs. Louis Bram

LEECH ADVISORY

Hi again, wow, I did not expect so many people to be interested in Camp Golden Oak. Some of you questioned what the hell was going through my parent's minds when they sent me there, and after reading that rule list, I completely agreed. I managed to get my dad on the phone and brought up that I'd found some of the souvenirs from Camp Golden Oak as a way to mention the old place.

One of my suspicions was correct—dad never saw this 'rule sheet', and I'm betting mom didn't either. I don't know why I didn't show it to them or talk about the camp's bizarre rules. The more I pick my brain about it, the more I feel like I've forgotten something really important.

But anyway, I'm getting off track. I dug more through the folder, there's a lot there, but the next thing that really caught my eye was the 'Leech Advisory'. Yeah. It's just going to get weirder from here.

The notice looked like it had been pinned to a wall, and judging by the rip near the top, I tore it down to take with me. Younger me was a little shit.

The paper has some sort of tacky stain near the corners, I'm assuming from a sticky child's fingers, and it's meant for the campers to read.

Greetings, campers of Camp Golden Oak! I hope you're having the time of your life this summer!

Now, we've had some heavy rain lately, I hope you've had fun with your extra time in the arts and craft room and are ready to go out and have fun! This week's activities will include more nature hikes through the woods and seeing who will be the first camper to climb to the top of the rock wall this summer!

However, part of the rain means the ground is quite muddy, and although they usually stick to the marshes, the leeches love to go exploring when the ground's like this. Don't worry! Leeches are nothing to be scared of! They're a part of nature, just like the raccoons we see reclining around the dumpster behind the cafeteria. Here are some things you can do to make sure you don't get hurt:

1—Wear long pants and tennis shoes, tucking your pants into your socks. It looks silly, but it prevents the leeches from hooking onto your skin! If it's too warm to wear a jacket, don't worry about it, but some of the leech species around here can drop from the trees and land on your arms and neck. You'll feel them a bit quicker, but it's better to be safe than sorry!

2—If you find a leech on your body, don't panic! First, call for your counselor. If they are a distance away, determine if the leech has bit into your skin. You shouldn't be able to feel it. Give them a quick tug, if they come right off, then place them on the ground and wait for your counselor to come and identify the type.

3—If the leech has attached itself to you, remember, do not panic. Wait for your counselor. Do not attempt to remove it by yourself.

4—Once your counselor has removed and identified the leech, you will either be taken to the main office where Mrs. Bram will clean off the wound and send you on your way, or to Chef in the cafeteria. Some of the leeches around here have some nasty germs in their mouths, but Chef knows exactly how to clean up the wound so you don't get sick!

5—Remember to tell your counselor immediately if you find a leech on your body. Don't be embarrassed if it's crawled somewhere that is covered by a bathing suit, we're here to help. If any young women are too embarrassed to have the Chef take care of their leech bite, then Mrs. Bram will do her best to treat it.

Thank you very much! Reminder that all horse related activities are suspended with the trails being in the condition that they're in. Be safe out there, campers, and remember to have fun!

—Mr. and Mrs. Louis Bram

———————

Okay, that one's not too weird. I do remember the leech infestation that happened when I think I was eleven, now that I think about it. One of the kids had to go home early because of a leech bite that had gotten infected. I guessed he just didn't go to the counselor about it.

I thought it was nothing until I got my finger stuck on the tacky substance in the corner, and realized that the paper felt a little thick. With a little careful tearing, I found that there was another paper stuck to the back. It's the same print, and it's also talking about the leeches... but this time it's directed at the counselors of Camp Golden Oak.

I remember my counselor, Maggie. She seemed a bit dippy but she meant well. I don't know how I didn't rip the back page to shreds attempting to get it unstuck from the front, but it's readable and... this has taken a bit of a turn. I'll let you guys read it for yourselves.

———

Counselors of Camp Golden Oak,

I hope you're having a good time. I'm proud of each and every one of you for taking care of your campers, you're all doing a great job. A special shout out to Margaret Wyler for handling the situation last week with the Lost Camper, you immediately took action and proceeded calmly and efficiently, and because of that you may have saved a child's life.

The leech infestation has invaded the main camp ground rather than just sticking to the marsh as usual. The heavy rain and high winds are likely to blame. Although this means we'll likely have a reprieve from the Lost Campers as they seem to have a distaste for harsh weather, it means we have to be on our A Game when it comes to these leeches.

If a camper tells you there is a leech stuck to them, immediately call your other campers to your presence and have them check themselves over for any parasites. Examine the child in question and the leech.

1—Is the leech brown/black, possibly with darker patterns on its skin? Immediately remove the leech, try to be gentle so as to not hurt your camper, and dispose of it by sprinkling it in salt and putting it in a dry place. If you have your partner counselor with you, the rest of the campers can stay with them as you take the bitten camper to the main office. My wife will clean the wound and calm them down. There is nothing to worry about.

2—Is the leech gray or white, with either red patterns on its back or what looks like green boils on its skin? Do not panic. Put on your gloves, take the salt you should have in your first aid kit and sprinkle some on its back. It should immediately detach, but be careful! It'll try to make a run for it and they are quick. Grab it and crush it beneath your foot multiple times until its black blood soaks the ground. Do not attempt to crush one if you're not wearing shoes or only wearing flip flops, use the first aid kit if you have to. Once it's destroyed, have your partner counselor bury the remains in salt.

3—Immediately after killing the infected leech, have your partner counselor look over each of the children while you take the bitten one to the cafeteria. Chef will likely be in the kitchens preparing the next meal or he'll be putting together a puzzle in his private quarters. Loudly knock three times on his door before entering and explain the situation.

4—Treating one of these leech bites is extremely painful for the one bitten. It involves burning the bite wound and spreading on some herbs that burn even more than the flame. Even though it might be frightening, please stay there for the camper. Hold their hand and remind them it will be okay. You might see something drip from the wound that is not blood, that means the treatment is working. I'd advise not looking though, it isn't pleasant to see.

5—Once the bite has been purged, take the child back to the cabin and put them on bed rest for a few days. The wound may have been purged but infected leeches will be attracted to the bite mark left by another of their kind. It's better to have them rest up while they heal. We have coloring books and materials in the office, request them for your laid up camper so they have something to occupy their time with. If they have to go outside, make sure they wear long sleeves and pants so the scent of their blood is at least partially masked.

6—There are some times when your campers do not tell you when they have been bitten by a leech. You must stay on high alert, especially after tramping through muddy trails or if you stray too close to the marsh. Do not be ashamed if the latter happens, this may be a huge campground but even I find myself walking towards the marsh on days my mind wanders. Keep your eyes open for:

- Leech bites, they should bleed quite a bit and they'll have a triangular shape if they're fresh. If they've aged a bit, they'll probably resemble a mosquito bite. Have Chef look at a bite you find suspicious, particularly if your camper is acting shifty about it.

- Your camper experiencing a combination of any of the following symptoms—insomnia, seeming to mentally 'check out' during activities, irritability, rashes on their necks and/or wrists, skin going pale, vomiting, sleep walking, reckless behavior, random bouts of uncontrollable and unexplainable giggling, reddening of the eyes and bleeding of the gums.

- Your camper purposely distancing themselves from you but watching your every move intently.

- Your camper daring others to either kiss them or drink their blood.

- Your camper is trying to attach leeches to others.

If caught early enough, Chef can still expel the poison and the child will be fine, although they'll likely have to be sent home early with how exhausted they'll be from the ordeal.

However, and I cannot stress this enough, if the infected camper attempts to attack another one of your campers, your priority is the healthy campers. Do what you have to do to not let others get bitten. The transmission is much more effective when going from human to human. If the infected camper runs off to the marshes, let them go. The Lost Campers do not tolerate Infected Campers, and if the Infected Camper manages to fight them off, Chef will make sure it's handled.

If the worst happens, you will not be blamed. I've personally interviewed each and every one of you. I know I can trust you with the safety of your campers, and if we escape this wet summer with only one or two Infected Campers, I'll consider it a good year. You can do all you can and there might be one that slips through the cracks.

May the Wild's God protect us this summer,
Mr. Louis Bram.

THE HORSE CORRAL AT CAMP GOLDEN OAK

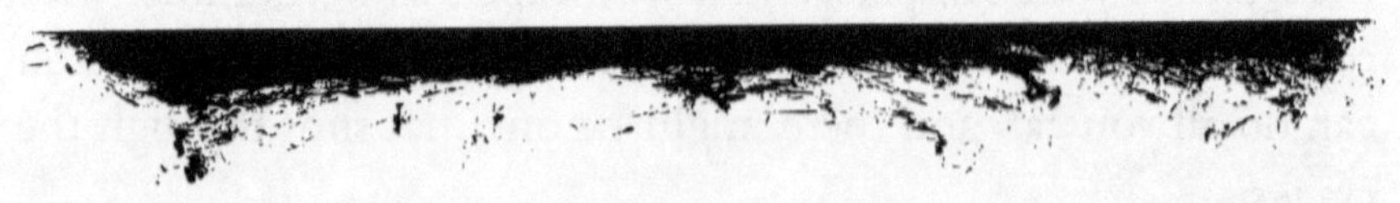

Hey, it's me again, the camper from Camp Golden Oak. Thanks for all the responses so far, I've even managed to get in contact with a few other people who have actually gone to the place. Nothing too exciting, other than some of the odder occurrences I've already mentioned, but at least I know I'm not alone.

I'm still going through the folder's contents, there is a lot of shit in here, not to mention some things seem to have fallen out and got shuffled around in the box. I think I found a series of notes passed between me and a friend at the time, her name was Marie, she was the kid with all the allergies, we've all had a friend like that growing up, I think. I haven't spoken to her since Camp Golden Oak, but I'm still working on reading the notes—some of them are smudged and it's probably going to be impossible to get them entirely legible but I hope to have them done soon. For now, I found another set of rules, specifically for the horse corral.

Yeah, there's more rules, who's fucking surprised. I had one of those disposable cameras as a kid, I took at least one each year I was at camp. I must've snapped a pic of the rules hung up in the stables. The picture's pretty dark, but I can make out the rules clearly enough. I doubt I'll post any of the pics here, mostly because ninety eight percent of them have my fingers in the way of the lens or they're incredibly blurry.

Listen, disposable cameras were not user friendly to a clearly oblivious ten year old.

If we're going by my memories alone, I loved the horses. I always wanted to ride this beautiful black one named Onyx. She was a sweetie and liked to have her neck pet. I'm learning that I can no longer trust my memories though. Which is probably the worst part of this experience.

Anyway, rules are listed below.

Welcome to the Horse Corral! We hope you're here to have a good time! The horses at Camp Golden Oak are gentle creatures who love to be fed carrots and to have fun. Just remember to follow the rules below and we'll all have a great and safe time!

1—Horses are living creatures who deserve our respect. They are not toys. You are not to hit, shout at, or kick the horses. If you are caught abusing one of our horses, you will be sent back to your cabin for the rest of the day's activities and will be strictly reprimanded. If you are caught twice, you will be sent home.

2—There is no room to fool around in the stables or the corral. Horseplay is reserved for the horses. Rough housing could lead to someone getting hurt, and we don't want that to happen.

3—If you want to help out with care of the horses, be sure to ask the Stablemaster, Ms. Grace Triggs. She always appreciates a gentle hand!

4—All the horses in the stable are for the campers to ride, except for Domino. He is to be ridden by counselors and Ms. Triggs only. Do not ask to ride Domino.

5—All the horses at Camp Golden Oak that are safe for riding are colored bay, black, or dapple gray.

6—There are group rides every week led by Ms. Triggs, be sure to sign up quickly as spots will go quickly!

7—Remember that horses can see things that we do not. You may have to go back early from a ride if Domino becomes spooked, but it's better to be safe than sorry.

8—Do not come to the corral alone. It isn't safe. Be sure to go with your counselor or Ms. Triggs! They know how to keep you safe.

9—If you're about to go on a ride and you see a white or palomino horse approaching the group, do not approach this horse. This is not one of Golden Oak's horses. Leave them alone.

10—These horses can occasionally be spotted near the lake and the marsh. Again, do not approach them. They will wander off on their own sooner or later.

11—If you see Domino walking around the camp with no rider, do not be alarmed. He occasionally likes to open his stall door and go for a walk. He likes to make sure we're all safe! He'll be back for supper time. Please do not attempt to pet him or distract him from his duties.

12—If you see your friend trying to play with one of the white or palomino horses, call them back to you. They might tell you that they think it's okay, but these horses are not safe. Under no circumstances are you to climb on their backs or attempt to guide them by their reigns, especially if they're near the lake or the marsh.

It's better to just leave them alone rather than get hurt.

13—If you see a camper riding a white or palomino horse, yell as loud as you can. Get the attention of a counselor, Chef, or Ms. Triggs immediately. They will handle the situation.

14—There may seem to be campers on occasion that seem to have control of these strange horses and are able to guide them. Take a closer look but do not approach. Does this camper resemble a Lost Camper? (See your camp rules.) If they're a Lost Camper, then immediately leave the area and tell your counselor.

15—If a Lost Camper attempts to approach you while riding one of these horses while you are alone, if you are near the stables, run inside and find Ms. Triggs. If you cannot find Ms. Triggs, get into Domino's stall. He might not be for you to ride but he will not hurt you.

16—If you want to give a horse a snack, ask Ms. Triggs for a carrot, an apple, or a sugar cube! The horses love a snack!

—Mr. and Mrs. Louis Bram

Update: I... think I remembered something.

I was trying to organize the series of notes that were exchanged between me and Marie when the memory just hit me. I suppose thinking about the damn place enough shook something loose. Part of me wonders if it's just something my mind made up, but after going through this folder, I'm not sure anymore.

I think this happened my second or third year at camp. I was running down one of the horse trails, it was late at night. My heart was pounding in my chest, but I didn't dare turn around. I heard a voice call out for me and I stumbled over a root and fell to the ground, my knee scraped against a rock.

That's when I heard it.

You know that squelch your tennis shoes make after they've been soaked? It was that. The sound grew closer, and I scrambled back to my feet and took off again.

I saw the stables, lit up by two lanterns at the front, and I ran faster. I didn't want to see what was behind me, but I knew if I stopped it would catch me. And I didn't want it to catch me.

I opened the stable door and slammed it behind me, my head whipping around, searching for something, anything... and then I saw Domino.

I was a pretty tiny child, but Domino was an enormous horse. Easily the biggest of the stables, he was jet black with a white spot over his right eye. He looked over at me before quietly nickering. I took that as my invitation. Feeling my fingers shake, I opened up his stall and slipped inside. My legs turned to jelly and I fell to the ground. Domino ignored me, choosing to eat hay and flick his tail.

The door opened and Domino's head raised.

I heard the squelching of wet tennis shoes slowly approach, and I managed to stand enough to peer over the stall door.

There it was. A Lost Camper.

He was a boy, probably around twelve, with sunken, pale cheeks and bangs hanging into his eyes. He was completely soaked, I saw goose bumps on his arms but he wasn't shivering. He didn't look up, but he knew I was there.

" Can we go play again? Like we did last summer?" His voice was so sad, and I was sad too.

I shook my head. "We can't play anymore, Michael. I'm really sorry. Go back to the other Lost, please, or Chef will come get you."

'Michael' rested a wet hand on the stall door, but withdrew it quickly as Domino lunged, his body slamming against the door. He gulped as he stared at the horse. And I saw his eyes.

They looked watery, like he was sick, but his pupils were shrunk down to pin points, black dots in a blue expanse. He looked at me and I felt like he recognized me. He opened his mouth to say something when the stable door banged open and a bright light shined in.

"Get your arse out of here, you lil demon! Out!"

Michael bolted, his shoes squelching slowly disappearing into the distance.

Ms. Triggs walked up to the stable door, lifting up her flashlight. She wasn't a very big woman, but the gun on her waist wasn't the prop one she used for telling stories by the fireplace at the meal hall. She sighed and shook her head.

"There's no bringing back the Lost, kid. Come on, I'll let you bunk with me tonight."

I don't remember anything after that, except maybe heading back in the morning. Ms. Triggs didn't bring up anything about last night, only lightly ribbing me for snoring like an old man. I laughed and ran to get breakfast. I knew Chef always made his blueberry pancakes on Saturday morning and they always went fast.

I'm only getting pieces of the puzzle, it's still filled with giant holes, but I can tell you this—

I know Michael. But I don't remember him like that. I remember playing soccer with him, and splashing each other while we swam in the lake... and I remember that he didn't come back to camp next year.

NOTES PASSED AT CAMP GOLDEN OAK

Hi guys, it's the camper from Golden Oak again. Sorry it's been so long, work got busy, some personal shit happened, I'm sure you all get it.

So last time I brought up the notes passed between me and Marie at Camp Golden Oak. It was a pain in the ass to get them sorted. Not to mention some weren't even legible, I've done my best to transcribe them below but you'll notice gaps, I'm sure.

I do remember a bit more about Marie. She went all three years of camp, we always ended up sharing a cabin at least two of those times. She was the camp friend, she lived in the UP (the upper peninsula of Michigan for the non Michigan readers) and we just didn't live close enough to be friends all year around. But she was a sweet girl, a little bit of a crybaby, but sweet. She loved the Arts and Crafts room the most. I'm glad her handwriting was as nice as it was, it was hard enough working out my chicken scratch. I labeled the notes as 'Marie' and 'Sarah', Sarah being my name.

Anyway, might as well get on with it. I don't have any memories of the incidents described below... but I think I know what happened to Michael now.

———

I'm so bored.—Sarah

If the Chef catches us passing notes during morning announcements again, we're gonna get in a lot of trouble. —Marie

He won't get us in trouble! He'll just glare before taking them again. You excited for riding horses today? —Sarah

Not really. That creepy Palomino keeps following me. It's scary. —Marie

Just ignore him! He's just a wild horse. He'll wander off when he gets bored. I call dibs on Onyx. —Sarah

What if Michael wants Onyx? —Marie

Don't be stupid. Michael always picks Patch. And why would I care what horse Michael wants to pick anyway? —Sarah

Sarah, you're not fooling anyone. —Marie

———

I think I like Michael. Really like him. —Sarah

Took you long enough. Whatcha gonna do about it? —Marie

I dunno. Probably just pretend I don't. Michael's nice, but he's also nice as a friend. —Sarah

He is. You should totally hold hands with him at the bonfire on Saturday though. —Marie

Ugh, I might skip. Who cares about the Wild's God anyway? —Sarah

Don't be like that! I think I actually heard the whispers last time. —Marie

You did not. The Wild's God isn't real. —Sarah

I mean, the Brams seem to think so, and so does Chef. —Marie

Girls, note passing during night announcements isn't allowed. —Unknown (Handwriting that's quite large and blocky, not either mine or Marie's.)

Well. That was embarrassing. At least Chef didn't confiscate our notes this time. —Sarah.

———

I think I saw a Lost Camper. —Sarah

What???? Is this why you were late to getting back to the cabin tonight? —Marie

Yeah, Michael asked to see me by the bathrooms after light's out. But on the way back, I heard someone calling my name and I turned... It looked like a Lost Camper at least. A really pale and soaking wet kid wearing a camp shirt. I ran as fast as I could back, luckily the door wasn't locked or I would be in trouble. —Sarah

You're not supposed to look back at them. —Marie

I'm fine, Marie. I promise. Nothing bad happens by just looking. —Sarah

So you didn't kiss Michael? —Marie

Go to sleep or I'm hurling a pillow at your face. —Sarah

———

That stupid palomino followed me nearly back to camp this time. I feel sick. —Marie

Ignore him! He's being a dumb horse. —Sarah

I told Ms. Triggs, and she seems pretty mad. She's gonna go out riding with Domino to chase him away, or at least try. I hope she doesn't shoot the poor thing. He doesn't seem mean. —Marie

Of course he doesn't. But rules say don't touch the wild palominos. —Sarah

I know the rules, Sarah. —Marie

Sorry. I'm gonna go to sleep. —Sarah

Did you see that thing on the hike today? —Marie

No, and you didn't see anything either. —Sarah

Sarah! It was the Wild's God! I'm sure it was! —Marie

It was just a stupid tree swaying in the wind. —Sarah

Trees don't walk. Except in movies. I swore it had a face too. And Domino didn't spook, so it wasn't something evil. And the Wild's God isn't evil. —Marie

Marie, don't be silly. The Wild's God is just something the Brams made up to make the camp seem special. Listen, I don't wanna talk about this. Can we just talk about something else? —Sarah

Please don't skip the bonfire this Saturday. —Marie

I'm going to skip the bonfire. —Sarah

Why? Couples hold hands around there all the time! You could be a real couple with Michael. —Marie

Michael thinks the whole ceremony about the Wild's God is a bunch of crap. So we're skipping and going to take a walk around the lake. —Sarah

Are you crazy!? What about the marsh? —Marie

What about it? We're not gonna go near it, it's gross and smells terrible. And we're not crazy, we just want to be alone. —Sarah

You're making a mistake. I'll tell the Chef if I don't see you. —Marie

If you tell the Chef, I'll never talk to you again. Ever. Leave me alone, and don't even think about sitting near me during arts and crafts. —Sarah

———————

(Here I found a letter folded up several times and pretty crumpled up. It definitely isn't from me or even directed to me, but I have no idea how it's in my things.)

Chef,

My name is Marie. I have a best friend named Sarah. She's going to try to skip the bonfire on Saturday night to go hang out with Michael. She doesn't want me to tell anyone, but I'm scared for her. She could get hurt. I know she saw a Lost Camper following her last week, and I'm scared it'll find her again. Please try to stop her from going. I know she'll never talk to me again, but I need to make sure she doesn't get hurt.

Thank you,
Marie

———————

Marie,

I'm really sorry about what happened. I know you're probably still sleeping after what happened, but I need to make sure you know I'm sorry.

You were right. I was being stupid. Michael was just so brave, and I want to be brave too. I wanted to impress him. And because of that, I'm never going to see him again.

The Lost Campers. Michael thought one of them was his friend. That was the one I saw after meeting Michael at the bathrooms. They're evil. They smell like a wet, moldy basement. They started singing the camp song and chased us into the woods. I almost ran into the marsh when you saved me. You stuck a foot in instead though...

you had like three leeches stuck to you, I'm so sorry. That must've really hurt.

Michael's still missing. The Brams and some of the counselors have been searching nonstop, but I don't think they'll ever find him. He's one of the Lost Campers now.

I'm so sorry. I should've believed you. Because I was stupid, you got hurt, and Michael's gone forever. I know you'll probably be going home after you feel a little better. I don't blame you if you hate me.

Please don't hate me.

—Sarah

Sarah,

The Wild's God spoke to me during my dream.

You need to open your ears to him or Michael's going to lead you to join the Lost.

I will be going home. And I'll miss you lots. But I'll see you next year, and we'll pick up right where we left off.

I don't hate you. You are and always will be my best friend.

—Marie

THERE'S A GIRL WHO LIVES ALONE IN THE WOODS

Down a long dirt road, past a mile or so of forest, there's a girl that lives all by herself in a big house. All of her relatives have passed, leaving her a treasure trove of valuables and money that she keeps on the property. There's not even a dog to keep her safe from people who would take those things away.

And when the wrong ears hear all those things, their eyes fill with dollar signs, and they decide to make the trek.

They always make the same wrong assumption, though—

That I'm really *alone*.

Four men came to my house a few nights ago. I saw one of them carrying a crowbar and another had a gun tucked into his pants. I only closed my curtains and locked my bedroom door. I've seen this happen many times and I can tell you exactly what came to pass, even if I wasn't a witness to all of it.

They enter through the front door. They're always surprised to see it's unlocked, but they likely assume it's because I live so far out and am comfortable in the safety of seclusion.

They split up in pairs, not worried about what they'll do if they find the owner of the house. She's just a girl, one who stares at the ground when she talks and who trips over her words in a rush to get them out. She's clearly not very bright and obviously not very strong.

One of my monsters is hiding under the couch tonight. When he saw they were coming, he slipped under there. One of their ankles strays too close and he's pulled under with not even a scream. In the morning, the man will wake up in a country where he doesn't speak the language and with no memory of how he got there, only that there's a bite mark on his leg and that he'll never feel safe in the dark again.

He is the lucky one. The monster under the bed is merciful.

The monster in the closet is not.

The one with him assumes that the missing man is pulling a prank, he calls his name and starts poking around for him. He asks the other two (who are going through my grandmother's music boxes) where their friend went. They have no clue. They didn't see it happen.

The searcher opens a pantry and out a clawed hand flies, wrapping around his throat and dragging him in. He screams, screams, and *screams* until his throat is cut. In seconds, all the skin is flayed from his body, landing next to his body in a pile of fleshy ribbons. Eyeballs are squished like grapes. Teeth fall from his jaws and to the ground with a sound not unlike dropping a handful of marbles. He isn't long in the world, but those remaining seconds are filled with some of the most excruciating pain a person could remotely comprehend.

When the other two throw open the door, they find the whole pantry is soaked top to bottom with blood. The remains of their friend are unrecognizable as such, other than the scraps of his clothing and his crowbar.

The two panic. They split up in their haste to escape.

One runs into the backyard. His mistake.

The monster outside the window lives out there, and he doesn't really interfere with trespassers unless someone bothers him. And when someone slams the back door open while screaming at the top of their lungs, well... that bothers him, as it would most people, I think.

I don't talk about the monster out there, only that once his target was in sight, the unlucky soul didn't have the benefit of a quick death. He was dragged into the shed and what happens in there I can't tell you. I just know that the man didn't expire until three nights later and when that was happening, he was begging for death.

The last one, in a blind panic, ran up the stairs to my room. He threw himself against the door once, twice, three times before it gave way. I screamed and ran to my corner, heart thumping in my ears.

The man got up and stared at me. Fear turned to realization that I was the girl in the house, and not only that, I was somehow responsible for the mutilation of his friend. He took out his gun and pointed it at my face, calling me a slew of horrible names.

He stops when he looks at my eyes.

Once blue, now one's turned green. The pupil is constricted to a pinpoint, the other one looks washed out compared to how bright the other is. He can't stop staring at my eye.

The gun nearly slips from his hand until I catch it, firmly pressing his hand to the grip. He's starting to shake, sweat dripping down the side of his face.

I stare at him until he turns that gun on himself, putting it in his mouth before pulling the trigger. Blood paints the ceiling as the body thuds to the ground.

I don't know what things people see when they look into my green eye, but I doubt it's anything good.

I go to bed after this, knowing the monster under the bed will clean up after tonight's debacle. Not the closet monster, he's always been a real dick about that. The monster outside the window isn't allowed in the house. He tracks mud everywhere and no one really likes his staring.

It's good that he cleans, though. Because I have to get back to work. I'm working on a book about thieves who think they can rob a girl who lives all alone, only to find out that she's not alone. And not only that, but that girl is the worst monster of them all.

Because she created the three monsters that live under the bed, in the closet, and outside the bedroom window.

I DON'T WANT TO BE A MERMAID ANYMORE

I mean, every kid went through that phase, right? When you'd go to the pool you'd dive in and imagine your legs fusing into one and growing scales of your favorite color. I wanted blue scales. More than once I'd surface hacking and coughing because I'd try to hold my breath for a second too long. Not pleasant. But by the time I was ten, I could do it for quite an impressive amount of time.

My dad thought it was hilarious. Mom treated it as just one of those childish things I'd grow out of. But my Uncle Craig actually encouraged it.

Uncle Craig was my mom's oldest brother, a big man with a thick stomach and a roaring laugh. Despite having four kids of his own, he loved coming to see me. He'd bring me seashells and tell me stories about his latest catch. And he always listened to me tell my mermaid stories.

I was an imaginative lil kid. I loved coming up with stories about this mermaid named Elora, who was pretty and looked just like me. My parents never cared to listen. But Uncle Craig would eat up every one. Every time he came around, he'd ask me, "So, what has Princess Elora been up to lately?" and according to him my face would light up like a lighthouse through the fog.

For my eleventh birthday, he took me on a fishing trip.

Mom tried to talk him out of it, saying I'd be bored the whole time, but Uncle Craig said that he'd 'show me a mermaid' and that was it. Mom knew I'd never shut up about fishing with Uncle Craig if he was going to show me a mermaid. So when Friday finally came around, Uncle Craig picked me up and we drove to the ocean.

Uncle Craig had his own boat, and it was actually pretty decently sized—big enough for us and three of his friends—Abe, Bobby, and Irvin. Irvin brought his twin daughters Ocean and River. They were quite a bit older than me, probably almost eighteen.

His friends were quite nice, asking my name and complimenting my Ariel backpack. Once we headed out on the water, Irvin turned and asked, "So Hazel, your uncle says you have stories about Princess Elora the Mermaid. Care to share a few?"

At first I was nervous, four adults and two older girls with all their attention on me, but once I got going about the time Princess Elora battled a hammerhead shark, I was chattering away with no fear at all. River would ask questions, like what was Elora's palace like and what she liked to eat for breakfast. Ocean didn't talk very much, but she braided my hair and made it super pretty.

I think my mom expected I'd be bored to tears or that my uncle and his friends would get drunk and rowdy. On the contrary, there were a few beers tossed around at night, but the men stayed sober the whole time.

Saturday, I fished for the first time.

That was kinda boring, but Ocean and River made it fun by singing. Both of them sounded just like the mermaids I dreamed about. Ocean would encourage me to join and even though my singing talent would make a deaf man's ears bleed, the girls would grin and bear it.

I caught a fish about midmorning. I don't really remember what it was. All I remember is screaming that I was catching something and my uncle was right behind me, encouraging me and telling me I had this, I had this!

And I did. It was a tiny little thing, but everyone acted like I had just broken a world record. Lots of cheers and slaps on the back, picture opportunities abounded, and Uncle Craig lifted me above his head and tossed me into the water. Apparently it was a tradition.

My clothes were soaked, but I was grinning from ear to ear when he pulled me back out. This was the best birthday present I could've ever gotten. I'd almost completely forgotten about the mermaid thing.

When I was shooed off to bed, Uncle Craig winked and said, "When we find a mermaid, don't worry—we'll wake you up." With a promise like that, it was almost impossible to go to sleep. I did end up drifting off sooner or later.

I was awoken by my shoulder being gently shaken and Abe's quiet voice.

"We spotted one. Come on up, lassie."

I stumbled to the deck, rubbing the sleep dust from my eyes and looking around eagerly for the mermaid. The mood had entirely changed from the day.

Ocean and River were sitting at the front of the boat. My uncle was sitting to my right while Irvin and Bobby were to the left. No one was talking, or singing, or even smiling. I frowned and opened my mouth when Abe pressed a finger to his lips.

"Shhh..."

My mouth shut. Abe stood next to me, his eyes flicking around. The only sound was water lapping at the boat.

Then Ocean gasped.

"There she is!"

I ran to the front of the boat with my uncle, my heart pounding. Was it her? Was it a real mermaid?

I saw the brief tail flip before my uncle threw the nets over her.

"Think we got it! Ocean, River, start singing!"

The sisters joined in unison, singing a song I didn't understand or know. The water turned to white foam as whatever was inside the net thrashed about. Beads of sweat dripped from my uncle's face and landed on the top of my head. He gritted his teeth and pulled harshly. "Irvin, grab hold! She's a fucking fighter!" He barked.

I got pushed out of the way as the other men grabbed the net and pulled, I heard the sound of something heavy coming out of the water.

The girls silenced their singing as the catch was hauled up and then dropped on the deck.

It was a real life mermaid.

The creature attempted to sit up as best as she could, trying to fold her tail beneath her as she looked around frantically. The lights on the boat flicked on brightly and she flinched, covering her face.

I could scarcely breathe. I'd always hoped I'd see a mermaid someday. I would pray that they were real. And the real deal was just as beautiful as I hoped. Her kelp green hair clung to her skin, patches of cerulean scales growing across her breasts and arms. Her tail flopped about uselessly, the fins translucent and glittering in the light.

Her royal blue tail, with gold flecks mixed in with the smooth scales. I barely realized I was reaching out to touch it.

Uncle Craig seized my hand before it got too close.

"Whoa, Hazel! Don't touch!"

The mermaid lowered her hands as she bared her teeth ferociously, and it showed I would've made a horrible mistake—her smile was more like a shark than a pretty mermaid princess'.

Bobby chuckled and lifted up his right hand, which was missing three fingers. "Rookie mistake. Been there done that, kiddo," he said.

I gulped and backed away.

Uncle Craig pulled a knife from the sheath on his belt, and my attention was hyper focused on that. "What are you doing?" I asked.

The mermaid's face had gone pale. She attempted to struggle away, but the twins grabbed the net and twisted it around her, making it impossible for her to crawl to the edge of the boat and jump off. My uncle paused for a moment before he turned to me.

"Remember how we gutted that catch of yours this afternoon?"

I nodded.

"This is the same concept. You can go back to bed if you don't want to see."

I swear time froze. I looked at the mermaid, who was starting to shake. Her eyes looked at me. She knew what that knife meant. I knew what that knife meant.

I didn't move. I didn't say anything. I just nodded.

Mermaids bleed an almost greenish red. She wasn't alive for much of it, Uncle Craig didn't prolong her suffering. He slowly began to cut her down the middle before he froze. "Holy..." He made the final cut fast and I saw dozens of reddish-black beads swirl about in her guts. The other men began to freak out, swearing and running their hands through their hair. Bobby's jaw dropped. "That... that can't be..." He stuttered.

"Mermaid. Caviar." Uncle Craig lifted up a handful of it, running the small beads between his fingers. He looked at me before he grinned. "I've been fishing for maids since I was your size, Hazel, this is the first time I've personally harvested mermaid eggs. You're a good luck charm."

I ran below deck to puke. I didn't make it to the toilet. I collapsed outside the bathroom and my dinner splattered across the floor. The stomach acid burned as I continued to dry heave, and it took all my strength not to pass out in my own vomit.

I don't know when the girls came down, but they didn't get mad about the mess. They cleaned me up and put me to bed.

I almost could've thought it was a dream, except in the morning when I walked up on deck to see the mermaid tails put on ice.

They'd caught one more since I was in bed. This tail was ruby red and thicker than the other. I ran my hand over the scales, and they were as smooth as they looked.

"We caught a merman after you went to bed."

I turned around to see Uncle Craig, who looked nothing but proud at his catch.

"You know how much last night's catch will pay out for me?"

I didn't answer. He continued.

"Enough to keep paying for your college. Already got my own kid's covered. Do you want anything else for your birthday? New bike? Trip to Disneyland?"

I looked back at the scaled tails. I couldn't speak. I couldn't say anything. I just remembered the look in the mermaid's eyes before the knife plunged in her chest, the spurt of blood covering my uncle's hands.

" I can understand if you're upset."

Uncle Craig sat a hand on my shoulder. "Your mom was the same when our dad took us for the first time. Mermaid catching runs in the family. Has been since your great great granddad. And it isn't pretty. But it's what we do." He ran a hand through my hair, and I flinched.

"Let's go home, kid."

Uncle Craig treated me to an enormous ice cream cone on the way home, my favorite flavor—cake batter. I ate it while trying to forget about the tails without mermaids attached to them.

I avoided my Uncle Craig a few months after that. I'd hide away in my room and pretend that I was busy. This didn't stop him from leaving me presents. I slowly grew to forgive him and soon enough, we were hanging out like old times.

It's been ten years. I'm already a published children's writer. I write books about Princess Elora the Mermaid. Kids love how she has these crazy sharp teeth, although parents not so much. Writing about her makes me happy.

Uncle Craig passed away two months ago from heart failure. He lived a good life. Long and full of happiness. One of the two things he's left me is his fishing boat.

I got in my car and drove to the ocean as soon as I could. When I got there, I saw two grown women waiting for me. It took me a second to recognize them as Ocean and River.

Ocean smiled and waved.

"Hey, Hazel! You're not so much of a kid anymore... up for a fishing trip?"

The other thing he left me was in my pocket. A list of coordinates. Places to fish.

"Can't wait. I'll drive the boat."

MY ANCESTOR'S JOURNAL

I found this journal among some things in granddad's attic. As far as I can tell, it belonged to some old relative of ours, but I'm not sure what I make of it? Maybe one of you guys can give me some help here. Maybe this is some sort of fiction the guy wrote while bored, I can't imagine running a farm was that entertaining. But at the same time, I really don't know. Some of the book's illegible, but I've inscribed what I can down below.

June 12

Another storm tonight. Real bad one too. Think lightning touched down a few times in the pasture. I'm gonna have to go out tomorrow to make sure nothing was damaged. Today was good though. Productive. Think Rose is going to have that calf soon—she's getting bigger by the day.

Alva's talking about going to Sara's grave again. I don't know if me or the boys will have time. She might have to walk there herself. And I wouldn't say it to her, but I miss Sara too. Almost too much. It's better if I stay home.

June 13

Someone was out last night in that damned storm.

Albert found him this morning. He'd let the cows out to graze and went to check on the chickens before he heard a hullabaloo coming from the pasture. He ran out there and found the poor fellow.

It was obvious he'd been out there all night, he was soaked to the bone, naked as the day he was born and for a moment I thought I had a dead man on my land. But when he started to murmur, I had Albert and Sven bring him inside while I finished up the chores.

The man's still not awake. We dressed him and set him by the fire to warm up. He's feverish, but Alva's a good girl and taking care of him. I'm surprised he's still alive after being out in the rain all night. Although I'm not holding my breath to see if he survives. The chills might take him before morning.

June 15

He finally woke up.

He'd been out since we found him, mumbling deliriously and didn't have a clue where he was. But this morning while Alva was sitting by him, he opened his eyes, sat up, and asked for water.

The man's got no memory of who he is or how he ended up in the pasture. I might end up making this month's trip to town earlier than planned, and start asking around. Someone ought to be missing him, and well, he sticks out. Handsome man, strong jaw, hair so blond it's almost white, and tall. He's head and shoulders on me in height. He also has this scar on his back. Not a whipping scar, looks like someone tried to skin him. It's only recently healed too.

In the meantime, I'll help him get healthy and see if he can handle farmwork.

June 24

We've taken to calling our guest Stefan. He seems amused by the choice and likes it, so Stefan he is.

Still no memory, but he's gotten strong enough to walk around and help keep the house neat. Alva already fancies him, practically lives to help him out and show him around. I can't say I dislike the man either. He's quiet, doesn't speak a harsh word. Since he's gotten so much better, I think I'll see about having him help me with the cows in the morning.

June 26

Cows don't like Stefan. I don't know why. But the minute Stefan steps foot in the barn, they panic, start making a ruckus and kick out at anyone who gets near them. I had to make him leave, I didn't want to panic Rose into losing her calf.

The two goats we got don't mind him, though. The male always seemed to be an ornery thing, especially when we got near his wife, but Stefan can enter their pen without getting butted. So that's his job now. Takes one more thing off of me and the boy's plates.

June 27

Alva had a nightmare last night that Rose lost her calf and gave birth to it dead. When Alva got close, the calf exploded into maggots that crawled onto Rose and ate her alive. Hell of a dream. She was pretty shaken up about it, Stefan took over her chores for the day. Good man.

Gonna make that run into town Monday. I'll bring Stefan with me. See if anyone can place him. It'll be a darn shame when he goes though. The bruises on my backside are finally fading since I don't have that damn billy goat charging me every time I go in there.

July 3

No one recognized Stefan. I'm disappointed but also a little relieved. Means he can stay around longer. We don't mind having an extra mouth to feed here, especially since he's willing to work. Sleeps in my room now, just so no tongues wag about him sleeping too close to Alva. I won't have anyone slandering my girl's name.

Stefan doesn't mind the bedroll at least. He's asleep now, his hair's still white as the day he appeared. It looks like a halo spread around his head now. His face sometimes twists in his sleep, as if he doesn't like what he's seeing. Maybe he's seeing pieces of who he used to be, but still can't put together who he is.

Poor man. I can't imagine not knowing who you are.

July 4

I had a dream last night.

Rose gave birth to her calf, dead like Alva's dream. But instead of turning into maggots, Stefan walked up to it. His mouth was turned into a grin so disturbing it made me break into cold sweats. He knelt by the calf and pulled it up by the head before biting its throat.

Worms crawled from the wound as Stefan chewed on the spoiled flesh, his teeth turned sharp as knives. He got up and walked to me. I couldn't run away, I couldn't move a muscle.

Stefan kissed me, his breath tasted like bitter rot. I could feel the worms from the meat squirming into my mouth and down my throat. I still couldn't move, and I began to choke on Stefan's tongue and the worms.

When I woke up, I'd found myself chewing on my blanket. Stefan had woken up and was getting dressed. Time for chores. He asked if I was all right. I lied and said I just had a strange dream.

My mouth still tastes like worms.

July 6

No more nightmares. None I can remember, at least. But I think I'm walking about in my sleep. When I awake in the morning, my feet are covered in mud and I got scratches on my legs like I've been walking through thorns. Feel like I've walked for miles too, my thighs ache.

Stefan's been a good help though. At night he's been massaging my back, trying to soothe the pain. Talks about his own dreams and what little he remembers.

I don't listen to all of it, the man has good hands but Stefan apparently had brothers once upon a time. Lots of them. He wasn't a farmhand, but he can't say what he used to do. Not sure if he can't or he won't.

Sven and Stefan had an argument. Don't know about what, but Sven seems to have the idea he's sweet on Alva. I don't know where the hell that idea turned up, but Sven's like his mother. Stubborn once his mind latches onto an idea.

If Stefan wanted to marry Alva, though, I'd give that marriage my blessing, if that's what the both of them wanted. He'd take good care of her.

July 7

The calf was born dead all right. Rose died too. Something must've gone wrong, the calf had gotten stuck and that's what caused the bleeding. Albert found their bodies, the calf still hanging out of Rose's body halfway as they lay in a pool of blood. The stench is so bad, I think it'll stick into the walls forever.

Trying to salvage what we can by butchering the two of them and salting the meat to save. I'm starting to think Stefan used to be a butcher. He carves meat professionally. I might see if he ever wants to leave to get him started in town.

I hate that I lost a cow. But it ain't Stefan's fault, no matter what Sven thinks. I think Sven's been paying a little too much attention in church. Devils don't walk among men, the son of the Lord made sure of that. They have no power over us.

July 15

I can't let my children know what happened this afternoon. They'd never look at me the same again.

Stefan and I were out there repairing the fence when he asked if we could go for a walk, farther from the house. So we could be alone. The look in his eyes wasn't the kind of 'alone' that I should've agreed to. But I did.

Stefan and I sinned together under the apple tree. I loved Sara, I did, but she never made me feel like Stefan did. It was bliss, like my wedding night all over again. I kissed his hands and praised his name, and I only feel guilty because of the risk of getting caught.

It's our secret. Stefan will live here, just a man with no home and nowhere to go, and we'll keep on making love like husband and wife. And no one has to know.

July 21

Sven and Stefan had another fight. At first I found it funny since Sven's still stuck on the idea that Stefan's wanting to marry Alva, but it turned into shouting and hot anger. Albert tried to get in between the two, trying to calm them down, but then Alva fainted, her skirts soaked with blood.

I took her into her room and yelled for Sven to run for the doctor. I had to undress her too if she was injured, and that's when I saw it.

A dead black kitten was curled between her thighs. As far as I can tell, she birthed it.

I hid the cat's body by the time the doctor came, and he diagnosed it as one of those 'monthly' things.

I have to talk to Alva tomorrow when she awakens.

July 22

Alva confessed to me witchcraft, but where she admits she learned it from has chilled me to the bone. Stefan gave her the tools to talk to The Devil Himself, to sell her soul to gain his power.

I didn't believe her, called her a liar and that she'll burn in hell for tarnishing a good man's name. She burst into tears and told me everything.

Stefan told her she had a gift, a power that could be unlocked. She at first resisted the idea of calling on the Devil, but he told her how much could be gained. I asked if he was a witch too. She told me he was not... but told me that he was no man either.

I'm going to have to talk to Stefan tomorrow. I don't know how I'm going to do it. But I will.

July 24

It's storming again. I still haven't talked to Stefan. I've let him sleep in my bed and kiss my body, but I can't ask him why he turned my daughter to witchcraft. I'm afraid of his answer.

Alva's strength has returned, and moreso, it's doubled. I've seen more cats. Black ones.

I had to set down my journal, I thought it was hailing, but it's not.

It's raining toads. Toads and blood.

Ju y 2

I asked Ste an what he was. What he was to have his very presence kill ca ves and turn God loving girls into witches.

He say (...) fallen from grace and that (...) end until he is gone.

(...)s go ng to k ll (...)

(This page was stained with bloody water. I can barely read it. The next five are entirely illegible.)

August 17

We buried Sven today. I've told the town there was an accident. That the cow had kicked him in the head, that he was killed instantly.

I wish I could say it was instant.

Stefan's missing. It still rains toads at night. Alva's gone too, left last night.

Albert's still here. He's all I have left. God have mercy on him please.

August 18

Stefan came back last night. He says he wants to stay but he knows I won't let him.

We both know now his presence brings hatred and death, and although he might not have borne ill will to the family who took him in, he could not stop his curse.

I kissed him through the window before I told him if he didn't get off my property I'd shoot him in the head. He laughed at that.

We both know who'd win a fight. I'm so sorry Sven. I should have listened to you.

All my animals are dead, minus that damned billy goat. Sven is dead. My daughters ran into the forest to dance with the witches and marry the Devil. All I have left in this world is Albert. And tomorrow we're packing up what little we have and getting out of here, so Stefan won't be able to find us.

I don't know if I can turn Stefan away again. I'm not strong enough.

THE WALLS SWEAT

I think I need to move again.

The doctor called it agoraphobia. I call it a rational reaction after being stalked for two years by an ex boyfriend. The moment he was finally jailed, I picked up everything and got out of there. Mom said I could move in with her, but I didn't want her to see what I'd become.

The new apartment was across the state, cheap, and had plenty of delivery services. Once I entered that building, I resolved the closest I'd get to leaving it was to get the mail every other day. I worked from home, freelance writing. Unpredictable, at best, but I'd managed to get it to work for me.

The place was actually really nice at first glance. No cracks, no drafts. The stove worked like a charm. The fridge was cold. Heck, even the lightbulbs didn't need changing. The building occasionally settled loudly, but it wasn't too loud. Maintenance made sure this place was nice.

Neighbors weren't too off either, although I only talked to one of them- an old lady who had lived there since the place was built. She was a widow, had a fat ugly cat, and she brought me chocolate chip cookies that tasted even better than my mom's shortly after I moved in. I never invited her in, but she was kind. She even brought me my mail sometimes. I figured this place was the perfect place for the new start I wanted.

At first, I blamed it on the open window during a rainstorm. I'd come into the room and found the wall next to my bed dripping water. I hadn't remembered leaving the window open, but I was pretty scatterbrained once I got relaxed in this place. I just closed the window and wiped down the wall, resolving to be more careful.

Then I noticed that the wall dripped a *lot*. Not like a leak from the apartment above. It was like condensation on a bottle, the walls would just grow little beads of water and drip. I complained to the landlord, but unsurprisingly, he told me the building 'just did that sometimes'. Ass.

Around the fifth time this happened, some of the water got in my mouth. I was just wiping down the wall, it had gotten exceptionally wet this time, and some just flicked into my mouth. I gagged, it tasted like... sweat.

It tasted *exactly* like sweat.

Disgusting, but I rationalized this wasn't too strange. Maybe it was the paint that gave the condensation that salty taste. Nothing too strange. I just had a wall... that sweat.

Then came the day I hit my head. I had tripped on a rug and knocked myself across the forehead on the cupboard. I fetched an icepack from the freezer and stumbled into my room, deciding to screw the rest of the work day and just lie down.

I had flopped down and the ice pack slipped from my fingers, landing against the dripping wall...

And the building *sighed*.

It was a genuine sigh of relief. Like when you stumble from the hot outdoors into the cool air conditioning of home.

I yelped and snatched away the ice pack, wondering if I had given myself a concussion. The wall was silent. Slowly, I slid the ice pack across the bed and pressed it against the wall.

The wall *moved*. Slouched, more like. Relaxed, with the ice pack pressed against it.

I was shaking. I wanted to scream, and cry. Instead, I just lied down and pretended I was dreaming.

The next morning I did a first—I left my apartment and went to the old woman's room.

Her ugly cat insisted on snuggling with me, and the old lady got me milk and cookies. After the typical small talk, how work was going, the weather, how her health was, I finally decided to bring it up.

"So, last night I had something kinda weird happen here. Have the walls ever... sighed? Like, made a sound like sighing, at least?" I felt like an idiot.

The woman's milky eyes looked up in surprise, before she smiled wide. "So you notice it too. It's been a long time since someone's put it together. So long, honey, so long."

I blinked owlishly. "Ma'am, I'm not sure what you mean."

The cat jumped off my lap and ran into the bedroom. The woman watched him go and sighed, eerily sounding like my bedroom wall. "This place is special, dearie. The original landlord made a deal with the devil, you see."

"A deal with the devil?" Maybe it wasn't the wisest idea to come to a person who likely had dementia and didn't know me from her grandchildren.

She bobbed her head up and down, quite pleased. "Yes! To get the money to build this place! But it's not a bad thing, this place only has a deal with the landlord. He *refuses* to step foot in this place, try and call him, you'll see. But this place has a few quirks, I'd suppose. Just treat this place with kindness, and it will pay that back. Your neighbors on your right, they always keep the heat so high! Makes the building uncomfortable. I swear on my father's grave, they're gonna pay for that soon."

I went back to my room feeling distinctly uncomfortable.

I had to know the truth, though.

I started a routine where every night, I'd get frozen water bottles out of the fridge and the ice packs and start pressing them against the wall. It certainly helped the wall's sweating, although the sighs were still unsettling.

But sure enough, the building started to pay me back. I'd find that the oven was preheating when I wanted to make dinner, I'd find coupons in my mailbox, the carpet was always clean, little things like that. I even left the room once to get a water bottle, and I came back to find that my laptop was booted up and plugged in, my writing program up and ready to go.

The building did take care of me.

In more ways than one.

My mom called me the moment my ex was released from prison. Apparently good behavior while locked up was good enough to let him go free, with community service.

I ran to the bathroom and immediately threw up. When I was done coughing up stomach acid, I looked up on the counter to find antacid tabs and a cold washcloth.

"Thank you." I croaked, taking the washcloth and draping it around my neck, throwing the pills down my throat to calm my sour stomach. "I... I really hope this isn't too much to ask, but... I'm scared. I'm so scared he's going to come find me."

The building made a groan, but this groan was sad. Like the place actually pitied me. I felt crazy, but I kept babbling. "Just don't let him in the building. Please. I know the doors are locked, but please, *please* make sure he stays away."

I heard the click of my deadbolt and the sliding of the chain on the door. Then the poof of the oven turning on, followed by something falling out of the fridge. I walked out to see a pack of cookie dough that my elderly neighbor had given me sitting on the floor.

I made myself some cookies and curled up on the couch in a blanket to watch television. I didn't have a subscription, but apparently the building didn't care, it let me watch trash TV all night. I fell asleep and felt perfectly safe.

Exactly one week later, my ex found me. I heard singing outside my window and my heart stopped. I glanced outside to see him walking down the parking lot, looking right at my window. How did he know? How did he *know*?

The window slammed shut and the building... growled. Like a mad dog.

I could still hear him yelling, though.

"I got out on good behavior, baby! I'm a whole new man! Let me in, we can talk, I promise, I can make your life so much better..."

Again, the building growled. And then I heard it speak. Clear as day.

'Get into bed. I'll take care of him.'

Didn't need to tell me twice, hiding under the quilts felt childish, but safe. He wouldn't get in. He wouldn't get in.

I heard the smashing of the glass door that was closest to my room.

Then I heard him scream.

And scream.

And *scream*.

The next morning, the cops knocked on my door.

Apparently my ex was drunk, and after breaking the glass, fell forward and his throat was cut open by the shards still sticking out of the door. I could smell the blood in the air. I told them I was in bed, asleep with the help of medication. I didn't even hear him.

Thanking me for my help, they left.

I sat in my living room, sipping the cup of tea that had been left for me on the counter.

My stalker was dead. I had taken care of the building, and the building had taken care of *me*.

Now you're probably wondering why I'm thinking about leaving.

Last night I heard the building growl again. And then the neighbors, who always had the heat turned too high, started to scream.

I'm still thinking about it, but I think it might be irritating to wake up to screams every time someone doesn't respect the building. Might be worth waiting it out, though. They just need to learn.

THE BEST DAY OF A GIRL'S LIFE

The best day in a girl's life is when they get married.

I met Henry while working a late shift at a diner. I just got yelled at by a cranky trucker and was about to cry when the guy sitting alone at the next table grabbed my hand.

"Ignore that creep," he said, gently squeezing his fingers between mine, "he's just pissed for the sake of being pissed."

Our eyes met, and I felt that flutter in my chest. Love at first sight is real, and I felt it with Henry.

I suppose I'm a little old fashioned, being a woman who only thinks about falling in love, but that's just who I am. My mother was the same way, even though she never found another man after Daddy walked out the door. But if you think I'm stupid, I'm not. I just want to be loved, and that's not something anyone should be ashamed of.

Henry was a salesman and a good one too. But in his spare time he loved to write poetry. I encouraged him to pursue that, even if it wasn't a masculine interest. I lived for the ones he'd write about me, how he loved my golden hair, my brown eyes. He never wrote anything sexual though, I'm the kind of girl who waits for marriage and he respected me for that.

He realized he was meant for me after the third date. For the fourth one, he took me to meet his parents. His father gently teased me, while his mother fawned over me. I was the daughter she never had. On the way out, I caught her whispering to Henry to 'not let her get away'.

I wasn't going anywhere, and neither was he.

Henry proposed a little over six months ago, on our first-year anniversary. I was so excited that I burst into tears when I saw the ring gently sitting on the top of my cake slice. He'd taken me to my favorite restaurant and let me order my favorite dessert. I should've seen it coming when I saw the grin on the waitress' face. She had a ring on her left hand too, a small golden band. Simple and pure.

She knew the joy that comes with being married to your love.

I know there's girls out there who want to have a big blow out wedding. But we didn't have that kind of money, and that was okay with me. It doesn't matter how much you spend on the wedding, and even who's there.

All that matters is that you're finally with the man you care about.

It was a small affair, just Henry's family and a few of our mutual friends. The only family member I was close to was my mom, and she passed away shortly after I turned eighteen. I was alone, until I had Henry. That's all I needed.

I did buy a new dress though, a halter neck with a shimmer pattern over the top half. I wore a veil with a tiara and I felt beautiful. Henry's mother did my hair, she even offered to let me use her dress, but there was no way I could do that. Her dress, her marriage, her memories. There was no possible way I was taking her son and her dress away.

I teared up during the ceremony but that was okay. Henry was choking back his own tears as he smiled and beamed down at me.

"You may kiss the bride."

Didn't need to tell us twice, Henry was tall enough to sweep me off my feet and plant one right on my lips. I could hear Henry's mother weeping from where she sat in the front row. Her baby boy, finally married.

I didn't take my eyes off of him for the whole reception. Several times people chimed their glasses to get us to kiss, and we did every time. I didn't even eat much, I was just too happy. The food was delicious though, I didn't hear a single complaint from the guests.

Our honeymoon was to take place at my cabin, it was the one thing Daddy left to me. Quiet. Peaceful. No one to bother us. You can't even get much cell phone reception out there, that's how far you're out. It's perfect.

I won't reveal much about our wedding night. Only that it was satisfying for the both of us. Henry was so gentle, and he made me feel so loved. After it was over, we curled up together and I set my head on his chest, hearing his heartbeat and soft snores. I never felt more happy.

When I woke up the next morning, I realized that my most wonderful day was officially over.

With a heavy heart, I got up and headed to the kitchen to make breakfast. Eggs and bacon, his favorite. I have a special recipe for eggs, a special combination of seasonings to make them the most delectable one could ever have.

Add in a dose of cyanide and he never knew what hit him.

Henry loves me with all his heart. The heart that's now beating far too fast, the eyes that looked at me with love now fill with disorientation and confusion. Why is this happening to him? Why am I just sitting there, not touching my breakfast, and just *watching*?

At least he didn't vomit. Grant vomited. Spewed all over me and the table, it was disgusting. Henry falls from the chair, seizing and his eyes rolling back. I remain still, I don't reach for my phone. I don't even try to call for help.

Not until his body stills, not until he goes lax. Then I get up and kiss him one more time. To thank him for all he did for me. But my happiest day is now over and it'll never get better with him.

Nothing Henry can do will make me happier than the moment he said 'I do'.

Now I can find someone else to have the best day of my life with.

TEACHER'S PET

I think every straight guy in my school had a thing for Miss Bell.

I'm the last dude you want to come to when it comes to judging 'female beauty', but even I could admit she was pretty. Blonde hair usually drawn back in that messy bun style, a bod that would make Venus jealous, and a round face that was nearly always smiling or laughing.

She was our English II teacher, and had just transferred in that year from California. During our first class, she talked about going to college and how she used to surf on the weekends. My friend Sean elbowed me and whispered a comment about how she'd look in a bikini. My practical ass said that she probably was wearing a wetsuit when she surfed. This got the back of my head punched and Sean whispering 'Gaaaaaaaaaay' into my ear. I mean, really not *inaccurate*, but the punch wasn't necessary.

Miss Bell wasn't a bad teacher, I don't think, but she wasn't the greatest. For one, she so clearly picked favorites. I think Sean nearly creamed his pants when she leaned down next to him when wearing a low button-down shirt to explain how to properly use an adverb. Me, on the other hand, she'd just tell me to check the notes when I had a question. The notes were useful, but Jesus Christ woman, would it kill you to take two seconds out of your day to teach?

The favorites in my class were my friend Sean and Elijah, the former being captain of the debate team and the latter being halfback on the football team. Now I can say without a doubt both of these guys were hot as fuck, so I guess that's why she liked them. Her least favorite students were so clearly the girls. She ignored them more than she ignored me and that's saying something. When she did talk to them, it was condescending as fuck. Poor Tracy had the nerve to ask a question about Edgar Allan Poe's 'Masque of Red Death' and the look that Miss Bell gave her could make plants wither.

I ignored this for the most part until the rumor spread that Miss Bell was sleeping with her favorites.

I know, lots of guys would think this was the greatest thing, scoring with the hot teacher... but all her students were around fifteen or sixteen at this point. That's not fucking okay, I don't care how 'hot' people think it is. It's a bit personal for me, if I'm honest. My older sister was preyed on by one of her teachers when she was a freshman. It only came out when she got pregnant at age fourteen.

That guy's still rotting in jail and when he gets out, I'm gonna probably punch his face till it breaks.

It's the double standard of it. Up until this point, I tolerated Miss Bell, but after that skeleton fell out of the closet, I *despised* her. I decided to follow up with Sean at his house, since he was a supposed favorite.

We were playing video games, eating mozzarella sticks and just chatting it up when I decided to bring up Miss Bell.

"Soooo... what do you think about her?" I asked, snatching another mozzarella stick off the Mt. Everest Mountain pile of them. Sean's mom always wanted to make sure I was fed, I think she genuinely believed I didn't eat anywhere else but her house.

Sean's face lit up in a way that made my stomach twist. "Oh man, she's the greatest! I got to study at her house last Saturday," he said.

I swallowed. "Did... all you do was study?" I asked, glancing up the stairs to make sure Mrs. Barnett wasn't within hearing distance.

Sean grinned and leaned in close. "We did it on her kitchen table," he said.

Well, that confirmed it. "Dude, she's like, thirty! That's not cool!" I said, jerking away and nearly knocking over Mt. Mozzarella.

Sean snorted and rolled his eyes. "Come on, it's not like I didn't want it. And she's not thirty, she's twenty-eight," he said, as if that made it all better.

"I'm telling you, it's kinda creepy that a *twenty-eight* year old woman wants to 'do it' with a sixteen-year-old," I said.

"It won't be creepy when I'm twenty-eight and she's forty... is that math right?"

I shoved him and was about to tell him exactly what I thought when Mrs. Barnett came downstairs with hamburgers and chattered our ears off. By the time she left, all the courage I had about broaching that topic again with Sean had left. I know that makes me a coward, but it's kinda hard to tell someone they're being victimized when they think they've reached cloud nine.

God, I really should've talked with Sean about it sooner.

That Friday I'd forgotten my copy of 'To Kill a Mockingbird' in Miss Bell's class and was heading back to get it when I saw she wasn't alone in class. Maybe hoping to get some evidence of her creeping on teenage boys, I listened in.

I recognized the other person as Malcolm. Malcolm wasn't the brightest bulb in the package, he'd been held back a year and thought of himself as a badass just because he graffiti'd the school with giant spray paint dicks once. Right now, Malcolm was crying, and I felt sick to my stomach.

"I just... I just don't wanna lose you, Tia," he said between choked sobs.

"Oh, baby," Miss Bell brought Malcolm into a tight hug, "You won't lose me. I love you, and you love me. That's why I know you'll do your very best to keep me."

Malcolm sniffled and pulled back, but there was this oddly peaceful smile on his face. "I'll do it. You know I can," he said.

"That's my baby."

I darted off after that, resolving on Monday that I'd go to the principal and tell him about the conversation I heard. I needed that much time to work up my nerve... I really wish I wasn't such a coward then.

That night Malcolm went into Taco Bell and put three bullets in Chase Stanford's chest.

It was all over Facebook. My feed went from cute animal rescue stories and memes to 'HOLY SHIT SOMEONE'S SHOOTING UP TACO BELL'. The only person killed was Chase and thank god no one else was injured, but it shook me to the core when it came out that the shooter was Malcolm... and that he was still at large.

It was like everyone went fucking crazy over the span of a single night. My mom ended up guarding the front door with a gun while my dad watched the back door while wielding a baseball bat. I was ordered to stay in my room and if I heard anything suspicious to immediately call 911.

How crazy, do you ask?

Well, Malcolm's murder spree had only just begun, and it wasn't only him who had suddenly gained a lust for blood.

An hour after Malcolm killed Chase, someone broke into a party at Elijah's house and proceeded to pummel the shit out of him before putting a bullet in his back. Unlike Chase, Elijah managed to survive after some serious surgery, although he'd never walk again. The cops weren't sure if Elijah's attempted murderer was Malcolm or someone else, although if it was Malcolm, well...

Malcolm ended up getting stabbed to death that night.

He was found with a dozen stab wounds in his chest and neck, bleeding out on a street corner. He didn't even make it until the medics got there. In his jacket pocket was a confession and a dedication. He was doing this all for his girl, to prove that he was going to be her true love forever and ever.

Murder. Murder everywhere. Everyone in my school made it their responsibility to keep everyone updated as soon as they could. All I could do was watch.

Max Reid broke into Brad Watson's house with a knife and after stabbing his mom, went after Brad. Brad ended up throwing Max down the stairs and the idiot broke his neck. It came out later that Max's knife was the one used to kill Malcolm.

Brad ended up trying to break into the hospital where Elijah was being treated (god knows how he found out) and tried to get to him. He obviously got arrested.

Someone broke into Jake Curtis' house and when he found out Jake wasn't there, ended up shooting his parents. They both died.

Jake wasn't there because he was choking Oliver Ballard to death. His hunter caught up to him and executed him.

The list goes on and on.

I found out the pattern real quick. Each of the murderers/victims were favorites of Miss Bell. I had a breakdown and told my parents what I'd figured out. They immediately called the cops and tipped them off. Of course the cops went to Miss Bell's house, but she was long gone, probably not even returning home after school let out. Her car was found abandoned a few miles out of town.

I ended up getting questioned about the other 'favorites' and I listed who else I knew was rumored to be one. I'd like to think I saved a few lives by doing that.

I didn't save Sean's though.

When the police caught up to him, he'd been in the process of shooting another student in the head. The mystery second shooter. I don't know how they talked him down from the gun, but he was brought in. He's going to spend a long, long time in prison.

The sun came up and over a dozen people were dead. Five favorites remained, and all of them were locked up in prison. Their stories were basically all the same, though—Miss Bell told them that they had to.

That fucking bitch. She'd managed to manipulate all of her teenage lovers into murdering each other before she skipped town. Why, we don't know. Miss Bell's gone with the wind. Heck, they found out that wasn't even her real name. Her real identity is a mystery.

I've graduated by now. Every week I go visit Sean in prison. He's gotten his GED at least. I'm proud of him for sticking around. At least two of the other kids that were caught committed suicide within a month of incarceration.

Last time I saw him, though, I noticed something on his left hand. A golden ring. I asked who gave it to him.

He just smiled and changed the subject, but I'm worried about him.

I wonder if Miss Bell is still lurking around, waiting for her favorite student to get out of prison.

WALTER THE GHOST

Two months ago we moved into our new place. It's honestly amazing, huge property, beautiful forests, and an old barn out back that my wife Lydia hoped to remodel into a workshop. She loves wood carving.

We have two sons and a daughter. Elliot is ten, Joey is eight, and Samantha is five. The old house is big enough for the kids to have their own rooms, but Joey still gets night terrors, so he bunks up with Elliot. Elliot doesn't complain, he's a solid big brother.

Course, no move is without its difficulties. The kids miss all their old friends, they're still adjusting to a new school, a new schedule. The job I had lined up told me I was no longer needed, so things went belly up there. Bills got a little tight.

So that's why I didn't bat an eyelash when Samantha started talking about Walter.

Samantha has always had a hell of an imagination. She tended to make up a new 'friend' every week. A few weeks before it was Paula, a girl about her age wearing a bright red dress. Before that it was Ruby, Mary, Nick... you get the point. Typical attention span of a little one.

But Walter stuck around. Walter was an 'old man', which by Samantha's standards meant probably around forty or fifty. He lived in the closet and Samantha would leave him strawberry

Kool-Aid in plastic cups and saltine crackers. Thankfully I never had to clean it up, Samantha was good about keeping after that. For being five, she's quite tidy.

I blew it off at first. Every kid has imaginary friends. I had them, my wife had them. The stress of the move probably just had her cling onto this one a little longer.

Then Joey started bringing Doritos into the closet.

Doritos were his favorite snack. Cheesy fingerprints typically stain his shorts, it makes laundry a pain, but that's life when you have kids. Joey was never the imaginary friends type though. He maybe had one when he was Samantha's age, and that phase lasted no more than a week. So this was a little weird.

I decided to ask more about Walter.

I walked into Samantha's bedroom to see Samantha and Joey kneeling next to the closet, quiet as mice. I cleared my throat, and both jumped like they heard a gunshot. Joey instinctively kicked the door shut. "Hi dad!" he said.

I walked in and opened the closet door. Nothing in there except an empty plate with Dorito crumbs and a cup that had spilled a single drop of red juice on the carpet. "So, Walter likes your Doritos, bud?" I said.

Joey nodded. "He likes snacks," he mumbled.

"What is Walter like?" Satisfied the closet was empty, I closed the door and turned to my kids.

Samantha and Joey brightened up before they both began sharing bits of info with me.

"He's blonde!"

"He's starting to go bald, just like Uncle Craig!"

"He wears suspenders!"

"He's very quiet!"

"He's got a big ole hole in the side of his head!"

"He's here to protect us!"

"He really likes Doritos!"

I raised my hand. "Hold on, back the train up. What do you mean to protect us?" I wasn't even going to touch the hole in the head thing.

It was like they knew they said too much. Samantha's hands flew up to cover her mouth while Joey looked at the ground. Samantha spoke up first.

" He says there's something in the forest. Something in the barn... something really, really bad," she said, barely above a whisper.

The bedroom door slammed shut, and I nearly screamed. I walked backwards to the door and slowly opened it back up.

No one in the hall. And today had been too cold to leave the windows open.

I'm probably different from most people in this situation. I actually believe in ghosts. I had some experiences as a teen that turned me into a believer. Lydia laughed out loud when I told her I think our daughter had a ghost in her closet, but I didn't expect anything different. She's the skeptic of the two of us.

So I decided to dig into the history of the house.

This place had been tossed around quite a bit, most owners didn't keep it for over a year. Heck, one couple and their daughter actually moved out after two weeks. I kept digging. And before the house was built, I found something.

I found Walter.

His full name was Walter Griggs, he had three kids. He was a widower. He hadn't remarried. But one day, the house was burned down with Walter inside. The kids were never found. The common theory was that Walter killed his kids and then himself when he couldn't live with the guilt. God knows what he did with the bodies.

I was chilled to the damn bone when I realized my kids were talking to a murderous ghost. I called a family meeting, Lydia was less than impressed but she went with it.

"Guys, we need to stop talking to Walter and giving him snacks."

Lydia rolled her eyes. "Kurt..."

"It's just to be safe. Walter might've done some bad things."

Elliot blurted out, "But he's nice! He tells stories and talks about the good ole days!" He immediately regretted speaking as he saw my face go pale. Even Lydia looked unsettled.

Elliot was too old for imaginary friends and far too practical. Even as a tiny tot he wrinkled his nose at the idea of having a friend he made up. This only confirmed my theory—Walter was a ghost and the original owner of the property.

Samantha sniffled, her eyes filling with tears. "But... but what if he gets hungry?" she asked.

"And what if the... the *folk* come around? The ones he warned us about?" Joey shivered.

I sighed. "Guys. I don't know what Walter really is, but I do believe he's not something Samantha made up, and I believe he's not safe. Samantha, we're going to move you into the other room for now. We'll start hunting for a new house as soon as we can, but until then, leave Walter alone. Do not talk to him. Do not give him snacks. All right guys?"

Samantha bolted from the room crying. Joey turned into the couch to hide his tears. Elliot was the only one who nodded and said yes, but I knew he was upset too.

I surrounded the closet with a ring of salt, I would've burnt sage or whatever you do but I had no idea how to get my hands on some. So salt was the best I could do. Plus, I'd be able to tell if the kids tried to approach the closet this way. I looked up tips on how to make ghosts fuck off, Lydia for once not laughing at my 'crazed paranoia'.

Samantha was the most resentful of the kids. I caught her at least twice trying to sneak into her old bedroom with a plate of Saltines. Each time she was scolded, and I reminded her it wasn't safe, but I knew she didn't believe me.

Perhaps she knew more than I did.

Things were finally settling, I got a new job, and we were house hunting once again. Samantha still sulked, but Joey was over it, running about in the big backyard we had and playing games with a few of the neighbor kids.

Then one night I woke up and there was Walter, sitting in a chair in the corner of the room.

He was as solid as you or me and exactly as the kids described him—middle aged, blonde, balding. Suspenders over his blood-spattered shirt. And the 'hole' in his head? It looked like half his skull had been blown clean off. One eye had gone with it while the other, a deep blue, stared me down.

I couldn't breathe. I couldn't even wake up Lydia.

Walter sighed before he got up and motioned for me to stand and follow him. Like being pulled on strings, I got up.

Walter's voice was quiet and hoarse, like he'd had strep and still couldn't speak. "It's not too late," he whispered. "Go, hurry. I lost my children to the Folk, but you can still save yours."

I ran to the kid's bedrooms, feeling Walter's cold breath on the back of my neck. Each bed was empty, the sheets pulled away and their windows open. I almost collapsed, but Walter's ice-cold grip dragged me back to my feet. "No time for panic, son. Go," he said between gasps.

I didn't even put on my shoes. I ran out into the backyard. The forest was now glowing with bright lights, I could hear the piping of flutes and the pound of drums. I took off running, Walter on my heels.

I pushed through the bushes and nearly tripped on piles of old leaves, following the source of the sound. I stumbled into the clearing, which was now bright as day.

My three children were standing around a woman wearing a white gown. She was in every way perfect, beautiful, with dark curls cascading down her back. She was tall, taller than me even, and

I'm no short guy. Her hands were spread out and Samantha was reaching for her.

I heard the scream of a man in agony.

"NOT AGAIN!"

Walter rushed in, growing bigger, bigger, bigger... his essence swallowing the light. The clearing was now ice cold. I could see my breath coming out in puffs in front of me. The woman stumbled backwards, eyes growing in shock as Walter now towered over her.

"These children are not going with you, Fair Folk!" He howled. "Not this time!"

The woman turned and fled. Before my very eyes she stepped into a ring of mushrooms and vanished into thin air. Walter shrunk back to the size of a man before he turned to look at me.

I couldn't say anything. I wanted to apologize. I'd horribly misjudged the ghost of a grieving father who'd lost his children to something otherworldly. And he'd saved my children from the same fate.

Walter smiled crookedly before he vanished. I ran up to my kids. They were still entranced, pupils blown out, and they didn't recognize my voice. I got them back home and rushed them to the emergency room.

The doctor had no explanation. About an hour after they'd been checked in, they came to with no ill side effects and no reason why they'd been out of it. Elliot said he'd heard a woman's voice outside the window and that she was offering treats, but that was the last thing he could remember.

They were in observation for a day before they were released, but by then I'd changed my protection plan. I didn't put scissors or knives in their beds but my wife did get ahold of some pieces of iron from a friend's garage and she created small statuettes of our kid's favorite animals with the iron set inside of it—a tiger for Elliot, a monkey for Joey, and a bunny for Samantha.

I've now taken to going up to that old closet with a glass of whiskey and a portion of whatever was for dinner.

I haven't seen Walter again, but I have caught glimpses of his smile as I'm closing the closet door. I think he was getting a little tired of strawberry Kool-Aid.

HUSH LITTLE BABY

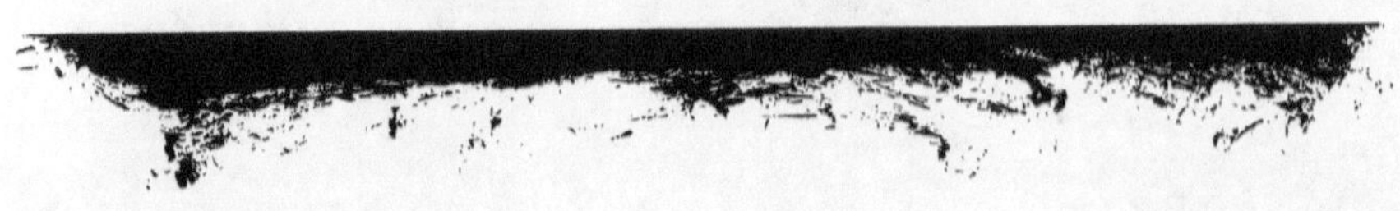

Dear Diary,

We're going on a vacation! I'm really surprised because daddy said we didn't have the money for one this year, but he came home today and told me and mommy to start packing. I don't know where we're going yet, but I can't wait.

I filled my suitcase to the brim with my clothes. Daddy hasn't said how long we'll be gone yet. I wonder if we're going to see grandma and grandpa down in Florida? I hope so! They promised the next time I came down they'd take me to Disney World. I've always wanted to go.

Mommy's really tired, so I'm trying to help her pack, but she keeps saying 'don't worry' and sends me back to my room. I wonder if the baby will be born in Florida?

Gotta go, dad's coming down the hall, he really wants to get going!

Bethany

Dear Diary,

We're on the road! Boy, we packed a lot of stuff into the van. Dad's put on my favorite playlist so we can sing Let It Go on the way to Disney World. He hasn't said that's where we're going yet, but I just know it! Why else would we pack so much?

I get to take up the whole back seat. When it's nighttime, dad usually lets me unbuckle so I can sleep. It's always so hard sleeping in the car, though. I hope mom doesn't need to puke. When she first told me that I was getting a little brother or sister, she was non stop barfing! Blegh! Barf is gross!

Oh, I think we're meeting with Uncle Harry and our cousins on the way down, too. I hope Uncle Harry brings his camper. We're not allowed to stay in it while it's moving, but maybe if I ask reeeaaallly nicely...

Bethany

Dear Diary,

I get to stay in the camper!

It was getting really dark by the time we met up with Uncle Harry. Traffic was really bad today and dad had to keep turning off Frozen so he could check on the radio. I dunno why, I think he wanted to hear the traffic reports.

For some reason Auntie Debbie isn't here. I tried to ask Uncle Harry why she wasn't but he seemed grumpy, so I just played Go Fish with Kevin and Macey. Kevin didn't even call it a baby game this time, so that was fun.

Macey said she thinks her mommy was working at the hospital when it was time to go. That's really sad. She's gonna miss Mickey Mouse.

Bethany

———

Dear Diary,

Ugh! I'm so BORED! We've been on the road for two days and I'm already so bored, bored, bored.

I think Uncle Harry's sad about something. He keeps crying at night and not looking at Macey. Whenever I get carsick and try to look out the window when we've stopped he snaps at me to keep the blinds shut.

Kevin's sad too. He's pretending like he's not crying, but I can hear him in the bathroom sometimes. I think he really misses his mom. Macey misses her too, but she's not crying.

I don't wanna play more Go-Fish but there's no INTER-NET out here so I can't watch anything on YouTube. This is gonna be a loooong trip.

Bethany

———

Dear Diary,

I think I saw someone who was really sick today.

We were stopped at a gas station to load up on snacks, I think we were the only ones there cuz I didn't see anyone else. I was playing Barbies with Macey just outside the camper and we were pretending to be dragon riders when I heard something. I looked up, and I saw a lady walking up.

She didn't look very good, her skin was all gross and her eyes were leaking green and white goo, sorta like whenever I have a cut that gets infected. She looked really scary. I yelled for Kevin, and he poked his head out to see her getting closer.

I think he was scared.

He grabbed me by the hair and Macey too, pulling us in and yelling to his dad that one of 'them' was out there. I dropped my Barbie and asked Kevin to go get it because I didn't want to see that ucky lady anymore, but he told me to shut up.

He must've felt bad because after his dad came back, he went and got my doll. I don't know what happened to that lady, but she was gone. I think Uncle Harry told her to go away.

Bethany

Dear Diary,

We're not going to Disney World.

Daddy held a 'pow-wow' when we stopped for the night to tell us why we were on vacation. It's not really a vacation. People are getting really sick and they're becoming very dangerous. If we're too loud, they'll come and they'll hurt us. The sick people are attracted to noise and they're very dangerous. They could get us sick, too. I don't wanna get sick so I wanna be quiet.

Aunt Debbie died. That's why Kevin and Uncle Harry have been so sad. They told me and Macey at the same time. One of the sick people hurt her really badly while she was at work. She's in heaven now with Great Aunt Julia and my dog Bucket. I'm gonna miss Aunt Debbie. She always liked singing in the car with us, even though she sang really badly.

Macey cried until she fell asleep. I haven't cried yet. I feel really sad, but I can't cry. I hope I'm not broken.

Bethany

Dear Diary,

I'm not broken, it just took a while. I was eating breakfast with Kevin and Macey when I started bawling my eyes out. I'm never ever ever going to see Aunt Debbie again. She's not gonna get to see Mommy's baby. And I'm scared that I'll get sick too and hurt Macey and Kevin and Mommy.

Macey hugged me better and told me that I wasn't ever evvver gonna get sick, we have her daddy and my daddy, and they'll make sure we're safe. That made me feel better.

I think Mommy's scared about the baby. We can't go to a hospital so she can have it. I hope she'll be okay.

Bethany

———

Dear Diary,

Mommy's having the baby right now!!!! Ahhhhhhh!!!!

She's hurting really badly, but she's trying not to scream, so the 'zombies' (that's what Kevin says they are) don't find us. I feel really bad for her.

I gotta stay in the truck right now. I'm keeping a look out for zombies with Macey and Kevin! Haven't seen any though. Just a lot of empty road and no cars. It's super quiet.

Take that back—mommy just screamed. Kevin has his dad's gun in his hand and he's looking scared.

I'm a little scared too but I know we'll be okay.

Bethany

———

Dear Diary,

I have a little brother. I'm so happy. We're all really happy.

He's so tiny and bald! He's got like maybe five hairs on his head, and dad told me to stop exaggerating but it's true! I love him so much. I want him to be safe and I promised mommy that I'll do my best to make sure he's happy. Mommy's tired, but she smiled so wide when I said that.

My brother's name is Nathan. I love him so, so much.

Bethany

Dear Diary,

It's been a crazy few days. Nathan really likes to cry a lot. Dad says I wasn't this fussy, but I think he's stressed out. We've seen a lot more zombies lately now that we're getting closer to a town and they can hear Nathan crying.

Uncle Harry and Dad go out when they start getting too close to bash in their heads with a baseball bat. It's a lot quieter than the gun, which can only be used in emergencies. I'm not allowed to look outside when they're getting rid of the zombies, but sometimes I take a peek.

I always knew my daddy was strong.

Ugh, Nathan's crying again. Mommy says he's having trouble 'latching'. I don't know what that means, but I'm gonna have a headache if Nathan keeps crying.

Bethany

Dear Diary,

Uncle Harry, Daddy, and Kevin are going into town. They have to get baby supplies. Mom is letting me and Macey take care of Nathan while she's lookout. I get to be a babysitter for my own brother!

Macey doesn't like holding him, she says he kinda stinks, but I love holding him. He's so still and he just looks at me and I love it so much. Because he loves me too.

It's getting dark. I hope Daddy gets home soon.

Bethany

Dear Diary,

It's been two days. Daddy and everyone else isn't back yet. Mommy's really scared. She's tried calling them a few times, but they don't pick up, it just rings out. She's crying.

I'm so scared that my daddy's dead.

Nathan needs to stop crying. The zombies are getting closer. And Mommy isn't strong enough to use the bat to bash in their heads.

Bethany

Dear Diary,

Daddy's back! Everyone's okay! And they brought back SO MUCH STUFF! I get to have potato chips at dinner tonight, I'm so excited.

Kevin told me what happened. Apparently they got cornered in a building and had to wait for the right moment to book it. It was so scary, he said, but it sounds exciting! I'm glad everyone's not hurt, though. Nathan's a lot happier than daddy's back too, I think.

I can't wait for potato chips. I have to wait until Daddy and Uncle Harry clear away the zombies, though. No dinner until we're safe.

Bethany

———

Dear Diary,

We didn't have dinner last night. Uncle Harry's dead.

He got torn to pieces in front of the camper. We thought the zombies were all gone, but they weren't, and Uncle Harry was heading on back when they all attacked him at once and they bit his neck and there was so much blood and it was so so horrible... there was nothing Daddy could do.

We all cried last night as we drove away. We couldn't even bury him. We had to leave him behind.

Macey and Kevin don't have a mommy or a daddy anymore. I don't have an uncle anymore. Daddy doesn't have a brother anymore.

I wish we were going to Disney instead.

Bethany

———

Dear Diary,

Mommy says that Nathan has a colic. I think that just means he cries a lot.

Kevin's teaching me and Macey how to drive the camper. He no longer teases us or calls our dolls stupid. He makes sure we have plenty to eat and reminds us to be quiet.

I keep waking up in the night crying. Kevin once had to smush a pillow into my face to keep me quiet because he couldn't wake me up. I can't stop thinking about Uncle Harry. How much it hurt when the zombies ate him.

Why is this happening to us? And why can't Nathan stop CRYING?

Bethany

———

Dear Diary,

Mommy and Daddy are going to get more supplies. Nathan needs more formula and diapers. Kevin is going to keep look out while they're gone, Macey and I are going to watch the baby.

He won't stop crying. We're trying SO HARD but he won't be quiet. We're trying to feed him, but he won't eat, and he won't nap, and his diaper's clean, and I don't know what to DO. I keep asking Kevin, but he doesn't know either.

I heard Daddy tell Kevin if they're not back in two days, we have to leave.

I hope Daddy comes back in time.

Bethany

———

Dear Diary,

I'm a murderer.

I killed Nathan.

It was an accident! The zombies were getting close, Kevin was in the front with his bat prepped and Nathan just wouldn't stop CRYING! Macey was crying too, she was so scared they were gonna get inside to get to the noise and then the zombies would eat us all up. I didn't know what to do, so I decided to make Nathan quieter by covering his face with a pillow.

It worked. He stopped crying. But when I took the pillow away, his lips were blue and he wasn't breathing. I tried to wake him up, but he wouldn't wake up. I shouted for Kevin and he tried to wake Nathan up, but he couldn't.

I killed my own little brother. I'm so sorry Nathan. It wasn't your fault you were colic-y. But it is my fault for not being able to help you.

Bethany

Dear Diary,

We had a funeral for Nathan today. I wasn't allowed to be a part of it, I had to stay in the trailer.

Mommy hit me when she found out what happened. Kevin tried to take the blame, but I couldn't let him do that. It wouldn't be fair. I killed Nathan. Not Kevin.

Mommy hates me now. Whenever I say something, she tells me to shut up. She hates me. I hate me too.

I think Macey hates me too. She doesn't want to play with me anymore. Daddy just makes sure I eat, even though I don't want to. He doesn't talk to me.

I think the only person who likes me now is Kevin. After dark I'll sneak out and put my favorite doll on Nathan's grave. So he isn't alone when we leave.

Bethany

Dear Diary,

Mommy isn't doing well. She keeps snapping and yelling at everyone, even though Daddy has to remind her that she has to be quiet or the zombies will get us.

Last night I woke up, and she was standing over my bed. I sat up and asked why she was up. She just glared and stomped back to bed, and started crying again.

I just make things worse by being here.

Bethany

Dear Diary,

I think Mommy tried to kill me today.

I was washing up at a creek we stopped by when my head was shoved down below the water. I couldn't breathe. I tried to scream, but I just got a mouthful of mud. I thought I was going to drown.

Then I was let go, and I popped back up so I could scream.

Mommy was being dragged away by Kevin, Kevin was calling her a lot of mean words I can't repeat, but I can write down—'bitch' was one of them. He called her a bitch a lot. Mommy just cried and screamed nonsense, and we had to get out of there quickly so the zombies couldn't find us.

My mouth still tastes like dirt. Mommy's just sitting on the couch and staring at me. Kevin won't leave my side. I'm glad there's someone who loves me still.

Bethany

Dear Diary,

We're almost to Florida. Maybe we can make it to Disney after all.

Bethany

Dear Diary,

My parents forgot me.

We stopped at an abandoned motel. There was no one there except for a few zombies, and Kevin took care of them. He's so strong. I went to sleep in a bed last night, Macey was next to me. But when I woke up this morning I was alone, with my backpack full of my favorite toys and my favorite foods.

The camper's gone.

They'll realize I'm gone soon and come back, right?

Bethany

Dear Diary,

It's been two days. I've spotted a few zombies, but they don't come close. They don't realize I'm here, I'm excellent at being quiet.

I'm still waiting for my mom and dad. I'm searching the motel for more food, so I don't go hungry. At least the sink works, so I'm not thirsty. Bethany

Dear Diary,

It's been five days. They have to come back soon. They have to.

Bethany

Dear Diary,

It's been two whole weeks. I think I found all the food that's left here. And Mommy and Daddy aren't ever coming back.

So I gotta go find them.

I packed my bag as full as I could and I'm gonna start walking today. Maybe they'll still be going to Disney, and we can meet there.

I'm so sorry, Mommy and Daddy, for killing Nathan. But maybe when I find you again, you'll forgive me.

Bethany

PROBLEM CHILD

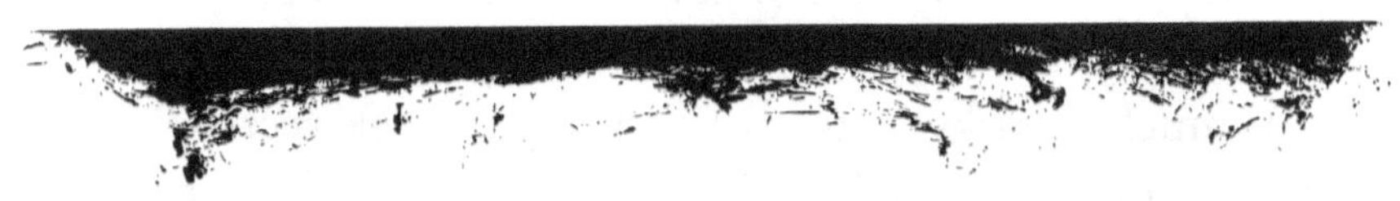

As a social worker, you're bound to come across some really messed up stuff. I've been at this job for nearly twelve years, and I've seen everything. Joel was raised in a kennel with a dog, he was so small I thought he was two years younger than he really was. Andrea went into a doctor's appointment only for the doc to find out the kid had contracted chlamydia. Sophia who had been tied to a bed and beaten to 'get the devils' out of her. Fynn had been choked for enough time by his stepdad to have permanent brain damage.

But all of those kids have homes now. They were adopted by loving families. I send them cards on their birthdays. Joel is now a complete Potterhead and went to Florida with his mom during summer vacation. Andrea now speaks regularly at sexual abuse seminars and helps other victims come forward about what they went through. Sophia wants to be an astronaut, Fynn is beating the odds and making us all proud with all he's accomplishing.

I can't say the same for Bonnie.

Bonnie only crossed my desk recently, her original caseworker had retired, and no one wanted to go check on her. I couldn't imagine why until she was sent back into the system. That's when I cracked open that file and gave it a long read.

No one knows where Bonnie came from. They found her in the backseat of a car that had been in an accident, the driver appeared to have suddenly swerved and ran into a tree. It killed him instantly. However, when the driver was ID'd, he didn't have children that age. The girl wasn't one of his relatives, and she was found in a worn out car seat that had the name 'Bonnie' scrawled on it in black crayon.

As much as it irks me to say this, she was the perfect case for an easy adoption. Blue eyes, blonde hair, six months old and perfectly healthy. Exactly the kind of child that anyone would want. It's no surprise to me that a lovely young couple brought her into their home within a week. I even found a newspaper clipping announcing that the Johnson's family has grown by one. Cheesy, but cute.

But not even three weeks later and Bonnie was sent right back into the system, with no explanation other than 'she's a handful'. I did some digging, and it does seem that the perfect Johnson couple were not nearly so perfect. A well check revealed that the garbage can was filled to the brim with wine bottles and Mr. Johnson had been fired from his workplace for embezzlement.

I actually looked them up to scrape up that last fact, I had gotten far too curious.

The next couple seems to be an even better fit, the Morrisons. They'd already adopted three-year-old Lily the year prior, and they were excited to grow their family again. Mrs. Morrison was a teacher, Mr. Morrison was an accountant. Lily was a happy, healthy girl.

Well, she was.

Two weeks after Bonnie joined their perfect family, Lily was diagnosed with leukemia. This was out of nowhere. It worked fast. Before the year was out the family had shrunk, and the Morrison family had to buy a coffin that should never have to be made so small.

Everything fell apart after this. Mrs. Morrison started having an affair with one of her students, Mr. Morrison came home to them in bed and in a rage he shot them both. The teenage boy didn't survive, but Mrs. Morrison did, although she'd never be able to walk again. During the trial it came out that Mrs. Morrison felt like she was no longer in control of her actions, and claimed she was sleepwalking when she seduced her student and brought him into her bed. Funny part is, Mr. Morrison said he had no idea where he even got that gun—he didn't own one, and it wasn't registered to him either.

Obviously, little Bonnie had to be sent back into the system while her parents were sent to prison for statutory rape and murder.

I wish I could say it got easier for her from here... but it didn't. Not at all. It got worse even. Not every house was as perfect as the Morrisons could've been. There are so many 'parents' out there that are in it for the paycheck. Frankly, they got what they deserved when Bonnie entered their house.

I was on the computer all night to see the path of destruction that laid in Bonnie's wake. Housefires. Unexpected deaths, some explained, some not. Illness. Erratic and violent behavior. The most saintly of people became depraved maniacs, devolving into sexual deviants that sold their kids to sickos and downloaded terabytes upon terabytes of illegal porn. Big brothers began gutting cats and big sisters were found with their wrists slit in the bathtub. Parents threw children out the window on the second floor. Jobs were lost. Homes destroyed.

And the only thing in common with each and every one was Bonnie.

The last house probably had it the worst, the Raders. This poor couple hadn't a damn clue what they were getting into when they adopted Bonnie, they'd already adopted three other 'problem' children who came from abusive pasts so they probably thought that Bonnie would be nothing new. Nothing unexpected.

Mr. Rader went into work last week and killed every one of his coworkers with a shotgun. No one was spared, and it ended only when he turned the gun on himself. The only survivor had managed to hide herself in the closet and she said that he didn't say a word until everyone else was dead. Then she heard him start to scream uncontrollably, the screaming grew louder and louder until it was cut off by the final shot.

I can't say the rest of the family had it easy. On the same day, Mrs. Rader drowned the youngest child in the bathtub, while the older children ran down the streets, naked and wailing. They finally managed to flag down a neighbor and told her, and I quote, 'Mom's gone crazy, she's going to kill us all just because of Bonnie!'

When the police finally got to the home, Mrs. Rader had hung herself off the shower rod while Bonnie was busy drawing flowers in the basement. It was like she didn't even know what was going on upstairs.

I've seen a lot of children, many who might be labled as 'problems'. But Bonnie takes the cake. This child is a jinx in human form, and I have no idea why.

So this is why I've agreed to foster Bonnie. I cannot let this child go into another home knowing what I do now.

Bonnie is one of the most beautiful children I've ever seen, dark golden curls and those wide eyes are such a bright blue they make the sky seem drab. She's quiet, always says please and thank you, and I've yet to see any typical trouble making behavior—stealing, hoarding, lying, destroying.

I questioned her about all her previous homes, how her entire life she's never spent more than seven months in a house. At the time we were enjoying dinner, and Bonnie looked up from her mac n' cheese to ask for some applesauce. When I poured her some applesauce in a bowl, she took it and then she started talking.

"I'm a very bad thing. I can't do good things, no matter how hard I try, and everyone around me gets hurt because of it. I'm sorry, I'll try to do better this time."

I pity this child. I don't know if I trust her, but I do pity her.

I only hope I can avoid the fate of Bonnie's other families.

MR. O'BRIEN'S PARTY PLACE

I just wanted to start saving money for college. I didn't sign on to deal with the rest of this bullshit.

I applied for practically everything in my area, but the thing is, so did all the other kids that graduated from my class. And luck of the draw, I didn't get hired at McDonald's, KFC or Panda Express.

I got hired at fucking Mr. O'Brien's Party Place.

It was like a circus and Chuck E Cheese had a drunk one-night stand and whoever carried the kid did cocaine laced with glitter. This place was awful, and I was stuck being the janitor. At least I didn't have to wear one of the eyeball searingly bright spandex costumes the waiters and other performers wore, which I have a feeling chafed like a motherfucker... but I did have to be the one to mop the pee and blood out of the ball pit. Seriously, don't let your kids play in those, they might get HIV.

But unlike most of my other friends, I didn't get paid minimum wage, I got paid pretty damn well. So I shut up, smiled, and let myself be pointed to the nearest pile of vomit because Billy ate his pizza too fast. I say pizza in the loosest sense of the word, but you get my point.

I figured out quickly I was the odd man out when I walked into the break room and not one person acknowledged my presence as I ate my packed lunch. I was okay with that, I mean, I was the janitor.

I didn't know anyone else there, none of my friends were hired, and I hadn't met anyone here before. I wasn't part of the clique.

Then one day I got a damn migraine and Bunny came to my rescue.

Bunny was just what I heard people call her, she wore these pink floppy bunny ears and had her face painted with a nose and whiskers. She wore this oversized magenta onesie and always sang the birthday song for the birthday girl or boy. That's really all I knew about her before the migraine.

I get migraines pretty frequently. And this was a bad one. I knew it was coming on by the time I clocked in, but I didn't exactly have someone else to call in for me. I just hoped it wouldn't be a bad one.

Yeah, it got to be a bad one after an hour of squawking children and flashing lights from the stage.

I felt like I was about to faint when Bunny popped out in front of me. "Robin? You look pale. Do you need to sit down?"

I opened my mouth to say 'yes, I really do' but all that came out was this pathetic gurgle. Without another word, Bunny lifted me up, put me over her shoulder, and carried me off like I didn't weigh any more than a feather.

She took me to the break room, laying me down carefully on the threadbare couch. "I'll bring you some water, would you like some Advil too?" she asked.

I nodded, and she gave me two thumbs out before skipping out of the room. She returned a few minutes later, handing me the pills. "What's wrong, lovely?" she asked, and this was the first time I noticed her British accent.

"Migraine. Sound. Light hurts. Didn't want to call in." I swallowed the Advil and took slow sips of water.

Bunny nodded before getting up and mercifully dimming the lights. "Just lay back here, I won't tell Mr. O'Brien. I'll go bring you a blanket too," she said, and before I could object, she was gone.

I was quite embarrassed to be treated like this, but Bunny wouldn't hear any apologies. Every half hour until the end of my shift, she came in to check on me, got me more water. And feeling her gloved hand run through my hair was so genuinely soothing, I almost cried.

Luckily, I could drive myself home at the end of my shift. Bunny put her finger to her lips and told me it was our little secret that I rested for a 'little while' of my shift. Bitch, I was useless for over half of it, but Mr. O'Brien never found out.

Bunny was sweet. But Bunny and the other employees had a secret.

Like I said earlier, I didn't know any of these other guys. Not that weird, I live in a small town, but it's not like you can know everyone. And I'm a bit of a hermit. I don't go out except for work. But over time, I began to realize that I never saw the other employees leave.

Sure, they'd sometimes disappear for part of the day, but I never saw one leave the building. Not even to chill out back for a smoke break. I didn't think too hard about it, it's really easier not to think when something weird happens. I bet some of you have witnessed something that was in fact quite bizarre, but just didn't think of it that way. You made an excuse.

Course, it's really hard to make an excuse when you walk in on your coworker literally pinning another one's back together.

I should've already gone home, but there was a nasty shit explosion in the men's bathroom, and I was late. I just entered the back room to clock out when I saw Bunny and another performer called Pumpkin sitting on the couch. Pumpkin's shirt was off and I nearly backed out, thinking I walked in on something a little private when I realized there was something very wrong with Pumpkin's back.

Between her shoulder blades there were two deep red gashes, painfully swollen and oozing pus. She had tears in her eyes and I realized Bunny was holding silver pins in her fingers. A few pins were already in Pumpkin's skin, forcefully keeping the skin together like a quilt my grandma would work on.

I dropped my water bottle, startling both women and Pumpkin yelping quietly as one of the pins slipped out. "Fuck, B... Bunny, it hurts so much," she gasped.

Bunny set down the pins. "I can explain!" she said.

"I hope you can," I hurried over to Pumpkin's side to examine the wounds, "Jesus Christ, she needs a doctor!"

You might as well have suggested I take Pumpkin out back and shoot her in the head with their expressions. I raised my hands in the air. "Or not! What do I know? Those wounds are infected, though! She needs serious medical attention!"

"I need my wings back."

Pumpkin sobbed quietly, holding her shirt up to cover her chest as she rocked back and forth. "I can't do this anymore, Bunny! It hurts so much, I can't dance like this!" she said.

Bunny rested her hand on Pumpkin's shoulder before looking at me. "You're a normal person, right, Robin?" she asked.

I nodded dumbly, wondering what the hell she could mean by that. Bunny nodded before she unzipped the back of her onesie and turned to let me have a look.

Right, I told you how Pumpkin's back looked, right? Well, Bunny's was about a hundred times worse. Same two wounds, leaking pus and painfully swollen, only Bunny had the added bonus of having actual maggots crawling about in sores surrounding the slits. I nearly threw up as one squirming grub fell onto the ground.

Bunny zipped herself back up before sitting down. "The best we can do is pin ourselves together. Mr. O'Brien won't let us leave," she said.

"Why?" I asked, shaking my head, unable to burn that horrid image from my head. "What did he do to you?"

"He took us." Bunny wrapped her arms around herself. "He took us from our home and took away our wings. We can't go back without them. If he suspects we've left... he'll destroy them."

"Then he still has them?"

Bunny nodded and picked up the pins, pushing them through Pumpkin's back to force the wounds together. "In his office. But we can't go in there."

I had already made up my mind by the time I walked to the door. "I'll go then."

Pumpkin's eyes filled with hope, but Bunny's were filled with fear. "If he catches you, he'll kill you," she said.

"Hope he does," I joked, although the joke was not taken well judging by Bunny's horrified expression. "I'm kidding! I'll be quick, he'll never even know I was in there."

I slipped out of the backroom and headed right for the office. Whether it was luck or fate, Mr. O'Brien was out, and he never locked his door.

I may have spitefully knocked the horseshoe off his door on the way in, I always thought that thing was stupid and really didn't match the theme of the place, but I didn't care. I don't know if I'd let it sink in what Bunny and Pumpkin were, but I didn't care.

I found the wings stacked in the closet. Each was sealed in clear plastic, in every imaginable color and shape. I grabbed the whole stack, not sure which ones were Bunny's or Pumpkin's, and walked on out.

I was almost back to the break room when I heard Mr. O'Brien yell after me.

"Robin! What the hell do you think you're doing?!"

I bolted into the room and locked the door behind me, throwing the plastic packaging at the girls. "He saw me! Find your wings!" I yelped as I held the door shut with my body.

Pumpkin pulled out a pair of monarch butterfly wings and crowed with joy as she stood, more bloody pins falling onto the ground. I felt Mr. O'Brien slam into the door behind me, I knew we didn't have much time.

Bunny pulled out an incredibly large pair of pink wings, and I saw her smile triumphantly before she held them to her back.

The door came off the hinges, and I was thrown to the floor the same moment the room was filled with a white light.

When the light died down, Bunny was no longer in bunny ears and a onesie... and her eyes were much colder. Both her and Pumpkin stood side by side as O'Brien came into the room, going white as a sheet as he realized he was too late. "What have you done, Robin? Do you realize-"

Pumpkin crossed the floor and, without so much a single moment of hesitation clawed out Mr. O'Brien's eyes. He screamed in agony before Pumpkin tackled him to the ground, from where I was pinned under the goddamn door I could see squirts of blood coming from Mr. O'Brien's general direction.

The door was lifted off of me and Bunny picked me up, setting me on my feet. She wasn't short and cutesy anymore, she looked almost feral and towered almost two feet above me in height. "We're even now, Robin," she said as she patted my head, "I knew you'd do whatever I wanted you after I helped you with your headache. You wouldn't like to owe a person, you'd hate owing a fae even more."

She pressed her lips to my cheek, and I was back in my bedroom.

Shit's gone sideways here since last week. People disappearing only to reappear saying they've been gone for years, people who have been missing for literal decades have popped up thinking they've only been gone for a minute. People have bizarre Rube Goldberg machine-esque accidents that result in horrific maiming or death. Kids are gone for just a second suddenly act completely out of character, laughing at nothing and never sleeping. Nature is reclaiming any place abandoned by humans. I see people dancing down the streets, people with glowing wings and beautiful faces.

So I might've screwed my whole town and now we're under attack by a bunch of fae who've been cooped up for fuck knows how long by a bastard who made them perform at his shitty pizzeria joint.

Hopefully they'll get bored and leave soon. I need to find a new job.

DOCTOR'S NOTES

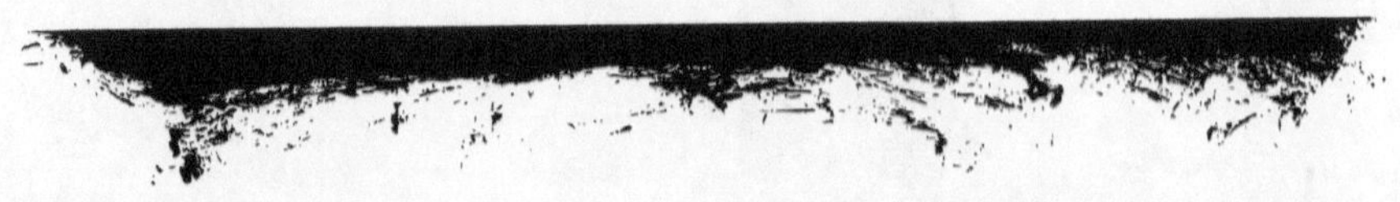

I cannot share all the details of what happened on March 3rd, 2018. As a doctor I'm not allowed to share certain private details, so names have been changed, and I do not mention what hospital I worked at at the time. There has to be some sort of logical explanation as to what happened.

So far, I haven't come up with any. Here are my notes I took that night. Three people are dead because of that woman's presence. And I need to find a reason why so I can continue going on with life. Everything has to have a rational reason. Or so I thought.

6:29 PM

Jane Doe was brought in about ten minutes prior. Age is somewhere in her early twenties. She would be quite tall when standing, almost six foot two. She's African American with two mirror injuries between her shoulder blades. The skin has been taken clean off and seems to be done expertly, I believe someone may have been trying to skin her, possibly to hide an identifying mark like a tattoo.

Jane Doe was found walking naked down a street in a daze. She was found by two young women who took her immediately to the emergency room. By the time they reached it, Jane was unconscious and unresponsive. I hold high hopes for her recovery, as other than the injuries on her back, she seems to be perfectly healthy.

7:01 PM

Had to calm down Derek Peterson again. Patient woke up screaming about demons and had to be given a sedative. He really needs a transfer to a proper mental ward but his parents only want him to be treated for his injuries before he's sent home. Like this time and every other time.

8:09 PM

Jane Doe has awoken. She seems to be all right in mind but claims to not remember who she is and what happened to her. I have reason to believe she's lying, but it appears she's gone through some form of trauma and I don't believe she's ready to relive it. I've ordered a rape kit, but she doesn't appear to show the typical signs of sexual assault other than being found nude.

The storm is picking up. I'm going to get a migraine from this.

8:38 PM

Jane Doe somehow escaped from her room and ended up in a room of the Agnes Church. She was sitting by the elderly woman and stroking her hand, almost comfortingly. I managed to guide Jane back to her room and apologized to Agnes, but she had already fallen back asleep. I imagine that's really all that's left for her, sleep.

Jane has been put back in her room and I've assigned a nurse to her door. We can't have her wandering around the hospital, she could hurt herself.

8:55 PM

Agnes passed away not five minutes ago. I cannot seem to shake off this odd chill about the uncanny timing of her meeting Jane and her death, but it is circumstantial. Agnes hasn't been right for days, I knew her end was coming soon. I'll miss playing board games with her on the weekends. If there's a heaven, she's likely playing Yahtzee with the angels now and somehow winning every time, even if it is a luck game.

9:23 PM

Jane got out of her room again, the nurse left to use the bathroom, and by the time she got back, Jane was gone. Because she was in my office.

She's incredibly sweet, all she wanted to tell me was that she remembered her name—Leah. I am not the kind of man to get captivated with his patients, but something about Leah tugs at my heart. I suppose she reminds me of my sister before the cancer weakened her spirit. I took Leah back to her room and told her that she shouldn't leave until we can find someone she knows.

She seemed mildly agitated with this, but did not object.

10:42 PM

Derek passed away.

This shouldn't have happened. One moment he was enjoying TV while chattering the ear off of the nurse who was checking his bandages when, as she describes, 'the eyes rolled back in his skull and he fell backwards, choking and thrashing about'. We tried to save him, but he was gone within minutes. It was like his body just ceased.

I'm going over his treatment, but he wasn't allergic to any of the medications we gave him and other than his mental disorders, he was perfectly healthy.

Leah tried to get out during the chaos, but I managed to catch her before she left her wing. She said she wanted to go outside for a breath of fresh air, but I have no doubt that if she leaves this hospital, we will never see her again. We're still trying to get a positive ID on her, there are no girls in the area matching her description with the name Leah who have been reported missing. We might have to widen our search.

The storm's only getting worse. I think there's something wrong with the air because I've had no less than two bloody noses tonight and my head is pounding.

11:01 PM

Once again, Leah tried to escape. She's begged to be released and claims she remembers how to get home, but she cannot name an address nor any relatives who can pick her up. She still doesn't remember her own surname. The police here now are trying to ID her.

I just got word. She escaped again.

11:32 PM

Leah was found attempting to get to the roof. She claims that's the way home. We've now had to restrain her to the bed as she is now classified a suicide risk. Officer Matthew Reynolds said she had taken off her hospital gown and was about to jump when he tackled her. I'm thankful she didn't succeed with her attempt to kill herself, but I'm worried she'll try again.

11:45 PM

Reynolds is dead. He just dropped in the hallway. Just like Derek.

I have an unsettling feeling that Leah may be connected to this.

12:01 AM

The power was knocked out by the storm, we're running off of generators now. The lights are constantly flickering. Two nurses have fainted, thankfully not dead, but both experiencing bloody noses and migraines. I can feel my own head start to pound.

I swear there's blood pattering against the window, but that's impossible. I might need to go home. Or go to the emergency room.

12:33 AM

Birds are flying into the windows. Like drawn to a beacon, they're flying to the building, smacking against the glass and falling to the ground dead. The sound certainly isn't helping my head.

I need to talk to Leah, but I believe she's asleep and is under guard by two officers.

It's foolish to believe that this girl could be causing such madness, but I don't know what else to think.

12:45 AM

The officers have fallen unconscious, and Leah is nowhere to be found.

I'm checking the roof now.

1:12 AM

L ah i go ne. S e fle w aw ay.

8:31 AM

I was found on the roof unconscious shortly after I wrote that nonsense message in my notes. My face was apparently covered in blood, and *they thought I might be dead, but I survived the experience... whatever that experience was.*

I must have hallucinated everything, but I shall take note of it anyway. I found Leah standing on the edge of the roof, once again nude and staring at the sky. She turned to look at me.

"Will you stop me?"

Her voice was hollow, tired. Lightning flashed, and I swore I saw something on her back illuminated by the lightning.

I tried to talk her down, show her there's a better way, but she shook her head.

"I have to try. I have to try to get home, Doctor. This is the only way to see if I can still fly."

She jumped then. I ran to the edge of the roof and peered over the ledge. I saw Leah's body on the ground.

But I saw her also stand, brush herself off like she'd suffered a minor fall. She looked up at me and I became overwhelmed with grief. I wept. I cried as she raised her head to the sky and screamed at the top of her lungs. The sound of loss, the sound of heartbreak.

I must have passed out then, because that's all I remember. Thankfully I seem no worse for wear and will likely return to work in a few days.

Leah is missing, but there is no sign of her body either.

I think she's going to spend the rest of eternity trying to find a way home.

WHO LIVES UNDER BRIAR ELEMENTARY AND HIGH SCHOOL?

B riar Elementary and High is a small school of just under three hundred students, from first grade all the way to senior year. It's spaced between two buildings and has been running since the early 1900's, although it was just a high school academy back then.

And apparently there's a monster in there now.

It's just little things that lead people to believe there's something supernatural lurking in the halls. The things that would go missing, only to turn up later caked in muddy fingerprints. The food theft, mostly lunchboxes, but sometimes whole pizzas would just vanish into thin air. Hearing something crawling under the floor. And the hissing you can sometimes hear while in the girl's bathroom in the highschool. If you go in there alone, sometimes you'll make out whispers.

There's three rumors about what it really is. I'll go over each one.

One. There's a creep who lives in one of the nearby caves and invades the school to get memories to jerk off to later and supplies. Around the Briar school area there are a lot of caves and tunnels that go underground. Kids have wandered in there and never come out. One of them's beneath the school actually but I'll get back to that in a minute.

Now, supposedly, there's a man by the name of Dale Horton who lives in these caves. Dale was a pedophile who preyed on little girls, inviting them to his house to model for him before he'd rape them and slash their throats, draining their blood so he could drink it later. He even shaved their heads, he liked how their hair felt. Dale was caught and sentenced to life in prison, but on his way to permanent lock up he broke free and hid in the cave system. They never caught him.

However, I'm gonna have to break your hearts on this one. There is no 'Dale Horton'. Dale Horton never existed. Seriously, I looked it up. No serial murder pedo either. The closest I can find to this sorta crime is a serial rapist that attacked three teenage girls before being caught. He was a fellow student by the name of Kyle. I think he managed to shake the charges off though, I never found evidence of an official case being brought against him. Eh, that's life when you're a boy with a 'promising future' and a sports scholarship.

Two. It's the ghost of a teacher killed by a spurned lover.

This legend's literally as old as the school. There was this woman, Miss Agnes Cherry, who taught the freshmen music. Beloved by all. Always pleasant to have around. And of course, had many admirers among the staff and students. One student in particular was downright obsessed with Miss Cherry. So much in fact, he got her alone and begged her to run away with him so they could get married.

Agnes told him to go away and that his actions were inappropriate. In response, he took out a knife and slashed her throat, dragged her out of the school into the mud before he killed himself. That's why everything's covered in mud when she touches it. People have even seen Agnes' ghost, a pale woman covered in mud and always sounding like she's gasping for air.

Okay. Agnes was actually real. So was her admirer. Her throat was slashed, too. But she didn't die. Nope! She actually survived the attack and went on to marry the principal. Her daughter teaches at the school, Ms. Patton. She's in charge of the Creative Writing class, I'm ninety percent sure she made up the rumor that Agnes died just to get a kick out of the students' stories.

There's one more. The one that has the least amount of detail. It's another ghost story, about a girl who used to go to this school. Feeling like she was ugly and had no one to love her, she broke a mirror and cut her throat in the girl's bathroom, effectively ending her life. This one doesn't explain the mud though, and doesn't even try to say who she was as it's clear bullshit. There's never been a suicide on grounds.

But I knew her name. And I knew what really happened.

Samantha Bishop. That was her name. She was a sophomore. Her favorite color was teal. She liked pearl earrings. Her favorite food was lasagna. She loved Garfield, even had pajamas with his face on it. Avril Lavigne was her hero. She was saving her money to one day go to one of her concerts.

But she also was socially awkward and suffered from a lack of self-esteem due to her glasses prescription giving her the appearance of having enormous, buggy eyes.

This just made her a target for people who didn't bother to look past the book's cover. One girl, in particular, and her friends. Audra Hart, Candice Whitfield, and Cindy Sweet. Audra was the ringleader. She used her nail polish to write nasty messages on Samantha's locker. Knocked her things from her hands. Would constantly talk shit about her, right while she was in the room. One time when she was on her period, Samantha bled through during class and when Audra saw the red stain on the back of Samantha's pants, she screamed out loud about how 'filthy' Samantha was.

Filthy Sam. By the end of the day, everyone was calling her Filthy Sam.

The tormenting just got worse. Her mother tried to stop it, oh she did. But Audra's father was a major figure on the school board and donated yearly to the sports program. So Audra got away with every damn thing.

But, of course, came the day things got taken too far.

Typically just before lunchtime, Samantha would go into the bathroom to just get away from the bullies for a few moments. And typically, said bullies would be too focused on getting something to eat rather than chasing down 'Filthy Sam'.

But this time Audra had to go to the bathroom. And when she saw Samantha, she couldn't resist the chance to pick on her again.

It started off simple. The name calling, 'Filthy Sam', 'Bug Eyes', 'Alien', 'Freak'. When Samantha ignored her, likely advice from the staff, Audra started to get meaner. Made cuts about her mom being a slut, her 'retarded' little sister.

'So stupid she can't even make it into kindergarten, huh?'

That was too far. Samantha loved her family. Her hard-working mom who'd divorced and remarried. Her little sister who schooled from home due to Asperger's. It was too much.

So Samantha turned around and slapped Audra across the face. A much overdue slap, if you ask me.

But Audra reacted back, much harsher. She grabbed Samantha by the hair and slammed her face into the mirror, shattering it with the force. Samantha dropped from the floor and stopped breathing.

The girls, panicked that they may have accidentally murdered their 'prey', remembered that in this particular bathroom there was a crawlspace in the floor where they kept the cleaning supplies. They opened it up and with a heave ho shoved Samantha's lifeless body into the crawlspace. They slammed it shut, cleaned the blood off the mirror, and went about their day like nothing ever happened. Cindy ever so kindly reported to the teachers that the mirror was broken. They plotted to return after school and somehow smuggle Samantha's body out in an instrument case before dumping the body wherever they could.

See, now we're getting to the part about the caves, and the fact one of those tunnels happens to be right beneath the school. When the girls returned and opened up the crawlspace, they found a hole that plummeted straight down to a bottomless pit. Perhaps throwing Samantha in there so roughly had broken the floor. Maybe it just couldn't support the weight of a teenage girl. Either way, Samantha was gone.

Assuming she was dead, the girls made a pact that they'd never tell anyone, boyfriends, husbands, teachers, or parents, that they'd killed Samantha.

Life went on. Samantha made the news when she turned out to be gone. Audra was questioned but let go, they had no proof she had anything to do with Samantha's disappearance. Soon her locker was emptied out. Her desk remained empty. Audra and her friends graduated. Went to college. Got jobs with the influence of their families'. They married rich, and no one knows about their dirty little secret of murder.

Samantha's mother became depressed but kept it together for the youngest child of hers, another daughter by the name Patricia. Patty for short. Patty grew up with all the love of her mother and stepdad. She found her love in poetry and writing, creating scripts for comics by the time she was twelve.

And she ended up going to Briar Elementary her sixth-grade year. Despite her social difficulties at first, Patty found a group she could blossom with. Bullies were laughed at in their faces, Patty never really understood their insults anyway. Where Samantha lacked self-esteem, Patty almost had more than her fair share. She found herself to be different from others, sometimes in ways that confused or angered them, but she was still worthy of respect. Her skills in writing blew away her teachers, and she was moved up several classes in order to keep her challenged. She won contests. She was the president of the writing club by her eighth-grade year.

I've always found communication tricky, by the way. It's so much easier to just write the words out. Sometimes I've had to have accommodations made for me, given my sensitivity to sound and difficulty eating in front of others, but rather than bother them each time I ate in the bathroom. And it was that bathroom where I found my sister again.

I heard the rasping breaths below the floor, and although I'd heard rumors of ghosts and pedophiles, I didn't believe in them. And rather than run away, I opened up the crawlspace.

She dropped away so fast I could barely make her out, but I caught a flash of her pearl earrings.

That night, I went to the school. More accurately, under the school.

It was tricky finding the right cave, but I took my time. Mapped myself through it. And soon I was under the school.

And I found where Samantha Bishop had been all these years.

I wouldn't go as far as to say she's become primal, but after receiving the head injuries and being completely isolated for so long, I think it's safe to say she's lost her mind. She's several pounds underweight from a strict diet of rats, toads, and rainwater, has torn out most of her hair, and is now completely blind from living in near total darkness. She knows it's me, though. She knows my voice, my scent. She knows I'm her sister.

I haven't attempted to force her out from her squalor, I can barely get near her without her darting away, deeper into the caves. She had moments of clarity where she told me what happened, but most of her vocalizations are hums and clicks of her tongue, similar to the croaking of the toads. I have helped her though. Brought her blankets, clothes—her uniform was nothing more than rags at this point. Brought her lasagna and other healthier food in attempts to give her more strength.

I don't know what to do anymore. Should I tell the police, and force her from this nightmare she's been living in into a whole new one? Make her reenter a society that tried to kill her?

Besides, I can't explain away the fact that Cindy and Candice were found dead in their homes, their ribs gnawed on, innards ripped out, and their throats cut with the glass shards of mirrors.

And I almost wish Audra hadn't moved out of town.

It's going to be hard to hide Samantha so long in the backseat of my car.

THE SUN'S NOT COMING UP

January 3

The sun's not coming up. The sun's not coming up.

I can't deal with this, school's starting Monday, how am I supposed to get to class when it's so dark you can't see your hand three inches in front of your face?!

When I got up, I figured it was just because it was winter, ya know? Sun goes down and stays down longer when it's cold. But I knew something was up by noon. The sun should've been up by now, it's starting to freak me out.

Neighbors have come by asking for some things they don't want to run to the store for, ignoring the elephant in the room that there's no fucking sun. Apparently the darkness gets even worse when you try to get out of the neighborhood. It's best to just stay here until this all blows over, while pretending it's not happening at all.

Dad was sleeping on the couch this morning. I think he and mom got into another fight, they're not talking, and mom's been crying, even though she does her best to hide it. God, it's bad enough that the world might be ending. I don't have time to worry about my parent's failing marriage.

January 4

The street lights went out, and haven't come back on. Outside now looks like Satan's Winter Wonderland, with all the snow and it being so dark. I can see other houses across the street, the lights shining through the window like beacons in the night. The only reason I can make out anything in my yard is from the light shining from my living room window.

Mom and Dad still aren't talking. Jesus Christ, you could cut the tension with a knife. I really wish I could go outside to smoke, but I swear Dad had a stroke when he saw me open the back door. I don't know how he expects me to go to school if I can't even go out on the back porch to 'get some air', but whatever.

For now I'm just cracking the window in my bedroom and doing what I can to waft the smoke out there. I'm sixteen, I can make my own decisions.

January 7

Okaaaaay. I guess I'm not going to school.

Sun's still not up. Weekend's just been boring as shit with just watching the outdoors get darker, if that's even possible. I even started getting ready before I realized 'what the hell am I doing' and went downstairs to ask if I could stay home. My dad gave me his approval and said I can stay home for as long as it stays dark.

First time we really acknowledged how absolutely bizarre that is, and it's the only acknowledgment.

I tried turning on the TV, to see if there's anything on the news about this, but all I got was static. Couldn't even connect to any local channels, it's all snow. Phone's dead too, I tried calling Isla and Lydia and got nothing. Not even a busy signal. It worked last night when I talked with Lydia. She lives just a few blocks away, and it's dark there too. Isla lives in the city though, not Bartonville, and apparently the sun's fine there. She said she'd come over today to see if I'm still making up bullshit.

It's not bullshit. Sun's gone, and it's showing no sign of coming back.

January 8

It's not just the sun disappearing. Lights are going out.

It started with the kitchen. I went down and tried flicking the light, but got nothing. I yelled for dad and said the kitchen bulb burned out and he went pale. He switched it and I heard him swear for the first time in my life when it still didn't work. I tried to tell him to check the breaker, but he was clearly losing his shit. By the time Mom came in he was babbling nonsense about the lights being taken away and Mom had to help him lie down.

I wonder if this has anything to do with why he was at work late for the last few weeks. I don't know what he works on, but I'm starting to go a little stir crazy and it's making me paranoid.

Isla never showed up yesterday. Stayed up until midnight and she never showed. Maybe she just got turned around or maybe she forgot, she's like that.

I bet she just forgot.

January 9

Half the house is stuck in the dark now, including my bedroom, but that's not the worst of it.

Watching the street is the only form of entertainment I have other than reading, and I'm getting too antsy to focus on that. I cracked the window while I street watched and then I heard it.

For the last few days, all I've heard while I've cracked the window is wind. Today I heard whispers.

Yes, I thought maybe I'd finally cracked and was hearing things, but I pressed my head against the screen to listen better.

It was then I heard the clack of something like claws climbing up the side of the house. I yanked my head back just in time to see those claws land on the sill. I was frozen when that... that THING hauled itself up to my eye level.

It was probably my height, maybe a bit bigger, pure black with tufts of hair or fur coming from the top of its head and its shoulders. It didn't have any facial features other than these large pointed ears and bright red eyes, eyes bigger than my balled up fist. It blinked a few times, like he was just as surprised to see me as well.

His claws sliced through the screen as I stared at it. I had to be going crazy, right? Its enormous hand groped around my desk before landing on my last pack of cigarettes. It yanked them back, waved them in my face, and then it dropped out of sight with a chittering madman's sound.

I screamed as loud as I could before slamming the window down. My dad came in and when I told him what I saw, he began to cry. Just crumpled into a ball on the floor and began sobbing.

I had to tuck him into bed. I asked mom what was wrong with him, but she couldn't answer me. All she knew for sure was that he came back late January 2, looking paranoid as all fuck and smelling like someone else's perfume.

I don't know what's worse, the fact that my dad apparently is having an affair or how calmly my mom said that. Apparently she'd been onto him for months, and it'd been likely going on for years. Years. It was only that night she caught him.

God, I wish I could just go back in my treehouse and hide for a bit, but I can't imagine leaving this house right now. Not with those things out there that laugh and whisper... even though they don't have mouths.

January 10

The darkness took an entire house last night.

The chittering from those freaks was so loud it woke me up. We crowded in front of the living room window and watched as dozens, maybe even a hundred of those monsters, surrounded the house across the street. Windows were busted in, the door was ripped off the hinges, and they flooded inside.

The Kinneys started screaming seconds after they got in. They screamed for what felt like ages. And all we could do was stand there and watch.

Dad bolted around the house after that, extinguishing every candle, turning off any lights we still had that worked. He's sure they were attracted to the light. I don't get it, but honestly I'm not gonna argue with the guy who's clearly two steps away from a mental breakdown. The Kinneys did have the most lights on still.

My thighs are going to be covered in bruises with how I keep bumping into everything every few steps. I can only use my flashlight to write in my diary, I have to leave it dark the rest of the time. All I can do is just watch the darkness outside the window.

January 11

Two more houses were ripped to pieces during the night... maybe at night, I can't tell anymore. I count days by sleep now. And now there's not much else to do but sleep.

I am getting better at seeing in the dark though, although all there is to see isn't great. The monsters just took the Kinney's house down, there's nothing left but a pile of wood. The Lotts' and Jarvis' house is also destroyed. In the wreckage, I can sometimes see dark shapes moving around them, more monsters, probably. I wish I could fucking see Lydia's house, but it's too far away. I hope she's okay.

It's clear my dad prepped for being here for a long time though, we have enough canned food to last until the end of the century. Something on that last normal night spooked him. And although he and my mom are clearly going to split the moment they can, he still cares about us. Even if he did betray us.

I'm too tired to be angry. And too scared. Maybe turning the lights off was the right choice, but who fucking knows.

January 12

Rhys Gill.

That's the name of dad's 'other woman'… or in this case, man. Boy, this just couldn't be easy, could it?

I was in the living room watching the snow when I saw a dark shape dart across the lawn. I almost screamed for my dad when I heard someone run into the door, but then I heard a voice.

"God, please let me in!!"

I don't know what made me turn the knob, but the guy nearly flattened me in his panic to get inside. The side of his face is all raked up from something's claws, and right after I closed the door I heard something else slam against it, followed by an angered scream. That thing was right on his heels, and I didn't even see it.

My dad admitted it all to my mom in the other room when Rhys practically fell in my dad's arms, sobbing about how they weren't just seeing things. Mom came out after a few minutes alone, dry eyed and holding a first aid kit. She patched up Rhys' face while Rhys explained what had been happening all over the block. The monsters, or 'Shadows' as he called them, are in fact attracted to the light. Dad was right. But they also like heat. Rhys saw a few of them curled up around a burning house like a bunch of dogs in front of a fireplace.

They didn't bring the dark though. The 'Other Thing' did. Dad and Rhys refuse to explain further, but apparently that night they saw something. Something… unknown.

I'm praying for the sun's return soon. Dad turned the heat off and we're all bundling up.

January 13

I like Rhys.

That sounds so bad, I know, he's the guy that's ruining everything for my parents. But he's super nice, he's helping board up the windows so as little light and heat escapes but leaves peepholes for me to keep an eye out. He's trying to keep the mood up by bringing up his travel stories, apparently he went all over Europe for summer vacation after he graduated. If I'm ever interested, he can recommend the best spots apparently.

I'll take going anywhere to get out of this damn darkness.

I think even Mom likes Rhys, or at least is playing nice. There's no room to be a dick while the world's potentially ending. And dad... he looks happy when he's with Rhys. Happier than he ever looked with mom.

Fuck if I keep crying all over my diary, I'm gonna make the ink bleed. I can practically see in the dark like a cat now, although Rhys gave me plenty of new batteries for my flashlight, so my handwriting is actually readable.

January 14

The monster that stole my cigarettes came back.

I know it was him because he's made the butts into a creepy necklace. Dickhole, I could use a smoke. He was just peering in through the slats of my window's barricade, tapping on the glass with his claws and making more weird warbling sounds.

Rhys showed me his gun, he says if the monster tries busting through he'll make sure to put it down. I've never felt so relieved.

In the meantime, I'm calling it Nic (short for Nicotine) and I'm sleeping in my parent's room. Well, mom's room, dad and Rhys are now occupying a room in the basement.

I wish they'd just tell us what they saw that night.

January 15

NicgotinNicgotinfuckfuckfuck—

I don't even know how! I just heard Rhys and Dad scream and came down to the basement to find dad bleeding everywhere and Rhys trying to put a bullet in Nic's head. He missed twice and ended up pegging it in the arm once. It bolted back long enough for Rhys and I to drag Dad to the main floor and to shut the door.

Nic is stuck in the basement, and he can't get up here, but I do hear him pacing up and down the stairs. Dad's... really fucked up. Mom started praying when she was patching up his neck, he looks super pale still and he's going in and out of consciousness. Rhys is holding onto his hand and he's bawling his eyes out.

I think my dad's dying.

January 16

Dad's dead.

He passed away sometime... well, I don't know really when, clocks have all stopped and haven't been going for days. It's like time's not even real anymore, it's just an eternal night until we all die.

I peered out the window to see the front yard's got a few more bodies in it, all pretty badly shredded, but I would recognize Lydia's hot pink coat anywhere. I think the rest of the bodies are her family but I can't tell. Won't be able to either probably, even if I could get up close to them.

We're all going to die. Mom's just laying in bed and Rhys is counting his bullets in between his sniffles.

All I need to know is that he has more than three.

January 17

After we stashed Dad's body in the office, Rhys sat both mom and I down and told us what happened.

They'd met by the old State Hospital, planning on going for a drive in Dad's car while leaving Rhys' stashed around there. Dad never once worked late in his life, which for some reason that of all things ticks me off. He always got on my case whenever I skipped a class or two and all this time he was practically gunning it from work to go meet his boyfriend.

At sunset they saw the monsters.

Two of them, not counting the Shadows that surrounded the one that almost looked human, except he was too tall and too pale and had eyes black as night. The other one was hunched over and some sort of drooling creature with a maw not big enough for all its teeth, but it was clear these two creatures were not friends.

The King (that's what Rhys is calling the one with the Shadows) apparently attacked first, but the Beast fought back. It was then the sky began to grow dark, despite the sun still sitting on the horizon. They watched the sky grow black while the creatures continued to fight.

They got the hell out of there before it became too dark, both going home and telling each other they'd been drugged. That was the only explanation for what unexplainable shit they'd seen. But they both still found themselves preparing, dad picking up all that canned food and Rhys digging that gun out of storage and making sure he had ammo.

This has nothing to do with us. The King and The Beast just put us in the middle of their shitfest and we're all going to die because of it.

January 18

Mom's going to kill herself. Rhys and I aren't going to stop her.

There's not going to be an end to this night. Mom knows this. The sun's never coming back. Nic is still in the basement, pacing up and down those steps. It's waiting for its friends to show up so they can kill us all, rip us limb from limb.

Rhys is going to make a last stand when that happens, but Mom can't bring herself to wait for the sun anymore. She sat me down and told me how much I mean to her, that she still loves dad even if he really, really hurt her. That she won't think badly of me if I'm not ready to end it.

I'm not. But I'm just glad she's going to take pills and peacefully go to sleep instead of taking Rhys' offer to use his gun. I'm not sure if I could take it if I heard the gun go off.

I'm such a coward, I should be joining her right now. But I'm too scared to die.

I'm only sixteen.

I don't want to die.

January 19

This will be my last entry.

Nic and the others broke through last night, right through the basement door. Rhys took out a lot of them, but I'm not sure if he's still alive since I'm not hearing any gunshots anymore. I'm barred up in my room, I keep getting whiffs of my parent's rotting bodies and it makes me want to puke.

Why why why didn't I go with mom yesterday? I don't want to die. I don't want to die

I can hear them in the hall. They're looking for me. They can feel my warmth, even if my fingers feel numb and my teeth can't stop chattering.

I can hear them whispering my name.

I'm going to make a break for it out my window. I don't have a doubt that I'll freeze to death, but I'll take that over being ripped to pieces.

I hear it's quite nice, freezing to death. You just sorta go to sleep. Goodbye.

I found this in the attic of a home I'm restoring. There was a horrible blizzard a few decades back that destroyed a fuckton of homes, but nothing like this. Maybe it's a joke. Maybe it's some creative writing homework or the beginning of a novel.

All I can say is that last night the sun went down... but it hasn't come back up yet this morning.

HAIR

Trichotillomania.

A mouthful of a name for the compulsion to pull out your own hair. All hair, the hair on your head, arms, your eyelashes, eyebrows. Lots of people have it, it's usually paired with anxiety and other lovely issues. Mine got worse when I felt anxious, my fingers would just curl up in my hair and I'd pluck a strand out. Then another one. And another one. During high school I'd beg the principal to allow me to wear a hat to school so no one could see the bald patches, but he told me 'just stop pulling out your hair.'

Needless to say, I got picked on. A lot.

I suppose it was a learned habit, though.

My mother pulled out her hair too.

I was raised only by my mother, but that didn't mean we were close. She was a mousy woman who never went out, only to work at the salon and to pick up some groceries. When I was twelve, she started giving me money so I could handle that.

My mom's trichotillomania was much worse. Her arms were bald, and she had no eyebrows. Her head was covered in bald patches that looked irritated and sore from where she picked at the exposed skin. When she went out, she did have the luxury to be allowed to wear a hat. People tried to get her help, I think. But as far as I know, she never pursued help.

Her obsession with hair went farther, though.

When I pulled my hair out, I just wad it up in a ball and tossed it. Not my mother.

In the living room as we'd watch TV, her fingers would curl into what little hair she had and pluck! Out came a strand. She'd set it across her lap, run her finger along it, before her hand went right back to her hair. Pluck. Pluck. Pluck.

Pretty soon, she'd have several dozen hairs stretched across her lap. She'd stroke them, ever so softly, before pulling out more. At the end of whatever movie or show we'd watch, she'd go down to the basement. At the time, I had no idea what she was doing with the hair, but she'd come back up without it and get to work on dinner.

My friends hated coming to my place. They'd pull faces at my mom's balding head and were disgusted by the hair. I'd gotten used to picking out hair from my sandwiches and stews, but one time my friend found a long strand of hair in her spaghetti and screamed before she ran to the bathroom to throw up. She refused to come to my house after that.

I'd grown ashamed of my mother and her compulsion, I'll admit, but it didn't stop me from pulling out my own. When I got to be eighteen, I moved out with a few other students. We weren't friends at the time, but I was the only one with a car, so they let me stay with them.

I learned to stem the habit when I was away from my mother, and after one of my roommates suggested I cut my hair, I went the extra mile and shaved it all off. A strange style for a woman, maybe, but it stopped me from pulling it out. At times I'd find myself tugging at the hair on my arms, but that wasn't nearly as strong a desire. More like an itch rather than a need.

The next time I saw my mother, I was twenty-four years old.

She hadn't attempted to call, or message me on Facebook, hell I didn't get even so much as a text from her. It was hurtful, maybe, but I figured that's just how it was going to be.

Then one day I found myself turning onto her street.

We'd only lived maybe half an hour or so apart, but I'd never bothered to go visit. She never invited me after all, but today I felt different. Someone needed to check up on her, after all.

When I got up to the front door, I thought the window was covered in cobwebs at first. When I managed to get the door open, I heard several familiar snaps.

Hair.

I forced the door open to the hair web of my mother.

It was the only real way to describe it, a web. Strands of hair had been woven together, over everything in the house. I covered my mouth to stop from inhaling the musty scent. God, had my absence made my mother's compulsion grow out of control?

Half tempted to call the police, I walked past the hall into the kitchen, where a similar sight of woven hair greeted me. It appeared that these hairs were woven first, they were starting to crumble and seemed more like efficient tangles rather than the smooth plaiting that concealed the couch.

Where the hell was my mother?

I heard something clank downstairs.

Let it be clear, as a child my mother always made clear I wasn't allowed down there. She said the stairs were steep and I could break my neck. As a teenager, I didn't want to go down there. It was dark and smelled bad.

But curiosity got the better of me, that and the possibility that my mother could be injured down there. So I walked to the door.

It had been entirely taken over by hair, I ended up having to take a pair of scissors from the kitchen to cut my way open.

The basement was dark, and the moment I set my hand on the banister to steady myself, I felt it.

Hair.

Even more hair.

But this wasn't my mother's hair.

See, I should've put it together when I was upstairs. That my mother had fine, brittle brown hair.

The hair upstairs varied from blond to black. And the hair I rested my hand on was thick, I could almost imagine the locks of curls that had been stretched out to weave together.

Feeling dread seep into every pore, I walked into the basement.

It was a maze of darkness. I could only feel my way through twisting walls of hair. I could feel textures, coarse, fine, curly, thick, frizzy... had she stolen it from work?

Then I turned to a room only lit by a dim desk lamp.

A woman was strapped to the chair, and I took notice of her luxurious and long red hair. She was unconscious.

I heard the buzz of a razor. And I saw a pair of hands extend from the darkness to stroke that lovely red hair.

I screamed and ran from the house. I ripped through so much hair, tore down all the sheets of it that I could. I was trapped for god knows how long.

I finally reached the kitchen and went out the back door, ripping away locks of dyed green and pink hair that had it tied closed.

Apparently, you look like a crazy person when you run down the street, covered in enough hair to make a whole new person and screaming your head off. Someone called the cops, and I was hauled in for questioning.

Someone had been going around and kidnapping people, returning them after three days physically unharmed save a few nicks, but telling stories of a dark basement and someone stroking their hair and complimenting it before shaving it all off.

I was partially relieved my mother hadn't become a serial killer, but the worse problem was when the police searched the house.

They hadn't found my mother.

But they did find a tunnel that led into the ground, covered by a mass of hair so thick they had to burn it in order to get through.

MORE CHILLS FROM VELOX BOOKS

SPIRALING
DOWN
DISTURBING HORROR STORIES BY
MICHAEL MARKS

"STRIKING, BITING, AND WICKED;
YOU WON'T WANT TO MISS THIS COLLECTION."
PLASTIC
FACES
UNSETTLING STORIES BY
MARTA ABROMAITYTE

STORIES THAT ARE
GUARANTEED TO
ENTERTAIN
VACANCY
R.K. KOMBRINCK
THESE LONELY
PLACES

I'VE DONE
THIS
"TRULY SPECIAL"
BEFORE
A BARRAGE OF
NIGHTMARES BY RYAN MAJOR

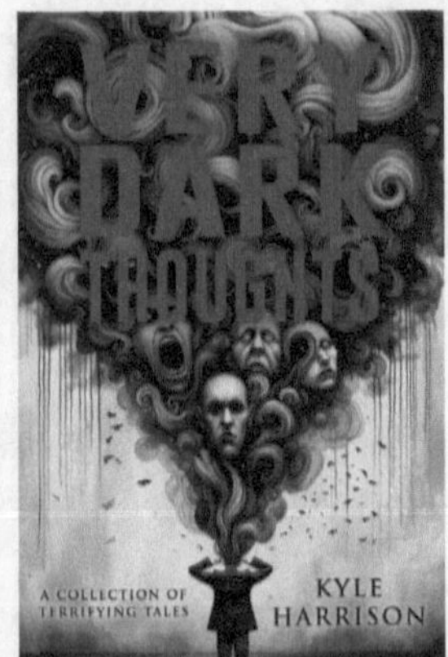
OUR
DARK
THOUGHTS
A COLLECTION OF
TERRIFYING TALES
KYLE
HARRISON

"AN EXCELLENT
COLLECTION
OF HORROR"
IRON
MAIDENS
TWISTED TALES OF KILLER WOMEN
SARAH-JANE HUNTINGTON

STRANGE
TALES
OF THE
MACABRE
TALES BY E. REYES

FACE DOWN
"A GREAT LITTLE
COLLECTION OF THE
BIZARRE [AND]
MACABRE"
IN THE
GRAVE
SINISTER TALES BY
THOMAS O.

TRIPPING
"T. W. GRIM CAN
TELL ONE HELL OF
A STORY"
OVER
TWILIGHT
DARK TALES BY
T.W. GRIM